Of Moonlight and Fire

Written by

J.N Wynn

Cover design: J.N. Wynn
Interior design: J.N. Wynn
Editing: Independent
Published by: J.N. Wynn
United States of America

ISBN (Paperback): 9798273755178
ISBN (Paperback): 979-8-9936147-4-8
ISBN (Hardcover): 979-8-9936147-3-1

First Edition: 2025

TERMINOLOGY

 **<u>Selvaran (the Moon Realm)</u>**
Morning: *Moonrise* (when the moon's first light touches the realm again)
Midday: *Halflight* (the pale silver glow that fills the sky when the moon reaches its zenith)
Night: *Moonfall* (when the moon's light fades into the horizon, marking rest and dreams) (Dawn)

 **<u>Solara (the Sun Realm)</u>**
Morning: *Sunrise* (first flare of golden light)
Midday: *Highflame* (when the sun burns brightest overhead)
Night: *Sunfall* (when the sky turns reddish pink) (Dusk)

The Realms of Sun and Moon

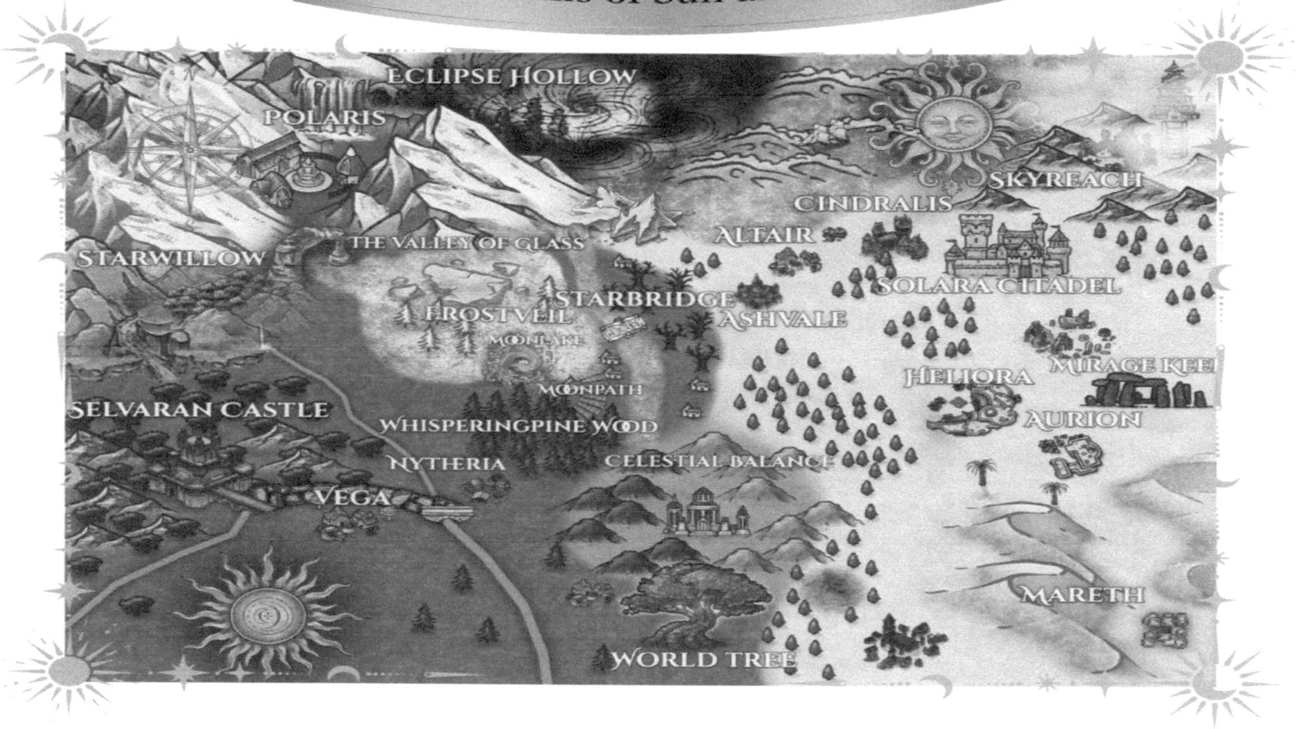

This novel contains material that may be distressing for some readers,
including depictions of child abuse, wartime violence, and graphic violence.
Reader discretion is advised

.

LUNA
SOLIS
ARGUS
CALISTA

ONE

LUNA

The arrow cut through the night, silver against the dark sky, gliding with preternatural precision before striking the rabbit cleanly through. The small body tumbled into the grass and fell still, its final motion fading into the tranquil whisper of the forest.

A gleeful sound escaped Luna as she did a small dance, or rather a little wiggle of triumph, given she was still mounted on her mare. At only ten years old, her aim already rivaled that of

Selvaran's most seasoned hunters. Perhaps even those of Solara. Pride tugged a smile across her lips as she swung down from her horse.

She crouched beside the creature, brushing her fingers across its soft fur as its warmth ebbed swiftly into the cool night air of Selvaran. Life had already slipped from its eyes, leaving behind only stillness.

"Don't worry, little rabbit," she murmured, her tone soft as she made her promise to the small creature. "Your life will not be wasted. Tonight, you'll be honored by the fire."

Hunting was only permitted in Selvaran when the creature's life would serve a purpose. Killing without one was considered a transgression. Her father, King Orion Velastra, forbade the taking of any life without meaning. Every resource, he said, must be treated with care and reverence. Every creature was part of the balance of life.

Luna lifted the rabbit gently by its ears and rose. The darkness of Selvaran dulled the white fur to a grayish hue. She wished her land held the brightness of the Sun, but the Sun belonged to the other side. The realm of Solara, ruled by the Aurelius bloodline. Selvaran had not known such light for centuries, guided only by moonlight and stars.

Once, the world had been united, the Sun and Moon sharing the same sky. Now, it bore the curse of the heavens, the Sun and Moon ascending together yet never coexisting.

The crescent at her chest lit up, a pale light pulsing beneath her skin.

Luna stilled.

The mark had been with her since birth, a quiet presence she scarcely noticed anymore. It had never reacted before.

Brushing it off, she turned toward her mount, just beginning to slip the rabbit into the leather pouch strapped to Moonshade, the silver-white horse her uncle Khael had gifted her, when a voice cut through the stillness of the forest.

She pivoted toward the sound and found a boy standing among the trees, no older than she was, with hair the color of sunlight, impossibly rare in Selvaran. His eyes, a luminous ocean blue and brimming with tears, met hers.

"You killed my rabbit," he said, his voice trembling. His shoulders shook with every word. He sniffed and wiped his nose with the back of his hand, making Luna nearly groan at the sight. For someone who looked around her age, he acted more like a helpless infant.

She scrutinized him with quiet percipience. Something about him felt incongruous. His clothes were finely woven, his boots spotless, not a worn mark in sight, and his hair neatly trimmed. Even his posture was unblemished by hardship. No village child could afford attire like that, and the colors, white and gold, were unmistakable. Solara colors. The enemy.

Her grip tightened on the bow. He might have been young, but Solaran nobles were trained in combat before they could even read. Even their games were built upon the concept of war. Still, there was nothing fierce or formidable about this one. The way he fidgeted, the way his lip quivered as he tried to hold back more tears, he seemed different, too soft for a Solaran.

Against her better judgment, she straightened and lifted her chin, just as Uncle Khael had taught her. Fear is vulnerability, he always said. Show courage and even the strongest opponent will hesitate. This boy looked like the kind who would cry over a bruised flower. There was no doubt he would cower.

"It is not your rabbit," she said, keeping her tone even. "The forest owns it. Anyone may hunt here so long as they obey the laws of Selvaran."

"But I chose that rabbit," the boy stammered, looking down at the ground. "I found him first and named him. He was my pet, and you killed him."

Luna blinked in disbelief. A pet. In the wild. The boy had named a wild rabbit and expected no one to kill it simply because he had claimed it. Unbelievable.

She lifted the rabbit by its ears, holding it out for him to see. His shoulders trembled again at the sight. She let out a quiet sigh. "What's done is done. I can offer you a piece of the meat."

He shook his head, tears spilling freely now. "I do not want to eat Flurry."

"Flurry?" Luna repeated under her breath. The moon helps her. Of all the names in the realm, this boy had chosen Flurry. Why not something grander and fiercer, like Sir Fluffer? But Flurry? No wonder the poor creature had run straight toward an arrow.

She lowered the rabbit and studied the boy. Her parents were probably already wondering where she had gone, yet this boy wept as though his heart had been cleaved in two over a rabbit, for moon's sake.

She crossed to him and placed a hand on his trembling shoulder. His gaze dropped to the limp body in her other hand, and he sniffed.

Battling the urge to roll her eyes at his reaction, Luna chose her words carefully.

"I am sorry," she said gently. "But Flurry is gone. You must let him go."

A shaky breath escaped him as he wiped his tears away. "Okay," he whispered.

Well, that was far too easy. She offered him a small, sympathetic smile, which he returned with one of his own. His eyes, an arresting shade of oceanic blue, gleamed beneath the moonlight, luminous and ineffable, far too lovely for someone from the enemy realm. Solara truly bred the most beautiful eyes.

She quickly shifted her focus back to the forest. She needed to return home before her parents grew anxious. But just as she turned, an arrow sliced past her cheek.

Luna froze. Someone was trying to kill her.

More arrows hissed through the air. She lifted her arm, light bursting from her palm. The shaft splintered mid-flight, scattering like molten sparks before they could reach her.

From her peripheral vision, she caught the boy's reaction. There was something in the way he looked at her, wide-eyed, knowing, told her he knew exactly who she was.

Before the thought fully formed, he seized her hand and pulled her deeper into the forest.

"Run."

They darted between the trees, their small feet pounding against the earth as arrows chased them through the dark. Luna could not tell how many attackers there were, only that they wanted them dead.

It was the first time she had ever experienced a true attack. Khael had warned her father that such things could happen, but never once had it occurred until now.

Her lungs burned as they ran. Each breath came faster, sharper, until it felt as if the air itself pressed down on her chest. The boy said nothing. He only held her hand tightly, leading her through the thick woods until the trees thinned and gave way to a riverbank.

They halted at the water's edge, panting, trying to catch their breath. Luna whipped around and scrutinized the surroundings, her eyes narrowing as she spotted them.

Masked figures emerging from the shadows. Five in total.

She could not tell which realm they served. Their faces were concealed behind black fabric, their eyes the only discernible thing. They discarded their bows and drew their blades. Moonlight struck the steel, gleaming like liquid mercury.

Luna raised her bow, her hands trembling, though she forced her voice to remain unwavering.

"How dare you attack the princess of Selvaran."

The assassins offered no reply.

They charged.

Her heart slammed against her ribs. She drew an arrow, but too late. It struck the ground at one of their feet, useless against their advance.

A sudden tug seized her arm, yanking her backward. The next instant, icy water engulfed her.

TWO

LUNA

The ice water swallowed her whole. The river dragged them under, the boy's grip anchoring her as the current tore them downstream.

They coughed and gasped, swallowed by the roar of the water. The world above vanished into a blur of darkness.

The forest, the assassins, the chaos—everything vanished beneath the unrelenting surge.

When they finally reached land again, both were soaked to the bone. The boy's golden hair plastered to his forehead, several shades darker when drenched. His body shook violently, teeth chattering. Luna crawled forward, hacking up river water as mud smeared across her palm.

He had saved her. He had also nearly drowned her. She wasn't sure whether to thank him or shove him back into the river.

She collapsed onto her back, arms sprawled across the damp earth. "When will this war finally end?" she groaned. Every breath carried exhaustion—the assassins, the running, the conflict that felt endless and puerile. Couldn't Solara simply call for a truce already?

The boy fell beside her, his chest rising and falling in rapid bursts. "When Selvaran decides to call for peace," he managed between shivers.

He did not merely blame her people. Solara's arrogance seeped from his words like heat radiating from embers. For years, it was Solara who had refused to halt their relentless assaults. Her people had only ever fought to defend themselves.

Luna turned sharply toward him, strands of soaked black hair clinging to her cheek. "Or when Solara calls for peace! They're the ones keeping this war alive."

He pushed himself up on his elbows, water dripping from his sleeves. "Solara isn't the only one at fault. Our people suffer just as much as yours. We want it to end too."

Her breath caught. *Our people. We.*

"You're Solaran," she said quietly.

He didn't answer. He didn't need to.

Silence settled between them, heavy as the clouds above.

Luna's heart thudded. She had escaped assassins… only to wash ashore with the enemy.

Selvaran and Solara had been at war for centuries, drowning generations in hatred no one truly remembered the origin of.

Blaming him felt pointless. He was only a boy, a child like her, born beneath the weight of someone else's hatred.

With a quiet sigh, she rose and wrung the water from her hair. "What were you doing on our side of the border? You should know Solarans are not welcome here."

He hesitated, his blue eyes flicking away, fixing instead on a nearby tree as if it held the right answer. "I… I was wandering."

"Wandering?" she repeated, unimpressed.

No Solaran child wandered alone into hostile territory. And his attire—white jacket embroidered in gold—betrayed everything. He wasn't merely a simple child. He was someone significant.

She crossed her arms. "Why are you really here?"

He stared at the river, watching the current sweep past them. Only after a long silence did he speak. "I came from a camp nearby."

"A camp?" Luna's voice hardened. "A Solaran camp inside Selvaran borders?"

He rolled his eyes, exhaustion dripping from his tone. "We're not camping inside Selvaran territory. We're stationed on our own border, just as you are on yours."

There were a hundred questions she wanted to ask, yet doing so meant revealing her own reasons for being here. She could not tell him why her people were stationed nearby, and she doubted he would confess his truth either.

Still… one question lingered.

"Who are you?" she asked.

He hesitated again, gaze dropping to a small stone he picked up, turning it over with restless fingers as though it were the most fascinating object in existence. With a swing of his arm, he tossed it into the river. The rock skipped before vanishing beneath the current.

"Just a son."

A son of whom?

Her eyes scrutinized him closely, taking in the fine stitching, the gold detailing, the posture too polished for common blood. No ordinary child wore clothes like that.

He must have come from wealth—perhaps even royalty.

Could he be… no, impossible. The Solaran king would never be so careless as to let his own son cross enemy lands.

Yet curiosity pricked her.

She tilted her head. "Whose son? And what is your name?"

His cheeks flushed. He looked flustered, caught between veracity and deceit. "I… I'm the son of a lord. Just a provincial lord. No one of importance." He extended his hand toward her, forcing a small, nervous smile. "The name is… Sol."

A son of a provincial lord? One from the border region? It could make sense, yet something in her refused to buy it. No lesser lord could afford gold thread. Fine. If he wished to lie, she could too.

"The name is…" She gripped his hand. "Nova."

His fingers tightened around hers, a faint smile tugging at his lip. "Nice to meet you, Nova."

The way he said *Nova* made it sound as though he didn't believe her either. Nevertheless, they held the fragile game of deception; neither intended to break it.

"So, Sol," she said, brushing mud from her knees, "what are you doing at the camp? Children of lords don't normally train in war camps."

His mouth opened, then closed again as though choosing his words carefully. He released her hand and stood, brushing mud from his clothes. His white trousers were stained brown, but he seemed utterly unconcerned—another sign of wealth.

"I'm training," he said.

"Training?" Luna raised a brow. "Aren't you a little too young for that?"

So the rumors were true. Solaran children began training young. No wonder Selvaran struggled to hold its borders. Her father was too merciful to send children to war.

He shrugged. "My father wants me to be capable. He says I am inadequate. If I am capable, maybe I can help end the war."

Sympathy stirred in her chest, though she wished it hadn't. Feeling pity for an enemy was dangerous. Khael would have lectured her for hours.

Yet she caved anyway.

"But Sol, you're too young to fight in a war."

He said nothing. His silence said enough. He had no choice. What the king commanded, he obeyed—even if it meant marching to death. She knew that feeling too well. She had never wanted to be a princess either, but duty never cared for wishes. Duty came first.

It always had.

She gazed down at her trembling hands. Her bow was gone now, probably lost somewhere in the river's depths. "My father says the war will end soon. But it never does. Someone always pays the price."

He turned toward her. "It is the same in Solara. Our people are suffering. My fa— the king says the war continues because Selvaran refuses peace."

She let out a sharp snort. "Your king could not be more wrong. Selvaran would give anything for this war to end."

"Well then, Selvaran should end it."

"Maybe Solara should end it first."

Their eyes met, stubborn and unyielding.

A long silence pulled between them before Luna sighed. This was why the war would never end. The repetition of history built on the same festering hatred passed down from generation to generation like a poisonous heirloom. And here they were, echoing the very conflict they had inherited. Perhaps, as the princess of Selvaran, she could be the first to break that cycle—start here, with him. Find common ground with her enemy's son.

"Maybe both realms are misguided," she said quietly. "Maybe we both want peace, but we're too stubborn to admit it."

He blinked. "What?"

"Maybe it isn't about who started the war," she continued softly. "Maybe it's about who ends it. Who drops their pride first and lets their people live."

He stared at her, uncertain, as if weighing her words. Then a faint, unexpected smile curved his lips.

"You're strange for a Selvaran," he said. "Where did you say you came from again?"

"And you're arrogant for a Solaran," she replied, a small smile forming despite herself. "Just a farmer's daughter."

If he could lie, so could she.

He studied her for another moment, then turned toward the river. The current rushed strong and steady, still a miracle they had survived.

"We should find our way back," he said.

She nodded. Together, they began walking through the forest.

Along the way, Luna asked him small, harmless questions—his favorite food, what Solara looked like, the sort of things she had always wondered about. It wasn't every day she met a child of the sun realm.

He confessed that he was an only child and that his father was exacting. No matter how hard he worked, it was never enough.

Luna listened with quiet percipience, empathizing with him in a way he probably didn't expect. She knew that feeling too well, the endless pressure to become the perfect heir her parents wanted her to be.

By the time they reached the edge of the forest, the moon was already sinking toward the horizon. They stood in silence, shivering as the cold tightened around them. Mist curled at their feet, rising thicker as Moonfall approached in Selvaran.

Luna was mid-sentence when the sound of hooves broke through the stillness, thundering against the ground. Her heart skipped. They had been found. But by who? Solara or Selvaran?

She snapped her head toward the noise. Through the drifting fog, riders emerged, their armor gleaming beneath the pallid light. The black-and-silver flag of Selvaran unfurled in the wind, its threads glinting with austere grace. Relief flooded her chest.

Uncle Khael.

They must have begun searching for her after she failed to return to camp for supper. A wave of comfort washed over her, steadying her trembling hands.

Luna cupped her hands to her mouth and called out, her voice echoing through the mist. "I'm right here!"

A relieved smile began to form, but when she turned toward Sol, it faltered. Panic flared in his eyes. His gaze darted toward the riders, his body going rigid as if preparing to flee.

Uncle Khael's horse came to a halt before them, hooves tearing into the earth. He glared down from the saddle, his black leather armor clinging to his frame, his cloak billowing in the wind. His expression was grim. Luna did not need to guess. She was in trouble.

"Princess, where have you been?" His voice carried the resonance of command, yet beneath it lived a restrained softness meant for her alone.

Luna winced. That tone meant she was about to get an earful about how the princess of Selvaran should never wander off alone, especially near the border.

"I got lost," she blurted, forcing a feigned innocence. But sweetness never swayed Khael. He was the commander of her father's army, a man forged by war, shaped by a lifetime beneath military law. A soldier molded by order and discipline. If coldness had a visage, it would be his.

Khael's scrutinizing gaze shifted. His lips pressed into a thin, severe line. He was staring at Sol.

Uh oh.

Luna's stomach dropped. "This is Sol," she said hastily, hoping to de-escalate the situation before it began. "He helped me find my way out of the forest."

Khael ignored her. His eyes never wavered. "Who are you, boy?"

Rigid with tension, Sol chewed his bottom lip, his gaze avoiding Khael's piercing eyes. Instead, it found Luna's, wordlessly pleading for help. But Khael was already in motion.

The commander dismounted with a fluid motion, his boots striking the ground with a heavy thud. In one swift movement, he caught Sol's arm and twisted hard. The boy flinched, his breath catching from the pain, yet he uttered no sound. His gaze shifted to Khael, unyielding now, his defiance almost audacious against the commander's imposing presence.

Luna opened her mouth to speak, but Khael silenced her with a raised hand. His grip on Sol's arm tightened, twisting further until a strangled cry escaped the boy's lips.

"The prince of Solara," Khael said coldly. "It seems the rumors were true. The ruler has sent his own son into the battle."

Her breath caught. The prince of Solara. Not a noble but a royal. The only son of King Leo. The heir of the Sun Realm. She was standing beside not only her enemy's son but the boy whose father had caused the deaths of hundreds of her people.

The truth struck her. King Leo had sent his own son into the fray. From her lessons, she remembered that the prince of Solara was merely a year older than she was. Eleven years old. A child hurled into the chaos of war. What kind of man would demand that of his blood?

Her gaze darted between Khael and Sol, disbelief anchoring her tongue. She could not speak.

Through gritted teeth, Sol managed, "My father isn't sending me off to the war. I was supposed to stay in camp, but I snuck out."

"Perfect," Khael replied as he drew his sword, the steel reflecting the moon's final rays. The silver shine illuminated Sol's features. "Then we shall rid the realms of the heir of that wretched throne and end their bloodline once and for all."

Solis struggled against Khael's restraint, golden flame igniting in his palm as he tried to break free, his fire licking across Khael's leather, yet the commander did not relent. Luna could only watch as the fire burned. So it was true. Sol was an Aurelius. Only the Aurelius bloodline carried a flame of such luminous gold.

His chest heaved, and despite his youth, his eyes held no fear. Only defiance. A kind of bravery Luna had never known a child could possess. His chin lifted, proud and unyielding, as if daring Khael to strike.

That was not wise. Khael was not the type to be swayed once his resolve had set.

The blade arched toward Sol's neck—

Luna moved before she realized it and threw herself between them.

THREE

LUNA

Her heart pounded hard against her ribs. Khael was going to kill the prince.

"Uncle, stop," she cried, her fingers scrabbling at Khael's grip on Sol in a desperate attempt to pull him free. "Spare him—he saved me!"

"Princess," Khael said, his tone implacable. "The son of a Solaran king is our foe. His father showed us no mercy, yet you want to spare his son? Blood does not change because of one good deed. His lineage is unchangeable."

"Please, Uncle," Luna pleaded, tears glimmering in her eyes. Her mind raced for a reason, for any thread of logic that might sway him. If his hatred could not be softened, perhaps his prudence could. Anything to save Sol. It was not that she cared for the boy, but the thought of someone so young—someone as innocent in this war as she was—being cut down before her eyes was unbearable. "Solara will seek vengeance if you kill him. He is Leo Aurelius's only son, the heir to their throne. If his death ignites a fury that drives Solara to strike in full force, Father will be absolutely furious. Think of your men. Think of our people. Bring him back to camp. Use him as leverage. He still has value."

Even at such a young age, Luna already understood the value of an heir. She knew what waged wars and what ended them, and killing Solis could spark a destruction neither realm could contain. A total bloodshed neither side desired. They could not afford to spill his blood.

Khael stalled. The blade of his weapon remained suspended in the air, poised directly over Sol's throat. Around them, the soldiers exchanged uneasy glances. Luna's voice trembled, but she persisted. "Please. Think of our people. He could change their fate. Use him. This might be our only opportunity to end this war."

Sol met her eyes. For a fleeting moment, gratitude flickered within the blue depths of his gaze.

Khael exhaled sharply through his nose, finally lowering his sword, though his tone remained edged in steel. "Fine. For your sake, Princess. But if he so much as breathes the wrong way, I will not hesitate to remove his head from his body."

With a rough shove, he pushed Sol to the ground. The boy struck the earth hard but lifted his chin nonetheless, still defiant. In a blur of motion, Khael stepped forward and delivered a solid blow to Sol's face, sending him stumbling, nearly losing his footing. He barely managed to steady himself as blood traced a thin line down his lip.

Khael's glare hardened. "I will not be looked at with defiance," he snapped.

There was wetness gathering in Solis's eyes, but he refused to let it fall. His spine straightened, silent and proud. There was no denying he was a prince. Luna could hardly believe she had not seen it sooner. Had the rabbit incident blinded her judgment?

"Get on the mount, boy," Khael barked, turning back to his horse. He swung into the saddle and waited.

Solis sniffed, swallowing his pain, and stepped forward. Khael hoisted him onto the horse with a rough hand.

Luna followed quietly. Moonshade was among the horses Khael had brought; the mare must have returned to camp on her own after Luna and Solis fled the assassination attempt. A rare occurrence—one she had never encountered before. Who would want her dead? Solara? A traitor among Selvaran? She shook the thought from her mind as she mounted Moonshade and fell in line behind the group as they turned toward her father's camp.

As they rode away, Luna watched Solis sit rigid in the saddle, the silver luminance of the moon catching the wet strands of his hair. A faint bruise was already blooming across the cheek Khael had struck.

He never turned to look back at her. His gaze remained fixed ahead, as though reckoning his fate with every step of the horse beneath him.

Luna knew her father would not kill a child. Children were sacred—rare. He would never inflict upon another father the same grief that haunted so many in Selvaran. She trusted he would show mercy. But she did not trust Khael.

The war had taken everything from him, carving tenderness from his soul. Solaran blades had claimed his wife and son. His hatred had hardened into something absolute.

The Selvaran camp came into sight, lying beneath an endless veil of stars in the clearing beyond the forest. Black-and-silver banners fluttered in the night breeze. They had arrived home.

Luna slid down from Moonshade, her boots sinking into the ground. She handed her reins to a nearby soldier. Khael dismounted as well, then yanked Solis from his mare. The boy stumbled, nearly falling, but Khael caught him by the collar of his mud-streaked shirt and dragged him forward toward the council tent.

"Change and get some rest, Princess," Khael ordered, his tone clipped.

"But what about Sol?" she called after him.

He did not slow. Solis dragged helplessly behind him. "The boy will meet your father, as you requested. Now, go."

With that, Khael pulled Solis deeper into the camp and out of her sight. Luna remained rooted, her pulse thundering with trepidation. If Khael had his way, Solis would not live to see the next Moonrise. She could only pray he kept his word and delivered the boy before her father.

Back in her tent, Luna stripped off her soaked garments and changed into something dry. Her hair was tangled and damp, but she was too exhausted to care. She lay down on her cot, her dark hair spilling like ink across the pillow, eyes fixed on the tent flap where moonlight filtered in with a spectral gentleness.

Sleep eluded her. No matter how she tried, she could not banish the image of the boy with the golden hair from her mind. The prince of Solara. The one who had saved her. The one who could have let her drown but didn't. The boy who cried over a rabbit. Sol was living proof that Solarans were not the monsters Selvaran made them out to be. Perhaps, in time, the two realms might bridge their differences and end this restless war.

She pressed a hand to her chest, feeling the rapid rhythm of her heart, wondering if the boy was out there, still safe. She prayed her father would be sagacious, as he always was, though Khael's influence could be perilous. A silent plea slipped from her lips.

He is only a boy. Please don't let him die.

Only then did sleep claim her at last.

The next Moonrise brought an unexpected relief. Luna's breath eased when she saw him at breakfast. He was alive. They had given him fresh garments in Selvaran colors, black trimmed with silver. In that attire, she could almost forget he was Solaran, if not for the gold of his hair and the vivid blue of his eyes. His sun-warmed bronze skin set him apart from their pale court, yet somehow he looked as though he belonged. The black made the blue in his eyes gleam brighter. Black suited him, ironic for the prince of the sun realm.

She hurried to her father and wrapped her arms around him, grateful for his mercy in sparing the boy.

King Orion chuckled softly and patted her hand.

"Sit, my little moon," he said. "I hear you met our guest, Prince Solis?"

Of course she had. She had found the reckless prince wandering near their border. He must have possessed a special kind of foolishness to trespass into Selvaran while bearing the Solaran crest. Luna would never have taken such a risk.

She pressed a kiss to her father's cheek. "Yes. We met in the forest."

King Orion smiled faintly, though curiosity flickered behind his calm, discerning eyes. He scrutinized Solis with quiet percipience. "I see. And tell me, child, why were you near the border? I cannot imagine your father allowing his only son to stray into enemy lands. What brought you there?"

Luna took her seat beside Solis, her curiosity mirroring her father's. A faint bruise still shadowed the boy's cheek where Khael had struck him.

Solis toyed absently with his food. "I wanted to see the stars."

For a heartbeat, silence enveloped the table. Even Luna forgot to breathe. The stars? The prince had risked his life for stars. Her mouth parted in disbelief. What kind of fool nearly died twice for something so simple? She fought the urge to roll her eyes but could not suppress a faint, incredulous smile.

Queen Astrid covered her mouth, a quiet laugh escaping. "My child, you risked your life to see the stars?"

Solis's face flushed. "We do not have them in Solara," he admitted softly. "I have read about them, and I wanted to see them for myself."

Something stirred within Luna. His wish sounded achingly familiar. She had always dreamed of seeing the golden oceans of Solara. Perhaps she understood him more than she cared to admit.

"So," King Orion said, folding his hands. "You entered our forest alone to see the stars? Did your father know?"

Solis lowered his spoon. "No, Your Majesty. I left the camp without permission. He will be angry."

King Orion's smile was gentle. "I imagine he will. I have written to him and asked that he come to collect his son from my camp. Do not worry. We will not ambush him. In truth, I see this as an opportunity to speak of peace."

Solis looked up, surprise illuminating his features. "Peace? You would call for peace?"

Luna's heart leapt. Her father had said the word aloud. Peace. The sound of it filled her chest like sunlight breaking through storm clouds.

Across the table, Khael's hand stilled above his plate. King Orion always dined with his subjects; that was the kind of ruler he was. Khael, his oldest friend and most trusted commander, sat among them with a hard, inscrutable expression.

"Orion," Khael said sharply, "you cannot invite the king of our enemy into our camp. It will endanger everyone. Think of your daughter."

King Orion lifted a hand, a quiet gesture for restraint. "King Leo loves his son as I love my daughter. He would not endanger his boy. We can make this work. I am weary of war, Khael. I have grown weary of watching our people suffer. It is time to end this. And what better place to begin than by bringing our children together?"

Luna looked at Solis. He met her gaze for a fleeting moment, and for the first time in her life, she felt something akin to hope. The war was ending.

After breakfast, King Orion dismissed them to meet with his council. Luna seized the chance to show Solis around the camp.

"See that tent over there?" she said, pointing ahead. "That is where I sleep."

He studied it curiously. "It is so colorful."

Luna's tent was dyed a deep violet, nearly the same hue as her eyes. She had begged her father to color it because she wanted it to stand out, unique and unmistakable, like her.

Solis raised an eyebrow. "Are you not worried assassins will know which tent is yours if it stands out so much?"

That was a fair point, the same one Khael had made when she first requested it. That was also why more guards surrounded her tent than anyone else's.

"I am a skilled fighter," she said proudly. "I am not afraid of assassins. Besides, they have not sent one."

Except for today.

They, of course, meant Solara. She did not need to say it aloud.

Solis's gaze lingered on her tent. His voice fell low, carrying a fragile tremor. "There have been assassination attempts on me. More than once. My father had them burned for it."

Luna blinked, comprehension striking like ice. The assassins in the forest had not been after her; they had hunted him. Yet they had loosed their arrows with her standing beside him. Whoever wanted Solis dead possessed no compunction about collateral bloodshed.

Could it have been Khael? Was he truly so ruthless as to send killers after a child? Had he known she was there that night? Would he have wanted her gone as well?

No. Khael's vengeance lay with Solara, not Selvaran. He would have wanted only Solis gone.

For a moment, she forgot what it meant for him to be a prince.

Being the only heir made him both a target and a symbol, a living emblem of his realm's power. Both kingdoms believed a single boy could raise an empire or shatter one. That was why Solis lived in peril. If he fell, Solara would fracture without an heir to its throne. It was the exact reason Khael would send assassins to hunt him. A throne without an heir was a throne doomed.

Solara would never send assassins after her because she was a woman.

She knew how Solara regarded women. In that realm, daughters were commodities bartered through marriage, their bloodlines absorbed into foreign houses. Power belonged to men, and women were little more than ornaments of alliance. She posed no threat in their eyes.

Let them believe that. Let them underestimate her.

The silence between them thickened. His words lingered like smoke.

It must be lonely, she realized, to be the prince of Solara. She could feel the weight of his solitude pressing against the quiet, and for once, she found herself bereft of words.

So she spoke the first thought that surfaced.

"Do you want to shoot arrows?" she blurted, her tone light and teasing, an audacious attempt to dispel the gravity that had settled between them.

And just like that, the tension dissolved. Solis's eyes brightened, and a grin curved his lips, warm and unguarded.

"Yes."

They crossed the field together and reached for their bows. Luna lifted hers, drew the string, and released. The arrow sliced through the air and struck the target's center with a resonant thud. Satisfaction bloomed in her chest. Archery had always been her forte, a skill that made her feel both fierce and free.

Solis raised his bow next. From his stance alone, Luna could already tell he would not strike the center. He released the arrow, and as she expected, it landed near the mark—commendable, but not perfect.

"How did you learn to shoot?" he asked, notching another arrow. This time, it missed the target entirely.

"Khael," she replied softly. "He is like a second father to me. He taught me everything."

"Must be nice," Solis said, his tone carrying a quiet wistfulness. "I trained with Argus. He is my only friend… and his father. Khael must be an exceptional teacher, because you shoot with incredible precision."

Luna felt warmth rise to her cheeks. "I suppose I do."

They spent the afternoon loosing arrows until the targets resembled pincushions. Luna continued to ask questions, fascinated by the boy beside her. Solis answered each one with patience, never irritated, never guarded. For a boy of ten, he carried himself with a composure far beyond his years. It was difficult to believe this was the same child who had cried over a rabbit only yesterday.

That night, Solis sat with her inside her tent. Luna had invited him after he mentioned a game he wanted to teach her, a strategy board called King and Queen. The goal was to conquer the enemy's pieces and capture their king. When the king fell, the people followed. As he spoke, his hand moved over the parchment, sketching the grid with careful strokes as he explained the rules.

Luna frowned. "What about the queen? Is she not significant too?"

"She is," Solis said. "She is the neck of the king, his strength. When she falls, the king loses his will. A powerful woman strengthens her king."

Luna regarded him for a long moment. For someone so young, his words carried a gravity that unsettled her. Solis fascinated her in ways she could not yet name. She had never met a boy quite like him.

FOUR

LUNA

At the next Moonrise, the announcement came. King Leo of Solara was coming for his son.

No one could believe it. The ruler of Solara setting foot on Selvaran soil after years of bloodshed was inconceivable, yet it was happening. The news rippled through the camp, carried on breathless whispers that darted between the soldiers like wildfire.

From a distance, Luna watched her father prepare for the meeting. He spoke with quiet composure to his advisers, but the faint crease in his brow betrayed a hidden unease. The two kings had never met despite decades of war. He masked his apprehension behind the polished veneer of command, the practiced restraint of a sovereign.

A low, resonant horn announced the arrival of King Leo Aurelius.

Luna followed her father outside, Queen Astrid and Khael flanking them, with Solis trailing close behind.

The Selvaran guards shifted uneasily as the Solaran banners came into view. White and gold, embroidered with a golden lion, shimmered beneath the moonlight—a brilliant contrast to Selvaran's black and silver. Even their standards were opposites, one radiant as dawn, the other veiled as dusk.

Luna stood beside her mother as her father advanced to greet their adversary. Solis remained near, his expression unreadable. Silence blanketed the camp as the two armies faced one another.

A towering man with hair like molten gold dismounted from his stallion. Where Solis bore gentleness, King Leo radiated iron. His features were chiseled and severe, the countenance of a lion carved from flame. A trimmed beard framed his mouth, and his golden eyes burned with cold, deliberate fury.

His black stallion halted a few paces away. King Leo's gaze found Solis at once, bypassing King Orion as though the ruler of Selvaran were no more than dust beneath his boots. Arrogant. Insufferable. Luna felt understanding settle within her. With a king like that, peace was a fantasy.

A flicker of something—anger or perhaps disappointment—passed across Leo's face. Solis shifted beside her, shoulders tense beneath the weight of his father's stare. Luna could not fault him. King Leo possessed no warmth, no mercy. For the first time, she truly appreciated the steady compassion of her own father.

"King Orion," Leo said, his voice deep and measured, cutting through the cold night air. "I see you have my son. Return him to me, and we will depart."

Despite Leo's brusqueness, Orion replied with composed civility. "Of course. It is not in my nature to hold a child hostage. Welcome, King Leo. It is an honor to host you. We meet not as enemies but as fathers." His gray eyes shifted to the Solaran retinue. "I do not see your wife, Queen Aurora?"

"My wife does not travel with me," Leo said curtly. "A woman's place is within the palace while a man fulfills his duty. Women on the battlefield are a distraction to men."

The remark made Luna's blood simmer. A distraction? The only distraction she could imagine was an arrow through the skull of any man who dared say such a thing.

King Leo tilted his head and looked past Orion to Solis, who stood rigid beneath the unrelenting scrutiny of his father's gaze. "Son, come to your father."

Solis took a hesitant step forward, uncertainty etched across his features. Before he could reach Leo, Khael seized his arm.

At once, the Solaran soldiers' hands flew to their hilts. Behind King Leo, a heavily armored man—likely the commander of his forces—fixed Khael with a glacial stare, a silent challenge.

The Selvaran troops mirrored the motion, palms resting on steel, their tension drawn taut as a bowstring. The air thickened, charged with the peril of a single misstep. Luna felt her breath falter and could not look away from her father.

The silence fractured when King Leo lifted his hand. At his signal, the Solaran soldiers lowered their weapons. His arm fell back to his side, the gesture of truce unmistakable. The violence that had threatened to erupt dissipated into brittle restraint, fragile as glass under strain.

"King Orion," he said, his tone cool and resonant. "I trust your commander does not intend to provoke a conflict. I want my son returned."

Orion turned to Khael. "Release the boy, Khael."

Khael did not move. His grip tightened, knuckles pale against the boy's sleeve. Solis remained motionless, silent, his gaze fixed ahead as the scene unfolded.

Challenging her father was one of Khael's many flaws, though perhaps it was also her father's for allowing such defiance. They had been comrades for decades, and that familiarity granted Khael liberties few others dared to take. In truth, he commanded the greater portion of Selvaran's forces; the soldiers were as much his men as they were the king's. Compassion, Luna realized, could be as formidable a weakness as it was a virtue.

"My king," Khael said sharply, "we should make arrangements before we hand him over. Once he has his son, we cannot predict what he will do next. I suggest we discuss terms first."

The tension in the camp thickened at Khael's words. Luna swallowed hard, each breath heavy with unease. This was a moment that could decide life or death.

The Solaran commander stepped beside King Leo and murmured something in his ear. Leo inclined his head as he listened, his gaze never leaving Solis. When the commander withdrew, his deference was unmistakable—an obedience Khael never granted Orion. At times, Luna wondered if Khael even regarded her father as a true king, given how often he defied him. Just as he did now.

In one fluid motion, Khael drew his sword and pressed the blade against Solis's throat. The edge glimmered beneath the moonlight, silver and merciless. Steel met sun-warmed skin, cold and unyielding.

"Do something foolish," Khael warned, "and I will have the child's head rolling on the ground."

He meant it. Luna knew that with chilling certainty. One reckless act could cost them everything—their lives, their fragile hope of peace. Her pulse thundered in her ears. They stood upon the knife's edge of war, and her mother was here.

Her heart pounded so violently it hurt. Please, she prayed silently, do not do anything reckless, Khael.

She held her breath and waited.

"That is unnecessary," King Leo said at last. Relief swept through Luna so swiftly she nearly gasped. "We have agreed to discuss terms. Shall we do this seated?" His gaze shifted to King Orion.

King Orion inclined his head, his expression composed. "Yes, of course. Please, this way."

Though the confrontation had ended, the air still trembled with unease. The soldiers had sheathed their weapons, yet the silence that followed felt precarious, as though peace itself were holding its breath. Luna could only hope that whatever terms her father intended would be enough to end the war once and for all.

Turning, she followed her parents into the council tent. Khael kept a firm grip on Solis's shoulder, guiding him forward with the sword still resting lightly against his back.

Once everyone was seated or standing along the perimeter, King Orion broke the silence.

"I would like to propose peace, King Leo," he began, his hands resting calmly in his lap. "Before anything else, I must tell you that I will return your son unharmed, regardless of your decision. As I said before, I do not wish harm upon a child." He turned to Khael. "Khael, remove the blade from the boy's neck. Let us speak as civil men. There is no need for such display."

Khael hesitated, then slowly withdrew the sword, though he kept Solis in front of him. The boy did not flinch. Even held at blade's edge, his composure remained unshaken—remarkable for someone so young.

King Leo leaned back in his chair. "What terms does this peace require?" His gaze sharpened. "I hope it is not my boy. I would not give my heir as a ward to Selvaran if that is your intention."

"No, no." King Orion lifted a steady hand. "I would never hold a child hostage from his father. I am a father myself." He paused, his tone contemplative. "Instead, I propose a union—a marriage. The boy will return home with you, but our realms can be bound through our children. I offer you my daughter in exchange for peace."

Luna froze. Marriage? To Solis? She had known him for only a few days, and now their fathers meant to bind them for life. Her stomach twisted. It took every ounce of strength not to cry out at such absurdity.

Solis did not look at her, but in the flicker of his eyes she saw it. He was thinking the same thing.

"Marriage?" King Leo's brows lifted. "The boy is eleven. Your daughter cannot be much older. They are far too young for such talk."

A faint smile touched King Orion's lips, his eyes glinting with quiet humor. "Not now, of course. When they come of age. I would never suggest one child marry another."

A long silence settled as King Leo weighed the offer. At last, he spoke. "This war has endured too long. I have no wish to see it continue. Your people have suffered as mine have. Perhaps it is time to end it. And if joining our children can bring unity, then I agree. But your daughter will bear the Aurelius name."

The audacity of it left Luna breathless. not only would she lose her freedom, but even her name. Her father's silence struck harder than any blow. Wetness blurred her vision, yet she refused to let the tears fall. Now was not the time to break.

King Orion nodded. "I agree to those terms."

No discussion. No glance her way. With a single handshake, her father sealed her fate.

And just like that, Luna Velastra, princess of Selvaran, was promised to Solis Aurelius, heir of Solara.

The betrayal burned. Women had always been bartered for peace, yet she had believed Selvaran was different—that her father was different. That he would at least speak to her before deciding her future.

The pain struck like a shattering star. A single tear escaped as she watched her father clasp hands with King Leo, sealing her destiny as though she were nothing more than a token to be traded. Her mother said nothing, though her silence carried the weight of fury. Luna could see the flare of wrath burning in Queen Astrid's unspoken eyes.

Solis stood beside her in silence, his expression unreadable. Of course he would not understand. He was a boy; he would never have to surrender his name, his home, or his freedom.

King Leo gestured for his son. Solis stepped forward, obedient yet hesitant. When he reached his father, Leo placed a hand upon the boy's head, giving it a firm, almost possessive rub.

"Thank your future father-in-law for his hospitality."

Solis turned and bowed. "Thank you, Your Majesty."

King Orion waved the gesture aside. "There is no need for thanks."

Father and son turned to leave. As Luna watched them, her heart began to sink. She was furious about the marriage, yet she could not bring herself to hate Solis. The boy who had made the last few days feel almost like a dream was leaving, and since they were now bound by betrothal, even if she despised the idea of losing her own choice, she wanted to give him something before he departed.

It was the Selvaran way to honor a promise with a token, even if she was the one offering it. Searching through her pocket, she found what she sought. It had once been a gift from her mother, and now she would entrust it to Solis.

"Wait," she called.

Solis halted and turned. Luna ran toward him and, without hesitation, took his hand. She pulled a small object from her pocket and placed it in his palm—a finely carved necklace bearing a crescent moon of polished stone.

"For a reminder," she said softly. "So you don't forget the stars. I hope to see you again, Solis."

A faint smile touched his lips. He closed his fingers around the pendant, then turned and walked beside his father. King Leo placed a heavy hand upon his son's shoulder, guiding him from the tent.

Luna watched until they vanished from sight. She prayed she would see him again soon, though reason told her that the next time they met, they would stand as betrothed.

Perhaps that was not entirely dreadful. Solis did not seem cruel. He was gentle, inquisitive, and far too soft for a prince raised for war. There could be far worse fates.

Her father's voice came gently from behind her. "My little moon, I apologize for not speaking with you sooner about this, but what is done cannot be undone. I hope you understand."

Before Luna could respond, her mother's voice sliced through the air, sharp as glass. "You should apologize to your wife as well. How could you make this decision, Orion, without a single word to me? How could you offer our daughter to lions?"

Oh no. Her mother was just as furious as she was.

Her father exhaled heavily. "Little moon, go get some rest. It has been a long night. Your mother and I have something to discuss."

"Oh, now you want to talk to me?" Queen Astrid snapped. "Go rest, little moon. I will give your father the earful he deserves."

Leave it to her mother to defend her. Luna knew how deeply her parents loved one another; they ruled together as equals. Unlike Solara, where a single throne belonged to the king, Selvaran held two. This marriage should have been forged with her mother's counsel as well. Knowing Queen Astrid, she might very well murder her father before Moonrise.

Slowly, Luna turned, leaving them to their quarrel. "Yes, Father," she murmured as she stepped outside the tent.

The camp had grown still. Soldiers had returned to their posts, and the Solaran troops had drawn back, granting their king distance yet keeping him within sight. Pale moonlight spilled across the encampment as though nothing had happened, though everything had.

From a distance, she watched King Leo and his son prepare to mount their horses. The path before them shimmered with torchlight. Their golden banners glimmered as they rode into the night, vanishing into the dark.

Luna remained there for a long while, her gaze fixed on the place where they had disappeared. Her thoughts drifted to that audacious prince who had crossed enemy lands simply to see the stars. Strange and unforgettable he was.

And even as she turned toward her tent, her reflections lingered on the boy who had only wanted to see the stars.

FIVE

SOLIS

The smoke was the first thing Solis saw when his father's army returned to the Solaran camp. Gold and white banners waved above the tents, the lion and sun sigil of Aurelius gleaming beneath the heat. His bloodline. His burden.

The sun scorched his skin, chasing away the lingering chill of Selvaran. Solara was born of fire; cold did not belong here. Yet the short time he had spent beyond the border had made him sensitive to its warmth.

King Leo dismounted and handed his reins to a soldier. He spoke briefly with Commander Ivan Korven, who saluted before hurrying away to fulfill his orders. Ivan was loyal to the Aurelius line beyond reason; obedience was his creed.

He had one son, Argus Korven, Solis's only true friend. Argus was three years older, yet he was the only person in Solara who treated him as an equal. The rest bowed, smiled, and wore their pretentious courtesy like fine silk. Their constant politeness was suffocating.

That was the curse of royalty. Everyone wanted his favor. Solis only wanted honesty, and Argus had always given him that.

Solis knew punishment awaited him the moment they crossed back into camp. He had trespassed into enemy land, been captured, and forced his father's hand into peace and into marriage. A Solaran prince bound to a Selvaran princess would be deemed a disgrace. The nobles would demand the union be dissolved as soon as word spread. Hatred for the Moonborn ran deep among the highborn. Only the commoners might not care, so long as their tables were full.

As the soldiers caught sight of him, they cheered. Their prince had returned. Their Sun, they called him.

Solis felt more like a fallen star. They did not yet know that peace had been bought through a promise of marriage to their enemies. And if they did, their celebration would curdle into something far less flattering. By the look on his father's face, even the king found no triumph in it.

His boots scuffed the dirt as he followed King Leo toward the royal tent.

King Leo looked over his shoulder. "Inside."

Solis obeyed and stepped through the tent flap. The air inside was stifling, thick with heat and the faint scent of charred parchment. Maps covered the table, scarred with inked symbols of conquest. His father picked up a scroll, studied it briefly, then dismissed it with visible disinterest.

"Son," King Leo said at last, "do you comprehend what you have done?"

Solis swallowed hard. "I only wanted to see the stars."

He knew that feeble explanation would not suffice, yet it was the only truth he possessed.

King Leo's brows lifted. "The stars?" His tone sharpened, edged with disbelief. He circled the table, eyes moving over the marks of war like a judge weighing sins. "You forced a peace that cost us victory. Solara was an inch away from conquering Selvaran, from expanding our dominion, and you ended it—for what? Stars?" His voice reverberated through the tent, heavy with disdain. "You embarrassed our name. You shamed your realm. Think of the soldiers whose lives were lost, their deaths rendered meaningless by your puerile foolishness."

Solis kept his gaze lowered, fixing his stare on his boots. "I am sorry."

"Sorry?" The word cut like tempered steel. "Sorry will not resurrect the fallen. Sorry will not console the widows or explain to our people why their sons died without glory. We could have claimed a tremendous victory, but instead we retreat because my son wished to gaze upon the night sky—and now you are bound to that cursed princess."

Solis's hands clenched at his sides. He had not meant for any of this. He had only wished to glimpse what Solara had never known. His throat burned, but he refused to cry. Nothing he said would restore his father's pride.

King Leo's boots halted before him. The king knelt, molten-gold eyes locking onto his son's as he lifted Solis's chin.

"Tears are for the weak. Love is for the weak. You must learn to be strong. Weakness invites death. Weakness brings ruin to our people. Do you understand me?"

Hatred brings ruin too, Solis thought, but he did not dare speak it. He merely nodded like the obedient heir his father demanded.

"Good." King Leo brushed a hand through his hair. "Now go. I have a mess to rectify."

No punishment? That was uncharacteristic of him. Yet Solis did not linger long enough to test his father's temper. He turned quickly, the tent flap striking against his back as he stepped outside.

The sunlight hit him full force, hot and unforgiving. Even a few days in Selvaran had dulled his eyes to its brilliance. Around him, soldiers waved and called his name, their jubilant voices a cruel resonance against the shame tightening his chest.

He lifted his gaze to the blazing sky. The light stung. The stars he had risked everything to see were now far beyond his reach.

A soldier passed and offered him a courteous smile. Solis tried to return it, but the gesture faltered. Their laughter felt hollow, their triumph meretricious. They did not know what he had done. They did not know their victory had been stolen by his hands.

Peace had once seemed noble, even sagacious. Now, with their cheers echoing in his ears and his father's words carved into his mind, all he felt was shame. Solara's triumph was gone. His bloodline was blemished. The soldiers had fought and bled for glory, and with one reckless act, he had tarnished it all.

He moved through the rows of tents, head bowed. The air reeked of dust and smoke, the heat pressing against his skin with oppressive constancy. Laughter trailed him, bright yet hollow, scraping against the heaviness in his chest.

He wished he could undo it all. The forest, the river, the promise. If he had obeyed orders, his father would not look at him with that veiled contempt.

His hand brushed the pendant at his neck. The small moon-shaped stone was cool against his skin, its silken edge unbecoming of a prince of Solara. He should have discarded it, yet something in him refused to let go.

Her voice lingered in his thoughts—the way she had shouted at her commander, the way she had looked at him without trepidation. She was nothing like the tales whispered of the Night Kingdom. She was not a cursed princess, not in the way his father believed.

The moon princess was everything Solara was not—brave when she needed to be, compassionate even to her foe. Love is not weak, he thought. My father is wrong.

He looked up at the sky. The sun burned bright, endless and merciless. Somewhere beyond that blinding light, the stars still waited.

SIX

SOLIS

Three years later…

The engagement had not lasted, just as Solis had predicted. In truth, he had not been permitted to see the moon princess again after that day. Only the crescent pendant resting against his chest reminded him that she had ever existed.

A year Into the engagement, his father had dissolved it after relentless petitions from the nobles, just as Solis had foreseen. Solara did not want the blood of the sun mingling with that of the moon. Such a union was deemed unnatural, an audacious defiance of tradition. Centuries of hatred could not be undone by a single vow.

Then the attacks began, sudden and inexplicable. Villages were found abandoned, with nothing left but ashes and distorted shadows where bodies had fallen. The realm whispered of curses. In time, Selvaran was blamed, though Solis was never convinced. King Orion did not strike him as a man driven by vengeance, but perhaps the annulment of his daughter's betrothal had wounded him deeply enough to provoke retaliation.

And so the war began anew, ending the fragile peace they had bled to secure.

In the years that followed, his father changed. It was as though something within him had splintered, altering his very nature in ways no one could explain. Even Solis could not comprehend what had happened, only that the man before him was no longer the father he once knew.

The rare tenderness that had existed between them vanished. The affectionate head rubs stopped. The kind words turned scarce, replaced by relentless fury that left Solis bewildered and hollow. Every mistake drew punishment. Every silence became an accusation. No matter how hard he tried, nothing was ever enough.

Just like today.

"Stand up, you weakling."

The sun seared against his skin as Solis stood in the training hall. Sweat slicked his back beneath the leather armor. Pain radiated through his shoulder as he forced himself upright, certain the bruise would bloom by Sunfall. At the far end of the room stood his father, eyes burning with the same cold disappointment that had become their only inheritance. Solis was no longer a son to him, only a failure draped in royal colors.

Why? Because he feared his own flame.

The fire that had once been his companion now felt foreign, estranged. It was as if he stood within a room that had once known his name, and now there was only silence. Since the day King Leo began using his own fire against him, that silence had grown deafening.

A burst of flame struck his ribs, searing through the armor. The heat bit into his skin like molten glass. Solis steadied his stance, refusing to cry out. He staggered forward, hands trembling as he pushed through the pain. With a swift pivot, he dodged his father's next strike and aimed a kick at his knee, but King Leo was faster. The king twisted aside and countered, his fist slamming into Solis's stomach. The air left his lungs in a hoarse gasp.

How was his father still this fast? For a man past his prime, King Leo fought with the fervor of a tempest. Solis knew he could match him if he dared to wield the fire that pulsed within his veins. But that meant surrendering to the very force he feared—the flame that had burned him, scarred him, and marked every failure.

"How can you call yourself an Aurelius," King Leo thundered, "when you cannot even command a single spark?"

With a flick of his hand, the king summoned fire. It coiled around his fist before slamming into Solis's back. Pain surged up his spine, sharp and scorching, but he swallowed the cry. Screaming was weakness. Fear was weakness.

And his father despised the weak.

And Solis was weak.

Frustrated, King Leo struck again, his boot driving into Solis's abdomen. Air burst from his lungs as he dropped to one knee, vision blurring. The guards at the edges of the hall did not move. None dared intervene when the king was "training" his son.

"You're no son of mine."

Cold trepidation rippled through him. He knew what came next.

Heat crashed against his back, searing through leather and flesh alike. The stench of charred armor thickened the air. Mercy had no place in the Aurelius creed. His father had proven that.

Solis gritted his teeth as flame ate at his skin. His fists clenched until his nails carved crescents into his palms. He had long since learned that crying only made it worse.

He remembered the first time his father burned him. He had been twelve, just two years ago. He had cried then, and that had only made his father angrier. King Leo had torn off his belt and whipped him until his back was raw, leaving strips of red that stung for days. Solis had gone to bed without supper that night, tears streaking his face.

His mother had come to him later, when the palace had fallen quiet. She rarely visited him now, not as she once did. He knew it had something to do with his father. A mother's love was another weakness he was forbidden to have. Love, his father said, was weakness. And he had burned that lesson into Solis's skin.

She had taken his small body into her arms, stroking his hair as she whispered,

"My sweet boy, do not cry. You must be strong. You must stand tall. You are the prince of Solara. You cannot show weakness."

Again that word. Weakness. Why did everyone care so much about it? Was he not human? Was he not allowed to feel?

Solis had rested his head on her shoulder and wept. That was the only time he allowed himself to cry—only with Argus or his mother, because neither ever judged him.

"But Mother, it hurts."

With the palm of her hand, she wiped away his tears. "I know, baby. I know. Endure it. Stand strong. You are the sun. You are the shield of this nation. Be strong."

Be strong. Be the sun. Be the shield.

He could not remember how many times he had repeated those words to himself during his father's wrath. Be strong.

What if he did not want to be? Why must he be the sun when all he wished was to be a single star, burning quietly on his own, with no kingdom to save and no crown to bear?

Why must he shine for others when he could not even shine for himself?

The next strike tore him from his recollection. His head bowed as his father's fury poured out in flame and flesh. When the final blow landed, the silence that followed was louder than pain itself. Sweat traced down his brow as his body quaked. His arms trembled beneath him as he struggled for breath. Heat crept up his neck, burning with humiliation.

King Leo's voice cut through the stillness, cold and sharp.

"You will never be a true Aurelius. Not while you cower behind your fire. Learn to control it, or it will consume you. Do you understand? An Aurelius does not fall to flame. They flare. They burn. They conquer."

Or they watch their fathers treat them like cattle.

Solis forced the words out, his voice hoarse. "Yes, Father."

"Speak up."

"Yes, Father." His voice came louder this time.

King Leo turned away. "Get out of my sight."

Solis rose. His back burned, but he did not waver. A prince did not waver. That was another lesson he had learned.

When the door closed behind him, he kept his posture straight even as his breath faltered. Straightening only deepened the pain, yet to show flaw would invite another lesson. And he was so very tired of lessons.

The scent of smoke and blood clung to him with every step, each heartbeat pressing its sting deeper into his back.

When he reached his chamber, a figure leaned against the wall. Green eyes, sharp as blades. Jaw tight with irritation. Arms crossed. Argus. His only friend, and now his assigned guard.

"What is the point of being your personal guard if you will not let me into the training hall?" Argus said. "You begged your father to bring me home, and now you hide from me like a child afraid of being caught."

Solis smoothed his expression, refusing to let the pain show, though he knew it was useless. Argus was too perceptive.

"My father asked me to come alone."

Argus rolled his eyes. Leave it to him to treat Solis like anyone else rather than a prince. He pushed off the wall.

"Show me."

Feigning confusion, Solis asked, "Show you what?"

Argus sighed, rubbing a hand over his short hair. "Solis, I know what he is doing to you. Just show me the damage."

Solis exhaled softly. It was impossible to hide anything from Argus. "Let us go inside first," he murmured, walking past him into the chamber.

Argus followed. Once the door was shut, Solis allowed him to unfasten the armor. Argus carefully lifted the leather from his back. Pieces had melted into the flesh, and when the armor peeled away, pain shot through him like fire. Solis screamed before he could stop himself. Hopefully no one would report it back to his father.

Argus did not flinch. He peeled the remaining pieces away one by one, setting them neatly on the floor. The touch of air against the wounds made Solis recoil. So much for being strong.

He lay on his stomach as Argus dipped a towel into the basin and began cleaning the burns. The cool water felt like deliverance, almost divine against the heat. When Argus lifted the towel, the white fabric was stained crimson. He rinsed it, then pressed it gently to Solis's back again.

"You will need ointment for the burns," Argus said quietly. "I will bring it after I meet with my father."

Silence lingered before Argus spoke again. "Why did you not fight back? I have seen you train. You are not powerless, Solis. You could have stopped him. Why are you so afraid of your father?"

Solis stared at the carved wood of his headboard. "Because I cannot use my fire."

"That is a lie," Argus said, his tone sharp. "I have seen you wield it countless times before."

Countless times when his flame had felt like home, not exile.

"Before he started burning me," Solis said quietly, striving to elucidate a fear too ineffable for words. "Ever since then, I have been trepidatious of it, shaken by the very fire that mirrors him."

In truth, he was daunted by what his power might unleash, apprehensive of the chaos coiled within him after years of suppression.

"And if you do not," Argus replied, his voice edged with conviction, "that fire will devour you from within. You know the peril of holding it in."

Solis shook his head, struggling to articulate what he hoped Argus might finally comprehend.

"I do not think you understand what I am saying. When it takes hold, I cannot harness the fire. I unravel."

Argus released a weary breath, the sound quiet and resonant in the tense air. With a steady hand, he wiped away the blood until the water in the basin clouded crimson and only heat and ache lingered on Solis's skin. When he was done, he rose and crossed to the dresser. Opening a drawer, he retrieved the hidden roll of linen Solis always kept for lessons like this, along with a small bottle of ointment.

Returning to his side, Argus uncorked the bottle and began to apply the salve to Solis's back. The cool balm soothed the angry heat the burns had left behind. Then, with deliberate gentleness, he bound the wounds in clean linen. He worked in silence, each motion precise and steady. Not a word passed between them until the bandages were tied.

"The king pushes you because he sees himself in you." Argus's voice came soft, almost a whisper, as though he was trying to convince himself as much as Solis. "But he has forgotten that even the sun can burn what it loves."

There was no denying the cruel truth of what King Leo had become. Argus had once respected the king as much as his own father did, but that respect had eroded with every wound he had tended. Solis could see it in the way Argus spoke of the man now. It was as though some part of him still fought to believe there was a fragment of goodness left within the king, that he was not entirely lost.

But Solis knew better. His father was gone.

A dull ache filled his chest, tearing at what remained of his weary heart. The words escaped him, fragile and final. "He does not love me. Not anymore."

Not anymore. When had he stopped? When had Solis become nothing more than flesh and blood instead of a son?

Argus swallowed hard as he stood, returning the remaining linen and ointment to the dresser. "No father simply ceases to love his child," he said quietly. "He loves you, Solis. He is simply too lost in his own pride to perceive it. Remind him who you are. Make him remember the son he once cherished, even if his heart pretends to forget."

No words could capture what passed through Solis's mind. The memory of his father's wrath lingered heavy and unrelenting, like the burns that seared his back. There was something different about him now, something hollow and cold. The man who had once laughed with him could no longer meet his gaze without shame or fury. No matter how rigorously Solis trained or how fervently he studied, it was never enough. What had fractured him so completely? Could a man's nature truly decay in so brief a time?

Whatever the reason, the man who had once been his father now seemed a stranger carved from stone.

"Rest, Your Highness," Argus said, his voice softened to something almost tender. "We will train again when you are healed."

The door closed behind him with a muted resonance, leaving the chamber steeped in silence.

Isolation seeped into Solis's bones, a cold that no flame could chase away. It was a loneliness carved deep, a wound he carried in place of his heart.

He let his eyes fall shut. Another day. Another lesson. Another scar to mark the ones that came before.

A constant reminder of what his father's love had become.

SEVEN

SOLIS

The nobles' endless chatter left Solis hollowed and exhausted. He stood beside his father in the throne room, enduring another tedious court session. As heir, it was his duty to attend to diplomacy, to learn the cruel architecture of politics and prepare himself for rule.

Under relentless tutelage, he had mastered the art of concealment, hiding every flicker of feeling beneath a stoic mask. Restraint was essential in Solara's court, where a single sigh could be read as weakness. He never knew when his father's temper might flare, so silence had become his safest currency. In that hall, his voice counted for little. He might as well have been a statue, an ornament reminding the court that the crown prince existed though he wielded no true power.

The nobles squabbled over the war. Some pleaded for peace. Others called for retaliation. Villages had been razed, one reduced to ash. The louder voices clamored for vengeance, pressing the crown to march into Selvaran, seize its castle, enslave its people, and hang its king for all to see.

Those were the kind of nobles Solis despised most.

Slavery? Humans have rights. They are not livestock.

"We have tried for peace, but Selvaran has refused it," King Leo declared. "Their forces have attacked the village of Dayreach. We cannot honor peace with a kingdom that cannot honor its word."

Solis stood silently beside the throne as the voices blurred into meaningless noise. His reveries wandered to violet eyes — the eyes of the girl he had met all those years ago. His fingers twitched toward the small crescent pendant that still hung at his neck. That pendant had been his only comfort through every brutal lesson and sleepless night. He could not imagine seeing her again. Not like this. Not when their realms were drowning in blood.

A hollow sorrow pressed against his chest.

Why did it ache? He barely knew her. Their nations had warred, made peace, and fallen into war again, yet the memory of her still stung more than it should. He missed her fierceness, her defiance. The girl possessed more courage in her small frame than half the men in this chamber.

His father's voice continued, but Solis no longer heard it. His reverie lingered elsewhere, on her, on that reckless smile beneath the moonlight. He had been only fourteen. What had he known then of marriage, of politics, of war? Nothing. Only the faint warmth that stirred whenever his fingers brushed the pendant she had given him.

Then a scream tore through the hall, shattering his sweet reverie. The acrid scent of charred flesh seeped into the air, dragging him back to reality. He blinked and saw it. A body consumed by flame, the screams fading into crackling embers. Within moments, what had been a man was reduced to ash.

He did not even know who it was. The fire had devoured every trace before his mind could register the face. Another life claimed by his father's fury. Only the stench of burning flesh lingered, clinging to the air like a curse.

King Leo stood with one arm raised, fingers curled upright, flame still coiling from his palm.

This was the very reason Solis wore a mask. For moments like this. Not a single expression escaped him. Any flicker of reaction would invite punishment later. A prince did not waver, even when his gut threatened to betray him.

He blinked until the pounding in his chest slowed, until the sickness twisting in his stomach began to subside. The stench of burnt flesh did nothing to ease the nausea clawing through him.

"Anyone who dares question my decision will share the same fate." King Leo's voice thundered through the hall, scorching into Solis's mind. The message was clear. Silence followed, heavy and suffocating, as though the nobles themselves were afraid to breathe.

To escape the cruelty of the Solaran court, Solis let his thoughts drift to the history of the magic that flowed through his veins. Magic had once been a gift bestowed upon the chosen, but centuries had worn it thin, leaving remnants only within royal bloodlines and a few noble houses.

From what he had studied, there was an age when the two realms had been one. The world had not yet been divided by light and shadow, but by those who could wield magic and those who could not. History did not reveal what calamity tore them apart, only that when the world fractured, it gave rise to two legacies. The golden flame of Aurelius claimed the lands of Solara, and the seers of Velastra shaped Selvaran.

He often wondered what it must have been like when the world was whole, when the sun and moon once shared the same sky. How did the magic-wielders live among those without? What had fractured them so deeply? What cause had turned unity into division?

Again, his reverie ended with an interruption. A noble, Lord Drabon if Solis remembered correctly, fell to his knees and pleaded with King Leo.

"Your Majesty, I implore you to consider the prince. His betrothal to Princess Luna could secure lasting peace between our realms. Severing that bond to force another match will not heal the kingdom; it will sunder it. It will bring suffering to the prince and perhaps to us all."

That revelation startled even him. There were nobles who still supported his marriage to Luna? He had thought the hatred for Selvaran ran too deep among the Solaran court, yet here stood a lord who dared to challenge that hatred with compassion, a quality rare among Solarans and rarer still in one who would openly defy the king.

When Lord Drabon spoke his final words, they echoed in his conscience. He was speaking of Solis's new betrothal to Duke Veyra's daughter, Calista. The very thought chilled him to the core. He remembered her all too clearly, the seraphic smile that never reached her eyes, the way she demeaned servants, the cruelty veiled beneath her beauty. To be bound to someone like her would not be a union. It would be a death sentence.

He opened his mouth to protest, but the flames spoke first, drowning his words in heat.

Drabon's scream tore through the hall, sharp and fleeting, before silence devoured it. Another pile of ash. Another life immolated.

Solis swallowed hard, heat creeping up his neck like a serpent.

King Leo turned his molten gaze upon him. "Go on, son. Surely you have something to say?"

Solis's throat constricted. "No, Father."

"Good," the king said, his voice low and searing.

Solis lowered his gaze. The stench of smoke clung to his clothes, his hair, his skin, a scent too heavy to wash away. It lingered in the air like guilt made tangible. Deep within, he buried what fragile remnant of his soul still survived.

The court meeting ended as swiftly as it had begun, yet the weight of it all felt heavier than granite. Only after the great doors closed behind him, sealing in the smoke, the stench of burnt flesh, and the ashes left within the throne room did Solis allow himself to breathe.

His chest rose unsteadily as his fists tightened at his sides. He blinked back the wetness threatening to surface, mourning the loss of someone's father, brother, and husband, lives taken today because of him — because they had tried to protect him.

He walked away from the throne room, each step faster than the last. He needed to move. To do something. Perhaps the training hall. Perhaps swing a sword until his arms went numb. Anything to feel again. The ache in his chest tore through his body with every breath.

His fingers found the pendant hanging from his neck. He held it tightly, drawing in a trembling breath as he swallowed the day's horror, forcing it deep where it could no longer be seen.

He was lost in the chaos of his shattered thoughts. His mind raced, his chest constricted until he could barely breathe. Footsteps echoed through the marble corridor, hurried and deliberate, closing in behind him.

A hand caught his shoulder and turned him around. Green eyes met his, steady and unreadable. Argus always carried himself like stone, unwavering and unshaken, yet Solis could see the concern flickering behind those sharp eyes. Argus's grip tightened, grounding him, studying him In silence.

Solis drew in several shallow breaths, each one a battle against the panic clawing at his chest.

Argus leveled himself to meet Solis's eyes. "Talk to me. Tell me what happened."

Solis could not speak. The words seared in his throat like fire, trapped and suffocating. His body trembled as he opened his mouth, trying to force them out, but nothing came.

Argus leaned closer until their foreheads met. His voice softened. "Come on, little brother. Breathe. Tell me what happened. Let me help you."

Solis's voice emerged at last, every word trembling as the memory clawed its way free. "He burned them alive. Two lords, for speaking against him. For speaking for me."

Argus's jaw tightened, his eyes hardening. "He made you watch?"

Solis gave a tight nod.

Argus exhaled slowly and placed a hand on Solis's head, the same gesture his father once used to make. A silent ache pierced through Solis's chest like a blade. He missed that touch more than he could ever admit. He missed the man his father used to be, not the tyrant who now sat upon the throne. That man was not his father. He could have been a stranger for all Solis knew.

"Hey," Argus said softly. "Look at me. You will be all right. I remember the first time I saw someone die. It stays with you for a while, but it fades. You will be fine, Sol. You hear me?"

Solis looked away as a tear slipped down his cheek despite his effort to hold it back. "They burned because of me, Argus. I do not know how I can endure that guilt alone. How can I survive this?"

Argus cupped his face, forcing him to meet his gaze. "Because I am right here with you. You are not alone. No matter what happens, I will be there. I would die before I allow him to break you."

Solis swallowed hard and gave a small nod. Only then did Argus release him, satisfied he would not crumble apart. They called Solis the sun, the shield of the realm, but to him, the true strength of Solara had always been Argus, the one who bore that light when Solis could not. Solis was not strong like Argus.

Argus swung an arm around his shoulders, ruffling Solis's hair in a teasing head rub as they started down the corridor. For the first time that day, Solis felt a little lighter. It had always been that way with Argus. He kept Solis standing through every battle, through every storm.

The memory of the burned still haunted him, though. He had never told Argus about the nightmares.

They walked in silence for a while before Solis broke it, his voice quieter than he expected. "They broke my engagement." The words hung uncertainly between them. Was there a part of him that still wanted that engagement to remain?

Argus let out a deep laugh. "Do not tell me you are upset about that. That engagement ended years ago."

Solis clicked his tongue. "That, and he has arranged another one."

Argus's lips tugged into a faint smirk. "You are rather popular, are you not? One engagement after another, and you are barely fourteen."

Solis's voice trembled before he steadied it. "He wants me to marry Calista."

The name tasted foul on his tongue. Of all people, his father had chosen her.

That made Argus stop mid-stride, his shoulders stiffening. "Did he say it was decreed?" His tone sharpened, edged with something Solis could not name.

"Yes," Solis replied softly. "He said I will marry her when I come of age. The decree has been sealed. That is why he burned the lords. They dared to oppose the union."

Argus exhaled sharply, his expression hardening. "That girl," he muttered. "All beauty, yet a heart rotten to the core."

Solis gave a humorless smile. "That makes two of us who think so."

They fell silent again. The marble floor gleamed beneath them, mirroring the golden light that streamed through the tall windows. That was the gift of Solara. There was always light.

At last, Argus spoke, his tone softening. "Sol," he said, using the nickname he had given him, "promise me you will not become him. Promise me you will remain as you are."

Solis looked up at his companion, the only person who saw him, not the crown. "Like what?"

Argus's lips curved faintly. "Soft. Kind-hearted soft. Like a fluffy little bunny."

"I am not soft." Solis frowned. "And do not ever compare me to a bunny, Argus. It would ruin what little pride I have left."

That earned a low, genuine laugh. "Whatever you say, kid."

They reached the end of the corridor, where the doors opened onto the royal balcony. The sky outside was dimming, brushed in the fading hues of sunset, the hour known as Sunfall. Solis stepped forward and gazed over the city below, rooftops glinting beneath the sun's dying light.

He lifted a hand toward it. The sun had always been his sanctuary, its warmth something he cherished as if it were a fragment of his soul. Slowly, he closed his fingers, letting the light fade within his palm.

"I want to see her again," he whispered.

Argus did not need to ask who he meant. His voice came low, almost reverent. "You were a boy then, and in some ways, you still are. What you feel is not love, Sol. It is merely the resonance of something kind."

"Maybe. I never claimed it was love," Solis murmured, his gaze still fixed on the streets below. "She was simply the first thing that ever felt real to me."

Argus gave a slight nod. "A girl can awaken parts of you that you never knew existed, but do not mistake kindness for love."

Maybe he was right. Could someone his age truly comprehend what love was?

Solis had no answer. He was not sure what he felt. But at last, he whispered, "I know."

Perhaps it was not love. Perhaps it was simply the kindness he needed in this gilded cage. Perhaps it was because the only time he had ever felt free was when he was with her.

EIGHT

SOLIS

The next morning, the palace stirred with life. Servants hurried through the corridors carrying boxes, bouquets, and silver trays of food. Some knelt to polish the marble floors until they gleamed like glass, while others exchanged quiet whispers with guards at their posts. The morning unfolded like any other, except today held the misfortune of his betrothed's arrival.

Solis stood beside his father as Lord Lucien Veyra and his daughter entered through the palace gates. Calista's pale blond hair caught the morning light, gleaming almost white beneath its brilliance. Her green eyes, so like Argus's yet stripped of warmth, locked onto Solis the instant she stepped inside, a fox studying its prey. He could not fathom how someone so young could carry such calculated intent. He turned away quickly as his father descended the steps to greet Lucien.

Solis remained at the foot of the grand staircase, the marble beneath him glowing under the soft radiance of day. The pendant Luna had given him rested beneath his tunic, cool against his chest. He never removed it. It offered the same quiet solace as sunlight on his skin.

Behind him, Argus stood in quiet vigilance, silent as ever, yet Solis could feel his presence like an unspoken promise at his back.

Lucien greeted the king with a smile so refined it seemed rehearsed, its sharpness betraying its falsity. Calista lingered behind her father, her gaze unwavering on Solis. There was something serpentine in that stare, a quiet hunger hidden beneath the charm.

"Solis," King Leo said, his tone measured and firm. "Come down and greet your fiancée."

Solis hesitated before descending the steps. Argus stayed where he was; by law, a personal guard could not intervene in royal matters. Still, Solis wished he could follow. He did not want to be alone with Calista.

Her lips curved wider as he approached, that practiced, venomous smile that always made his chest tighten. He shifted slightly and glanced toward Argus for reassurance. Argus met his gaze and gave a small, grounding nod. Solis swallowed hard and stepped forward.

When he reached her, he placed his right hand over his chest and bowed slightly, a prince's courtesy performed out of duty. Calista dipped into a flawless curtsy, her arms spreading with deliberate grace, each motion as rehearsed as the smile upon her face. These rituals were something Solis obeyed rather than embraced. His father would have his head if he dared to do otherwise.

"Lucien," King Leo said, placing a hand on the duke's shoulder as though they were lifelong allies rather than king and subject. "We have much to discuss. Let us leave the children to their duties."

Lucien's gaze flicked to his daughter. "Calista, I leave you with the prince. Try to behave yourself." Then his eyes shifted to Solis, cold and calculating. There was cruelty in that look, a silent challenge that made Solis's skin prickle. It was not the way one should look at a prince of the realm. If his father noticed, he chose to ignore it.

"Your Highness, I must trouble you to watch over my daughter."

With that, Lucien and King Leo turned and ascended the staircase together, their voices fading into polite conversation.

Solis remained where he was, shifting his weight uneasily. He stared at his feet, searching for words, but his thoughts tangled in disarray. The only ones he managed were, "Hi, Calista."

She stepped closer, each movement slow and deliberate, sending a chill down his spine. Her pale hair shimmered like silk, and her golden gown caught the light like molten sunlight. She was beautiful; everyone said so, yet beauty meant little when it cloaked a serpent.

"Your Highness," she said softly. Her voice was sweet, melodic, carefully practiced. "It is such an honor to see you again, and as your fiancée. What a dream it is to be engaged to a prince."

Fiancée. The word turned in his stomach like something spoiled.

Her smile widened, all grace and pride. "I hope you missed me."

He had not. Not once. He would rather be back in the training hall beneath his father's temper, anywhere but here. Memories of her cruelty flickered through his mind: the servant girl she had forced to her knees, the stray dog she had kicked for amusement. He had told his father once. It changed nothing. Calista never faced consequence for anything she did. That part still baffled him. Lucien was a duke, not a king, so why did his father fear him?

"You have grown," was all Solis managed to say, because it was the only safe thing to say.

"So have you," she purred. "You have aged well. I have heard of your training. They say you outmatch seasoned warriors. My father calls you the pride of Solara, the sun itself."

The sun of Solara. What a joke. He felt more like its eclipse.

Solis forced a thin smile. "Your father flatters me."

"Does he?" Calista tilted her head, eyes glinting like polished glass. "I thought truth was hardly flattery, Your Highness."

Behind him, Argus cleared his throat softly, breaking the tension. The sound alone brought Solis a fleeting sense of relief.

Speaking with Calista always felt like draining the very essence of his soul. Her gaze flicked briefly toward Argus before returning to him, refusing even the courtesy of a word. Her impeccable manners were precisely what made her so insufferable.

"Your guard seems to have forgotten his manners," Calista said smoothly. "I was under the impression that servants speak only when spoken to. Perhaps my father should remind him of what becomes of dogs who bark without permission."

Solis's gaze hardened. He was done feigning civility. No one touched Argus, not while he still drew breath. He cared little for Calista's lineage or the influence her father wielded in court. Before Argus could utter a word, Solis stepped forward and fixed her with a stare sharp enough to cut glass.

"Argus is the son of Commander Ivan Korven," he said, his voice low yet edged with frost. "In case you have forgotten, Calista. He is no servant."

A flicker of gratitude crossed Argus's face, brief and unmistakable.

Calista's smile did not falter. It was the smile of a serpent disguised as a courtier, languid and calculating. She glided closer until her breath brushed his ear, her perfume cloying and sweet, leaving a bitter trace in the air.

"You should speak more sweetly to me," she murmured, her voice a silken coil of mockery. "Or I might ask your father to remind you of your manners, my prince. I hear his lessons are quite unforgettable."

Heat crept up Solis's collar, fury coiling in his chest like a living flame. He shifted his head until their faces hovered mere inches apart. His blue eyes glimmered with glacial restraint, the kind of cold that could freeze blood.

"That is not how you should speak to your fiancé, my lady." His tone was chill, each syllable daring and edged with contained fury. "Perhaps your father should learn to teach his daughter how to address a prince. Because that is what I am," he added, his voice razor-sharp. "If you have forgotten, Calista." His final words cut clean. "Remember your place."

A quiet, derisive laugh slipped from her lips, soft and venomous. Her eyes held his with the smugness of a predator toying with prey, untouched by fear.

"You are learning to talk back," she said lightly, amusement twining with provocation. "How charming."

With languid grace, she reached into her gown and drew out a small satin pouch, as though she had not just mocked him.

"I brought you something," she said brightly, her tone shifting with unnatural insouciance, as if no venom had passed between them.

Solis studied her in still silence, his stare unblinking. Beneath her pulchritudinous exterior, he discerned the fracture that ran deep, a mercurial temperament that turned without warning. To her, cruelty was sport. A perverse fascination. A chill of intuition stirred within him, whispering that her allure was nothing more than an exquisite façade, hollow and perilous, crafted to conceal the rot festering beneath.

From the pouch, she withdrew a golden chain adorned with a ruby pendant shaped like a blazing sun. Her jasmine-and-rose perfume thickened the air, suffocating with each breath she took. She held the pendant before his eyes, tilting it so the light danced across its surface.

"I saw this and thought of you." Her voice carried that same rehearsed sweetness. If madness had a name, it was Calista. "Fire, like the Aurelius bloodline. Does it not resemble the sun?"

Solis regarded it in silence. The pendant glowed with the fervor of his crest, yet it felt hollow to him—like Calista herself—a meretricious symbol of warmth wrapped around a venomous heart. Instinct urged his fingers toward the chain beneath his tunic, Luna's moonstone pendant. His reminder of the stars.

He had never taken it off. He could not imagine replacing it. Calista must have known that. Why else offer another?

Before he could refuse, she took his hand, turned his palm upward, and dropped the pendant into it. Her fingers folded his hand around the chain.

"There," she said, her tone delicate as silk. "Now you will have a piece of me with you always."

Solis's hand tightened around the cold metal. The ruby glinted like fresh blood in the light. To him, carrying a piece of her felt like carrying decay. The pendant burned against his skin, unwanted and heavy, another burden forced upon him.

He disguised his distaste behind a polite, strained smile. "Thank you."

A wiser part of him knew better than to ignite the fire simmering beneath the surface. Calista was as unpredictable as the tide, shifting between calm and chaos without warning.

"Try it on," she said, that wicked smile curving her lips. "I always see you wearing that unsightly crescent. It hardly befits you."

The moon suited him more than he could ever articulate. Its light called to him, a quiet, ineffable pull that felt almost alive. It was the calm to his fire, the serenity to his storm, the light that had guided him through darkness.

His grip tightened around the ruby. "Perhaps later."

His voice emerged more strained than intended. For the briefest moment, her smile faltered. Her green eyes darkened, revealing the real Calista—cruel and calculating. Then the mask returned, bright and artificial.

"Try it on, Solis."

"No, thank you," he said coolly, each syllable a quiet defiance. He would not wear something tainted by her touch.

She stepped closer. Faint shadows gathered at her fingertips, distorting the air. Calista was a shadow-wielder, like her father. No one knew how they had gained such power. Lucien Veyra's origins were a mystery—he had appeared from nowhere, married a noble's daughter, then ascended Solara's hierarchy with unnatural speed. Now his influence stood just beneath King Leo's.

No one questioned it. Not even the king. And that was what unsettled Solis most. Shadows did not belong in Solara. Darkness had no place in the realm of the sun.

A firm hand seized Solis's shoulder and drew him aside. Argus stepped forward, his gaze unflinching. "The prince said he does not wish to. I suggest you heed his words and step back, my lady."

Calista tilted her chin, her expression venomously serene. "When I am queen, Argus, remember this."

When I am queen.

The words cut like a blade. Something sharp and furious twisted inside him. He would do whatever it took to ensure that day never came.

For now, he forced himself to remain composed. His father would punish him if he caused a scene, and this was already teetering close to one. To defuse it, he swallowed his pride.

"Calista, he meant no offense," he said carefully. "I simply do not wish to risk damaging the pendant. Perhaps I will wear it later. You have my gratitude for the gift."

Argus shot him a look that said, *You cannot be serious*, but stepped back, granting Calista room once more.

She smiled and slipped her hand through Solis's arm as though they were already bound. "Indulge me, my prince," she said with saccharine poise. "Show me around your radiant palace."

Show her around. The thought was laughable. The Veyras had been entrenched in Solaran politics for decades. Calista had practically been raised within these walls. She needed no tour — only an audience.

But he led her anyway.

As they walked through the corridors, the maids bowed and the guards straightened at the sight of him. Solis acknowledged them with a polite nod. Calista held her chin high, her eyes glimmering with disdain, as though everything beneath her were unworthy of notice.

He hated her already.

She spoke without pause, extolling her brilliance and recounting how everyone envied her, mocking those too petty to recognize her worth. She listed her virtues like debts the world owed her. Solis listened in silence, bile rising at her self-adulation. She was the kind of noble who found pleasure in cruelty, too self-absorbed to care for anyone beyond herself.

Argus followed a few steps behind, silent and vigilant. His hand rested on the hilt of his sword, his eyes occasionally rolling at Calista's endless monologue. Solis caught each one from the corner of his vision and had to keep from laughing. Calista, absorbed in herself, noticed none of it.

They encountered his father and Duke Veyra in the main corridor on their return from the so-called tour. By then, Solis was ready to tear his own ears off just to escape the sound of her voice.

Duke Veyra bowed low, a hand pressed to his chest. "I am honored to join our houses, Your Majesty. May this union strengthen Solara and ensure heirs of true Solaran blood. Imagine mingling our line with that of a Selvaran. Truly abhorrent."

King Leo's chest swelled with pride. "I agree. I cannot have our blood sullied."

Solis bit the inside of his lip. Luna was not filth. Her family had shown him kindness—more kindness than his own parents ever had. Calista, in contrast, embodied everything rotten in the nobility: self-centered, cold, and venomous.

Calista drifted to her father's side, announcing their arrival with an affected grace. Solis longed to vanish behind one of the marble pillars. There had been enough formalities for one day.

King Leo turned his head toward him. "Solis, you will dine with Lady Calista tonight. She will remain here in the palace for now."

His mouth fell open. She would live here. Next to him. Every waking day would be a slow, exquisite torment.

"Father," he began. The walls seemed to tighten around him. Now he would have to endure both his father and Calista.

King Leo's voice cut through like a blade. "I do not wish to hear it. The only words I expect from you are yes, Father. Do you understand, boy, or must I remind you of your manners?"

As always, there was that temper—burning like wildfire, uncontrollable and consuming.

With no choice and fear tightening in his chest, Solis swallowed. "Yes, Father."

"That is what I thought." King Leo waved them away, his tone glacial. "Show her to her chambers. They are next to yours."

Another tour. As if one were not enough. Even Argus showed signs of irritation despite his usual composure. Calista was exhausting in every possible sense, her arrogance grating even on someone with his restraint.

As before, when Solis led her up the stairs of the eastern wing toward his chambers, Calista's voice never ceased. Her words filled every quiet space, self-praise woven through idle complaints about the décor, the servants, the food. He wondered if she ever grew tired of hearing herself speak, because he certainly did.

They reached the door beside his own chamber. Solis stopped and stared at it, resentment coiling in his gut. The air felt heavier here, as if the palace itself disapproved of her presence. He exhaled slowly, forcing his composure, then turned the handle.

"Your room," he said curtly. "I trust it will suffice."

Calista brushed past him without a word, her perfume lingering like poison in the air. Solis watched her cross the threshold, already dreading the days to come. He closed the door behind her and stood there for a long moment, steadying the quiet fury beneath his skin.

Argus watched Calista with narrowed eyes, as if glare alone could set her ablaze. She tipped onto her toes and pressed a kiss to Solis's cheek, a calculated gesture meant to claim him like property, the same way she treated everyone else. He wanted to burn his own face clean.

When they were finally released from Calista and her torturous tongue, Solis ascended toward the main hall.

Anger pooled beneath his ribs like molten heat. His fire pulsed, demanding release. He forced it down and turned toward the training hall instead.

Argus fell into stride beside him. "She is charming enough to burn the patience out of a man," he muttered.

Solis's lip twitched. "Charming like a rotten fruit. She contaminates everything around her."

Argus's mouth curved faintly. "If you ever decide to torch her, tell me first. I might assist. It would spare the realm a great deal of trouble."

Leave it to Argus to threaten a duke's daughter without a flicker of hesitation. Truthfully, Solis would not have minded. Calista was an insufferable thorn lodged beneath his skin, one he could never remove.

He glanced down at the ruby pendant still in his hand. He had not yet found the chance to put it away. Keeping it in his pocket would likely burn a hole straight through it. His palm flared with heat as the gem caught his light. "I wish I could," he murmured. "But she is someone's daughter."

Someone—as in the man who now stood at the king's right hand, rising in influence with every passing season. The someone they could not afford to offend. Solara did not need a civil war.

"That someone's daughter will become your nightmare, Solis," Argus said quietly. "Mark my words."

Probably true. Calista would be his nightmare.

Solis slipped the ruby into his pocket, feeling its unwelcome weight with each step. He made a mental note to rid himself of it the first chance he had.

The moon-shaped charm at his neck rested cool against his skin, steady and familiar. It belonged there. It always had.

NINE

SOLIS

Dinner with Calista proved just as insufferable as Solis expected. He picked at his meal, idly swirling his fork while she went on and on about herself. Again.

The dining hall of Solara Citadel shimmered in gold and sunlight that streamed through the clerestory windows above. Only the clink of utensils and Calista's voice disturbed the still air. His ears felt as though they might start bleeding. Perhaps they already were.

A hand fell upon his head, smoothing through his hair. Solis shifted slightly, realizing the touch belonged to his mother. She could have sat at his father's side, yet she chose to sit beside him instead.

"My sun, do not play with your food," she said softly, her fingers threading through his hair. A faint comfort settled over him. He wanted to lean into her touch, but doing so would only draw his father's wrath. Love was weakness. A mother's affection, according to King Leo, interfered with discipline and the strength of one's fire.

Solis met her eyes. Blue, like his. "Yes, Mother."

She pinched his cheek with a small smile.

"Do not baby him," King Leo's voice thundered. "The boy is old enough not to be smothered by his mother."

His mother flinched.

Beside him, Calista let out a sharp snort of laughter. Heat crawled up his neck. His fist tightened around the fork, his gaze locked on his plate. He bit down on his tongue until the metallic taste spread across his mouth.

On his other side, Queen Aurora lowered her gaze. The hand that had comforted him withdrew. Her smile faded as she quietly resumed cutting her meal. Solis despised the tone his father used with her.

Calista turned and smiled at him. His blood turned cold. The hairs on his arms rose, a chill sweeping through him. That monster smiled at him, smug and calculated, as if mocking him in silence.

"Solis, I think we should honor our engagement with a celebration," she said brightly, her pale lashes fluttering. "A feast, perhaps."

A feast. A waste of gold while people starved and war still burned along their borders. Was she truly that blind? And those lashes. Did she think batting them made her charming?

Solis set his fork down. "I believe we should focus on political matters rather than a marriage festival," he said evenly. "The people do not need a celebration. They need hope. They need their rulers to show strength and end the war."

Lucien looked up, his lips curling into something that resembled a smile, though it never reached his eyes. "Well said, my prince. King Leo, your boy has a fine head on his shoulders. I am honored that my daughter will marry such a promising young man."

Promising young man. Solis nearly scoffed. He was still a boy, not yet a man. The marriage was absurd, a political farce that could unravel what little peace remained with Selvaran. The kingdoms had already agreed he would marry their princess. To turn away now, without proof that Selvaran was responsible for the attack on Dayreach, could shatter any hope of reconciliation.

"May I suggest," Solis said carefully, "that we meet with Selvaran to discuss peace?"

The sharp crack of his father's hand striking the table reverberated through the hall. Solis stiffened, the sound cutting through him as King Leo's eyes flared with fury.

"You will hold your tongue. The affairs of the realm are decided by men who can comprehend the weight of this kingdom, not by a mere boy who has yet to earn his place. Finish your meal. You will report to my study later."

A small tremor passed through him before he could suppress it. His mask returned as he lowered his head. "Yes, Father."

He said nothing more for the remainder of dinner. Calista's voice became a blur of meaningless sound. All he could think about was what awaited him later. His back already ached with the ghost of old punishments.

When the meal concluded, Solis rose from his seat and excused himself. He had barely stepped into the corridor before Calista followed. Her arm slipped through his before he could stop her.

"Leaving so soon?" she asked, her voice dripping with affected sweetness. "How discourteous of a prince."

"I do not recall being commanded to escort you like a servant," Solis replied evenly. "I would appreciate it if you afforded me some distance, Calista."

He wished Argus were there, but Argus had not been permitted to dine with him. He was likely in the guard quarters with his father, Commander Ivan Korven.

Calista's lips curved, her voice lowering to a purr. "Then I hope you value the lesson your father will teach you soon."

Solis halted, heat crawling up his spine. "What did you do?"

She lifted one delicate shoulder, the gesture infuriatingly casual. "I merely informed His Majesty how insolent his son was toward me. How he allowed his guard to humiliate me before others. He agreed such behavior required correction."

She slipped her arm free, her smile sharpening into something triumphant. "Consider it a favor. A prince should learn obedience early. Especially one destined to be my husband. I expect nothing less than complete discipline."

Obedience. His blood boiled. His gaze followed her as she turned and glided down the corridor, her footsteps fading into silence.

Solis stood motionless, fury coiling in his chest until it threatened to consume him. His hands trembled at his sides, the urge to summon fire rising beneath his skin. Words eluded him. Breath eluded him.

"Learn well, Solis," she called over her shoulder as she drifted farther away. Her voice lingered long after she disappeared.

Solis tried to stop his hands from shaking as he walked to his father's study while the sun went down. The sky was streaked with red and pink, the only sign that night had come to Solara, where the moon never rose. It was called Sunfall in Solara, and Moonfall in Selvaran.

His fingers twitched as he knocked on the door. Why was he so afraid? This was not his first punishment, nor would it be his last. Yet his body quivered as if he stood atop a frozen peak with no escape.

He drew a slow breath when his father's voice came from the other side. "Get inside."

Solis obeyed, closing the door behind him. He kept his head low, though his eyes lifted enough to see his father standing behind the desk, the hearth light sharpening the austere lines of his face.

"Do you know why you're here?"

Because Calista is a venomous little witch and I wish I never had to see her again, he thought bitterly, but he said nothing.

"Have you forgotten how to speak, boy?" His father's voice thundered. Solis tensed. The sound made his heart pound against his ribs like a trapped bird in a gilded cage. His thoughts scattered, searching for words that might defuse his father's fury, but none came. He said the only thing he could, repeating the accusation Calista had given.

"Because I spoke out of turn," Solis whispered. "And I did not treat our guest with proper respect."

King Leo's tone dropped, cold enough to chill bone. "You embarrassed me before our guests. Before your betrothed. You dared to question my rule and speak of peace with an enemy that has slaughtered our people for generations?"

Solis bit his tongue until he tasted iron. His jaw clenched so tight it ached. He wanted to remind his father that once, long ago, he too had sought peace. The words sat in his throat, heavy and burning, but he forced his gaze to remain fixed on the floor. His breath tightened in his chest. "I only wished..."

"You do not wish," King Leo cut in sharply. "You obey. You listen when spoken to and remain silent when you are not. A prince who cannot hold his tongue is a liability to his crown."

Solis swallowed hard. "Yes, Father."

The king stepped out from behind the desk, his shadow stretching long across the floor. "Since you wish to be treated like a man, you will be disciplined as one."

He crossed to the wall and unhooked the whip that hung there. The sound of leather sliding free made Solis's breath falter.

"Remove your shirt, boy."

Solis hesitated, rooted to the spot. His fingers twitched at his side, then curled into a fist, a futile attempt to steady himself. The room seemed to shrink around him. He was afraid to lift his eyes because he already knew what awaited him the moment he did.

"Now."

A shiver slipped through him as he obeyed. The air felt cold against his bare skin. Old scars prickled, warning him of what was coming.

The first strike cracked through the study. Pain split across his back like lightning. Solis gritted his teeth and stayed silent. Foolish, reckless him for ever opening his mouth.

King Leo's voice followed each lash, unwavering. "You are an Aurelius. An Aurelius does not yield to weakness. He does not plead for peace. He seizes it. He commands it."

Another lash struck, deeper than the last. Then another. Solis's knees threatened to give, but he steadied himself before they could. He would not give his father the satisfaction.

"Do you understand me?"

"Yes, Father," Solis forced out, his voice rough with pain. His back burned as if fire had been carved into his skin.

"Good." King Leo flung the whip aside. The sound of leather striking marble echoed through the room, sharp against the ringing in Solis's ears. "Remember this, boy. A king does not speak of peace. He seizes it through conquest."

Solis bowed his head. "Thank you for the lesson, Father."

"Now get out of. My sight."

Bending down, Solis seized his shirt and turned toward the door, shutting it softly behind him. His hands clenched around the fabric until his knuckles whitened. The corridor air stung his skin as he slipped the garment back on, every movement pulling against the new welts. He did not look back.

Argus would not be waiting this time. He had departed earlier with his father. The halls were empty save for the sentinels stationed throughout the palace, mannequins of flesh and armor who neither spoke nor moved. They never offered comfort after punishments. No one dared touch him except for Argus... and Calista, though Calista did not count. Her touch was poison. Solis had never felt so utterly alone.

When he reached his wing, the demon herself lingered by her chamber door. A slow smile unfurled across her face.

"Did you enjoy yourself, prince?" Calista tilted her head, the glint in her eyes as cruel as her words.

He had no answer. The punishment had stolen his voice. He turned sharply and strode past his own chamber, deeper into the corridor, ignoring her laughter echoing down the dim hall.

He did not know where he was going, only that he had to get away from her.

He found himself in his mother's garden.

Outside, the air hung cold and still, a quiet contrast to the rage within him. His flame fumed through his veins, pressing against his spine, demanding release. He could not contain it any longer. His anger, his humiliation, his sorrow… they erupted at once.

He bent forward and screamed. Fire burst from him, surging into the air like a living storm. Flames devoured the garden, climbing across stone and flowers alike. The ground burned. The night burned. The world itself ignited with him.

Tears streaked his face as he fell to his knees. The world blurred into smoke and firelight. He looked down at the crescent pendant hanging from his neck. It glowed faintly amid the flames but did not burn. Gratitude swelled in his chest. Losing it to his fire would have broken what little was left of him.

He gripped it tightly and wept until his voice failed him.

He did not know how long he remained there. The fire spread quickly, curling across the marble like living veins of gold. The air shimmered with heat, the garden reduced to smoke and ash. He wanted to stop it but could not. His fire kept answering the ache that burned inside his chest. The guards stood frozen at the threshold, too terrified to Approach. One of them would soon report what he had done. He no longer cared.

A voice cut through the flames. Someone was calling his name.

Through the haze, his mother emerged from the inferno. He had reduced her garden to ruin. She loved this place. Tears spilled down his face as she approached. Her maids lingered at a distance while she knelt beside him. Her arms came around him, warm and steady, and she pressed a kiss to the crown of his head.

"My baby, it is all right," she whispered. "Breathe. Stop fighting it and breathe, my love. My sun. My heart."

He clutched her arm and buried his face against her shoulder. "Mother, I do not want to be king. I do not want to marry. I do not want to be an Aurelius."

I just want to burn. Burn to ashes.

She stroked his hair, her touch gentle even through the smoke. "My sun, you cannot choose your fate, but you can choose how you live."

His throat ached. "What if I choose not to rule?"

She drew him closer, her voice quiet but resolute, her fingers tracing the line of his neck in a soothing motion. "Then you may do as you please when you are king. But for now, you must endure. You must rise. Master your emotions, my sun. Master your flame before it consumes everything you love."

Maybe that was not such a terrible idea. Let it all burn.

"I cannot," Solis said, his voice cracking. "I do not want to."

She lifted his face in her hands, her touch unwavering. "Look at me. You are the sun of this realm, the heir to the Aurelius bloodline. Your fire is your own, not your father's. Burn as you were meant to burn. Do not let anyone extinguish your light. The sun does not falter, my boy. Look at the sky. Has it ever lost its light? No. The sun always endures, answering only to itself."

Solis choked back his tears. His mother brushed them away with her thumb. "Rise, my sun. Rise."

At her words, he rose like Sunrise across the world, radiant and defiant. His arm lifted toward the sky, and with a subtle twist of his hand, the flames receded, fading into the night until only smoke and ash remained.

"I am sorry your garden is gone, Mother," he whispered.

She stood and cupped his face in her palms. A soft laugh escaped her. "We can always rebuild it, my sun."

TEN

LUNA

The moon hung high above the mountains, silver and full, washing the forest in pale light. The air was cool, threaded with the soft hum of nocturnal life, life that Luna had always known.

Like any other night, she stood at the center of the training field, flipping her daggers between her hands and catching them with ease. Khael stood across from her, a wooden staff gripped firmly in his weathered hands.

"Ready, princess?" he asked, tilting his head. His beard had grown whiter with each passing year, a mark of his age. How old exactly was Khael? Luna had no idea. She only knew he was old, old in the way ancient trees were old, unchanged and immovable.

Her lips curved as she lowered her stance. "I was born ready."

She charged forward. Her right dagger swung upward toward Khael's neck, but his staff struck her arm before her blade could reach him.

"Watch your elbow, child."

She spun, switching hands, her left dagger slicing toward his ribs. Khael sidestepped with a speed that should have been impossible for a man his age. His cloak melted into the shadows as he moved, his expression calm and unreadable.

"Better," he called. "But do not lose your momentum. Keep your elbow bent. Never hesitate. Strike to kill. The moment your enemy sees an opening, they will strike first."

She attacked again and again, her blades flashing in the moonlight, but Khael deflected every blow with infuriating ease. Frustration bloomed in her chest.

"And control your temper," Khael added, his tone unshaken. He talked too much, but she loved him all the same. He was like a second father to her.

"What has you so tense tonight?" he asked.

She drew a sharp breath. Her mother had told her about Solara's decision, how they had ended the fragile peace that had lasted only a year, how they dared to strike Selvaran, and about the shadow attacks no one could explain. Khael should already know. He was her father's commander, and if war began again, he would be the first to bleed for it. She did not need to explain that.

Yet her temper slipped.

"Because of that stupid realm," she shouted. Her anger made her reckless, and Khael's staff cracked hard against her ribs.

"Focus," he said firmly. "You know how ruthless Solarans can be. I warned your father this peace would not last."

He had. But her father had trusted that cursed king too much, and now they were paying for it.

She struck again, her voice sharp. "I cannot believe they would rather have war than see their prince married to me. It is not as though he was even worthy of me."

Khael huffed a quiet amusement. "No one is worthy of you, princess."

Luna thought of the boy she had met three years ago—the ocean-blue eyes, the soft voice, the kindness that did not belong to a Solaran. She had lied. He *was* worthy of her. Solis was not his father. His heart had been pure. She had never met anyone who would cry over a rabbit before.

The memory made her smile. Stupid boy.

That smile earned her another strike to the arm.

"Ouch," she hissed, rolling her shoulder to ease the sting.

"That is what happens when you let your thoughts wander," Khael said, shaking his head. "What occupied that restless mind of yours?"

The foolish prince of Solara. The one they had stolen from her. The realm that had betrayed its promise of peace. The shadow attacks that defied explanation. The missing villagers whose names haunted their silence. Too much to say, too much to carry.

"Nothing of consequence," she replied, though a thousand thoughts collided in her head like clashing storms.

She lowered her daggers and exhaled slowly. "Khael, what will happen if this war never ends?"

Khael rested his staff against his shoulder. "Then our people will suffer," he said gravely. "I have already doubled the border guards, yet steel alone cannot stem the tide of blood. Your task, princess, is to temper your focus. I will not see you defenseless when the battle reaches our gates."

He paused, his eyes narrowing with sagacious percipience. "Your true war is not fought with blades, but with mastery. Master your light, Luna. When the time arrives, the realm will depend upon it."

Luna tilted her head, curiosity gleaming in her gaze. "And how will that help?"

"The rumors of villages devoured by shadow," Khael murmured, his tone lowering. "Creatures unlike anything we have faced. Your light may be the only force capable of dispelling them. Your father claims it was written in the stars."

Again with her father and his stars. He was a seer who read the heavens like scripture, though his visions were riddles cloaked in ambiguity. Sometimes they illuminated truth; more often they dissolved into confusion and reverie.

"And what if it is not enough?" she asked, her voice barely above a whisper.

Khael's expression softened. "Princess, your light is the miracle Selvaran has awaited. Have you not heard the prophecy? The one foretelling seven warriors who will shield the light, the light that will end the darkness? You are that light."

There it was, the prophecy that had shackled her destiny since birth. She was the realm's shield, its savior, the luminous force destined to drive back the dark.

Luna lowered her gaze as uncertainty coiled through her chest. "How can you be certain?"

Khael let out a low breath of amusement. "Have you seen another born with light in their chest? You carry the moon within you, child. That is no ordinary gift; it is providence."

The light within her chest. Her divine inheritance. The god-given gift she had been born with. A crescent moon etched into her skin, glowing with luminous radiance, the living mark of prophecy that bound her fate to the stars. It was the light her people placed all their faith in.

Luna fell silent. Doubt pressed like frost against her heart. What if she failed them? What if her strength was nothing more than a fragile illusion? How could she stand against both the shadows and Solara's wrath? They called her a miracle, yet she did not feel like one.

She lifted her eyes to the night sky. The constellations shimmered faintly, shifting as though whispering her name.

I wanted to see the stars.

That was what Solis had said when they caught him trespassing near the border. He had only wanted to see the stars.

Why was she thinking of that foolish prince again? Their betrothal was over. They were nothing more than adversaries born of rival realms.

And yet he lingered in her thoughts. Perhaps because, deep within, she believed he could end this war. If they met again, she could reach him, persuade him. She could make him remember what they once shared, even if it was small.

Perhaps he could stop this before it consumed them all.

He could.

She just had to make him believe it.

ELEVEN

LUNA

Luna entered the palace gardens after training, her steps light but her thoughts heavy, each one sinking like a stone. The air smelled of silver dew and the faint sweetness of moonpetals blooming along the palace walls. The sting of Khael's staff still lingered across her ribs. He never went easy on her during lessons. He loved her too much to show mercy. Mercy meant death in war, and Khael would not lose her to it.

Her shoulders sagged as she knelt beside the fountain and dipped her fingers into the cold water. The reflection that looked back at her was not the same girl she once knew. No longer carefree. A quiet sorrow lingered behind her eyes, something a child her age should never have carried. She should have been dancing in the gardens, laughing with Nova, visiting the villages. Instead, the title of princess had become a tether, binding her to obligations far too heavy for her small shoulders.

How was she supposed to end this war? She was only thirteen. Yet everyone looked to her with faith that trembled on reverence. What if she failed them? Would they all suffer for it? Would her parents? Would Khael? Would Nova?

She twirled her fingers through the water until her reflection dissolved into ripples.

"Still awake, my little moon?"

Luna turned. Her mother stood beneath the archway, a soft smile touching her lips. Queen Astrid moved with the grace of twilight itself, her midnight gown trailing like mist across stone. Strands of moonpetals were woven through her dark braid. Though the years had passed, her face remained ageless. People often said Luna was her mirror: the same heart-shaped face, the same gentle lips, the same violet eyes that carried the night within them.

"I feel restless," Luna said softly. "Too much on my mind."

Astrid crossed the garden, each step quiet as moonlight. "You are too young to think so much. Thinking is for adults. Enjoy your youth, my moon."

"I cannot help it," Luna murmured. Her voice held no insouciance, only weariness. The world already seemed cruel and unjust. "Khael told me the war is inevitable. But part of me feels as though it does not have to be. Perhaps if we spoke to that king, maybe we could change his mind."

The Queen knelt beside her and folded her hands in her lap. "Khael has seen many wars. His fears are reasonable, but even the sagacious can be wrong. Perhaps we can change things. Perhaps not. Nothing is inevitable. Even the stars can be rewritten."

Luna's gaze fell to the water. Her fingertips traced idle circles across the surface. "I just do not understand why the Solarans would break the peace. Why would they throw everything away? What could they possibly gain?"

"Because pride blinds even the wisest men," Astrid said gently. "And fear makes them cruel."

Luna lifted her eyes. "What is King Leo afraid of?"

Astrid did not answer at first. Her gaze drifted toward the sky, starlight settling gently in her eyes. "Some things are beyond our understanding," she said quietly.

"Stupid king," Luna muttered. "Foolish, selfish king."

Astrid smiled faintly. "A foolish, selfish king indeed. Let your parents worry about him. Focus on what a child should worry about."

"Like what? How can I be a child when everyone keeps telling me I am the light, that I will save Selvaran, but I do not even know how? What if I am not strong enough?"

The Queen reached forward and placed her hand over Luna's chest, where soft luminescence pulsed beneath her skin. "Trust in yourself. Strength is not in how fiercely you strike, my little moon, but in how long you continue to shine when darkness tries to smother you."

Luna blinked back the heat behind her eyes. "What if I fail?"

Astrid kissed her forehead. "Then rise again. Rise as many times as you must. The stars never surrender their light, even when the world turns away."

Luna looked down at her reflection once more. The faint glow beneath her skin shimmered across the water, haloing the moon above.

"I do not want there to be war," she whispered.

"Neither do I," Astrid said softly. "But sometimes peace must be broken for the truth to be seen. And sometimes it takes a moon to remind the sun how to shine."

Luna glanced up, uncertain what her mother meant, but Astrid only smiled, her gaze distant as though she could already see what was to come.

"Go rest, my little moon. The stars will watch over you tonight."

Later that night, sleep refused to come easily. Moonlight spilled across the chamber floor, silver and delicate, illuminating the canopy above her bed like spun silk. Luna lay awake, her mind burdened by her mother's words.

Would the stars still watch over her people when Solara invaded? How many would be forced to bury the ones they loved? How many more would be lost to fire and ruin?

She rolled onto her side, resting her head upon her arm. Could she truly save them?

When her eyes finally closed, her thoughts drifted like petals on wind.

And the world changed.

She stood beneath an endless sky, surrounded by silence and light. The ground beneath her feet was made of clouds, soft as breath. Constellations shimmered overhead, fracturing with each exhale, scattering like shards of glass across eternity. A melody drifted through the air, woven by a flute and a guqin, their notes rippling like wind threading through water.

"Where am I?" she whispered.

Her voice echoed and dissolved into starlight.

She walked forward. Then she saw him.

His ocean-blue eyes met hers. His golden hair fell across his brow. He stood across the expanse as though waiting for her, the air between them pulsing with quiet energy.

Luna's heart quickened. "Sol?"

He did not answer. His image wavered like a reflection upon water. His face was the same, the same eleven-year-old boy she had met in the forest, yet sorrow lingered in it now, a heaviness that had not been there before.

She took a step forward, reaching for him, her fingers trembling in the light. Concern threaded through her voice. "Are you all right?"

As she drew closer, the clouds stirred, the air shifting with an otherworldly pulse. Light rippled through them, separating her from him. When it dimmed, seven figures appeared behind Solis, their forms wreathed in mist, each surrounded by a different hue of light, their faces hidden by shadow.

Solis extended his hand toward her, his fingers reaching for hers, but they never touched. The air shimmered between them, gold and silver folding together, sun and moon entwined. The vision felt like a reverie, illusory yet painfully real.

His lips parted, but no sound emerged. Her body moved without thought, drawn to him as if by fate itself call for it. She reached for him, desperate to close the distance—but fire erupted around him, a light so fierce it blinded her. She lifted an arm to shield her eyes.

When the brilliance faded, her breath caught. Shadows spilled through the void, twisting around Solis's form, consuming his golden glow until only his eyes remained, blue and desperate like the distant ocean she had only read about. Oceans belonged to Solara. Like him.

His form fractured, and with it the golden light vanished, an eclipse devouring the sun. The world split apart, light and darkness colliding in a soundless storm. She tried to call his name, but only silence answered.

Then, faintly, from the distance, her name echoed across the emptiness.

She spun in every direction, but the darkness had dissolved. Only silver light remained.

"Sol!" she cried again, her voice trembling with urgency.

It was not him who answered.

"Princess, wake up."

Nova's voice pierced the dream, soft but resolute.

Luna's eyes flew open. Air rushed from her lungs in uneven bursts. She blinked rapidly, the remnants of the vision dissolving as she focused on Nova's face framed by black hair tied into two small buns.

"Finally," Nova said with a relieved sigh. "I've been calling you. Time to get up."

Luna turned toward the window. The moon still hung high in the sky, serene and luminous. She must have overslept.

What a strange dream.

Why had she dreamed of him?

He had appeared in her dreams almost every night since. Day after day, Luna followed her usual routine; training, studying court matters, and retiring at Moonfall, only to meet those same blue eyes again. Eyes full of melancholy, calling for her light to save him. Save him from what, exactly? She never knew. No matter how far she reached, she could never touch him. His presence vanished the instant her fingers brushed the air where he once stood.

A repetition she could not escape, a longing she barely understood, as if her soul remembered something her mind had forgotten.

A few days later, Solara officially declared war on Selvaran by striking the border villages without warning. For two years, tension between the realms had lingered in fragile silence. War had existed only in words, confined to politics and empty threats, but this attack made it real. It marked the first blood of a conflict that would ignite hundreds of battles to come.

And with that, the dream ended, as if the boy had dissolved with it.

Khael was dispatched to reclaim the fallen villages while Luna remained behind to train, her heart weighted with apprehension for her people. The peace treaty was shattered.

Her engagement to Solis dissolved like smoke. There was no turning back. Peace had become a dream long extinguished, and only one realm would remain when the smoke cleared.

Rumors soon spread that King Leo had arranged a new union for his son, binding Solis to the daughter of a Solaran lord. A noble in place of a princess. The insult cut deep, wounding the pride of her people. They cried for Solara's downfall, demanding vengeance for their dishonored heir.

Yet Luna herself did not feel humiliated. In truth, she was grateful to be unbound from that realm. Solara had proven itself faithless and cruel. The boy she once knew, she told herself, no longer existed. He had been shaped into the weapon his father desired him to be.

Rumors claimed he had been seen during the attack.

If that were true, then he had chosen his side. Anyone who brought ruin to her people would never have her heart. She refused to ache for someone who lived for blood and fire.

Years passed, and the war dragged on. Nova lost her brother, as did countless families who buried their dead beneath the moonlight. For what? A greedy king's ambition.

Worse still, the shadow attacks continued to strike their villages alongside Solara's assaults. No one knew if the two were connected or if another force hid behind the chaos. If there was, Luna could not fathom who would want Selvaran to fall. Her father, King Orion, ruled with compassion and honor. Who would wish to destroy a realm built on mercy? The question lingered unanswered.

By the time Luna turned eighteen, she was finally permitted to join the fight. Khael rode beside her as he always had. Her light became the weapon of Selvaran, burning through the shadows that plagued their lands. The prophecy had been right; her light was a beacon against the darkness.

Yet even her brilliance could not match Solara's fire.

The golden flames of Prince Solis Aurelius tore through villages with merciless precision, leaving ash in their wake. Luna had never hated anyone more.

Even when she heard stories of him—how he had been forced into battle at fifteen, how his flames were wielded for ruin, how his enemies feared his name as much as they pitied his youth—Luna felt no pity. He had a choice. He could have defied his father. He could have fought for peace. Instead, he chose destruction and chaos.

He chose blood.

And blood was what he would receive.

TWELVE

LUNA

The wind tugged at her braid as she stood upon the crest of the hill, mounted on Moonshade. The air was sharp with frost, heavy with the scent of rain gathering beyond the horizon. Mist coiled through the valley like the breath of unseen spirits. Below her, the dark forest stretched vast and endless, marking the borderlands of Selvaran.

After hearing of an attack, she had ridden from the castle for three days, racing to defend a border village before the next strike. Khael and several of Selvaran's finest soldiers followed close behind.

Luna lifted her gaze to the moon above. Its light shimmered faintly across her armor, cool and resolute. "Please," she whispered. "Guide me tonight."

She pressed her heel to Moonshade's flank, and the stallion began her descent into the waiting darkness.

The village of Altair lay in ruins when they arrived. Shadow smoke drifted through the air, the unmistakable mark of the creatures of darkness, not Solara. The golden flames of Solara left no smoke; those embers burned pure. This reeked of corruption.

The night was unnaturally still. The air hung thick with iron and ash. Houses once built of pale stone stood blackened and broken, their roofs collapsed into shadow. Smoke coiled toward the moonlight, twisting like lost spirits searching for home. No living soul remained.

Luna dismounted, her boots sinking into the scorched earth. The silence was worse than the ruin itself. Not a single sound stirred except the faint crackle of dying embers.

This was the work of the shadow creatures. When they struck, nothing survived. Sometimes she and her soldiers arrived in time to stop them. Other times, like now, they were too late.

Khael approached and lifted a hand, signaling the soldiers to fan out. "Stay alert," he murmured. "They could still be here."

Luna's heart hammered as her eyes swept the devastation. "Are there survivors?"

She already knew the answer. She still asked. Hope was a stubborn thing. Perhaps this time fate would show mercy. Perhaps this time they were not too late. But reality was as merciless as the creatures themselves.

A guard emerged from the smoke, his hand pressed to his chest as he bowed. "No signs of life, Commander."

And just like that, hope slipped soundlessly through her fingers once more. Why couldn't the heavens spare Selvaran even a moment of grace? At this rate, her kingdom would crumble.

Khael's jaw tightened. "Keep searching."

Luna moved deeper into the ruins, each step stirring ash into the air. Her white bow shimmered with lunar light, steady in her grasp as the glow in her chest pulsed with every breath. Instinct whispered caution. Something was wrong. The air grew heavier the farther she ventured, pressing against her skin like an unseen weight, as though the night itself urged her to turn back.

Then she saw it.

Something moved between the burnt houses, a flicker so swift the naked eye could barely catch it.

Her body reacted before her mind did. Fingers brushed the bowstring, drawing light from within as she formed an arrow of pure radiance. She aimed toward the shadow, breath held, waiting.

The creature that emerged made her pulse seize. Its body twisted unnaturally, limbs bending at angles no living thing should move. Smoke wrapped around bone, shaping something almost human but grotesquely distorted. Two crimson eyes gleamed with unholy hunger. Its claws scraped the ground, leaving trails that hissed and burned through the scorched soil.

This was the abomination that haunted Selvaran's villages.

Before she could process the terror of it, the creature lunged. Claws sliced toward her throat. Luna pivoted aside, her body moving with trained precision, and released the string. The arrow struck its chest, bursting in a flare of silver light. The creature disintegrated into mist.

No sooner had the first fallen than another emerged from her right. Luna twisted, conjuring another arrow mid-motion, and released it in one fluid breath. The second beast staggered before it dissolved into radiant vapor.

Around her, the clash of steel and claw reverberated through the village.

There were more.

Luna sprinted toward the nearest sound of battle. The sight wrenched her stomach.

A soldier was impaled on the claws of a third beast. Where its face should have been, a jagged split tore open, lined with serrated teeth. They clamped down and crushed the man's skull as though he were clay.

Luna raised her bow, releasing several arrows in quick succession, each one striking true. The creature shrieked before collapsing into a wisp of smoke.

Blood stained the ground where the soldier had fallen.

His name was Alex. She forced herself to remember it. She always remembered their names. None of her men would fade into nameless ghosts swallowed by meaningless death.

Chaos surged around her. Luna loosed arrow after arrow of radiant light, each one cleaving through the shadow creatures one by one. Desperation quickened her pulse as she fought to save whoever still drew breath. But not all were fortunate. Death claimed them swiftly and without mercy.

The stench of blood and smoke thickened the air, clinging to her skin. Her stomach twisted.

She hated war.

She hated death.

She hated the sight of blood.

THIRTEEN

LUNA

In the aftermath of the battle, Khael found her. His armor was slick with blood, dark crimson drying across the steel. Luna could only pray it was not his. If it was not… then it belonged to her men, for shadow creatures did not bleed. The sight made her stomach twist.

"Princess, are you hurt?" His voice carried the weight of concern. Khael had long petitioned to keep her from the front lines, but she had insisted her people needed their light. If Solis could wage war at fifteen, then at eighteen she was old enough to stand beside her soldiers.

Luna lowered her bow. "No. But please, tell me that it is not your blood." Her gaze sharpened, scrutinizing his armor as she searched for a wound.

A low, dry laugh escaped him. Luna found nothing in this ruin worthy of mirth.

"Wounds are inevitable," he said, as if he wasn't covered in blood. "You should not concern yourself with me."

She had every right to worry. Khael was as close to a father as the battlefield allowed. But arguing with him was futile. The old commander was resolute to his marrow.

She said nothing as she turned away, only for a faint glow to catch her eye.

Luna knelt beside the spot where the last creature had vanished. The earth was scorched black, the soil split by a perfect circle of ash. At its center, a ring of silver light flickered, pulsing like a dying heart. The shape resembled the sun being swallowed by the moon.

An eclipse.

An eclipse had not occurred in centuries—not since the realms were divided. It should have been impossible now that the sun and moon each ruled their own skies. Yet Luna recognized it from her studies. Scholars of Selvaran had devoted their lives to the stars and the moon. Eclipses, though long buried in history, had always been a fascination.

She reached out and traced the ring. It was cold beneath her touch when it should have been warm. Who possessed the power to distort the balance of nature itself? The hairs on her arms rose. The magnitude of it both awed and terrified her. Would she be able to stand against such a force?

"What is this?" she whispered. The tremor in her voice betrayed her wonder.

Khael joined her, towering over the glowing circle. His expression darkened. He said the same symbols had been found at several sites, yet no one understood what they meant.

Luna brushed her fingers along the edge again. The light pulsed beneath her touch, strangely familiar, like a voice calling from far away. Where had she seen this before? Nothing surfaced. She rose, brushing ash from her knees. The thought would return to her eventually.

For now, they had to search for survivors.

She doubted there would be any. If anyone had lived through the first assault, the second wave of creatures would have finished them, just as they had taken half her men. Their bodies lay torn apart, scattered among the ruins.

A chilling thought struck her.

The soldiers' corpses lay where they had fallen. But there was no sign of the villagers.

If the creatures killed the villagers the same way…

Where were their remains?

There should not have been emptiness. There should have been bodies.

What had happened to them?

The question weighed on her mind as they searched through the night, combing the ruins for answers. Only shadow and smoke replied.

Later, when Luna returned to her tent, a heavy weight settled in her chest. No survivors. Not this time. Perhaps not ever. How many more would they lose before this ended? How many more lives would the darkness claim before it was satisfied?

If only Solara could set aside their pride and stand with them, Selvaran might have a chance. Instead, her realm was caught between two wars: one waged by a foolish king, and one by a force far more insidious.

The next morning, seeking relief from the weight of war, Luna told Khael she would go hunting. It was the only way she could feel useful when everything around her felt hopeless.

Their numbers had been cut in half, grief hanging over the camp like a shroud. Khael would soon return to the capital to report what had happened in Altair. Luna knew this would be their final day before the journey home.

For now, she needed the forest—the silence, the stillness, the faint illusion that something in this fractured world remained within her control.

When the moon reached its halfway point, Luna guided Moonshade through the forest. The mare's hooves pressed softly into the dirt, their sound swallowed by the drifting mist. The trees stood silent, listening. Even the wind seemed to hold its breath.

After a while, she dismounted and tied Moonshade to a low branch near the forest's edge. Her gloved hand brushed the mare's neck. "Stay here, girl."

The deeper she walked, the colder the air became. Her hood shadowed her face, her breath a faint cloud in the chill. She moved with deliberate grace, her boots gliding soundlessly across the forest floor. The bow rested in her grip, poised for anything.

A faint flutter broke the stillness. Luna's head snapped upward. A flock of birds burst from the canopy, scattering silver light beneath the moon.

She drew her bowstring back. Light stirred at her fingertips as her arrow formed, humming with the pulse of her lunar power.

She released.

The arrow sliced the night and struck a bird midflight. A brief flare of silver lit the trees, then faded.

Luna followed its fall. Her cloak whispered behind her, brushing ferns and roots. Her steps were silent, fluid—a rhythm long mastered. Hunting was second nature to her, a dance of instinct and patience.

She crouched low, scanning the undergrowth.

Then something shifted.

The light in her chest flickered, faint but insistent. She froze, gaze drawn deeper into the woods. Between the trees, a glow shimmered. Not her own. Not moonlight.

Something else.

It called to her.

She followed, pushing past the tree line where shadows yielded to an open slope. Warmth brushed her skin. The mist thinned, replaced by brightness. The scents of soil and pine faded, replaced by sun-dried grass and salt.

And then the world changed.

Darkness fell away behind her.

Before her stretched a valley awash in gold.

Solara.

Luna stood frozen at the border where the two realms met. Behind her, Selvaran rested beneath a sky of silver stars. Before her, the world burned bright and endless, the air almost too hot to breathe.

The sun felt alive here. It pressed against her skin like a living flame. She raised an arm to shield her eyes.

If Khael discovered she had crossed the border, he would lose his mind. If her parents learned of it, she would never set foot outside the castle gates again. Yet curiosity burned hotter than fear. When would she ever see this realm again before war reduced it to ash?

She stepped forward. The field stretched wide before her, a sea of flowers painted in shades of gold, rose, and ivory. Petals brushed her dark trousers as she walked, their color so vivid it made her eyes ache.

She bent and plucked one, rolling the stem between her fingers. It was soft, simple, beautiful in its ordinariness. Selvaran flowers always glowed beneath moonlight, kissed by magic. These Solaran blooms held no enchantment at all, only sunlight and soil. Simple beauty. She liked that.

Heat pressed against her hooded face, beads of sweat sliding down her temple. Solara was unbearably warm compared to home, yet the light carried a strange comfort.

When she lifted her gaze, a column of pale smoke caught her eye, rising in the distance. A village. Not the black plume of war, but the gentle curl of chimney fires.

Curiosity tugged at her feet. She followed it.

The wildflowers thinned until the dirt path gave way to cobblestone. Buildings rose ahead, pale stone washed in sunlight. Open archways lined the streets, spilling laughter and music into the warm air.

Luna's breath caught. The village was alive in a way Selvaran never was. People filled the streets, their voices weaving together in a symphony of chatter and trade. Merchants called from stalls overflowing with fruit, fabric, and trinkets. Children darted between them, laughing.

Her home was a kingdom of quiet halls and whispered reverence, shops enclosed and streets hushed beneath the moonlight. But here, everything was open. Loud. Restless.

There were guards patrolling the village, yet with the crowd pressing in from every direction, slipping past their notice was almost effortless.

She pulled her cloak tight, keeping her face hidden just in case. Every color, every scent, every sound pressed against her senses until her mind spun. The heat. The movement. The light. She barely noticed the corner until she turned too sharply.

Her thoughts scattered.

She slammed into something solid. Hard. The impact sent her stumbling backward. Her bow clattered against her hip as she caught herself.

"Watch where you're going," a voice snapped.

Luna blinked, startled. The wall she hit was not a wall at all. It was a man.

He towered over her, easily six feet or more, a white cloak draped across broad shoulders, sunlight threading through the gold embroidery. His hair was a tumble of golden waves, framing a face that looked sculpted by the gods themselves. Sharp cheekbones. A strong jaw. Lips held in an impatient line. And his eyes were blue as a summer sky, flecked with gold. Cold. Focused. Unnervingly familiar.

Her breath hitched.

Oh stars, he was beautiful. The kind of beautiful that stole the breath straight from her lungs.

She blinked hard, dragging her thoughts back into order. No, she did not find him beautiful. He had, after all, just yelled at her.

The stranger crossed his arms, gold catching along his vambraces. "Are you even listening to me, lady?"

Her pulse jumped. A Solaran soldier. Perfect.

The last thing she needed was to run into one of them and get caught. Their king would rejoice if he learned the princess of Selvaran had wandered off into his realm. She adjusted her scarf, ensuring her face stayed hidden.

"I—" she began, planting her feet. "I'm sorry."

"You call that an apology? That is the weakest apology I have ever heard."

Her spine stiffened. A simple bump, and he spoke as if she had insulted his entire lineage.

"Are you dense? An apology is an apology. There is no such thing as a pathetic one."

"There is if you do not mean it."

Heat flared in her chest. "Maybe you should open your ears before accusing people, you arrogant—"

She caught herself, spun on her heel. "What a self-absorbed peacock," she muttered.

He let out a low amused laugh. "I can still hear you."

She raised her hand and flipped him off without looking back.

Her pace quickened as she put distance between herself and the Solaran soldier. Would he report her? Judging by his attire, he was someone of rank. Finery like that was not worn by common foot soldiers. Only the elite strutted around in gold-threaded uniforms. She would know; she had fought men like them before, officers who mocked her for being a woman on the battlefield. They had fallen as swiftly as their insolent words left their tongues.

For every Solaran man she struck down, one of her own had fallen to the blade of that spineless prince, Solis.

If Khael learned she had picked a fight with a Solaran in the center of their capital, she would never hear the end of it. But saints above, that infuriatingly beautiful man had deserved it.

Her anger carried her forward so quickly that she did not notice she'd reached the edge of the city until the light began to fade. The field of flowers stretched before her again, swaying softly in the wind. Relief swept through her.

Selvaran lay just beyond the horizon.

Her home.

The glow of the moon guided her path back through the trees. By the time she reached the Selvaran border, her boots and cloak were streaked with dirt and pollen. The light in her chest had dimmed, pulsing faintly in rhythm with her heartbeat.

Realizing she had forgotten to hunt for their meal, Luna headed into the forest once more. It did not take long to catch several rabbits.

Rabbits.

You killed my rabbit.

That boy again. Why did he still haunt her thoughts? Did his eyes have golden flecks like the soldier's? She could not remember. Eight years was a long time to cling to something so small.

She shook the ache from her shoulders and turned toward the camp Khael had set.

When the scent of campfire smoke reached her, Luna slowed. Torches burned ahead, their silver flames flickering against the soldiers' armor. Khael stood among them, arms crossed, his black cloak snapping in the wind.

"Where have you been?" His voice was low but sharp enough to slice through the night. "I nearly sent a search party after you."

Luna kept her tone even. "Hunting, remember?" She lifted the rabbits for him to see.

Khael's eyes narrowed, shifting between the rabbits and her face. "Hunting does not take hours, princess. Not for you."

She dropped the rabbits beside the fire and brushed a loose strand of hair behind her ear, refusing to give his glare the satisfaction of a reaction. She'd dealt with enough tempers today. Why were men always so uptight?

"It does when the prey is harder to find," she said coolly. "You should know that, Khael."

His jaw tightened. "You know Solaran patrols could be near," he replied, stepping closer. The torchlight carved the hard lines of his face, the youth long burned away by war. "I do not want to worry about your safety."

Annoyance hit her like a stone wall.

"I can take care of myself, Khael." Her voice bit at each word, her patience worn thin by his constant lecturing. His fatherly vigilance was both comforting and suffocating, a chain born from all the loss he carried. He treated her as though she were still a child, even after all the battles they had fought side by side.

"You forget I've been fighting beside you this entire time," she reminded him.

"And you still have plenty to learn," Khael said. "You cannot disappear for hours in the midst of war, especially when we are this close to the border. One of these days, you are going to give this old man a heart attack."

There he went again, being all fatherly.

"No one babies the other soldiers," she muttered.

His brow lifted, but she pretended not to notice. Firelight flickered between them, thickening the air with unspoken tension.

"Next time, I'm coming with you." Khael broke the silence between them.

Luna resisted the urge to groan. She did not need a shadow hovering over her shoulder. She could handle herself.

"Can we just let it go?" Her voice thinned with exhaustion. "I'm going to my tent."

She turned before he could argue. Fatigue tugged at her limbs, but it was not weariness that pushed her away. It was his unrelenting watchfulness, that iron grip of protectiveness she could neither escape nor fully reject.

Tonight, she needed silence more than she needed him.

FOURTEEN

SOLIS

He had never met a girl quite like her. He should have questioned her further. She was clearly not of his kingdom. The obsidian cloak alone made her conspicuous, even if she hadn't realized it. No one in Solara wore colors that dark, not beneath such blistering heat. She was too cloaked, too cautious. Undeniably Selvaran. A Selvaran at his border.

He should have taken her captive, as his father commanded for all who trespassed from the shadowed realm. What became of those captives, Solis preferred not to know. Over the past five years, he had learned to silence his tongue and obey. His father would have his head if he dared defy a direct order. Every Selvaran found within Solara's reach was to be reported and handed to Duke Veyra and his sanctimonious militia. Even Solis held no power over what followed. Just as he had no say when it came to Calista and her capricious whims.

In only a few years, Solara had transformed so drastically that he scarcely recognized his own realm. Bodies hung from the city gates, charred and lifeless, displayed as grim warnings to any who dared defy the crown. Those accused of consorting with Selvarans were punished with public beatings or death, their fates resting upon the duke's volatile temperament.

King Leo sanctioned every cruelty without the slightest hesitation.

It was as if Lucien were the true king, not his father.

And Calista. She had become more insufferable with every ascent in her father's power, a tempest of vanity and venom draped in gold.

Solis was exhausted. Weary of battle. Weary of capturing Selvaran soldiers only to watch them vanish into the duke's prisons. Weary of injustice disguised as duty. He had grown disillusioned with the war, with Solara, with the hollow obedience that ruled his life. Yet defiance was a luxury he could not afford. His father reminded him often enough.

He was not a prince. He was a possession. He obeyed. He complied. He performed as commanded. And pain was the only lesson his father had ever allowed him to remember.

His mind drifted to the woman's face. He hadn't seen her clearly, but those eyes, violet and bright as starlight, had burned into his memory. Something about her lingered. Even through shadow and distance, he had felt their pull. Just her eyes, yet he found himself unsettlingly enchanted.

Was that why he had disobeyed his father's orders? Why he had allowed a Selvaran to walk free? Why he suddenly felt the faint, dangerous edge of rebellion?

Since when did he allow a woman to interfere with his duty?

Solis pressed a hand to his face. The heat of his palm could not banish the ache inside him. His body was weary, filthy from the so-called glory of war. He had only just returned from the front. They had not faced Commander Khael, but another Selvaran general instead. Solis had killed him, burned him alive until nothing remained but ash and the acrid stench of seared flesh. The Selvaran men had watched in silence, trembling at the sight. It was the spectacle his father wanted, a performance of dominance meant to instill fear. Yet that smell clung to him, heavy and sickening.

The prisoners they captured afterward would meet a fate far worse than death.

His father wanted a weapon, not a son. A ruthless heir who would fight without hesitation. And that was what Solis had become, a creature of fire and command trained to kill without mercy, molded to obey without question. He had become the very man he despised. Whatever remained of his soul had long been scorched away.

He exhaled slowly. He should return to the castle, yet fatigue anchored him in place. Before he did, he needed to find

Calista a gift. Returning without one would be unbearable. She would never let him forget it, and neither would his father. He had never loathed anyone as deeply as he loathed her. Yet his father refused to end their engagement, and Solis had no desire to invite another punishment for displeasing her.

For some unfathomable reason, King Leo adored Calista. Any perceived slight against her became a personal affront. The last punishment had been brutal enough to remind Solis of what defiance cost.

He had learned then that shadow magic could be used for torture. He had not believed it until it became part of his lessons, his father's lessons. A prince tortured for a noble's daughter. The irony was almost laughable. His worth meant less than hers, even though he was heir to the throne of this cursed kingdom.

And he was too tired for pain. His body already carried enough reminders of it.

The streets were crowded as usual, yet none dared touch him. Not when he wore the white and gold of Solara. Not when his attire reeked of rank and privilege. Even the commoners feared the nobles. The divide between them had grown insurmountable. The poor had become poorer while the rich remained indulgent and untouchable, their greed consuming everything within their periphery. Each city of Solara had its own duke, each one audacious enough to tax the people into destitution while the crown remained complicit. Fear had become the realm's pulse.

The people smiled uneasily as he passed. Unspoken words flickered in their wary glances. Whenever a soldier strode by, the people lowered their eyes and murmured rehearsed pleasantries, a reflex carved by survival. Fear of saying the wrong thing had become a way of life. It lingered in the silence between conversations, in the way merchants flinched at the sight of the royal crest, their hands trembling as coins exchanged. Some even offered their wares freely, praying the soldiers would leave them in peace. Mothers clutched their children whenever patrols marched past.

This was not the Solara Solis had envisioned. A sagacious ruler governed with wisdom, not terror. A king should not rule through fear. Not like this.

He crossed the main square, his armor gleaming in the light, earning both reverence and trepidation. His expression remained impassive, a mask he had mastered long ago. Those who recognized him whispered his titles in hushed tones. Prince of Solara. Golden lion. Embodiment of victory. Monster of the war. Weapon of the crown.

And to Solis himself, a disgrace. There was no glory in murdering the innocent, no valor in burning homes, no honor in enslaving the helpless. Only the stench of ruin, ashes, and the hollow echo of a life he no longer recognized.

The patrols saluted as he passed. Every man in the force knew his name. He crossed the square, passing the great fountain where sunlight fractured upon the water like molten glass. Banners of gold and white adorned every building, each emblazoned with the lion and the sun. Symbols of loyalty and subjugation. At the heart of the plaza, the royal seal of Solara was etched into the stone, circled by garlands of perfumed flowers. The sight was meant to be magnificent, but beauty in Solara always came at a cost. A cost paid in blood.

His gaze drifted upward. Bodies hung from the city gates, charred and disfigured beyond recognition. Their presence defiled whatever elegance the square once held. The perfumed blossoms surrounded them to disguise the putrid scent of death. The fragrance made his stomach twist.

Solis turned away, his thoughts fracturing beneath the weight. He scanned the market stalls, not from desire but obligation. He needed to find something for her. It was futile. Calista possessed more than any noble could dream of. Jewels, silks, indulgences purchased with the kingdom's coffers, as if she ruled beside the king. Yet if he returned empty-handed, her shrill complaints would be endless, and his father's disapproval far worse.

He stopped before a jeweler's stall, its awning striped in gold and silver. The merchant, a thin man with trembling hands, bowed so deeply his head nearly touched the counter. When he finally spoke, his voice wavered with trepidation. "Your Highness," he said softly. "It is an honor to serve the son of the sun."

The son of the sun. What a hollow title.

Solis ignored the flattery. His gaze swept the rows of jewels, all gleaming with the same opulent brilliance. Rings. Bracelets. Necklaces. Symbols of vanity. All meaningless.

He reached for a necklace at random without even glancing at it. It would suffice. He had no patience left for Calista's indulgent whims.

The merchant fumbled the coins as Solis handed them over, his hands trembling so violently that the silver nearly spilled onto the street. Solis regarded him for a moment, unease coiling in his chest. The man looked petrified, as though expecting a blow instead of payment.

What had the soldiers done here when they were not under orders?

The question hovered at the edge of his thoughts, but he forced it away. There was nothing he could do. To question Duke Veyra's authority was to question the king himself, and Solis had long learned the price of defiance.

"Sol!"

The familiar voice cut through the clamor of the market. Argus pushed through the crowd, the golden insignia of the royal guard catching the sunlight. Solis had chosen simpler clothing, nothing that screamed royalty, yet even simplicity could not hide his status. Nothing he owned could ever pass as ordinary. Attention always found him, whether he wanted it or not.

Argus stopped beside him, green eyes keen beneath the glare of the sun. "Your father sent a messenger. He's wondering why you still haven't returned."

Solis exhaled through his nose. He was supposed to have been back two days ago. The skirmish had delayed him, and then came Calista. He could not return without a gift for her, which was one of the many reasons for his delay. She was a constant thorn in his side. It was always a matter of pleasing his father or pleasing her, and for reasons he could never understand, he feared her temper more than his father's.

"Let's go," Solis said quietly, slipping the cursed necklace into his pocket before focusing on Argus again. "Did General Velin send his troops back already?"

"Yeah," Argus replied as they walked toward the stables. "They left earlier this morning. I told him you and I could handle the rest."

"Thanks," Solis murmured. "I was hoping to stay a little longer."

Argus cast him a knowing look. "You know your father's patience, Sol."

Solis sucked in his teeth. His body was already a ruin, covered in scars that burned whenever he remembered the last time he defied his father. Each one was a lesson carved into flesh. And then there were the wounds that left no visible trace, the kind Calista favored.

They reached the stables where their horses waited. Mounting up, they rode toward Solara Citadel at full speed. The wind tore through Solis's hair, carrying the scent of salt from the sea. To their right, the ocean shimmered beneath the dying light of the sun, vast and endless.

He looked at it briefly, a pang stirring in his chest. He could not remember the last time he had truly seen Solara's beauty.

The wind softened as they rode farther from Auravale, the coastal town they had just left behind. The road stretched ahead in a pale ribbon of sand and stone. Far below, the crash of waves still echoed against the cliffs, their sound fading with each stride.

Neither man spoke for a while. The rhythm of the horses' hooves filled the silence, steady and deliberate, like a heartbeat against the earth.

Argus broke it first. "Did you manage to find that lovely soon-to-be wife of yours a gift?"

Solis rolled his eyes. Leave it to Argus to tease him about the engagement. "Yes, but I highly doubt she will like it. It might not fit her standards. I am already preparing my eardrums for the inevitable storm of complaints."

Argus let out a laugh, the sound carried by the wind. "Wait until she officially becomes your wife. You might just tear them off yourself."

A faint smile tugged at Solis's mouth. "That would be merciful."

Argus's grin lingered as he glanced over. "I do not know how you plan to live with her. You cannot stand being in the same room with her for more than five minutes."

"Maybe I'll get lucky and meet my end before then. It'll be a perfect mer—" Solis said, but the words died in his throat. They had reached the ridge overlooking the valley, and something in the air shifted. The tang of salt faded, replaced by the acrid scent of smoke.

Smoke. His pulse quickened. Had Selvaran forces reached the border already? He was certain they had crushed the last regiment that attempted a crossing when that general fell. Could it be that girl?

Solis scanned the horizon, his gaze sharp as the wind stung his eyes. Black plumes coiled upward in the distance, twisting against the rose-tinted sky. A village was burning.

His heart hardened. He had just returned from war, only to ride into another. How many more battles would there be before the bloodshed ended? With only Argus beside him, they stood little chance against a full assault, but instinct urged him forward.

Argus slowed his horse, brow creasing. "An attack?"

"I am not sure," Solis replied. "We should be cautious. Approach from the outer ridge. We need to see what we are walking into."

They descended into the valley. The closer they came, the worse the devastation became. Fields once golden now lay gray with ash. Homes lay in ruin; walls crumbled to blackened bones. Strange dark flames still burned, licking at the air like phantom fire and filling the sky with a thick veil of smoke. For a place so ravaged by heat, the wind was unnaturally cold. There were no Selvaran banners, no soldiers, no villagers. Nothing.

A chill rippled through Solis's spine. The silence was so absolute he could hear his own breathing. His eyes narrowed, fury stirring beneath the surface of his calm.

"Check for survivors," he ordered, dismounting. His boots sank into the soot-soft earth as he stepped toward the ruins, the air heavy with dust. Fragments scattered across the ground shifted as he moved deeper into the wreckage, his hands blackened by ash as he searched for even the smallest sign of life. But there were none. There were no bodies. Only emptiness. It was as if the people had simply ceased to exist.

The sight before him brought back a memory he had tried to bury. Months ago, a farmer's wife had burst into the throne room, her cries echoing through the marble hall. Solis had only just returned from the front and was standing beside his father when she fell to her knees and begged for justice.

Her husband had gone to a nearby village to sell their harvest when an attack struck, leaving nothing but charred ruin. No survivors. No bodies. She claimed it was the work of dark magic, something not even the Selvaran could conjure. A shadow-born magic… the kind that spread through fearful rumors and mirrored a lineage no one dared to name.

Yet Solis had believed her.

His father had not. King Leo called her a liar, declaring that monsters were tales for frightened children, not fables to spread in a royal court. When she persisted, pleading for him to send soldiers to investigate, he silenced her with fire. He burned her alive before the entire court. The smile that crept across Lucien's face as the woman screamed made Solis wonder if the man possessed a soul at all.

And yet, like every time before, Solis had stood there and watched. He had not spoken. Not even a whisper of protest. He had been taught that silence was obedience, so he obeyed. He let her burn. The scent of scorched flesh still clung to his memory like smoke to cloth.

Whenever he was not on the battlefield, he was forced to attend every court session, no matter how weary or blood-stained he returned. His father insisted he learn what Solaran justice meant. But there was no justice in Solara. Only fire. Only death.

She was not the only one. Countless villagers had come after her, desperate for answers, begging for the war to end. Some had been audacious enough to question Lucien's origins. They claimed the shadow beasts were linked to his power, that the magic corrupting their lands was his. But why, they asked, would Lucien destroy his own people? The duke had laughed and claimed that shadow magic did not belong to Solara at all. He said it came from Selvaran, from an ancient wielder whose cruelty had once eclipsed the sun itself. What became of that wielder, no one knew.

Solis had spent hours in the royal library searching for answers, but every record that mentioned shadow magic had vanished. It was as though someone had purged the knowledge from history itself. And each time a new attack came, Selvaran was blamed. Each time someone dared to question it, his father burned them for treason.

Once, Solis had found the courage to ask if he could investigate the attacks himself. He wanted to believe the villagers. He wanted to help them. His father's response had been as merciless as always. King Leo seized his arm and burned him until the flesh melted away. He did not release him until Solis screamed. It took the healers a week to mend the damage. The Sun Realm still possessed magic, but it was reserved for the royal family and for his father's cruelty.

Leo had warned him that if he ever raised the subject again, the punishment would be worse than fire. Solis believed him.

The scar on his arm remained as a constant reminder to stay silent.

He despised himself for it. He despised the man who had taught him obedience through pain. He despised the coward he had become. The blood on his hands could never be washed away. Not after what he had allowed to happen.

His thoughts fractured as he stared at the ruins before him. Another village. Another atrocity. Another wave of death he could not prevent. Shame burned through him like poison.

His eyes wandered until they caught a small shape half-buried in the dirt. A doll. It rested against a collapsed wall, as if its owner had set it down just before their final breath. A child, most likely. An innocent life lost in the chaos. A reminder that war spared neither the young nor the old.

Solis knelt and picked it up. The fabric was icy cold. The button eyes stared back at him, lifeless and accusing.

Something twisted low in his chest. His stomach sank like stone. Swallowing what little emotion he had left, he turned away and let the doll fall back into the ash. His steps were slow as he walked toward his horse, each one heavier than the last. His people were suffering, and he could do nothing. His father would not act. Years of injustice. Years of silence. Solis had never felt more ashamed to bear the name Aurelius.

When he reached his mare, he pressed his forehead to her neck, the warmth of her breath grounding him. For a brief moment, he let himself breathe, trying to ease the hollow ache in his chest.

A hand came to rest on his shoulder. He turned slightly to see Argus beside him. The look in his friend's eyes said everything. There were no survivors. Not even a child had been spared.

"Let's go," Solis said quietly. His voice cracked under the weight of it.

Argus nodded and mounted his horse in silence. The air felt sombre with grief, the kind that left nothing but emptiness behind.

Solis climbed onto his own mount. Together, they rode from the ruins, leaving the smoke curling behind them. But as he looked back one last time, he froze.

Burned into the earth was a mark, faint yet unmistakable, glowing like a dying ember. It resembled the sun swallowed by darkness. The shape of an eclipse. The same mark found at every other village that had fallen. Just as the farmer's wife had claimed.

FIFTEEN

SOLIS

The marble halls of Solara Citadel shimmered beneath the afternoon light. Golden veins ran through the pearl-white stone, reflecting the sun from the great glass ceiling above. Everything gleamed, immaculate and proud, as though the citadel had been built for gods rather than men. Yet nothing about it felt beautiful to him. The splendor was hollow. The castle was a monument to vanity, ruled by an inhuman king.

After three days of riding without rest, Solis and Argus finally returned. Exhaustion settled deep into Solis's bones as he crossed the corridor, his boots striking sharp against the marble floor. Servants bowed as he passed, their gazes fixed to the ground. No one dared meet the prince's eyes. That, too, was one of his father's rules, meant to ensure Solis was seen as divine, not mortal. Not someone worthy of love, care, or compassion.

For a kingdom of light, the Citadel felt suffocatingly dark. This was his cage. His gilded prison. There was little difference between walking these corridors and being locked in the dungeons below, except that his cell was made of gold.

Solis kept his hands clasped at his sides as he walked. The nearer he drew to the council chamber, the heavier the air seemed to grow. He closed his eyes and let out a quiet sigh. His heart hammered against his ribs, driven by the knowledge of who awaited him beyond those doors. If dread had teeth, it would have torn him open already. Audience with his father was never pleasant. King Leo's temper flared hotter each time his molten eyes met Solis's, as if his son's very presence was an insult to his rule.

Two guards stood before the great double doors. They saluted crisply, then pulled them open.

Solis wished Argus were beside him, but his friend had been summoned to the barracks to report to his own father about the aftermath of the campaign. That left Solis to face the king alone.

Inside, King Leo sat at the head of the council table, his presence dominating the room. His golden armor gleamed beneath the sunlit windows, a mockery of valor, for the king had never fought a single battle himself. He had his son to do that. The armor caught the light with a cold exaggeration, like a lie polished to perfection, his face impassive and carved from stone. Solis stood at the threshold, hands clasped neatly behind his back, waiting for acknowledgment. The council murmured among themselves until the king lifted one hand. Silence fell instantly, heavy and absolute.

Then every gaze turned toward Solis, as though they had only just realized he was there.

"I see you finally decided to come home, boy," his father said. The words carried a chill that sank deep into Solis's spine.

Solis placed a hand across his chest and bowed low. A strand of his hair fell across his face as he spoke. "My apologies, Father. We encountered an unforeseen event. An attack by a Selvaran force."

When he lifted his gaze, a smile spread across King Leo's face. The sight made Solis's stomach twist. That smile never meant kindness. It meant pride in cruelty. Pride in something Solis wished he could forget. His father must have already heard what had happened at the border. The thought alone made him sick.

"I heard you burned that general," Leo said, his tone casual, as if they were discussing the weather and not the brutal death of a man.

Solis swallowed hard, trying to drive the image from his mind. "I did."

The word tasted like ash on his tongue, scorching his soul with it.

King Leo clapped his hands once, the sound echoing through the chamber like mock applause. "Bravo. My son has finally grown a spine."

Heat crawled up Solis's neck, but his expression remained still as carved stone. The council erupted into laughter. Solis kept his gaze fixed ahead, unflinching. He was used to the mockery his father so loved to inflict.

With a dismissive wave, Leo silenced them. "New reports have arrived. The Selvaran fools are gathering near the border once more. Commander Ivan will lead the response. You will accompany him."

Solis's head lifted slightly. He had only just returned, and already his father was sending him out again—to burn, to destroy, to kill. The imagined blood on his hands thickened, vivid and inescapable. His body ached from battle, his mind heavier still, but defiance would serve no purpose. He was a weapon, and a weapon did not question its master. It obeyed.

"Father, may I remain for the night?" he asked quietly. "I wish to see Mother before I depart again."

The king leaned back, his tone sharp as steel. "Rest tonight. At Sunrise, you will ride. This war has lingered long enough. Show them the sun does not kneel before the night. We rule it."

Solis inclined his head. "As you command, Father."

Those were the words his father cherished most. Words of submission. Words that kept Solis alive.

Leo waved a dismissive hand. "You are dismissed."

Solis bowed and turned to leave, but before he reached the door, his father's voice struck the air again.

"One more thing," Leo said. "Spend time with your fiancée."

Solis froze. His fingers curled tightly into his palms. Calista was punishment in another form. He did not look back. "Yes, Father."

He stepped into the corridor and lingered in the silence. His heartbeat was steady yet hollow. Another battle awaited him. Another cycle of death. Another stench of burning flesh. Flashes of battle seared through his mind, threatening to tear him apart. He blinked hard, steadying both his breath and his composure before continuing down the hall.

The towering windows overlooked the horizon. Beyond the rolling hills lay the border, and beyond that, the Kingdom of the Night, a reminder of the cruelty he would soon be ordered to carry out. The imagined scent of charred flesh lingered in his nose, thick and nauseating, though the air was clean. Had his mind finally begun to fracture? Had the battlefield driven him toward madness, leaving behind only a quiet trepidation he could no longer conceal?

Like a distant melody, a face rose within his thoughts. Violet eyes. Eyes like starlight. The same eyes he had seen in the market. Was she truly the same person? No. It could not be. King Orion was far too sagacious to allow his daughter into Solara amid such unrest. Solis could imagine all too well what his father would do to her if she were caught. King Leo would make an example of her.

And Solis was not certain he could stop him.

He reached beneath his tunic, his fingers brushing the crescent pendant that still rested against his chest. He had never taken it off. Not in eight years. For reasons he could not explain.

The stone was warm against his skin, offering a fleeting comfort he knew he did not deserve. Perhaps it was only an illusion, a cruel trick of memory. The warmth mocked him, reminding him he did not deserve peace while so many Selvaran families suffered because of him.

The corridors leading to the east wing were quieter. That was where his mother resided. The air carried the faint scent of lilies and parchment, her favored fragrance.
And his as well. The scent of parchment reminded him of books, of the worlds he used to escape into before the battlefield claimed his days. He had once found solace in the realm of words, losing himself in a brief reverie rather than enduring reality. That small comfort had vanished when his father sentenced him to war. The luxury of reading was a dream long forgotten.

Solis slowed as he neared her door. The soft hum of her harp drifted through the stillness, weaving through the silence like a fragile thread of memory. For a moment, he closed his eyes and listened. That melody had carried him through sleepless nights as a boy. It was the sound of warmth. The sound of home. A song shaped by love, something he no longer believed belonged to him.

He knocked once and waited. The melody faded, and then her voice called softly from within.

"Enter."

He pushed the door open and stepped inside. Queen Aurora sat beside the tall window, her fingers hovering above the harp strings with ethereal grace. Her golden hair had begun to silver, yet she remained luminous; her presence held a quiet pulchritude untouched by time. Where his father burned with fire, she shone with dawn, gentle and constant, sorrow veiled beneath her serenity.

When she saw him, her lips curved into a tender smile. "My son. You have returned."

She reached out her hand, and he bowed his head before taking a seat beside her. When he sat, she enclosed his hand within her own, her touch soft and familiar.

"You look weary," she murmured. "Have you been eating? Do they at least care for you on the field?"

Solis nodded faintly. His mother had wept the day his father sent him to war at fifteen. She had fallen to her knees before the throne, pleading for mercy, begging King Leo to spare her child. The king refused. *A prince who hides behind castle walls is no heir of Solara. I am raising a son, not a daughter.* The words had branded themselves into Solis's memory, searing deeper with every passing year.

Even then, a bitter thought had flickered through him. What did that make a king who hid behind his own walls? His father commanded others to die in his stead, yet he had never stood amid battle. He had never breathed the fetid stench of rot, death, and ruin. He knew only the comfort of marble and gold while the men of Solara and Selvaran bled for his pride.

Solis studied his mother closely, scrutinizing her delicate features. She had aged waiting for his return. Each letter she sent had carried the same tender inquiries: *Are you safe? Are you eating? Are you well?* And each time, he had lied. *I am fine.* But he had not been fine. The war had hollowed him out, burning away whatever softness or sapience he once possessed, whatever fragment of humanity still lingered within him.

"I missed you," he said quietly.

Aurora's smile trembled as she clasped his hand. "My son, your father is proud of what you have accomplished."

The words cut through him. Proud of what? Of burning men alive? Of turning sons and fathers into ash? He had slain soldiers who had only sought to defend their homes, all because fear had chained his will to obedience. There was no pride in that. Only shame.

"Pride," he muttered, "always leaves behind ashes."

Aurora's fingers stilled above the harp strings. "You sound like your great-uncle. I met him only once as a child, but I remember what he said. Fire that destroys brings ruin. Fire that builds brings life."

Solis lifted his gaze. He had never met his great-uncle, the man exiled long ago for defying the crown. His father never spoke his name, as if silence could erase his legacy.

"I have done nothing but burn," he whispered.

Aurora set the harp aside and cupped his face. Her hands were cool against his skin, soothing the heat that lingered beneath. "You have your father's fire, but your heart is mine. Do not let him steal that from you. Fire is not born for ruin, Solis. It can protect. It can give light. You must remember that."

He searched her eyes, voice low. "What if there is nothing left to give? What if I am already lost?"

Her gaze softened, sorrow gleaming within it. "You are not lost, my son. You are weary, but not lost. I still see you. Your heart burns bright, not with destruction, but with love. Let that be the flame that guides you."

He covered her hand with his own. "And if I can no longer love? If I am too broken?"

Aurora's lips curved into a faint smile. "The sun cannot break. Even when the world turns away, it still burns. Remember that, Solis."

His throat tightened. "I will try, Mother."

She leaned forward and pressed a kiss to his cheek. "Then eat something before you face that wretched girl. Even soldiers need strength for battle."

He let out a low groan at the reminder. "You mean Calista."

"Yes," Aurora replied, lifting her harp once more. "That girl. Honestly, I do not believe she is suited for you, but your father insists. Perhaps she will change once you are married."

That was like asking a serpent to shed its fangs, or a fox to befriend a rabbit. Calista would never change. Solis was convinced there was no soul within her body, only venom. She was the spawn of something merciless, cruel, and wicked. An insufferable piece of—he did not even wish to finish the thought.

"Do I have to?" Solis muttered. "I would rather marry a cow."

A cow would have better manners. Likely more pleasant company too.

Aurora laughed, the sound soft and mellifluous. "Your father and I did not love each other at first, either. He was impossible to reason with. In time, I learned to endure him, and you will learn to endure her as well." Her smile softened, touched with quiet knowing. "Go on now. She has been waiting all day."

Solis exhaled through his nose. "Of course she has."

He rose and pressed a kiss to her cheek before turning to leave. Her harp began to sing again, the melody following him through the corridor, light and wistful, long after the door closed behind him.

The corridors leading to the guest wing gleamed beneath the light of a thousand chandeliers. They had moved Calista to these chambers after his mother insisted he was older now and therefore capable of temptation. She had no wish to see the daughter of Duke Veyra and her son compromised before marriage. As if Solis would ever touch Calista that way or even consider it. He would sooner offer himself to a brothel than endure her touch.

Calista, on the other hand, was quite the opposite. While he valued restraint and purity, she treated desire like a weapon. She crawled toward him whenever she found the chance, her touch as venomous and revolting as her nature.

His mother's decision had been a blessing. Having Calista's chambers far from his own was the greatest mercy ever granted to him. His sanity had not felt more intact than the day he no longer woke to her face lingering at his door each morning like a predator waiting for prey. It was as though she could not comprehend boundaries or the meaning of the words *leave me alone*. Her obsession baffled him. Why she regarded him like a doll to possess and parade remained beyond his percipience.

He turned the corner, following the corridor that led to the woman who would one day enslave him for eternity. The air thickened with the scent of jasmine, cloying and almost narcotic. His jaw tightened. There it was, her favorite poison.

Two maids stood at her door. When they saw him, they curtsied but did not move. Calista preferred her attendants stationed outside, ever waiting, ever wary. Solis wondered how long they had been standing there but chose not to ask. The answer would only stoke his temper, and he was already too weary for wrath.

He drew a slow breath and prayed she was asleep so he could turn back. He hadn't even changed out of his travel clothes, and every muscle in his body throbbed from exhaustion. He knocked.

"I told you not to disturb my peace!" Calista's voice cut through the air, sharp and imperious.

Solis paused, his fist still resting on the door. Well, she had said not to be disturbed. He might as well oblige her. He turned, ready to leave, granting her the solitude she demanded.

But then one of the maids spoke, her voice trembling with trepidation. "My lady, it is the prince."

Solis's eyes narrowed to a slit. Of course. Announce me to the one person I least wished to see. His gaze fell upon the trembling maid, her shoulders quivering under the weight of fear. Compunction rose within him, sour and immediate. He might be ruthless on the battlefield, but striking fear into women's hearts was not a cruelty he relished. If he had a choice, he would choose no cruelty at all.

"She would punish us if we said nothing," the girl whispered, still shaking. "Please forgive me, Your Highness."

He exhaled slowly, the sound heavy with resignation. "Of course she would." Calista never missed an opportunity to make someone bleed for her amusement.

He faced the door again. "May I come in?" he asked, steadying his breath though his patience had already begun to fray.

A few moments passed. It was like her to keep him waiting, to remind him of his place. Everything with Calista was a game, a performance of dominance, a constant assertion that she owned him.

"Of course, my prince," came her reply, smooth and saturated with feigned warmth.

He stepped inside.

Gold. That was the first thing that struck him. Gold fabric, gold candles, gold light. The entire room shimmered like a shrine to her vanity. If arrogance had been metal, she would have forged herself a palace from it.

Calista sat before her mirror, brushing her pale hair in languid, deliberate strokes. Her reflection turned toward him, emerald eyes glinting with calculated charm.

"My prince," she purred, rising from her seat. "I have missed you."

Solis almost laughed. *Missed me? You missed the pleasure of tormenting someone new.*

But he had learned not to provoke her. He remained where he stood as she crossed the room and looped her arms around his neck. Her skin prickled against his like frost, sending a chill down his spine. Her perfume enveloped him, cloying and narcotic, its sweetness thick enough to choke. His body went rigid as he allowed her to feign whatever passion she imagined between them.

"When did you arrive?" she asked, pressing her body against his, making the moment even more unbearable.

"This afternoon. I went to see my mother first."

"Of course you did." A faint curve touched her lips as her gaze lingered. She tilted her chin up, brushing her lips against his. The heat of her breath sickened him. "I was beginning to think you had forgotten about me."

That would have been merciful.

He stiffened as her fingers traced the line of his jaw. The reaction was slight, but she noticed. A mistake. Her smile faltered.

"And here I thought discipline was taught in every regiment," she murmured. "Shall I remind you what happens when you anger me?"

"I had something in my eye." His jaw locked. "It was not because of you."

It was because of you. You insufferable—

Calista's hand shot upward, gripping his jaw with predatory precision, stealing the air from his lungs and the thought from his mind. "I detest liars, Solis."

He knew what was coming before it struck. The pain came swiftly, not fire nor ice but something more insidious, as if his mind were being torn apart from within. His knees gave way under the weight of it. His skull throbbed with invisible pressure. He stumbled, gasping for air as his vision blurred.

"Please." The word scraped out of him. "Calista, make it stop."

Her voice lowered. "Only when you remember your place, my love."

As if she would ever allow him to forget it.

The agony surged again, coursing through his veins like molten iron. His breath fractured, his body trembling violently. He collapsed to the floor, sweat beading across his brow, every muscle convulsing as he fought not to scream.

She held the torturous magic within him until his teeth ground together and his body shook from the strain. Only then did she grant him mercy. Even after her power withdrew, he remained on his knees, hands braced against the floor, air rasping in and out of his lungs as he fought to steady his breath. The ache lingered, pulsing through every vein like a cruel echo.

Calista watched him with quiet satisfaction. "I trust I will not need to remind you of your place again, my love."

No word escaped him. He did not look at her. *If there were any justice in this realm, you would be the one on your knees.* But justice had long since withered in Solara. Calista and her father had seen to that. His title of prince was nothing more than a jest, a gilded illusion of power.

Solis straightened slowly, forcing his trembling body upright. Every movement sent shards of pain through him, like glass tearing along the inside of his skin. What made it worse was the silence he was forced to keep. He could tell no one. His father would never defend him. King Leo believed this was necessary, that pain would forge a man worthy of a throne.

Solis had never understood why his father favored her. He was the son, the heir, the bloodline of Solara itself. Yet whenever he spoke of Calista's cruelty, Leo's gaze softened for her and hardened for him. Was it the influence of Duke Veyra, the alliance his father clung to, or the convenience of keeping his heir leashed by fear? Or had his father simply decided that pain made a better king than love?

The question gnawed at him. It always did. His father had chosen a duke's daughter over his own blood, and that betrayal festered in his heart like a wound that refused to heal.

Calista's voice cooled as she stepped closer, her hand lifting to caress his cheek. Her touch offered no comfort, only contempt wrapped in silk. "I didn't want to do it," she murmured. "You made me."

"If you think hurting me will earn my love…" His breath hitched. "Then you're delusional."

There was still fire within him. For now. He did not know how much longer it would last. Each day stripped away another fragment of his pride until soon there would be nothing left. It was ironic that he found the battlefield more tolerable than the palace. At least in the field, he had control. He had dignity. Here, he was nothing more than a pet Calista could command at her whim.

Her lips twitched. "You're right. But I don't need your love to own you, Solis."

And there it was. The words that curdled his blood and turned his stomach. Own. As if he were a chained beast, something to command, to break, to humiliate.

"I must confess," she continued, her tone light and mocking, "I dislike how often you linger away from the palace. Perhaps I should ask Father to end this war. I would rather have you warming my bed than wasting yourself on blood and ashes."

His stomach twisted. He would rather die. He would rather fall upon a thousand blades than share her bed. She was the reason he had never given himself to another woman. The thought of touch repulsed him. Every brush of skin felt like hers, cold, controlling, laced with venom and deceit.

He had no words for her. None for the madness that governed her, none for the hatred seething in his chest. No words for the promise that one day she would pay for what she had done to him. Nothing, because he was powerless against her. The fire beneath his skin trembled, begging to be released, to reduce her to ash. Yet he could not. If he did, he would become his father. He would burn like the fiend he despised.

Yet a thought slithered in. Was it monstrous to burn a monster?

He wondered if he could, if he could set her alight before her shadows devoured him from within. But doing so would ignite civil war. Lucien would never tolerate the death of his precious daughter. Still, the thought stirred something darkly exhilarating within him. Perhaps he was already becoming the abomination his father had always intended him to be. His lips twitched at the thought of Calista burning, but he caught himself before she noticed.

Calista's gaze had turned pensive, her eyes dropping to his mouth. Without warning, her lips found his, a swift touch that still managed to sear him from the inside.

"Talk to me, Solis," she whispered against his mouth. "Tell me how much you missed me too."

Her lips brushed over his again, hot and heavy. He could feel her hunger, the feverish need that coiled through every movement, a need he could never return. He wanted her gone, but that was impossible. Not yet. When he became king, it would be his first decree. For now, he endured.

Just kiss her, he told himself. Just kiss, and the charade would be over. Just give her what she wants.

He closed his eyes and pressed his lips against hers, granting her the illusion of control she so desperately desired. She wasted no time deepening the kiss. The moment her tongue met his, revulsion clawed at his throat. His soul was slipping further away from his body. Duty, sacrifice, pain. Soon there would be nothing left of him. Just an empty shell of obedience.

But then, like a flicker through smoke, something else broke through the haze. Violet eyes. Bright as starlight. So luminous, so impossibly divine, like something sculpted from the heavens themselves. A small solace to his own desolation.

His body softened for reasons he could not truly comprehend, as though a calling reached deep into his essence. For an instant, he imagined it was her, the girl from the market, the one whose gaze had carried the night sky within it. The memory steadied him, cooling the fire in his chest until only light remained. He did not know her, yet something about her had awakened an ache he had never known he possessed.

Calista deepened the kiss, but Solis no longer felt her. All he saw was the night and, within it, the girl with starlit eyes. For a fleeting moment, his mind drifted into the illusion, distant from reality. But the instant he felt Calista's nails drag along his jaw and heard the soft, breathless sound she made, the vision shattered and pulled him back into the present, into his nightmare. Her breath was hot and possessive against his own.

He pulled away, breaking their seal. His lips still burned from her touch, the taste of her clinging to his tongue. Disgust welled within his chest, sharp and suffocating. Calista's lips curved into a smile of insouciant satisfaction, pleased with what she had stolen from him. He pushed himself back until his shoulders struck the door, his chest heaving as he struggled to steady his breath. He despised the helplessness she made him feel, the dissonance of his body's obedience against his mind's revulsion.

Silently, he rose before she could reach for him again. Her perfume clung to his skin, heavy and cloying, a scent that felt almost venomous.

"I should go," he said quietly. "I'm expected to leave before Sunrise."

Please, just let me be.

Her expression tightened. She stood, twirling a lock of her hair between her fingers with practiced indolence. Her voice edged with quiet accusation. "You always leave."

And he would never return if given the choice. Perhaps it was better to die on the battlefield than to live bound to her.

Solis forced himself to meet her gaze. His words were as level as he could manage, though irritation simmered beneath the surface. "You know why." His jaw clicked. "I don't get to choose. The battlefield decides for me."

She laughed softly, a sound devoid of warmth. "Everything is a choice, Solis. Even obedience."

Obedience. The word reverberated through him with bitter resonance. To obey or to suffer for defiance, where was the choice in that? He almost smiled at the irony. "Not for me," he murmured, voice low and frayed, scarcely more than a whisper. "Not anymore."

The words dissolved into silence.

Calista said nothing. Her attention had already drifted, disinterested in his weariness. She turned to her vanity, adjusting a flawless curl of hair as she admired her reflection in the gilded mirror.

"Have a safe journey, my prince," she didn't look away from the mirror. "Let them tremble before the will of Aurelius. My sun. Perhaps you can bring me their princess as a serving girl—a wedding gift worthy of me."

A smile curved her lips. His stomach turned to stone.

He knew what became of the women taken in war, how they were stripped of dignity and turned into possessions. The thought of them reduced to such cruelty made his blood run cold. This was his doing. He had not signed the decrees, but his hands had carried them out. He was as complicit as his father. As Lucien.

A hollow stillness spread through his chest, guilt festering until it stripped him of everything human. An empty shell. That was all he had become.

"I'll keep that in mind," he muttered, each word cutting through him like glass.

He turned toward the door, but Calista's voice halted him.

"Where is my gift, Solis? Did you think I had forgotten?"

His fingers lingered on the knob. After a long, ragged breath, he forced himself to turn back. He reached into his pocket and drew out the necklace he had bought her, placing it carefully around her neck. Her pale hair brushed against his fingers as he fastened the clasp. A satisfied smile curved her lips.

"It's beautiful," she said.

"Only the best for you," he replied. The words rang hollow, drained of all meaning. He could no longer summon even the illusion of warmth.

Her hand grazed his as he finished. He bent and pressed a perfunctory kiss to her cheek, only to appease her enough to let him leave. As she turned back to the mirror, admiring her new trinket, he slipped away.

He caught the door handle, releasing himself into the corridor. The maids still stood there, motionless and rigid, their eyes downcast as he passed. Each step grew heavier, as if the air itself had turned to poison, seeping into his lungs and veins, killing him from within. Only when he reached the threshold and put distance between her and himself did he finally breathe again.

The silence of the hall steadied him. Faded light from the dying sun spilled through the window, brushing pale gold across the marble floor. He leaned against the wall and pressed a hand to his chest, searching for it. The edge of his pendant met his palm, the crescent stone cool against his skin. It grounded him, reminding him there was still a fragment of himself untouched by the hollowness of his life or her cruelty. A reminder that he still had a soul. A star in the night sky, free.

He closed his eyes. For a fleeting moment, he saw it again, the endless expanse of night scattered with thousands of stars. The world had felt lighter then, unburdened by the weight it carried now. Then violet eyes pierced through his thoughts, drawing him in. They reminded him of the stars, of the freedom beyond them. Those eyes made him forget, even for a breath, how much of him was burning. How much of him was dying, leaving behind only the memory of the stars he had loved so fiercely.

He tilted his head back, gazing at the ceiling, imagining the starry sky and the violet eyes that mirrored its light.

SIXTEENTH

SOLIS

The morning came too soon.

The sky was still pale when Solis mounted his horse.

A faint chill lingered over the courtyard, the kind that clung to stone long after the sun had fallen. It felt almost like mockery, the sun's fervent devotion, burning and blazing, only to bow before the horizon once more. Like him. Forever kneeling to a world that returned nothing but pain and servitude.

Around him, soldiers prepared in quiescent order. Armor clinked, saddles creaked, steel caught the first glimmer of dawn. The rhythm of it all was steady yet hollow, the familiar requiem of men marching toward death for reasons he no longer comprehended nor cared to. This was not justice. It was a conquest. The audacity of taking what was never theirs to claim.

Argus appeared beside him, the sunlight spilling across his gilded armor. His green eyes still held the spark of life that Solis could no longer feel. "You look like hell, Sol."

A humorless laugh escaped him. "Thanks."

Sleep had eluded him. His thoughts had wandered restlessly through the night, haunted by Calista's scent even after he had scoured his skin raw in futile attempts to purge her from it.

Argus cast a glance toward the yard where soldiers loaded the final supply wagons. "We might not be back for a month. Did you say goodbye to your mother?"

A month. A reprieve from one prison to another. A month of duty and ruin, yet somehow a relief. A month without Calista.

"Yeah," Solis said. "Her… and the witch who calls herself my betrothed."

Argus's grin said everything. They both knew the kind of woman Calista was, though neither could alter Solis's fate. War, for all its carnage, had become his sanctuary. It had delayed the wedding, perhaps the only mercy the gods had ever granted him. Still, the thought coiled within his chest, festering with quiet disgust.

What kind of man found solace in bloodshed simply to escape his own bride?

A broken one.

Commander Korven rode in soon after, his eyes darting through the ranks, scrutinizing the supplies and ensuring every detail was in order for battle. Argus's father looked as though he had been carved from the same steel he wielded. There were no soft edges in him, only hardness and unyielding strength. Even his eyes, green like his son's, held a glacial sharpness, but when they met Solis's, a fleeting warmth surfaced, a fatherly warmth Solis had always yearned to see from his own.

"Ready for another taste of glory, boys?" the commander asked, his voice deep and rough, a faint smile tugging at his mouth.

"Never been more ready," Argus said with a half grin. Growing up as a commander's son had attuned him to the chaos of battle. This was just another day for him.

Solis let out a dry laugh. "Glory. My father's favorite word."

Glory and conquest. Take. Take. Take. Until there was nothing left to take. Solis wondered if his father ever realized the kind of monster he had become.

"Besides worthless," Argus muttered. "I don't see him out here swinging a sword. Maybe next time he calls you that, he should prove it himself."

That almost made Solis laugh. Argus never failed to defend him, even against the king himself. One day, that sharp tongue would be his downfall.

Commander Korven's eyes narrowed, his tone cutting through the morning air. "Argus. We do not speak of the king in such a manner."

As loyal as Argus was to Solis, Ivan Korven was equally devoted to his king.

"My apologies, Father," Argus said, the words stiff and insincere. "Got carried away."

Well, truth could never hide, could it? Solis held his tongue, though a hundred words clawed for release.

Korven gave a curt nod and turned his horse toward the gate. "Move out. We cannot wait any longer."

The gates opened with a heavy groan. Sunlight poured through, gilding the courtyard in bronze. Solis urged his horse forward, leading the column beneath the rising sun. The lion sigil blazed across the sky, brilliant and hollow, the promise of valor masking the truth of blood and ruin. The soldiers followed in silence, their faces blank, their futures uncertain.

"Solis."

The voice froze him. He didn't need to turn to know who it belonged to.

"Let me through."

He exhaled, weariness already tightening his chest. Argus shot him a look of pity as Solis dismounted. His boots struck the stone hard, echoing through the courtyard. Of course, Calista would halt an entire army just to make a spectacle of herself. Even his father hadn't come to see him off.

As he made his way past the soldiers, he caught the flicker of envy in their eyes. They thought him blessed. They saw only a prince adored by his betrothed, not the gilded chain beneath her silks. Not the invisible collar she made him wear.

Calista glided toward him, draped in white silk that shimmered like sunlight on glass. He might have found the sight ineffable if it had been anyone else. Her pale hair curled flawlessly over her shoulders, moving like wind over water. The moment she reached him, her arms wound around his neck. He resisted the urge to recoil and let his hands rest lightly at her waist, detaching himself from his own soul.

To an onlooker, it might have seemed a lover's farewell. To Solis, it was mockery. Another form of torture.

"My lady." His tone stayed level, hiding the irritation simmering beneath. "It's cold. Why are you outside?"

Go inside and let me leave, you insufferable witch.

Her lips curved faintly as she leaned into him, hair spilling across his armor, her jasmine perfume clinging to him like a curse. "I wanted to see you go. One last goodbye."

She said it as if she cared. As if she truly wanted him to return. For a fleeting moment, he wished it were one last goodbye. Perhaps the sun would grant him mercy on the battlefield, an honorable death to free him from her thralldom.

Her grasp tightened around his neck, pulling him closer.

"Come home safe to me, Solis."

She rose on her toes and kissed him. Her lips were soft and wet against his. Her eyes were closed, but his remained open. There was nothing tender in the touch, nothing real. Only performance as hollow as her affection. His lips moved against hers because duty demanded it, each taste souring his tongue.

When she drew back, her green eyes met his, cold and covetous, gleaming with that same predatory hunger.

This time, her voice dropped to a whisper, stripped of the pretense and pageantry.

"Come home, Solis."

He wished he wouldn't.

SEVENTEEN

SOLIS

The march to the border took three arduous days. Each Sunrise bled into the next until Solis could no longer tell one morning from another. It became an endless cycle—the sun rose, the army moved, the dust followed. Thousands of feet beat against the road, leaving trails of gold and white. The air carried the scent of sweat and leather, tinged with the faint sting of smoke that lingered from distant fires long extinguished.

Laughter still drifted through the ranks. Hope, faint and fragile, clung to their tongues. Many believed they would return home to their loved ones. How naïve they were. Solis knew better. He had seen death, smelled the blood, witnessed what remained when the light was gone. He had burned countless bodies before, his own soldiers And his enemies alike—each indistinguishable in the end. Charred silhouettes, lifeless and soulless, sent away to meet the gods.

In Solara, the dead were burned to return them to the light. The Selvaran buried theirs, believing their dead would rise again beneath the moon. Only a single belonging was kept—a token to deliver home as a memento of loss.

Most soldiers carried metal charms around their necks, their names engraved in silver, a final testament to the time they had lived.

Solis carried none. His father needed no reminder of the son he had already turned to ash. If death found him on the battlefield, it would be mercy long overdue. Only his mother would grieve. For her sake alone, he almost wished he had something to leave behind. The moon pendant hidden beneath his collar would have to suffice. Perhaps it would be the only piece of him left when he was gone.

Argus rode beside him, posture loose, whistling a low tune that pierced the quiescence of Sunfall. Solis recognized it instantly—the song of war and farewell.

The words surfaced in his mind as he listened to the melody, an old sorrow song whispered by soldiers before they took their final breath:

Farewell, my love, the drums now call,
Through fire and smoke, through rise and fall.
If death should claim me, do not weep,

For in your light, my soul shall sleep.
Just beyond the sun,
And into the unknown.

The melody settled In his chest with somber resonance. It was a song for lovers, an elegy for those left behind, a wife's prayer for the husband who would never return.

Did Argus have someone waiting for him? Solis had never asked. If he did, would this war steal him from her too, leaving her with nothing but a name and memory's ashes?

Would he ever find a love that reached the depths of his despair? Would he die before knowing what it meant to be truly loved—not the kind of love Calista offered, but something real, something that could unravel him completely? Perhaps he would never know. Perhaps such love was not meant for him.

Love was weakness. His father had carved that lesson into his skin, branded it into his bones with every scar. Love was a weakness he could not afford.

He closed his eyes and let the tune sink deeper, its sorrow fusing with his own reverie, feeding the melancholy he could never escape.

Then came the roar—a thunder of arrows cleaving through the air. Death hissed from the sky, a merciless omen descending upon them.

Solis's mare reared, screaming. He reached for the hilt of his blade and, with a single fluid motion, severed one arrow, then another. Splinters and sparks scattered through the haze. The arrows were enchanted, carved from shadowwood, their magic weaving a caustic veil meant to blind the Solaran forces.

Horses shrieked, soldiers shouted. The haze thickened, swallowing the ranks whole.

Solis blinked against it, but the world was already dissolving. The air clawed at his lungs and burned his eyes until all color faded into grey. Argus was nowhere in sight. Panic constricted his chest. He called out, but his voice was lost to the cacophony of war.

Steel clashed, and the forest erupted. Arrows rained from above like a tempest of iron, embedding themselves in earth and flesh alike. Blood spattered across soil and leaves, darkening the ground beneath the dimming light. Through the haze, Solis discerned the fallen, bodies trembling once before the reaper claimed them. Lives severed too soon, sacrificed for the hollow grandeur of war.

Horses thrashed, their hooves gouging the ground as terror rippled through the ranks. The air pulsed with the clash of blades, the cries of the dying, and the suffocating weight of smoke that refused to lift. The world had narrowed to chaos and blood, to haze and the stench of death.

This was what war bought: ruin, grief, and unending loss. Families robbed of the living.

Solis leapt from his mount before it could throw him. The ground quaked beneath his boots as another volley fell. He spun his sword in a wide arc, cleaving arrows mid-flight so that smoke and splinters burst around him. Heat flared from within, searing through the haze, illuminating his path as the darkness tore apart under its brilliance.

An enemy lunged from the side. Solis turned and struck, his blade cutting clean through armor and bone. He did not think. He could not think.

Do not think of who they were.

Do not think of who loved them.

Kill.

Kill.

Kill.

They were not men. Not a husband. Not a brother. Not a child. They were shells emptied by war. Kill. Do not think.

His sword swung again and again, movements faster and sharper, the inferno within him roaring for release. He surrendered to it.

Then the world ignited.

Flame burst from his core, scorching through the haze. Smoke split beneath its brilliance as fire leapt to the fallen trees and devoured everything in its path. The battlefield became a sea of burning silhouettes, steel glinting through the rising heat. The cries of men and beasts merged into a single terrible chorus.

Through it all, Solis stood at the heart of the blaze, consumed by the very fire that had answered his surrender.

All the suffering he had buried, every injustice he had swallowed, rose with the flames and fused with the heat. His rage, his grief, his pain—all of it burned until even the dying could feel the weight of his despair, the mourning of the sun.

His chest heaved as he strode through the infernal light, cutting down any who dared stand before him. Bodies ignited the instant his blade met flesh. Screams fractured the night, mingling with the storm of ash that fell like rain, like his own heart, like the creature he had become.

Then he saw her.

EIGHTEENTH

SOLIS

Through smoke and ruin, a figure emerged. Cloaked in shadow, daggers glinted in her hands as she lunged toward him, movements fluid and defiant, eyes burning with purpose, violet as starlight.

She moved like the wind. Like a force of wrecking. Like a sin made flesh.

His blade rose instinctively to meet hers. Steel met silver, sparks scattering like constellations across the blaze.

Her strike arced toward his neck. Little violent thing. So fierce. He ducked low, sweeping his sword toward her legs, but she moved like wind, each motion a dance of steel and tempest. She leapt through the fire's haze, her cloak trailing behind her in ripples of darkness. For a heartbeat she seemed unreal, her motion defying the ruin around her as though the inferno itself existed only to frame her light. Radiant as the moon.

Then her right dagger flared with silver brilliance, a burst of lunar glow that tore through the smoke. She twisted mid-air and brought it down across his arm. The blade struck deep. Pain seared through him, cold light carving the heat from his flesh. Yet it felt almost welcome. What madness was this, that his body yearned for her even as she became his undoing? Every fiber of him longed to crumble beneath her chaos, to let her ruin him in ways he could never name.

Solis staggered but did not yield. His eyes remained fixed upon her. He caught her next strike with his sword, steel locking against silver. His gaze flicked downward, tracing the slender line of her waist, the curve of her hips. A woman fighting alone in a man's war. It should have been unthinkable, yet it enthralled him — fierce, impossible, divine.

Her black armor shimmered beneath the firelight, every motion fluid and flawless, reminiscent of a dragon born from flame, his flame. Even chaos seemed to bend around her. The sight of her stole his breath. How could she move so fast, so precise, so beautifully? A grin unfurled across his face, wild and unbidden. Excitement coiled through him. She was intoxicating, reckoning made flesh.

Her dagger swept close enough to brush his cheek. He turned with her motion, blade rising just in time to meet hers. Their weapons locked, sparks bursting between them. It felt almost like a dance of steel, a waltz carved from fury and fire. Not the kind of dance he would have chosen with her, but one he did not mind. There was something about the way she wanted to kill him that made he want her more.

In that instant, he saw her clearly.

Silver light from her dagger washed across her features, pale skin framed by black hair bound in braids, the reflection of his fire glinting along her edges. Her expression was sharp, determined, and achingly beautiful. Not the polished beauty of Solara's court, but something wild and luminous. Something ineffable, like the horizon at dusk, elusive and eternal.

Her eyes lifted to his. Violet. BrIght. Endless. The same light that had haunted his dreams for years. The same light that had once cut through the darkness he could never escape.

His body still fought on instinct, blade meeting dagger, but his mind had fallen into those eyes. The fire, the screams, the turmoil — all of it faded, consumed by that impossible violet gaze.

He wanted to lose himself there, to remember what freedom had once felt like.

She stepped back, annoyance flickering across her face. Wind stirred the smoke between them, her braid catching the firelight until it gleamed with a copper hue. Her voice cut through the din, sharp as her blades, the faint light pulsing at her chest beneath the leather, the mark of the crescent moon.

"Stop looking at me like that."

"Like what?" He blinked, finally aware of how long he had been staring. Hard not to, when even fury looked beautiful on her. He lowered his sword a fraction, striving for composure, though the trace of amusement in his tone betrayed him.

"I didn't realize killing came with rules," he murmured, tilting his head slightly, eyes glinting with audacious mischief. "Tell me, what expression should I wear when I end you?"

It was madness to speak so lightly in the heart of battle, as though they stood not amid carnage but in a ballroom trading verses. Then again, she was verse — dangerous, ineffable, a stanza he would not mind reading to its final line. Perhaps he was mad after all.

She rolled her eyes — those perfect, infuriating eyes that managed to both irritate and enthrall him. Yes, he was insane. Entirely.

"Well, to start, that look." She pointed her dagger toward him, the blade glinting through the burning forest as she made a small, deliberate motion in the air, glaring as though she might hurl it at his face at any moment. "That's not the expression of a man about to kill. It's the opposite. It's almost like you want to—"

Her voice faltered. The words caught in her throat. Realization flickered across her face. A flush bloomed across her cheeks, softening the fierceness of her glare into something almost innocent, turning the indomitable warrior into a shy maiden undone by a thought she dared not finish.

He liked the warrior, but this fleeting glimmer of innocence captivated him more. So unpredictable.

His gaze lingered on her lips, his thoughts dangerously close to crossing a line he should not. Would her touch carry the same poisonous allure as Calista's, or something entirely different — something sincere, alive, and real? He wanted to know. Those violet eyes, luminous and arresting, had haunted his reverie through countless nights. And now she was here.

His brow arched, a smirk tugging faintly at his lips. A silent challenge lingered between them. Say it. Tell me what I want to do.

He should not have found it amusing. He should not have felt this pull, this desire. Not here. Not now. Yet amid the fire, the screams, and the suffocating stench of blood, he fought the irrepressible urge to smile — to marvel at the way she made his pulse quicken against his ribs.

"Please enlighten me," he said, tone low and edged with amusement despite the blood still dripping from his arm, a visceral reminder of where they stood. "Look like I want to do what?"

She said nothing. The flush on her cheeks deepened. Then her lips parted slightly as her eyes widened.

Her head tilted, studying him. Recognition flickered there, subtle at first, then brightening, dawning like the first sliver of sunlight breaking through a storm. Did she remember him? It had been years — eight long years — yet he had never forgotten her.

When she finally spoke, her words struck harder than any blade. The sting bit deeper than the wound on his arm.

"You're that peacock."

Peacock. The word echoed through his mind, absurd and cutting in its simplicity. Did she truly not remember him? Had he meant so little? They had been engaged, for the sun's sake.

Then it hit him like a flare of revelation—the market, the scarf, the violet eyes. Of course. It was her.

His eyes widened as the memory settled. He should have known. Who else possessed eyes like starlight? Who else could captivate him so effortlessly? Even now, amid the chaos, those eyes burned brighter than the flames around them. Yet she did not remember him.

He smoothed his expression into something languid, mocking. "Peacock? Sweet princess, are you calling me colorful?"

Her glare could have cut steel. "More like insufferable. Dull. A pain where no color would dare shine."

"Quite the temper," he mused. "Never thought a princess would have that kind of spark."

"The only spark I'll have is when I drive my dagger into you and—" She stopped. Her eyes narrowed. "Wait. How do you know I'm the princess?"

He choked, unable to help it. Even the trees could tell she was the princess. Who else bore the crescent light pulsing at her chest? Who else wore Selvaran black in a battlefield of Solaran flame? It was almost comical how long it had taken her to realize he already knew.

"Your light," he said slowly. "Tell me, who in Selvaran bears a crescent that glows like a pulse?"

He spread an arm, sword still in hand, gesturing toward the scorched earth around them, simply showing her how obvious her identity was.

Through smoke, a soldier lunged from the flank but never reached him; the man turned to ash where he stood. They did not call him the Sun for nothing.

He watched her closely as confusion folded into recognition, then disbelief, then hatred, each emotion plainly visible. So easy to read, like an open book. She was as formidable as she was entrancing. When she bit her bottom lip, something within him fractured. She looked adorably fierce, utterly irresistible. He was going to need saving, and not the kind his soldiers could give him. Even in those eyes that swore vengeance, he found himself drawn in.

Then her expression hardened, the moment it clicked.

"You're that prince," she spat. "That monstrous beast who burned my men."

Yes. That was him. There was no denying it, and still the hatred landed like a verdict. He had expected it, had even earned it. But it was not as if he had started the war. His hands were far from clean, yet how could she judge him when she had slain just as many Solarians as he had slain Selvarans? Who was keeping tally anyway? What point was there in defending himself? War made monsters of them all.

If she wanted a villain, someone to blame for this merciless war, he would become it. His expression darkened into the mask he wore for survival, the cruel curve he had learned from Calista's playbook.

"Did I become famous overnight?" he asked, relishing the accusation, masking every trace of feeling, sealing his heart the way he always had. No one loved a creature born of ruin. No one would ever love what his father had made of him. "Monster, you say. Then why are you so composed, princess? Aren't you afraid I'll finish you here and now?"

"Not before I end you first," she snarled, lunging with audacious precision.

He sidestepped her strike with the ease of someone forged through rigorous discipline. Lavender brushed the air as she passed, hollowing his chest with its comfort. He breathed her in, burying the ache it stirred, taking what he could of her before they crossed a point of no return.

For a heartbeat, he had almost believed she might see beyond the fire and ruin. But she saw only the monster she wished him to be. So he let her. Hatred, after all, was better than nothing.

"Princess," he murmured, amusement curling through his tone, "don't tease me with good times. If you intend to end me, then do it."

NINETEEN

LUNA

The battlefield roared around her, ember and ash colliding in a storm of screaming and steel. And still, she couldn't believe her ears. In the middle of a burning forest, with soldiers tearing each other apart, the idiot had the audacity to joke?

"Princess," the fool said, amusement warm in his voice, "do not tease me with good times. If you intend to end me, then do it."

The only teasing she intended was to slit his throat. Solis Aurelius was ruin made flesh. Because of him, her people suffered. Because of him, they fought two wars at once, one of shadow and one of steel. And now he had the audacity to mock her.

Her daggers flashed. One skimmed his cheek, drawing a single line of crimson. The arrogant prince moved with a swiftness that made her blood boil. She swung her leg, aiming for his stomach. He caught it and pulled her down in a single, effortless motion.

Her back struck the ground. His face hovered above hers, a smirk planted like a banner of victory.

"Well, that is unfortunate, and here I thought you were going to bleed my throat out," he remarked, "if only your dagger skills were as good as your archery."

"Excellent advice," she answered, her voice cold as glass. "Next time I will bring my bow and shoot an arrow through those pretty eyes of yours."

She lunged again, dagger arcing for his throat. He caught her wrist with maddening ease. The smirk did not falter.

"If your face were the last thing I saw, it might be worth it," he murmured, each word sliding from his tongue like smoke. She wished he would stop speaking, wished she could silence him once and for all.

Heat climbed her neck. Why was she blushing at this insolent prince's words like a foolish girl? She said nothing. She would not play his game. Her other dagger rose, but he caught that hand too, pinning both her wrists above her head.

"Nice try, princess," his breath brushed her cheek.

Frustration surged through her veins. She drove her knee hard into his groin. His face twisted; he staggered back with a strangled groan.

Luna rolled to her feet in a single, fluid motion. A faint, satisfied smile touched her lips. The smirk was gone. Good.

"Nothing to say now, prince?"

His eyes narrowed. He had left his sword behind when he caught her wrist. Now he stood empty-handed while she held two blades.

She lunged. His stance shifted the instant she closed in. With practiced precision, he deflected her daggers and torqued her wrist until pain raced up her arm, forcing her grip to falter.

Light pulsed from her chest. She released it. The burst struck him squarely. He lifted his arm to shield himself.

Flame burst from his palm, spreading in an uncontrollable surge that devoured the field. The heat rose between them, a living inferno. Before the blaze could touch her, his hand shot out. The fire curved away, as though the flames themselves refused to touch her.

He drew her against him, the inferno coiling around them in a sphere of gold. The roar of it filled the air, radiant as a newborn sun. For a heartbeat it felt as if they stood inside the sun itself. His power tore through the world, destroying everything except the space that held them.

Screams echoed through the burning field. Her body remained pressed to his, his arm still around her. He shielded her from his own destruction. Her heart stumbled against his. Warmth surged through her armor, through the chaos, through disbelief.

Why would he protect her when moments ago he had sworn to kill her?

Questions braided through her mind, yet she chose the one that trembled on her tongue.

"So why did you save me?" Her voice barely carried over the roar, uncertain. "I'm sure your king would reward you for the glory."

"A prince does not need glory, sweetheart," his tone dipped, "I already have plenty of that."

He raised one hand while the other held her still, drawing the fire inward until only embers remained. How could he command flame so easily and yet lose control so easily? She had read that Aurelius fire fused with emotion. What had happened to him to make him fuse his flame with such rage? What had happened to the boy who once cried for a dead rabbit—the boy so kind-hearted he could not bear to see something fragile die?

"What happened to you?" she whispered. "Solis, what happened to you?"

He said nothing, but his eyes answered. Melancholy lingered there, a sorrow deeper than she had ever seen. They had broken that boy. They had carved something into him she no longer recognized. They had remade him into a weapon. She remembered the cold set of King Leo's gaze and knew, without doubt, who had shaped this ruin. It took a beast to destroy his own blood.

"Princess, do not tell me you are concerned for my wellbeing," he drawled, "given that you just told me you wanted to end me."

She glared at him for the audacity of teasing her, then realized he still held her and their bodies were so close she could feel his heart beating through his chest.

Her face flushed. She pushed herself away.

Mad to cling to the enemy like a lover while the world screamed. The ground still smoldered from his fire. The scent of blood and ash hung heavy in the air, yet somehow she had spoken to him as if the two of them stood alone.

His gaze swept the battlefield; hers followed. A terrible stillness haunted the ruins.

Bodies lay scattered. Blood. Ash. Burned trees. Everything gone.

This had to end. It had to, before more lives were lost.

An unreadable expression crossed his face as he looked across the devastation. After a long pause of quiescence, he finally spoke.

"I'm sorry, princess," the words dropped low, "but I think we have a war to fight."

She raised her daggers. She agreed with him. This could only end with him gone. As much as she pitied him, as much as she longed to spare him, he was the reason her people were dying. He had taken too many lives. With him alive, the destruction of her realm would never cease. She could not allow that.

"Then I am sorry too," she said softly, "because I will miss the boy who once cried over a rabbit."

Something fragile shifted in his expression. He blinked, as if her words had pierced through armor.

When she lunged, he did not defend himself—not fire, nothing—as though he had no will to fight her. No will for anything at all. As if he wished her to end him. He stepped forward as her dagger struck. It stopped just shy of his throat as she drew back, a single bead of blood tracing down his skin.

Her breath caught. "Why?"

"Take me hostage," his voice was barely a breath, "call off your men, princess."

She stared at him, unable to believe what she had heard. Her hand trembled as she weighed ending him now against letting him live. Blood glimmered on the edge of her steel.

"Take you hostage? Have you any idea what you're saying?" she demanded. "Khael might not even consider it. They'll kill you."

He released a weary sigh, his eyes sweeping the ruin once more. "Maybe then it would all stop. Maybe the killing would finally end. Maybe the war would not claim another life. Maybe this is my only way to save what little innocence still lives inside me. Please, princess."

TWENTY

LUNA

Around them, the war raged on. Steel clashed. Fire burned. Men screamed. The world bled red and gold, yet she saw none of it, only him. The prince of Solara stood unarmed before her, his ocean-blue eyes locked upon hers. Always watching. Always calm. She could drown in those eyes and forget the ruin consuming the world.

"Take you hostage?" she asked, her voice nearly lost to the fervent roar of flame.

He met her gaze without hesitation. "Yes. Use me. End it. Tell the Solarian line you have me. Tell Commander Korven you will slit my throat if they do not stand down."

His certainty struck her like a gelid wind, audacious in its composure. Too sure that he could be sacrificed. Too sure she would not simply kill him. Too sure Khael would not.

Or perhaps he longed for death. There was a hollow in his eyes, an ocean dimmed by melancholy. Had they always been that sad? Was this his way of finding quiescence at last?

She could have ended him then, severed Solara's line and left the kingdom heirless. Yet the thought of driving her blade through that sorrow made her chest ache. He was a broken man.

And perhaps taking him hostage was not such a terrible notion. They could use him to end this merciless war. He was the only son of King Leo, the crown prince, the Sun of Solara. If Selvaran held him, Solara's morale would waver.

Her hand lowered. "You are insane."

"Maybe," he breathed, "but you're tired too, aren't you? Tired of watching them die."

She was. Saints, she was so very tired of this war.

Luna's gaze swept the field. Bodies smoldered in the grass. Flames licked the timber. The pride of kings had spilled enough blood to drown the night itself. Her throat tightened, heavy with compunction.

"Fine," she murmured. "I'm borrowing your neck for a bit."

His mouth twitched. "Go on, then."

He was clearly mad, yet she allowed him his folly. He crossed the scorched ground and retrieved his sword, then turned to face her. His figure towered above her, and for the first time, she realized just how tall he truly was, how easily he could have overpowered her if he wished. Instead, he turned again and sank to both knees, the blade clutched tightly in his hand.

"It must look convincing. My commander will not surrender easily. Neither will his son."

Before she could comprehend his intent, he drove the sword into his own side.

"Wait—" The word escaped too late. He doubled over, a ragged sound tearing from him as blood spilled between his fingers. Saints above, he was insane. Brave, or too broken to care.

She caught him before he could fall, her fingers tangling in his hair. It was softer than she expected, warm silk against her trembling hand. For a fleeting heartbeat, the fire, the screams, the ruin around them faded as her gaze fell to his wound. His white uniform was staining crimson fast, blood seeping through the fabric in dark rivulets. His breathing slowed, his lashes lowering as if to shield himself from the agony.

A stone of dread anchored in her stomach, yet she forced herself to move. She pulled his head back carefully, wary of worsening the wound, and pressed her dagger to his throat. The pulse beneath her palm was slow but palpable, steady in its defiance. Whatever came next, they had to act quickly. She was no longer certain how long Solis had before he bled out. Audacious fool.

"Stop the fight!" she shouted, her voice breaking through the roar with fervent strength. "I have your prince."

The battlefield inhaled and held its breath. Every soldier froze, the clash of steel dying into silence.

Then a voice cleaved the hush. "Let him go."

A man stepped through the smoke, armor streaked with blood, a greatsword at his side nearly as tall as he was. Luna's breath caught. He moved as though the weight were nothing, as if the blade itself obeyed him. There was a sagacious composure to him, a tempered strength that defied the surrounding chaos.

Her grip tightened in Solis's hair. A strained sound escaped his lips and her heart jolted. Perhaps she had tugged too hard, but there was no undoing it now. They needed the capture to look real. They had to make the Solaran line believe the carnage must stop.

Her dagger pressed to his throat. She could not falter, even as every instinct screamed to let him go. His skin paled; his breath came shallow.

"I said, let him go." The man's voice carried cold certainty, his stance coiled to strike.

Before she answered, Solis's voice cut through the crackle of fire, ragged with effort. "Argus. Surrender. Please."

So that was his name. Argus.

The man froze. The fierce wildness burning in his green eyes softened when they found Solis, folding into something like mercy. The bond between them stood plain in the air. Luna saw it at once. Argus loved Solis more than his own life.

"Solis," Argus said quietly. "I cannot watch you die."

"She will not kill me," Solis rasped, "not yet. Tell our men to fall back."

Argus's jaw tightened. "Solis, I—"

"Do it." The command scraped from his throat. "That is an order."

Argus swallowed the protest and obeyed. He faced the field, his voice hardening into command. "Solaran army, fall back! The prince has been captured. Regroup on the flank, now."

The order ran through the ranks like wildfire. Solara's lines folded, white and gold streaked with red as they withdrew from the burning field, leaving a hollow silence behind.

Only the crackle of flame remained, the air thick with smoke and the iron scent of blood. Solis's breathing grew louder and heavier, each ragged inhale a fragile testament to his will to endure.

Heavy boots ground through ash as Khael stepped from the haze, Selvaran troops fanning out behind him, black leather catching the last light. Cold pride sat in his dark eyes; the hard set of his mouth showed it. He looked from Solis to Luna, a wolfish grin tugging one corner of his mouth.

"Well done, Princess," he drawled, "you captured the Aurelius heir."

Luna kept her chin high, feigning the composure of a victorious princess while her stomach clenched at the prince's ragged breaths. Her dagger stayed steady though her hands wanted to tremble. An unfamiliar concern rooted itself in her. Why did she care so much for him? He was her enemy, and still she found herself daring to care.

"Kill him," Khael said. "End the war. One stroke and Solara's line will falter."

"No."

Disbelief crossed Khael's face. "No?"

"We'll take him to my father," she said. "He will decide his fate."

Khael studied her. Silence thickened between them. His jaw tightened before he gave a single, curt nod. He would not embarrass her before the Selvaran troops, not under Solaran scrutiny. Whether he kept that restraint once the soldiers were gone remained another matter.

"As you wish." Khael flicked his hand toward his men. "Bind him."

A voice rose from the Solaran ranks.

"I'd advise you to take your hand off my prince, princess."

A middle-aged man stepped forward, armor stained with crimson, yet white and gold still visible beneath the smoke. The way he carried himself spoke of an unmistakable bearing of command. Luna thought she recognized him from eight years past, the man whose loyalty to King Leo ran deeper than blood. His green eyes shared Argus's sharpness yet carried the weight of experience. This was Commander Korven.

Khael's head tilted. "And if we refuse?"

Commander Korven stopped a few paces away, expression unreadable. "Then I will claim him back myself."

The threat in his tone left no doubt he meant it.

Khael's lip curved into a mocking smile. "My apologies, Commander Korven. I do not take orders from Solara. You should be grateful for the princess. If it were up to me, your prince's head would already be rolling."

Korven met him with even resolve. "Then thank your princess indeed, for she shows more restraint than her commander. If not, I would not be so merciful. Return my prince now. This is your final warning."

The tension cracked like distant thunder.

Luna's mind raced for a solution and found none. She pulled Solis's head back harder, ignoring the pained gasp as she bared the wound to Korven. Blood darkened the fabric at his side and trailed down his leg in scarlet ribbons, soaking the charred ground. The sword still lodged there made every motion perilous. The dagger pressed cold to his throat, a promise of what she would be forced to do if Korven pushed further. She could only hope the commander would choose caution over valor.

"Commander Korven," she said, voice steady despite the cold tightening her hands, "no harm will come to your prince while he is in our care. Look at him. One more strike, and he will not see another Sunrise."

Korven's gaze shifted from her to Solis. The lines in his face deepened, carved by restraint, yet he did not move. After a long, somber pause, he gave a single, rigid nod.

"I will return to my king and report what has transpired here—and the prince's condition. I trust you will keep your word, princess."

Relief coursed through her veins, leaving her breath uneven.

"I will."

Khael smirked but did not press further. "Bind him," he ordered.

Two Selvaran soldiers stepped forward with ropes, binding Solis's hands behind him. He did not resist—or perhaps he could not. His head hung low, his breath shallow, as though he balanced on the edge of oblivion. His eyes were half-closed, his jaw tight with pain.

From the Solaran ranks, Argus called out, voice rough. "Ropes? Really? For a fire wielder? Solis, what in the hells are you doing? At least tell me what this is."

It was clear his men did not believe this ruse, yet they followed it. There was something about Commander Korven and this Argus she could not yet discern, a bond woven through loyalty and something fiercer—devotion, perhaps.

A sheen of sweat slipped down Solis's neck. His breath hitched, but his tone held. "There's nothing to explain. Argus, tell my father I was captured. Tell him to wait for King Orion's word. Tell him to do what is right."

Argus's jaw tightened. "Fine. You'd better live. If they harm a single hair on your head, I'll hunt them all down. You hear me? Live, Solis."

His green eyes burned toward the Selvaran soldiers with feral intensity, and Luna almost pitied the men who met that gaze.

Commander Korven turned as the Solaran army began to withdraw. "Princess." He didn't look back. "I trust you will keep my prince safe."

"You have my word."

Korven said nothing else as he walked away.

Luna sheathed her dagger, the metallic click echoing through the hush. For now, the battlefield had quieted into quiescence. Her pulse still thundered as she watched Solis, shoulders bowed, wrists bound, blue eyes unwavering even through pain.

He did not look defeated.

He looked free.

TWENTY-ONE

LUNA

The aftermath of battle came into full view once the Solaran troops withdrew. The air reeked of smoke and blood, and the forest that had once echoed with screams now sagged into silence. Only the faint rustle of armor and the rhythm of distant hooves broke the hush, small sounds of soldiers gathering the dead and tending the wounded.

Solis still knelt amid the ruin, lifeblood seeping through his armor like ink through parchment. Khael stood before him, a wall of iron and judgment.

"Khael, stop!" Luna shouted, her voice trembling.

He ignored her. With one swift, merciless motion, he wrenched the sword from Solis's side.

Solis's scream tore through the stillness, a raw, human sound that made even the crows take flight. Her heart sank as he collapsed forward, air leaving his lungs in a jagged gasp.

Her body moved before her mind could think. She was at his side in a heartbeat, knees striking the blood-wet earth. Her hands pressed against the wound, her pulse stuttering, a rush of panic crashing over her as she knelt by him. The heat of him clung to her palms, refusing to fade. Compassion for an enemy was not something she had ever expected to feel, yet there it was. She hated him for what he was, yet pitied what he had become.

"Khael." Her voice cracked through the quiet. "He's losing too much blood."

The commander turned the blade in his grip, studying it as though it were merely steel and not the reason kingdoms might burn if Solis died. "A fine sword," he murmured. "Nothing less for a prince."

Luna's pulse quickened. "Get the medics," she ordered. "Now."

Khael turned without a word, a faint curl of satisfaction shaping his mouth as if Solis's suffering were a victory to savor.

Her gaze settled on the man who had once stood tall as flame and now burned only to survive. Sweat glistened along his neck, his skin drained to a gelid pallor.

When the medics arrived, they worked quickly. There were no healers among them; healers were sacred, too rare to risk on a battlefield. Yet for the first time, Luna wished one were near.

"We need his armor off," one said.

She reached for the clasps, but Solis caught her hand. His fingers trembled, slick with sweat.

"No," he rasped.

No? Did the fool not realize he was bleeding out?

"This is no time for pride," she said, frustration cutting through her composure.

He only shook his head. "Later." His voice was soft and frayed, the sound of a man held together by sheer will.

Foolish prince. Stubborn to the end. If he wanted death so badly, she might let Khael finish the job.

She withdrew as the medic pressed crushed herbs against the wound. Solis's jaw tightened, teeth grinding while the scent of blood and mint thickened the air. Luna watched the flicker of pain in his eyes and felt something twist inside her that she could not name. She was pitying the very thing she ought to despise.

Hours passed before the column began to move, Selvaran banners unfurling through the smoke like dark wings. Luna rode beside Khael at the head of the line, though her gaze drifted back more often than she wished to admit.

The prince rode bound between two soldiers, wrists tied, posture slumped yet unbroken. He looked less like a captive and more like a fading sun refusing to set.
It was hardly believable that this was the same boy she had met eight years ago in the Selvaran forest, crying over a rabbit. He

had grown, his features sharper, the youth long gone, replaced by the hard edges carved of war. Yet, within those blue eyes, she still saw the little boy.

"He should have been executed." Khael's voice was gravel against the rhythm of hooves. "You do not comprehend the peril of keeping him alive."

Luna kept her eyes on the road ahead. "And ignite another war before this one dies? We need him alive if we ever want peace to happen, Khael."

His gaze stayed forward. "You saw what he did out there. Power like that never comes without cost."

"Perhaps." Her tone softened, weariness threading through each word. Her fist clenched the rein as she forced herself to ignore the prince behind her. "But for now, he is the only one who can secure peace. We need him alive."

Khael's jaw flexed. "I hope we do not come to regret this mercy. Sparing a monster. What a jest."

A monster. If he was a monster, then who had made him become one? And would a monster surrender himself for the fate of both realms?

Luna turned her head, the wind brushing strands of hair across her cheek. "Or perhaps it means he is more human than we believed."

When she looked back again, Solis's head had bowed forward, his body swaying with the rhythm of the horse. Blood still seeped through his bandages, dark and unrelenting. He looked exhausted, yet there was no fear in him, only quiet resolve. Was this truly a monster?

Something within her stirred, a pull she could not define, a yearning to understand the creature forged of sunlight and ruin.

She slowed her mount until she rode beside him. The guards reined back at her gesture.

"Solis."

His head lifted as if the act demanded what little strength remained. Their eyes met. His were the color of the sea she had only ever read about, endless and vivid, a blue too beautiful for a man who had burned her world to ash.

"Hey, princess." The faintest ghost of a smile touched his lips.

Her throat tightened. He was fading, the life draining from him like light slipping from a dying sun. She could almost feel it, that fragile thread still binding him to the world.

Luna's gaze dropped to the crimson spreading across his abdomen. Pride and politics no longer mattered. Not tonight. Enemy or not, they would show him mercy.

"We're stopping here." Her voice cut through the wind. "I need a break."

Khael halted. His neck turned slightly, eyes narrowing at her command. She lifted her chin, daring him to speak. He said nothing.

The moon hung low when they made camp beneath the dim sky. Luna stayed close to Solis, wary that Khael might slit the prince's throat before they reached her father.

When the tents were raised, she gave her order. "Bring him down."

Solis's head drooped, so low it nearly brushed the mare's mane. Her fingers twitched with the urge to touch him, to feel whether he still drew breath.

Two soldiers obeyed, lowering the prince from his horse. His weight sagged between them as his body slid free. His skin had lost all warmth, the gold in him dimmed to ash.

"Prepare a tent for him," she ordered. "He'll stay separate from the ranks."

The men complied, but Khael's voice cut through the night. "A tent for a prisoner? Princess, even our own soldiers do not get that privilege. Yet you would grant it to him?"

"He's injured, Khael." Her tone remained even. "We cannot leave him in the cold."

"You'd coddle an Aurelius?" He spat the words, voice sharpening. "He's better off dead. One less Aurelius to plague the realm. You saw the bodies he left behind."

Luna turned toward him, gaze cold and unyielding. "I already told you, Khael. I. Need. Him. Alive." Her tone hardened, each word carrying the authority of her blood. "His death would shatter what peace remains. Do not argue otherwise."

Khael fell silent as she slipped an arm beneath Solis's and helped him stand, leading him away from the dagger stares of her men. His body was cold beneath her touch, breath faint as mist. He leaned against her, the weight nearly crushing. Guilt coiled inside her, sharp as a blade. Perhaps she should never have let him drive that sword into himself. If she had stopped him, he would not be bleeding out in her arms now.

She guided the wounded prince toward the tent.

Inside, the air was cool and still, laced with the faint scent of smoke from the campfires outside. A single lantern glowed near the wall, its argent light trembling against the canvas. Luna guided him down and called for the medics again. When she reached for the clasps of his armor, his hand caught hers. His skin was cold against her own, his grip faint as breath.

"Don't."

Her gaze lifted to his. "Your wound needs tending. The armor must come off, prince."

His breath hitched. His gaze faltered, head lolling. "Don't… touch me."

Irritation flared beneath her fatigue. The audacity of him, half-conscious and still refusing aid. She wanted to let him bleed, to let arrogance finish what the battlefield had begun, but she could not. His life had become the hinge on which two realms turned.

"Stay still. Let me take it off."

"No."

Heat rose within her, sharp and impatient. "What are you so afraid of? I have seen worse wounds. You're no different."

None of them, however, had ever tested her patience as this one did.

"Don't," he murmured, voice cracked, eyes lowered again.

Her brow furrowed. "Don't what, exactly?"

His lashes lowered fully, the words slipping out as if against his will. "I just do not want you to see."

See what?

She exhaled through her nose. "Then how do you expect the medics to stitch you up?"

"I will do it myself," he whispered, lids falling shut. "I've done it countless times before."

She studied him, uncertain whether he was a fool or simply delirious. His eyes looked diluted, the color fading like water over paint. He could barely stay conscious yet still clung to that pride.

"Fine." She rose to her feet, too tired to argue further. If he wanted to bleed out, then she would let him. The tent flap brushed her shoulder as she stepped outside. Moments later, the medics arrived, and she instructed them to leave the thread, herbs, and tinctures for the stubborn prince. They obeyed without question and disappeared into the night.

She left the prince to himself and returned to her tent. Moments later, Khael summoned her for supper.

They ate in silence. The anger did not fade; it coiled beneath her ribs. She loved Khael like a father, yet there were times he tried her patience beyond measure.

When the meal ended, she excused herself. Her eyes kept drifting toward the prince's tent until, without realizing, her steps carried her there.

Light bled through a slit in the canvas, a narrow blade of gold cutting through the dark. He was awake.

The sight stole her breath.

Solis sat half-turned from her, armor discarded, the lantern's glow tracing the scars that marked his back. Pale and cruel, they crossed one another like constellations carved into flesh. Some gleamed silver; others lay dark and raised.

No battle had done this. These were the marks of cruelty.

Her heart dropped. Was that why he had resisted her help? So she would not see what had been done to him?

Her throat tightened. She let the flap fall and turned away, but as she walked off, the weight of compunction pressed hard against her chest. She could not leave him like that.

Drawing a breath, she stepped back inside.

His gaze snapped to hers, startled. His hands stilled mid-motion, the needle and thread poised above the open wound. Shadows bruised the skin beneath his eyes.

"You should leave. Your help isn't needed, princess."

He turned away. His hand trembled as he pierced the skin again, crimson slicking his fingers as the thread pulled through.

A soft gasp escaped him, barely audible, as though he feared to let the world hear his pain.

Unbelievable. Luna debated whether to leave him to his misery or—

"Are you sure you don't need help, prince?" The words slipped right through her reluctant heart before she could stop them.

He gave a faint nod, stubborn to the bone. "I can do it on my own."

He winced as the needle bit again, though no sound followed, as if control itself were the only dignity he had left. The lantern's glow flickered across his shoulders, catching the sheen of sweat and the tremor of his hands.

Luna stood motionless, watching him fight the thread. His fingers slipped through blood, trembling with exhaustion. She let out an irritated sigh and reached for his hand. His blue eyes met hers.

"You are impossible," she murmured. Her fingers closed around his, the coldness of his skin startling her. His gaze lifted. "Let me help you."

He hesitated, then finally relented. His hand dropped to his side as though his strength had run dry.

She stitched the remainder of his wound, her focus steady. He remained mostly silent, only small, stifled sounds slipping through. Was this how he had always survived? Tending to his wounds alone after every battle? After everything they had done to him?

She wanted to ask about the scars, but the look in his eyes changed her mind. Still, the questions gnawed at her.

"You know," she started, "you don't have to do everything on your own. It's okay to ask for help."

He said nothing.

He swiveled his head away, staring at the canvas of the tent. She could see the way his eyes flinched as she stitched him.

When she finished, she rinsed her hands in the basin and took a fresh cloth to wipe the blood from his skin. He leaned his head back slightly, the argent light glancing across his face. For all the fire and ruin he had wrought, he looked fragile now, like a flower withering through a crack.

For a long moment, silence lingered before he finally spoke.

"I thought you would have left."

She knelt beside him, uncertain what to say. Her hands were still damp from the cloth. Her gaze traced the scars across his chest, his arms, the plane of his torso; some were deep, some faint, scars aged and settled into his skin. She swallowed, the words rising and dying in her throat. The questions burned until one slipped out.

"How did you get those scars?"

His body went still. His gaze met hers, and the warmth once in his voice turned cold.

"It doesn't concern you."

Irritation pricked through her, dissolving what pity remained. "Why do you have to be so insufferable? I was only asking because… those… they look intentional."

His features stayed carved in stone. "Because they are. And like I said, princess, it doesn't concern you."

"Fine. It's not like I care anyway."

He said nothing. Then his teeth caught his lower lip, a small, unguarded gesture that made him look almost boyish beneath the scars and the hardened veneer of a soldier. It reminded her of the boy she had met years ago. Perhaps he was still in there somewhere.

"You cared enough to come back."

"I was making sure you were still alive," she replied. "It would ruin my night if you died before Moonrise."

She winced inwardly. She must have sounded foolish. She could have been kinder. He looked like someone who hadn't known kindness in a long time.

If her words stung him, he gave no sign. He reclined on one elbow, body slack with exhaustion. There was something in the unguarded way he rested, a quiet surrender that made her heart falter. A faint smile curved his lips.

"Didn't know the princess of Selvaran could show such concern for her hostage. I'm truly blessed."

Luna's patience thinned. "Don't flatter yourself. I only care about avoiding another war."

She rose to leave, but his hand caught her wrist. His fingers were cold, yet they burned against her skin, a fleeting warmth that unsettled her. His grip was light, unexpectedly soft for someone who had spent a lifetime on the battlefield.

"Thank you," he said.

Luna froze. The words sank deeper than they should have.

Her eyes dropped to his. The lantern light softened his features, lending him an almost tranquil glow.

"Why did you surrender?" she asked quietly. "Why not take me hostage instead?"

Solis's gaze drifted toward the tent's ceiling. Heavy silence settled between them like a gathering storm.

"Because there was once a boy who only wanted to see the stars."

The words struck her. A memory flickered. A young boy beneath a silver sky, whispering to the wind. Once a dreamer, and now that same dreamer lay before her, bleeding and broken, his light fading beneath the weight of war.

"I hope the stars were worth your freedom."

He gave a faint laugh, steeped more in ache than humor. "I lost that a long time ago."

"Why then?"

His voice softened. "Because no one deserves to lose the people they love for a war no one even remembers the reason for. Not for a king's greed, nor for the glory of it all. People deserve to be happy."

Her throat tightened. "That's brave of you. You could have died."

"Bravery is a special kind of stupid. Guess I'm not that smart."

"Perhaps that's what separates the strong from the weak—being brave even when it hurts."

"Perhaps."

Their gazes locked. The air between them felt fragile, warm, alive. Luna's heartbeat faltered. She did not know why she could not look away, why her enemy suddenly felt like someone she needed—wanted—to understand.

Outside, the frost of the night chilled the air, yet a strange warmth settled in her chest.

TWENTY-TWO

LUNA

The night stretched long and heavy. Moonfall had settled over the camp, casting everything into a hush that felt almost sacred despite the war. Soldiers slept in loose ranks beneath a vault of cold stars. Only royals and commanders rested beneath canvas, with one exception made for the captured prince.

Luna lay awake, sleep refusing her. Lantern light swayed against the tent's fabric, its gold trembling through the seams. The wind murmured outside, brushing the walls like a steady breath. Thought after thought gathered until her temples ached.

Would this fragile peace hold, or only stir something worse? King Leo would not take kindly to the capture of his heir. Would pride drive him to madness, or would reason guide him toward peace? She prayed for the latter.

The scars on Solis's back lingered behind her eyes. They were not marks of valor but of cruelty, carved deep by a hand that should have protected him. Instinct told her Solis was not the prince the world believed him to be. The radiant hero of Solara was nothing more than a vessel cracked by suffering, shaped by pain into endurance. How could any father do such a thing? What kind of heart carved ruin into its own blood?

Pity sat uneasily in her chest. He was tragic in a way that unsettled her, too human beneath all the arrogance. Her parents would never have done such things. She could not fathom what it meant to be betrayed by those meant to be one's shield, to be born into light only to be broken by it.

She turned onto her side, restless beneath the linen. Sleep mocked her. The journey ahead would be long, and Moonrise would not wait. If it were her choice, Khael could have ported them to the citadel in a single breath, but there were too many soldiers. Too much duty tethered her here.

Still, forcing Solis to travel that distance felt cruel. He could barely sit upright. She sighed. Why was she worrying over a prince who had once turned her world to ash? Why did he linger in her thoughts?

By the time the first trace of moonlight touched the horizon, her eyes burned with exhaustion. The cold bit softly at her skin as she stepped into the open air. Mist drifted over the camp, silvered by the faint gleam of Moonrise, a quiet herald of morning.

And still, he was the first thought to surface. Her feet moved before reason caught up.

Two guards stood outside his tent, faces drawn with fatigue. They said nothing as she approached. Leave it to Khael to post sentries around a man who could barely stand. She dismissed them with a nod, lifted the flap, and slipped inside.

The lantern had gone out. Moonlight crept through the seams of the canvas, tracing faint silver across the walls. His face was half-hidden by a bent arm, his chest rising and falling in steady rhythm. The tension that had sharpened his features earlier was gone, leaving something almost gentle.

She stepped closer. Even pale from blood loss, he was beautiful in a way no man should be. Strands of gold hair brushed his cheek, and his lashes, long and fair, rested against skin too unmarked for a soldier. His lips softened the cut of his jaw. The innocence of it felt like mockery from Solara's god of war.

"I didn't take the princess for someone who enjoys watching her hostage sleep."

Luna froze. Heat rushed to her cheeks.
When had he woken?

"You're awake," her voice fought for composure, the tremor betraying her.

Solis shifted, eyes half-open, blue softened by moonlight. Even half-asleep, he was unfairly handsome. A few loose strands of hair fell across his brow, and his lashes cast faint shadows over his cheeks.

She caught herself staring and turned away, biting her lip. Gods, she was admiring the enemy's son. Again.

"Hard to sleep," he murmured, "when I can feel your stare burning holes through my skin. Thought I was under attack."

"I wasn't staring. I was checking if you were still alive. Which you are. So… good. Goodbye."

The words tumbled out too quickly, and she winced at how ridiculous she must have sounded. She quickly turned to leave, trying to hide the fluster burning through her. But his words halted her.

"So you make a habit of watching your captives sleep? I'd start to think you like me."

Unbelievable.

She spun toward him. "Like you? Please. I was making sure you didn't stop breathing."

Her denial rang sharp, but her pulse betrayed her. She wanted to sink inward.

He smiled, slow and knowing. "So, you were worried."

"I was being thorough." She hated how defensive she was getting.

"Thorough." His smile deepened. "You must be very dedicated to your duties."

"You talk too much for a dying man." Irritation thinned her voice.

"Maybe that's why I'm still alive."

Her breath caught, though she didn't know why. "You're impossible."

He gave a languid smile, eyes closed. "And yet, you're still here."

Everything about this man was infuriating, yet her heart struck hard against her ribs as if it had forgotten whose side it was on.

She looked away before he could see her blush. "Only because you're my responsibility."

"How lucky am I," his voice sliding smooth with mockery, "to have the heir of Selvaran care for me so deeply? You must be incredibly short-staffed."

"I… someone had to keep you alive."

His eyes glinted. "How generous. Is there any other service the princess can offer, since she's so determined to keep me breathing? Perhaps she might keep my bed warm too?"

Her mouth opened, then shut again. The audacity of him. The thought of sharing a bed with him sent heat crawling up her neck.

She turned sharply, refusing to dignify him with an answer. Her steps quickened as she pushed through the flap into the night. The air struck colder than before, biting her flushed skin. She exhaled slowly, her breath unsteady.

Why did his words unravel her so easily?

The camp had begun to stir around her. Soldiers moved between the fading fires, packing gear and preparing for the march ahead.

Her hand rose to her face, brushing against the heat still clinging to her skin. Beneath her palm, her pulse betrayed her, thudding far too fast. That arrogance of a man had a way of getting under her skin.

"Something amusing, Princess?"

Her head snapped toward the voice. Khael stood a few paces away, arms folded across his chest. His expression was unreadable, though curiosity edged his tone.

"Nothing," she said quickly, straightening her posture and lifting her chin as if she had not been flustered moments ago. "Just enjoying the Moonrise air."

Khael's brows lifted. "In front of the prisoner's tent?"

She froze. Right. She was still standing there. She could almost hear Solis's laughter from inside. Stupid, arrogant prince.

Luna exhaled, forcing calm back into her voice. "Only checking if the prisoner is still breathing," the word projecting loud enough for Solis to hear. "Wouldn't want to return his corpse to his father too soon."

Khael's gaze lingered, sharp and searching. "Wouldn't want that, would we?" His tone carried quiet mockery.

A shadow of intent flickered through his eyes, and Luna's stomach tightened. Khael had lost too many friends in this war. Killing the son of the man who started it would feel like justice to him. But she could not allow that. Solis's death would unravel everything.

"I don't see the point of this conversation," she said, keeping her tone level.

"Unfortunately, I disagree," Khael replied. "But that is a matter for another time. We'll be departing soon. I trust you'll be ready."

"I'll be ready," she answered.

He gave a curt nod and turned away. Luna watched him go, her breath misting in the cold air. Then she turned toward her tent, refusing to look back.

Solis was a distraction she could not afford. He was not here for her amusement. He was here to end a war, and that was how it had to remain.

By the time the pale glow of the moon climbed high over the mist, the army was already in motion. Every trace of their camp had vanished, swallowed by the frost of dawn. Luna had ordered it so; Solaran scouts could not be allowed to follow their trail. She would not risk the enemy coming for their prince. Commander Korven knew nothing of Solis's surrender. If he pursued them, it would shatter the fragile peace holding both realms together.

Luna stood at the head of the column. Her black cloak swept the frozen earth, a dark river beneath the moonlight. Her breath drifted before her, a pale ghost dissolving into the cold. The steel of her armor caught the light, its edges traced in liquid silver as the soldiers brought Solis forward. The rope that had once bound his wrists had been replaced with chains. Khael had insisted. Rope could not hold a man who carried fire in his veins. Luna had not told him it was needless. Solis had surrendered willingly. His brilliant and reckless vision of peace was the very reason he now knelt before them.

The soldiers shoved him down. Her shoulder flinched as his chest struck the ground, the dull crack of impact echoing through the stillness. He drew a shallow breath, pain flickering across his face. She prayed the wound at his abdomen had not reopened.

Beneath the moonlight, he looked almost unreal. His bronzed skin gleamed against the pallor of her soldiers, and his hair shone like molten gold. Even among shadows, he was light incarnate, a living flame caged by frost. She should have ordered a hood to conceal him. One glance and anyone would know he did not belong to this realm. He was a walking target for those who still hungered for vengeance.

When he lifted his head and met her eyes, a faint smile curved his mouth, all teeth. Arrogant, even now. It stole her breath all the same. She looked away, pulse hammering in her chest. Fool.

A sharp crack split the air.

Khael's knee struck Solis's jaw, hard enough to send him sprawling. The sound fractured the night.

"Do not look at her." Khael's voice was cold, sharp as cut glass. "Keep your eyes down when you stand before the Princess of the Night. You are Solaran filth."

He raised his leg again, but Luna's voice cut through the chill. "Enough, Commander. My father will want the prisoner alive." Her tone was firm, though strain edged her words. "We have lingered long enough. Prepare to move out."

Khael straightened, a muscle ticking in his jaw. "As you command." He mounted his horse, the leather creaking beneath his weight. "The path ahead is clear. It should be safe to ride to the capital."

Luna swung herself onto Moonshade, the reins cold beneath her gloved hands. "Keep the line tight," she ordered, voice composed. "No one falls behind."

The signal rose. Hooves struck the valley in rhythm, the sound rolling like distant thunder. Selvaran banners unfurled like black wings beneath the argent sky.

She rode beside Khael in silence, her composure a fragile mask that revealed nothing of the thoughts circling back to the man behind her. She could feel him even without turning. Solis. His presence pressed faintly against her awareness, steady as the pulse of fire beneath ice.

When she finally turned her head, she found him watching the world instead of her. The cliffs fell away beside them, revealing a river winding through the dark below. It glowed beneath the moonlight, soft and alive, as though breathing magic into the air. The water shimmered with silver-blue light, stars scattered across its surface. Trees leaned over the banks, their leaves glinting with quiet enchantment, while fireflies drifted above the current like fragments of light.

Without meaning to, Luna slowed her horse. Solis's gaze followed the river, his eyes filled with something she had not expected. Wonder.

"First time seeing our river?" she asked.

He did not look away. "It is beautiful," he said quietly. "Is everything in Selvaran like this?"

A firefly floated near his cheek. Before she could stop herself, Luna reached out and brushed it away. His hands were still chained behind him. She could have ordered them freed. For a moment, she wanted to.

"Yes," she said softly. "I was surprised to hear your realm had lost its magic."

Solis's lips tightened. "We lost it long before I was born. I wish it had remained. Our lands might still look like this."

His voice carried a weight that did not belong to a prince. His eyes followed the fireflies, and Luna found herself watching him. His face was unguarded, softened beneath the moonlight.

It struck her how easily the smallest things seemed to move him—the way he watched light, the way he listened. She should have looked away. Instead, she let herself smile.

"You are staring again, Princess."

Luna's heart stumbled. His words pulled her sharply from her thoughts.

"I was not staring," she said quickly.

Solis turned his head, that faint, knowing smile returning. "You were."

"Hardly. I was ensuring you could still sit upright without falling from your horse."

He gave a low hum, quiet and amused. "How thoughtful of you. My captor, ever so concerned for my balance. Using her eyes to protect me from my fall."

Her face flushed. "You are mistaking concern for duty. Did you forget I need you alive for this to work?"

"Then keep me alive, Princess." His voice softened, still laced with that impossible calm. She noticed the faint bruise forming along his jaw where Khael's knee had struck.

Luna looked away, heat rising again to her cheeks. The audacity of him. The way he spoke, so calm, so careless. She tightened her grip on the reins and urged Moonshade forward. The cold air stung her face, but nothing cooled the warmth beneath her skin.

Behind her, Solis's quiet laugh slipped through the night.

"Something amusing, Prince?"

Khael's voice cut through the air. He had turned in his saddle, his gaze narrowing on Solis, and Luna felt her stomach twist.

"You." Khael gestured toward one of the guards. "Silence him."

"No." The protest left her too late. The soldiers dragged Solis from his mount and threw him to the ground. The first blow landed hard. Then another.

He did not fight back. His hands were bound, yet she knew the fire still lived in him. He could have burned them all. But he did not. He bore their cruelty in silence, as though punishment itself were familiar.

Her gut tightened.

"Stop! I did not give that order."

The command fell into emptiness. The soldiers ignored her. Her gaze snapped to Khael. Had he finally decided her words no longer mattered, as he had defied her father's so many times before?

"Khael," her voice shook, "order them to stop."

Her throat ached. Please, Khael. Do not become the monster we claim the Solarans to be. Be better.

He met her eyes, unreadable. She knew then the plea was wasted. She turned her mare toward Solis, but Khael's hand seized her reins, halting her.

"Ride on, Princess." His tone carried no warmth. "It is not your place to protect him."

But it was. She had promised to keep him alive. The words pressed at her lips, but the warning in Khael's gaze silenced her. If she interfered now, Solis would only pay worse for it later, and she could not shield him forever.

Each strike landed like a stone in her chest.

The dull thud of fists and boots filled the quiet between the trees. Solis did not cry out. When they finally pulled him upright, blood traced his jaw, running over the bruises darkening his skin. He lifted his chin, unbroken. His blue eyes found Khael's, and a faint smile touched his mouth, widening the split on his lip.

"Thanks for the wake-up call, Commander. Nothing like a little beating with a view."

Luna's chest constricted. The fool had the nerve to mock him even now, bleeding and broken. The fabric at his abdomen was soaked through, crimson blooming over brown. His wound had reopened, yet still he refused to yield. The only sign that he was in pain was the stiffness of his shoulder, the press of his lips, and the color draining from his sun-kissed skin beneath the moonlight.

Khael said nothing, but the look he gave promised this was not finished.

They forced Solis back onto his mount. His jaw clenched as he shifted. He could deny it all he wanted, but his expression showed otherwise.

The column began to move. Luna pressed forward, her fingers tight around the reins, but she could not stop herself from glancing back.

Solis rode behind her, head bowed, eyes closed. Moonlight traced the bruises along his face, softening what violence had carved there. The sight of him, silent, bloodied, and unbroken, stirred something deep within her that she could not name.

She looked ahead again. The memory of Khael's cruelty followed her through the trees, echoing long after the sound of the blows had faded.

They stopped again when the moon sank to its lowest point, its silver light thinning across the forest like the last breath of night. The river widened beside them, whispering softly against the stones.

Khael was the first to dismount, signaling the guards to make camp. Luna followed, her boots sinking into the damp earth as she watched the soldiers move with practiced quiet, building fires where the mist hung low. The air smelled of pine and cold water.

She froze when they dragged Solis from his horse with deliberate cruelty. Her jaw tightened. She should have turned away, gone to her tent, but the sight held her. He was not his father. He had not chosen this war any more than she had. Yet they treated him as though he wore the Solaran crown himself. The bruises on his face and the blood dried along his lip made her chest twist tighter.

When Khael left to inspect the perimeter, Luna moved.

Solis sat near the edge of the camp, apart from the others, his back against a tree. Two guards stood watch, his hands still bound behind him. She wondered when they would finally release him. He would need his hands to eat. Had they even given him food? It was a small cruelty, but small cruelties were the kind Khael preferred.

"Princess," one of the guards began, but Luna silenced him with a glance.

"Leave us," she said.

The man hesitated, then bowed. The other followed.

She knelt beside Solis. His head lifted faintly. The bruises along his jaw had deepened, and a thin cut traced his lower lip.

Luna sighed and drew a small vial from her pouch. The balm shimmered in the moonlight, the scent of mint and starroot curling between them as she uncorked it.

"I told you not to provoke him," she said.

Solis's voice came quiet, dry with humor. "Last I checked, laughing wasn't provocation. Your commander seems to disagree."

"It isn't personal," she murmured. "Khael lost his wife and son in the war. His hatred for Solara runs deep. You, being its prince, are the face of it."

Solis's expression softened. "That explains the temper."

"Hold still."

Her fingers brushed his chin as she dabbed the balm along his split lip. His skin was warm beneath her touch. She felt the small flinch beneath her fingertips, and when she looked up, his gaze met hers. For a moment neither of them moved. The world seemed to still around them, quiet and perilously fragile.

She wasn't sure she was breathing, and neither was he. Then Solis blinked, the spell breaking.

"You should not be here," he whispered.

"Neither should you," she replied softly. "Yet you are, because you gave yourself up for your people, and for mine."

Silence lingered between them, heavy but unspoken. The river murmured beside them, its rhythm low and steady, threading through the night like prayer.

Moonlight curved across his face. Even bruised, he was beautiful in a way that felt unreal, like a sun god forced to walk among mortals. His lashes cast faint shadows, his nose caught in the silver light.

Her fingers twitched. For a breath, she wanted to trace the bridge of that nose, to feel if it was as smooth as it looked. The thought startled her. This was not what she should feel for him. He was not someone to be desired. He was her enemy, a hostage meant only to secure peace.

She drew her hand back, her pulse quickening as she fought the warmth threatening to surface.

"I should go," she whispered.

Then he looked at her.

That look—the one that stilled her breath. His eyes held her, tranquil as sunset over distant water, where the light drifted like ink through a silken current and the melody of the tide sang in place of words.

"You should." His voice was low.

"Good night." She rose, ignoring the heat that touched her cheeks. Yet part of her lingered, caught in those ocean eyes that seemed to hold both sky and sorrow, like water breathing a song that refused to fade. "Rest. I will see that Khael does not come near you tonight."

"Protecting me again, Princess." His smile tugged faintly at the corner of his mouth. "I am beginning to think you wish to be my savior."

Luna said nothing as she turned away. She was not his savior. A savior would not have stood and watched them beat him.

TWENTY-THREE

LUNA

Night had already fallen when the castle of Selvaran rose into view. It loomed high upon the mountain, carved from the rock as if born of it. Obsidian towers veined with argent gleamed beneath the moon's faint reverie. Between those towers, a broad stairway climbed toward the gates. Banners of black and silver draped the walls, each bearing the crescent sigil of her bloodline, glinting at their centers like captured starlight.

The army gathered at the foot of the stair. Khael, Luna, Five guards, and the chained prince stood before the citadel. A gelid mist coiled around Luna's boots, brushing her cheeks in a quiet greeting as she began to climb.

The air felt thinner with each step. A tightness gathered beneath her rib. Her father was a man of unyielding justice. Would he grant mercy to the son of the realm that had razed their own? Would he see Solis as anything beyond the monster his father had forged? She hoped the prince grasped the gravity of his surrender, for this moment could end the war or… end him.

Behind her, Solis followed in silence, his wounds darker beneath the pallid moonlight. The chains at his wrists sang through the air, their metallic clatter an echo of penance. Luna longed for them to be removed, but Khael refused. He called it prudence, insisting Solis's true power remained unknown. Perhaps it was a trap, a ruse to breach Selvaran's heart and annihilate her bloodline. The thought settled in her chest like slow poison.

She forced the darkness down and clung to hope instead.

If he betrayed her, she would be the one to strike the final blow—if she could. His power was formidable, his flame unbounded. Yet should she succeed, Solara would call for vengeance the moment his blood touched Selvaran stone. The idea of life leaving those blue eyes sickened her. She prayed for an alternative, a path that did not end in his death.

In the hope of softening his resentment, she had kept to his good side. As promised, the final day's journey had been as merciful as she could make it, though Khael had done his best to make it otherwise. She kept her distance to avoid provoking his ire, shielding Solis from further harm where she could. Even so, their passage through the village of Vega had been fraught.

The villagers had stared, their gazes sharpened by grief and derision. Some had turned violent, forcing Luna to order Solis's face veiled beneath a hood. Yet hatred still hung heavy in the air, thick as smoke. To them, he was not a man but the living shadow of their sorrow, the monster of Solara.

Now, as she climbed, she glanced back. The hood concealed most of his face, yet she caught the faint bruise along his jaw, the fading green and yellow beneath his cheekbone. The guards trailed behind him, shoving when his steps faltered. Khael had called it precaution. Luna knew better. It was punishment, a quiet cruelty meant to humiliate the prince.

"Princess, look ahead," Khael said, his tone flat. "It would not reflect well for the heir of Selvaran to look upon a prisoner with soft eyes."

Heat touched her face. She was not gazing with soft eyes. She was calculating what awaited beyond those gates.

At the top of the stairway, her mother awaited them.

Queen Astrid's hair flowed like ink over her shoulders. A crown of silver, set with small gems shaped like stars, rested upon her head. Her midnight gown shimmered with faint galaxies, as though the night sky itself had wrapped around her.

"My moon." Her mother spread her arms, waiting for the embrace she had been denied for too long. An ache bloomed in Luna's chest as she stepped forward. The warmth closed around her, stealing her breath.

"Mother," Luna choked, falling deeper into her arms. The comfort of it nearly undid her. "I'm home."

"My little moon is home," her mother whispered into her hair.

A single cough broke the quiet.

Khael stood behind them, his throat clearing as if to cut the moment clean. Luna stepped back, brushing the tears from her lashes.

"My queen." He dipped his head as he spoke. "You will have received my letter by now. I recommend we discuss the matter at once."

Queen Astrid's gaze shifted past him to the hooded figure surrounded by guards. "Is that the prince you captured? My, how he's grown since last we met. Look at him. Poor thing. Bring him inside. The king is waiting."

She turned and glided toward the great doors. Luna followed, the guards shoving Solis forward. The rattle of his chains struck the marble floor, their echoes trailing through the corridor toward the throne room.

Two thrones of midnight marble stood at the end of the hall, etched with constellations that shimmered faintly in the torchlight. Between them, carved into the floor, was the sacred crescent of Selvaran, its silver lines gleaming against the black stone.

King Orion sat upon one of the twin thrones, his presence composed yet imperious. His robes of deep silver and black caught the flickering light, the fabric glinting like dragon's scales.

Queen Astrid took Luna's hand and guided her to the vacant throne beside him. "Sit, my moon." She brushed a loose strand from Luna's face before stepping back to stand at her side, her gaze steady ahead.

Luna's fingers tightened around the armrest as Khael advanced. The guards forced Solis to his knees before the crescent carved into the floor and tore back his hood, revealing disheveled golden hair and bruises darkening his features. The wounds had worsened; the discoloration had deepened, spreading along his cheek and jaw, shadowing the sharp lines of his face. Still, he lifted his head, proud and defiant despite the pain.

That defiance shattered when Khael's hand came down upon the back of his neck, forcing him to the ground.

King Orion rose from his throne. "Khael. That will suffice."

Yet Khael did not relent. "With respect, my king." His palm pressed harder against Solis's spine. "He is Solaran—the sun of Solara—the very kind who burned our villages. If we treat every enemy as a guest, especially one who showed us no mercy, they will call us fools."

"Release the boy." Orion's tone cut through the hall, controlled but glacial. "We will hear what he has to say before judgment is passed. I will not have cruelty paraded in my court."

Reluctantly, Khael withdrew his hand and stepped back, the tension in his stance betraying his irritation at being forced to spare Solis.

Solis lifted his head. His blue eyes met the king's, clear, defiant, unyielding. No words left him.

King Orion regarded him in silence before speaking. "I apologize for the treatment you have received." He paused, the hall seeming to narrow around the words. "I do not wish you harm. You must understand my duty. My people have suffered at your father's hands."

Luna studied Solis's face. His expression remained blank, unreadable, no trace of emotion.

His reply came hoarse, his voice scraped raw. "May I speak freely, Your Majesty?"

Khael's gaze sharpened, cold with the hatred buried beneath it. The sight made the hairs on Luna's arms rise. Her father inclined his head, granting permission. "You may."

Solis swallowed, a rasp catching in his throat. His voice carried the weight of exhaustion. "I am aware of the damage I have caused. If punishment is due, I will accept it. But as for my father—" he drew a slow breath "—he is not a man who yields. If we wait for him to choose peace, he never will. This war will not end until one realm falls. I propose we offer him a deal, a bargain to end the slaughter."

King Orion's gaze did not waver. "And what deal do you propose?"

Solis drew a steady breath, gathering what little strength remained in him. "Long ago, Selvaran and Solara stood divided by war, as we do now. To end the bloodshed, our ancestors built a keep between the realms, a sanctum where rulers could meet beneath the same sky without violence. It was called the Celestial Keep. The stronghold holds magic of its own. It senses hostility and shields those within its walls. No weapon, no spell, no act of malice can touch anyone inside. It was forged to preserve peace when words alone would fail."

He lifted his head. His voice, though faint, carried unbroken conviction. Luna could see the toll in every breath. Khael had shown him no mercy on the road. Though the beating had ceased, they had marched him beside the soldiers in chains. His wounds, crudely stitched, had reopened twice. Luna doubted they had fed him properly during the journey. Watching him kneel before her father, she saw how exhaustion hollowed him. He needed rest. He needed food.

"I suggest we restore that tradition," Solis continued despite it all, stubborn to the very end. "Let Selvaran and Solara meet once more within the Keep, as the ancients did, and declare a truce—a Celestial Summit to remind both kingdoms what unity once felt like, when we lived beside one another without shedding blood."

He paused. "Use me to make it happen. Demand that my father meet you there, or he will lose his son."

Silence swept through the hall. Luna was not sure she was breathing. He had asked them to use him, a pawn against his own father, a bargaining chip that could become his death sentence. Fool. Reckless, self-sacrificing fool. What was he thinking?

She did not know why she cared so fiercely for the idiot, but to hear him offer himself as though he were something to be exchanged, like a piece of an object, was heartbreaking. Did he have no will left to live? Or did he truly trust his father so deeply that he believed he would not betray him? Luna prayed it was the latter.

Orion's gaze sharpened, disbelief flickering across his face. "You would offer yourself as a weapon against your own father?"

"If it ends this war," Solis said, his tone firm, "then yes."

Luna's breath caught. Her pulse beat like thunder in her ears. He could not mean it. If King Leo refused, the choice would end in execution. It was not a wager to stake a life upon. From the scars along Solis's back to the quiet resignation in his eyes, she doubted his father would care whether he lived or died. Greed twists a man. It blinds him. It drives him to destroy what he once loved in pursuit of power. Luna prayed she was wrong.

"Are you truly willing to die for this?" her father asked.

"Yes. I am willing to give my life for my people," Solis said. "Use me to end the war. If I cannot, then I do not deserve to be called their prince, nor do I deserve to live."

For a long moment, silence held the hall. Luna could hear her heartbeat against her ribs. Then King Orion's eyes softened, the faintest smile touching his lips. She almost doubted she had seen it. Her father's warmth was usually reserved for his own people, never their enemies. Until Solis.

He rose from his throne and crossed the marble floor to where Solis knelt. The chains around Solis's wrists caught the silver torchlight. When Orion stopped before him, the air seemed to still.

The king lowered himself slightly and placed both hands on Solis's shoulders. Solis flinched, jerking back from the touch. The sudden recoil caught Orion off guard, but he said nothing. For a heartbeat, neither moved. Then Solis's expression shifted. Whatever fear had flickered there sealed itself away, replaced by an unreadable mask as if he was accustomed to locking every emotion behind it. A practiced composure born of someone who had survived and endured in silence.

A searing ache flared in her chest. How many times had he been forced to retreat behind that mask of his? What remained of the boy she had once known?

King Orion's voice carried through the chamber, composed. "Solara should be proud," he said. "It is no small thing for a prince to offer his life for peace. That kind of courage does not come easily."

He turned to Khael. "Remove his chains. The prince is our guest now, and he will be treated as one."

Khael's jaw tightened. Irritation flickered in his eyes, but he obeyed without a word, signaling the guards to comply.

The sound of metal striking marble echoed through the hall as the shackles fell away. Solis exhaled softly, as though taking his first true breath in days. He rubbed his wrists, the skin raw and red. "Your kindness honors me, King Orion."

Orion's smile deepened, faint yet sincere. "Kindness costs little, and it builds more than war ever could. You have come a long way, and I imagine this journey has not been easy. Rest will serve you better than formality tonight." He paused. "Come. I will walk you to your chamber myself."

Solis blinked, surprised. "You would walk me there yourself?"

Orion's eyes glimmered with quiet humor. "I have long been curious about the prince who was once meant to be my son-in-law. I think it would be good for us to talk. We have both lost too much to this war; perhaps understanding will serve us better than bitterness."

Luna froze, warmth rising to her cheeks. She had almost forgotten the betrothal that once bound them, a political promise lost to war. When she looked up, she saw the same faint flush on Solis's face. Her father, as always, had a gift for turning solemn moments into something mortifying. She groaned softly and covered her face with her hands.

Her mother's laughter filled the hall, soft and mellifluous. "There is no shame in affection, my daughter. To be fond of someone is as natural as the moon that watches over us."

The words lingered like a spark within Luna's chest. She scarcely knew Solis, scarcely trusted him, yet something in the way he carried himself awakened a quiet ache she could not comprehend.

She said nothing.

She watched as her father guided Solis toward the great doors, ignoring Khael's muted protest. King Orion ruled through compassion rather than fear, and his gentleness bore more authority than any blade. Perhaps that was why Khael defied him so often. Compassion could be both a strength and a frailty.

Her mother reached for her hand. "You must be weary too, little moon. Go wash and rest. We will see you at breakfast."

Luna inclined her head, though her thoughts were far from rest. As she turned to leave, her gaze lingered upon the doors where her father and the Solaran prince had vanished.

She sent a silent prayer to the moon that her father might restrain himself from further humiliation, though she knew better. That was his greatest talent. With a muted groan, she started toward her chambers. Tomorrow, she might have to walk the palace halls with her face concealed behind a veil.

TWENTY-FOUR

SOLIS

The doors closed behind them as Solis followed King Orion down the marble corridors of Selvaran. Though he had traveled through the realm for days, his body still had not acclimated to the cold. The air was biting and thin, sharp in a way that felt unnatural to him.

Lanterns lined the walls, burning with argent flame. Their light rippled over the stone like moonlight caught in glass. He found himself staring at them. In Solara, light was endless, golden and alive, spilling from the sky and drenching the world with warmth. Even when the rain came, it fell hot and heavy, turning the air thick as steam. He had never known a place that could feel so devoid of heat.

He drew in a breath. The air filled his lungs like cold water, clean and piercing. Each exhale drifted before him in a pale mist. The first time he had seen that, he thought his soul was escaping his body. He had been a naïve boy then. Now he knew better, yet the cold still felt wrong to him, a sun meant to burn in a land of frost, a spark trapped in a world of ice.

Even now, he could not stop shivering. He clenched his fists, holding to every ounce of control he had left to keep from revealing how cold he was. His gaze fixed on the back of King Orion, a few paces ahead.

His muscles still ached from days of travel under Khael's command. The man had done everything to torment him, short of killing him outright. Compared to Commander Korven, Khael was cruelty made flesh. Korven had at least fed his prisoners. Solis had never witnessed him mistreat anyone the way Khael did. What became of the captives afterward was beyond their control, but under Korven's watch, they had been safe and fed. Khael granted neither.

The throbbing in Solis's wrists reminded him where the irons had bitten deep. The skin was raw and bruised. He flexed his fingers quietly, more to feel something through the gelid numbness than to ease the pain.

"You've grown since the last time we met," King Orion said at last, breaking the silence between them. His voice, surprisingly gentle, carried easily through the corridor. "You were barely taller than my daughter then."

Solis allowed himself a faint smile. "Time has a talent for that."

Orion chuckled. "It does, though not everyone grows into themselves so well. I see my daughter's fondness for you has not dimmed."

Heat crept up his neck, biting against the chill around him. He had not been aware of Luna's fondness. If anything, it had seemed the opposite.

"I owe your daughter more than I can say," he said quietly. "She is the reason I am still breathing. If your commander had his way, I would have been sent back to my father without a head."

"Ah." Orion's tone softened. "Khael's loyalty burns hotter than his mercy. I apologize for his behavior. He has lost too much to this war, and grief makes men cruel. Still, you have my word that no further harm will come to you while you remain under my roof."

He glanced over his shoulder, his expression kind. "You carry the will of a warrior, much like your father, but you wield a restraint he never learned. Few would offer themselves for peace. Some might call it foolish, but I believe it takes a man of great heart to lower himself for those he loves."

Solis kept his gaze forward. "It is not bravery when it is the only path left."

Orion nodded, his voice turning thoughtful. "Choice. Such a fragile word, isn't it? Rarely meant for kings. We make decisions for others, not for ourselves. And yet, why not change that? Why must duty be the only thing that defines us? True strength is born of the heart, not the sword."

"My father thinks otherwise," Solis murmured.

"Your father is blinded by greed," Orion said quietly. "Greed changes a man. You, however, are not him."

His pace slowed, eyes turning distant. "You remind me of someone I once knew, a man who believed peace was worth every sacrifice. Most learn that lesson only after half a lifetime. You seem to have learned it far sooner. Solara should be proud of its prince."

Solis lowered his gaze. He wished his father shared that pride.

They passed a window framed in black marble, stars stretching endlessly beyond the glass. The sight caught his breath. The sky felt nearer here, as if he could reach out and brush its surface.

"Do you think our realms can ever live free of war?" he asked. He almost added *like the stars above, alive and unbound,* yet stopped himself. Foolish hope.

"Perhaps one day," Orion admitted. "When two kingdoms can look upon one another without reaching for their blades, that will be the beginning of harmony."

Solis's chest tightened. "That would be something worth dying for."

Orion studied him. "That was why I agreed to your engagement with my daughter. I never believed anyone could deserve her, yet for peace, I was willing to try."

"It must have been an insult when my father withdrew," Solis said.

"It was," Orion conceded, calm though steel edged his tone. "He treated my daughter as if she were unworthy of his son. Yet my little moon is worth more than all the stars above."

Violet eyes flashed through Solis's mind, bright and unyielding. He doubted he was worthy of her at all.

"I can understand your father's fear," Orion said gently. "You mean a great deal to him as well."

Solis doubted that. If Orion had seen the scars carved into his back, he would not speak of love so freely. Instead he asked, "Do you think he will agree to the peace?"

"I believe he will. Your father loves his power more than his people, but I think he loves you more than both. I saw it once, when you were a boy. He may deny it, but the love was there. It might yet be enough."

A dull ache spread through Solis's chest. If that love existed, it had long extinguished.

They walked in silence until Orion halted before a tall door of black oak inlaid with silver. "This will be your chamber. Rest, Prince Solis. Whatever comes next will come soon enough. Have faith in the path you have chosen."

Solis inclined his head. "Thank you, Your Majesty."

Orion placed a hand on his shoulder, an unexpected gesture of warmth. "Sleep well, my son."

The words struck something deep within him. He lifted his eyes to meet the king's gaze. Nothing but gentleness resided there. His heart ached. Once, long ago, his own father had looked at him that way.

He watched Orion's figure recede down the corridor until the footsteps vanished into quiet. Stillness seeped through the hall. A heaviness settled in him, not from the pain that throbbed through his body, but a warm sensation, like the first trace of light bleeding in after too many years in the darkness.

He released a slow breath and turned toward the door. The carvings shimmered faintly, silver filigree catching the lantern glow. He pushed it open.

The chamber breathed of cedar and something faintly floral. The walls were dark stone veined with argent streaks that gleamed under the lantern light. Curtains of deep indigo framed a wide window that opened to the night.

Solis approached it. Frost crowned the mountains beyond, moonlight spilling across the floor in quiet reverie. Yet what held him were the stars, thousands strewn across the heavens like fragments of shattered glass.

He watched one fall, trailing a ribbon of silver fire. What had they called a star that fell again? The word drifted back to him: a shooting star. He had once read that those who witnessed one could make a wish. The thought almost made him smile. Wishes belonged to those with dreams. He had none left.

Still, it was remarkable how something could fall and yet gleam with such unyielding tenacity.

If his father chose war over peace, then perhaps it would not be such a terrible thing to die in a realm that could make even darkness beautiful.

He turned back to the room. The bed stood against the far wall, layered with furs and a comforter the color of storm clouds. They had given him a chamber fit for a prince, not a prisoner. Orion's kindness unsettled him more than cruelty would have. His own father would have cast him into a dungeon by now.

The thought stung. He wished King Leo were half the man Orion was.

His gaze lowered to his clothes. The Selvaran soldier's tunic was stiff with dirt and dried blood, abrasive against his skin and heavy with dust. Better to wash before the chill sank deeper into his bones.

He opened the smaller door beside the bed and found a bathing room within. A wide stone basin waited in the center, its surface shimmering faintly beneath the lantern glow.

He pulled the tunic over his head and let it fall. The scars surfaced with the movement, pale ridges twisting across his skin like rivers through earth. His throat tightened.

The sound of the whip returned first, followed by the scent of iron and smoke, and the voice that called this pain love. This was his father's love.

King Orion was wrong. His father did not love him. This was far from love.

Solis lowered his gaze, tracing one of the old marks with his fingers. Obedience. Devotion. Punishment. The scars had faded with time, yet the memory had not. Some nights they flared anew, as if freshly carved. In his father's kingdom, endurance was love. Love was proven through pain.

He stripped the rest of his clothing and stepped Into the tub. The water was cool, almost biting yet welcoming. He sank until the chill settled through him. The wind drifted through the window, carrying the scent of pine.

He leaned back and closed his eyes. When he finished, he dressed in the obsidian garments laid out for him. A memory from eight years ago surfaced, soft and unbidden. The corner of his lips tugged upward. They had given him Selvaran attire then too, when he had fallen into the river with Luna. He had always felt like his color, not the white and gold he had been born into. Letting the memory settle within him, he returned to the window. With a soft whistle, he called into the night.

A flicker of gold broke through the darkness. Halo, his celestial messenger, appeared. The bird's feathers glimmered in the moonlight as it descended, alighting on the sill with a soft trill. A small capsule gleamed at its leg.

Halo had been a gift from his father on his tenth birthday, a rare celestial breed said to outfly every creature alive. Even that memory carried an ache. His father could be benevolent when it served his image.

Solis removed the capsule and unrolled the parchment. The handwriting was Argus's.

Your father is furious. It took all of Father's restraint to stop him from marching on Selvaran. He wants you returned. He wants fire. Calista is beside herself, which means the rest of us are suffering. I told her if she wants to find you, she should swim across the sea. Predictably, she did not appreciate the suggestion. Solis's shoulder shook as he read the lines. Trust Argus to torment Calista. *The soldiers are restless, but we are holding the lines until your word. Father doesn't believe you were truly captured. He knows you too well, but he's waiting. He trusts you have a plan. Don't disappoint us. Be safe, little brother.*

A faint smile touched Solis's lips at the last line. He ignited the letter with a flicker of flame. The parchment burned bright before crumbling to ash.

At least Calista would stop haunting his days for a while. One small mercy.

So his father wanted him back. The revelation stung more than it should have. But there was no time to dwell on it. He needed to send his reply before the man's fury reached its inevitable inferno.

He sat at the desk, pulled a fresh sheet toward him, and began to write. His message was brief and precise. Agree to King Orion's terms. There will be no victory in ashes. Only graves.

When he finished, he sealed the letter and fastened it to Halo's leg. The bird gave a soft trill before taking flight, vanishing into the night like a spark swallowed by stars.

After Halo disappeared, Solis lingered at the window. The castle was still, almost unnaturally so compared to Solara. He thought of the reports: the vanished villagers, the scorched towns, the traces of Eclipse magic left in the soot.

Something bound Selvaran to those disappearances. He could feel it, though he did not yet comprehend it. And if Orion's kindness tonight had been genuine, then the king was not the culprit.

Perhaps Khael was. The man carried cruelty in his eyes, a darkness Solis could not ignore.

He turned from the window. He would find the truth. Whatever tethered these shadows to Selvaran, he would uncover it before it devoured them all.

Restlessness stirred within him. The need to understand this kingdom of moonlight and frost pressed against his ribs until it drove him from the room.

He stepped into the corridor. The palace was still, almost unguarded. He remembered his walk with King Orion earlier. By his count, there had been no more than five guards in total. It was habit now, the instinct of survival, to take measure of what surrounded him. Still—five guards between the throne room and here? King Orion must have been mad.

In Solara, soldiers stood at every corner. His father trusted no one, believing safety was born from suspicion.

Here, King Orion trusted his people. Trusted that the walls of his home were strong enough, or perhaps that kindness itself could serve as a shield. Foolish, perhaps. Or brave. Solis could not decide which.

He did not know where he was going, only that the corridor opened into what seemed like a garden. The air smelled of earth and rain.

The plants glowed beneath the moon, their petals lit from within in shades of silver and blue. Each leaf caught the wind and shimmered like wet glass. It was nothing like the gardens of Solara. There, the flowers were sun-fed and heavy with heat and perfume. Here, the green drank starlight. The night itself seemed to nourish them.

Then he saw her.

Luna.

Her hair hung loose, black as the night behind her, and her sword moved through the air with the grace of a dancer, precise, fluid, free. The blade sang softly as it cut through the dark, silver light rippling along its edge like water in motion.

Solis stopped where he stood.

The way she moved reminded him of an old illustration he had once found in Solara's library, an ancient dance where the sword became an extension of the soul. Watching her now, he thought the Selvaran moon itself must have taught her how to move.

Her eyes remained fixed on every strike. Beautiful. Fierce. Untouchable.

Captivating.

He forgot how to breathe. She was beyond anything he had ever seen.

Leaning against a pillar, he lost track of why he had come at all. All he could see was her beneath the starlight, the way her body twisted and turned, the quiet power in every motion, the way her hair flowed like silk through the air. He wanted to step forward, to take her hand, to lead her into a dance beneath the moon, to lose himself in those violet eyes. Her beauty silenced his reason, hollowed his thoughts, consumed him whole.

Luna turned her wrist, the blade dipping toward the earth. Her breath left her lips in a soft cloud.

"Look who's staring now."

Solis found himself smiling. A quiet laugh escaped him. "You caught me." He lifted his hands in surrender. "Forgive me. I thought if I interrupted, you might murder me on the spot."

Her violet eyes rolled. His heart skipped a beat. His little starlight.

No. Wrong. She isn't his. Not yet.

He pushed off the pillar and walked toward her. Her gaze followed every movement, and with each step he took, it grew harder to breathe. Breathe, he reminded himself. Just breathe.

He stopped in front of her. "Couldn't sleep, Princess?" His tone turned teasing.

"I couldn't sleep knowing the most infuriating prince in existence is under my roof."

"Oh, is that so?" Solis grinned wider. "Would you like me elsewhere?"

"Yes," she said flatly. "Probably buried somewhere in this garden." She glanced around, gesture crisp as her tone, then pointed at two trees. "Would you prefer under the one on the right or the one on the left?"

Solis followed her gesture. "Definitely that creepy one. It fits the tragedy of my demise. Just leave a stone for me—killed for the crime of being unbearably handsome."

Her face flushed crimson. "I never said that!"

"You didn't?" His tone dripped with mischief. "I must have misheard it somewhere between the murdering and the burying."

Luna huffed, turning away, though not before he caught the faint pull at the corner of her mouth. "You're impossible."

"I prefer charming."

"Annoying suits you better."

He stepped closer, the distance shrinking until he caught the scent of lavender on her skin. Calming. Gentle. He liked it. She didn't move, her head tilting, meeting his stare as if daring him to try her patience. She held her ground even when they stood close enough for him to feel the warmth of her breath.

He lowered his head until their faces nearly met. Maybe it was his imagination, but did she forget to breathe? Her violet eyes widened, luminous under the moonlight. The eyes that seemed to see right through him. Yes, that's her. Starlight. His starlight.

"You don't really mean that," he murmured.

And there it was again—the faint flush blooming across her cheeks. Was it because of him? Did any other man make her blush like that?

Why was he even letting his mind drift there? It wasn't as if he felt anything for her.

Did he?

The necklace around his neck said otherwise.

He had hidden it when she entered his tent, not wanting her to see how much he still remembered.

The little defiant thing lifted her chin and met his gaze head-on, her nose almost brushing his. Her lips were so close he could almost lean in and...

"And if I do?" She tested him.

He smiled at their nearness, fighting the urge to do what he shouldn't. "Then I'd say lying doesn't suit you."

Her mouth opened, closed, then opened again before she caught herself. His eyes fell to her lips—soft, heart-shaped, too close for reason. A shiver ran through him, a want he had never known.

Calista had ruined desire for him, left him hollow at the thought of touch, sickened by what it meant when she took what she wanted. She had taught him that desire could wound, could take, could destroy.

Yet looking at Luna now, something within him stirred awake, like light brushing against a closed door. A forbidden door. She was meant to be his enemy. He couldn't have her. She could be his ruin. His father would never allow it. He would be punished—beaten until he bled dry. But none of it seemed to matter now.

He didn't care that she could ruin him. In truth, he wanted her to. He wanted to break. To shatter in her hands. Let her be his destruction.

Her kind of ruin would not leave him hollow. It would make him feel alive. It would make him feel human.

For the first time in years, the thought of closeness did not make him recoil. It made him ache. It made him want.

He had promised himself he would never want again, not after Calista. Yet something in the way those violet eyes held his made every reason, every rule, every duty fade into nothing. His heart screamed for her. He wanted to forget everything—his title, his throne, his cursed engagement—just to fall into those lips.

Then her gaze softened, and he felt himself slipping deeper, his will to resist unraveling with it.

He leaned into her, letting their lips brush, feeling the heat surge between them. Her body went still. Her eyes froze. Then the words that came from her mouth shattered whatever impulse had drawn him in.

"What about your fiancée, Solis?" Her head tilted, breaking their connection. "I didn't realize the prince of Solara could be such a player."

The words cut deep. His spine straightened as if her voice had driven a blade between his ribs. "My fiancée is none of your concern," he said, forcing his tone flat even as his pulse raced. He forced a smile, lying through his teeth. "I only wanted to see your reaction."

Luna's eyes shot daggers at him. It hurt worse than the memory of Calista. "Well, you got your reaction." She stepped back, creating distance. "It does concern her when you're about to—"

"When I am about to what?" He pressed. "Tell me, Princess, what do you imagine in that little head of yours I wanted to do to you?"

Her face flushed. "Nothing," she said quickly. "You should go. Before someone sees you."

She did not look at him again. He wanted her to, wanted her to convince him that what he felt was not madness, that it was worth something. But her eyes stayed fixed on the ground, her hand white around the hilt of her blade, reminding him of his place. Reminding him of who he belonged to.

He stepped back, then turned away, his back to her. He did not want her to see how unraveled she had made him.

"Good night, Princess."

He did not look back. Because if he did, if those violet eyes found him even once more, he knew he would not have been able to walk away. He would have stayed. He would have forsaken everything he was for her, even if she did not want him.

He reminded himself of the truth. He wasn't someone who deserved the love of another. He wasn't someone who got to want. Not someone worthy of her.

TWENTY-FIVE

SOLIS

It was the same nightmare again. Darkness. Absolute darkness. No edge, no floor. Just the void. Insults cracked through it like splintering bone. The snap of a whip. The stench of iron. Burnt meat. Charred flesh.

He blinked, and the darkness peeled back. A Solaran camp sharpened into focus. His fifteenth birthday. The day his father decided he should become a man. A soldier had been caught stealing bread for his family. His father ordered Solis to punish him. A boy with a whip.

His hand trembled around the leather. The weight felt wrong. He had never wanted to hurt anyone. He had wanted to be a shield, fire that could protect, just as his mother had told him. But his father's lesson crushed whatever compassion he had left. Break him, or I will break you. That had been the warning.

Heat pressed against his skin as they dragged the man forward, bound in ropes. His father declared the sentence: theft, punishable by whipping. Ironic. Solara starved its own people for war, then branded hunger treason.

Sweat slicked Solis's palm. They forced the man to his knees. Nausea climbed the back of his throat. He did not want this.

He met his father's eye, pleading for reprieve. His father's gaze was iron. Do it.

He lifted the whip. Leather hissed in the air. His arm shook. Then the man spoke, and the words struck deeper than any lash Solis could have delivered.

"Solara deserves to burn. I have no regret."

Solis froze, the whip suspended midair. The defiance echoed inside him. He had spoken those same words once. Hearing them now felt like being cut open. He could not make his hand obey. Then came the voice he feared most.

"Then you will burn with it." King Leo's gaze pinned him. "Burn him. Show me the fire of Aurelius still runs in you. Show me I did not raise a coward."

The soldiers were silent. Their gazes were knives. Solis wanted to retch. He could not do it.

"Torch him," his father snarled. "Or I will fetch his kin and burn every last one for treason."

Solis flinched.

The man lifted his head, defiant to the end. "Go on. Burn me. One day Solara will face its reckoning. My family has been starving long before this. I have nothing left to lose." His voice lodged in Solis's ribs. Each word struck bone.

Solis looked at his father one last time, begging for mercy. Nothing. Solara had no mercy for the weak.

"Bring his kin," the king said. "Let them share his judgment."

Solis could not breathe. His mind swarmed. The truth settled like a vice. He had no choice.

Tears slipped down his face as he let the whip fall. Fire clawed through his veins, rising with a violence he could not contain. He released it.

The screams came then, a single chorus that ripped through him. His own voice. The man's. He couldn't tell them apart. The hollowness felt all the same. Everything burned. The air stank of charred flesh and with it the world burned.

TWENTY-SIX

LUNA

At the crack of Moonrise, Luna was still awake. Sleep refused to claim her. Each time she closed her eyes, he was there—the prince of Solara—standing in the garden beneath the silver light, lantern fire threading through his hair, that maddening look in his eyes. The look that made her heart stumble, that made her forget which side of the war she was meant to stand on.

She turned onto her side with a groan. "Fool," she muttered to herself. "He is promised to another, and not just anyone—the daughter of a duke. And he is the son of the man who brought chaos to our realm. You should not be staring at him like some fairytale prince from those ridiculous romance books. He is not one."

A voice chimed from the doorway. "What kind of fairytale prince are we talking about?"

Luna froze. Her head snapped up to find Nova—her best friend, her shadow, her worst influence—leaning against the doorframe with that infuriating grin.

"How long have you been standing there?" Luna demanded.

"Long enough," Nova said sweetly, stepping into the room.

Luna groaned and collapsed back into her pillow. Nova ignored her entirely and leapt onto the bed as if she owned it. That was Nova. Maid by title, sister by soul—spoiled, fearless, and far too curious for her own good.

"Princess," Nova purred, stretching out beside her. "Who are we talking about?"

"No one," Luna blurted, pulling the blanket over her head.

"Oh?" Nova teased, laughter bubbling in her voice. "No one like that insufferably handsome prince you brought home yesterday? He is one fine no one, I will give him that."

Luna groaned louder. A thousand ways to smother her best friend flickered through her mind. She did not want to think about that prince. That arrogant, impossible, stupidly handsome prince. No. Not handsome. Not cute. Absolutely not.

She shoved her face into the pillow and let out a muffled scream. Nova laughed until tears gathered in her eyes.

"Just kill me now," Luna mumbled.

"Not until after breakfast," Nova said brightly. "And you might want to hurry. He will be there. I must say, black suits him far too well."

Luna sat up so fast she nearly struck the bedpost. "No. Absolutely not."

"Oh, yes," Nova flashed a wide, playful grin. "Maybe we should just keep him here in Selvaran. He would look lovely beside you."

Luna threw a pillow at her. "You are insufferable."

But Nova was right about one thing. If Luna had to see Solis every day—if she had to feel those blue eyes watching her the way he had last night—she would lose her mind. There had been something in that look. Something that reached inside her and refused to let go. Why did he have to look at her like that? Like she was the universe and he was a star forever caught in her gravity.

Her cheeks warmed. She flung the blanket aside and swung her legs out of bed.

Nova handed her a gown of deep violet, its silver stitching shimmering like starlight. Luna frowned. "Why this one?"

"No reason," Nova said, feigning innocence, though her grin gave her away.

"What are you up to?"

"Nothing," Nova bustled behind her, delight written all over her voice. "I only think the prince might like it."

Luna glared. "Nova."

But it was too late. The memory of last night returned—his voice low and alluring, the warmth of his breath as he leaned close, the way her heart betrayed her by answering his.

She shook the thought away. No. Bad. He was a guest. A temporary inconvenience. Soon he would be gone, and she would never have to see those infuriating blue eyes again.

"Come on, Princess," Nova hummed softly as she laced the gown. "The king and queen are waiting."

Luna recognized the tune immediately. A song about star-crossed lovers.

Oh, she was absolutely killing Nova later.

As they passed through the gardens, her gaze betrayed her. Through the morning mist, she saw the place where she and Solis had stood the night before. The memory struck like a pulse, her cheeks warming as if the moonlight still brushed her skin. She turned away before her heart could betray her again.

The scent of jasmine bread and starfruit drifted through the great hall. Silver light streamed through the arched windows, spilling across the long table where—Moon help her—Solis was sitting.

Nova had said black suited him. She had not been wrong. The color looked dangerous on him. The shirt clung to his frame as if woven from sin, every movement drawing her eyes where they had no business wandering. The black made his sun-kissed skin glow, turned his hair molten gold, and when he brushed it back with his fingers—stars above—her heart nearly stopped. And those eyes. That piercing Solaran blue against the dark. Even the Milky Way could not compare.

He was too perfect. Too elegant. Too effortless.

She barely noticed the fading bruise along his jaw because the rest of him made it irrelevant.

Luna hesitated in the doorway, pulse quickening. Her parents were already seated. Khael sat to her father's right, his expression carved from stone, and her mother to his left. Solis sat one chair away from the queen, a single empty seat between them. Her seat.

"Little Moon. Nova." Queen Astrid lifted a graceful hand. "Come. Sit."

And then he looked at her. Only a heartbeat. Perhaps less. But it was enough. Heat rose along her neck. She tore her gaze away and crossed the hall, pretending she did not feel his eyes follow every step.

She might have chosen the seat beside Khael, but her traitorous best friend swept forward and slipped into it first, all grace and feigned innocence. Nova's smile brimmed with mischief and apology.

Who even needs a best friend? She was going to bury Nova beneath the very tree she had once promised to bury Solis under.

"Good Moonrise, my little Moon," her mother said, eyes bright with far too much knowing.

"Good Moonrise, Mother." Luna sat beside Solis, leaning toward the queen just enough to avoid looking his way.

"My moon," King Orion rumbled, his tone deep with affection. "You rise late today."

"Couldn't sleep last Moonfall," she muttered, reaching for her fork.

From the corner of her eye, she saw it—the way Solis looked at her. His gaze swept down, then up again. That traitorous dress. Curse Nova forever. And was that a hint of color along his cheeks as he looked away? What right did he have to blush? He was the one promised to another.

"Princess couldn't sleep because she was planning to take the prince out today," Nova said sweetly. "She stayed up all Moonfall thinking of how to ask him."

Luna's mouth fell open. That traitor.

Words caught in her throat, strangled before they could form.

Solis froze mid-movement. Even his breath stilled. The bronze of his skin deepened, shading toward red. Then, as if in a desperate attempt to regain his composure, he turned to her father, fixing his attention anywhere but on her.

"Your castle is magnificent, Your Majesty," he said quickly. The warmth climbed his neck, and she could feel the heat radiating from him. So his fire did answer to emotion. And right now, she could feel every trace of it.

King Orion smiled. "I am sure it is not as magnificent as Solara's citadel. I have heard the marble there is threaded with gold."

"Gold and white, Your Majesty," Solis replied. "The colors of Solara. But I prefer the obsidian of Selvaran. The way the moonlight lives in your walls is… remarkable."

"Remarkable," Khael repeated, his voice cold as ice. "Until Solara decided to stain it with our blood. Tell me, Prince Solis, there's an old boast: cut an Aurelius deep enough and the wound bleeds gold."

The table went still.

Solis met his stare, lifting his chin. "If that were true, Commander, I would have been leaking gold the night your princess stabbed me."

She hadn't stabbed him. He had stabbed himself. Not that anyone at this table needed that truth.

"Perhaps," Khael hissed through his teeth, "the wound wasn't deep enough."

"Khael, enough," Queen Astrid said softly, her voice smooth as silk drawn over steel. "We will not speak of blood at the table."

"Thank the moon for that," Nova muttered. "All this talk of blood makes me queasy."

Then, with a brightness that could only mean trouble, she leaned forward. "Prince Solis, would you like to visit the village of Vega with us?"

"He has already been there," Khael snapped.

"As a prisoner," Nova countered. "Not as a guest. I thought he might want to see Selvaran for what it truly is."

"That is an excellent idea," Queen Astrid said smoothly. She turned to her daughter. "Luna, would you like to show him around?"

No. She would not. But the quiet expectancy in her mother's gaze told her the answer had already been given. As Princess of Selvaran, it was her duty to host foreign guests.

Luna tried not to groan. Spending an entire day with Solis was the last thing she needed.

From the corner of her eye, she caught the faintest curve of his mouth. The infuriating man was smiling. He didn't mind at all.

The path to Vega wound through argent forests and frost-lit fields, the air cool and still against Luna's cheeks. Perhaps it only felt that way because she wasn't breathing.

She walked beside Solis, pretending not to notice him. Impossible. The black leather of his Selvaran cloak clung to him like a second skin, lined in fur that caught the moonlight and turned it to ink and smoke. No Selvaran man had ever worn it so well.

Her own gown had been exchanged for supple leather, tailored for movement and warmth, her fur cloak drawn close around her shoulders. It had been Nova's brilliant idea to take Solis to Vega, but when Luna went to fetch her after breakfast, the girl was already curled up in bed, claiming the jasmine bread had made her ill—the same breakfast Luna had eaten perfectly fine.

When she pointed that out, Nova only grinned. "Have fun," she'd said. "And tell me later if Solis Aurelius burns as hot as the rumors say Solaran men do."

Luna had nearly thrown a pillow at her.

Now she walked in silence, reminding herself she was here because duty demanded it, because her mother had ordered it. Not because of the man at her side.

The man who had barely spoken to her since breakfast. The man who smiled like he knew exactly how much he unsettled her.

The village of Vega unfolded before them, hushed and dreamlike beneath the light of Moonrise. Lanterns hung from silver-barked trees, their glow spilling across cottages veined with ivy that shimmered black-green in the mist. Wildflowers of violet and crimson framed the cobbled streets, and a narrow river meandered nearby, its surface glimmering with drifting blue lights like fractured constellations. Even the earth seemed alive beneath them, fungi pulsing faintly between the roots. The air smelled of frost and honeyed pastry.

Solis halted in his tracks, his eyes widening as he took it all in. Her pulse beat with every breath he drew. A part of her adored the way he cherished Selvaran. A prince who loved and admired his enemy's realm. How could they call him a monster when all she could see was this soft-hearted fool who knew nothing beyond the suffering he had endured?

"This is Vega," Luna said quietly, "the closest village to the castle."

Solis studied everything with a quiet reverence that made her chest tighten. His brows drew together when something caught his attention, eyes flicking from one sight to another as though memorizing each detail. His lips parted slightly, then closed again. Those lips. Perfect. Symmetrical. Like the rest of him. Even his ears were infuriatingly well-shaped.

She needed help.

When he finally turned, she caught the faint flush along his ears. Was he nervous because she had been staring?

He blinked once. "Can we visit a store?"

"Sure," she said quickly, grateful for the distraction. She led him toward a small cottage with a wooden sign swinging gently above the door. Bakery was carved in elegant script.

The moment they stepped inside, the scent of sugar and warm spice enveloped them. Trays of pastries gleamed behind glass: star-shaped tarts glazed in black sugar, airy puffs dusted in silver, honeyed buns with violet drizzle, crescent loaves, and sticky black rolls that shone under the lantern light.

Luna's mouth watered.

Solis leaned over the counter, studying the display as though it held relics of a forgotten age. "They're so different from what we have in Solara."

"How so?" Luna asked, smiling despite herself. He looked so curious, like a scholar lost in a living dream.

The baker, a woman with greying hair, approached. "See anything you like?"

Solis hesitated. "I'm not sure."

"Two shadowrolls, please," Luna said before she could stop herself.

The woman bagged them with a knowing smile. Luna paid, then led Solis to a table near the window. He sat across from her, holding the roll gingerly. The glaze clung to his fingers as he examined it as though it might breathe.

Luna laughed softly. "Just eat it."

He took a bite, and her pulse faltered.

The chocolate smeared his lower lip, glinting faintly in the light. Then, without thinking, he licked it away. Slow. Unhurried. She followed the motion, her breath catching somewhere between awareness and something far more perilous.

Oh, Moon help her.

His eyes widened a heartbeat later, wonder illuminating his face. "Your pastries change emotions," he said, turning the roll in his hand as if studying a sacred thing. "That's extraordinary. How does it do that?"

"Magic," she said. "The berries we use carry it. Some bring joy, others ease pain. Some even mend heartbreak."

"I feel… comfort," Solis murmured. "Warm and soft. Like a mother's embrace."

"Yeah." She met his eyes for a heartbeat too long, heat rising across her face before she looked away. "Shadowrolls can do that to you."

She lifted her own pastry and took a bite. The rich chocolate melted across her tongue, sweetness unfurling in her chest. Solis's gaze flicked to her mouth.

Before she could ask what was wrong, he reached across the table and brushed his thumb against the corner of her lip.

Her breath caught. His skin was warm despite the cold around them. Their eyes met, violet to blue. For a heartbeat, the world fell away.

"You had some chocolate," he said, his voice low.

"Thanks," she murmured. Her pulse thundered in her chest.

He leaned back, clearing his throat, the tips of his ears tinged red.

"Do you want to go anywhere else?" she asked.

"What's your favorite shop here?" he said, rubbing the back of his neck. He still wouldn't meet her eyes.

Luna hid a smile. For someone so arrogant, Solis Aurelius was terrible at concealing when he was flustered. And stars, she liked it.

"The pawn shop," she blurted. "My second favorite place besides this bakery. It's full of strange things—sometimes even items from Solara."

That caught his attention. The curiosity that had softened his features vanished, his expression cooling to stone.

"Solara?" he said quietly. "I thought travel between our realms was rare. Especially now, with the war."

"It is," Luna admitted. "But some people find ways." Dangerous ways that would earn punishment if her father ever discovered them.

Solis nodded. "Let's go."

TWENTY-SEVEN

SOLIS

The shop was tucked between two ivy-covered walls, a crooked little cottage with a tarnished sign that simply read Pawnshop. When they stepped inside, a rusted bell chimed above their heads. Dust clung to the air like fog.

Shelves crowded the space, burdened with relics of the forgotten.

Solis moved through the clutter, his fingers gliding across the edges of objects dulled by time until he stopped before a pendant that glimmered faintly beneath the dust. A sun wrought in gold, a ruby burning at its heart. The Solaran crest.

He lifted it, studying it for a moment. Memory surged like a tide. He was certain it was the same pendant.

"Anything catch your eye, young man?" a rasping voice called.

Behind the counter stood an older man, a scar carved deep across his right cheek.

"These look… rare," Solis said carefully, masking intent behind courteous curiosity. "They don't seem like they belong to Selvaran."

The man didn't blink. "Neither do you. That hair of yours—blonde isn't common here. Where are you from, young man?"

A snarl edged his tone, the old resentment that still clung to Selvaran hearts after years of war.

Luna stepped quickly to his side. "We should go."

But Solis didn't move. His fingers tightened around the pendant. "I remember the prince of Solara had one of these," he said lightly. "A gift from his fiancée."

He felt Luna tense beside him. The word fiancée still cut her. He hated that it did. If only she knew what Calista truly was to him. Not a love. Not a choice. But now was not the time. He needed answers.

The man froze, saying nothing.

"I wonder," Solis continued, his tone composed, "how a pawnshop in Selvaran ended up with it."

The shopkeeper's throat bobbed.

Then Solis smiled faintly, as if offering reassurance to gain the man's trust. "Relax. I also heard that prince despised the pendant so much he gave it to a soldier during his first campaign. Poor man went missing after a battle, didn't he?"

The man nodded. "Yes. Some of these items come from the dead. From the battlefields."

"So Selvaran soldiers collect from the fallen?" Solis asked, voice deliberately easy. "Just curious."

"Not exactly." The man's eyes flicked toward the window, wary, as if expecting someone to appear. "That one was found at a site where the shadows attacked."

Solis's brows lifted. "Shadows? What do you mean by that?"

This was it. The truth he had been searching for—finally within reach.

Before the man could answer, a tug on his arm pulled him back. Luna had seized him. "We should leave."

Why was she in such a hurry? This was the closest he had come to answers since the war began. It could expose whoever was truly behind the attacks—and she wanted to walk away?

His gaze caught hers. Violet to blue. Her face strained to hold something back. Her eyes flicked aside, avoiding his. Her grip tightened. Her throat moved. Luna never hid things from him. Not until now.

His heart sank. Please, not Selvaran. Not her. If his father was right, then everything he believed in was a lie. He needed her to be real. He needed her not to become like his father.

Solis let her pull him away. The pendant slipped from his fingers, striking the floor with a muted clink. He followed her out, his face unreadable, his heart sealed in ice.

TWENTY-EIGHT

LUNA

She pulled him out of the shop, her heart pounding in her ears.

When they reached the street, Solis finally spoke. "Your realm is being attacked. People are vanishing, aren't they?"

Luna's pulse faltered. She could not answer. If his father knew, everything would unravel.

Such knowledge was forbidden to Solara. If King Leo learned that Selvaran was being struck not only by Solaran raids but by shadow creatures as well, he would see it as an invitation to invade. It would mark Selvaran as fragile. Defenseless. She could not allow Solis to know. Not when he could carry that secret home.

And what if he already knew? What if he was behind the attacks himself? No. She refused to believe that.

"I ask because," Solis said quietly, "the same is happening in Solara."

The words hollowed her chest. She had not known. Solara was suffering the same fate—the same disappearances, the same horrors. Was that why they had reignited the war? Because they believed Selvaran responsible? The realization twisted through her like a blade.

Before she could answer, a small figure collided with Solis, knocking him back a step. A boy, no older than ten. Solis steadied himself, then knelt with a grace that made Luna's chest tighten.

He placed a hand upon the boy's head, his voice low. "Are you hurt?"

How could a man who once turned battlefields to flame touch the world with such gentleness?

The boy did not answer. His eyes widened, color draining from his face. He was not looking at Solis. He was staring in the direction he had come from, frozen in terror.

Luna followed his gaze.

And froze.

A shadow towered at the end of the street, taller than any man, its form a writhing mass of smoke and bone. Its limbs twisted at unnatural angles, its edges rippling like torn silk caught in the wind. Smoke curled from its body, dense and black. When it opened its mouth, rows of glasslike teeth gleamed crimson, and two burning eyes fixed upon them with a hunger that turned Luna's blood to ice.

The creature lunged, its body unraveling as it tore toward them with a shriek that split the air.

Solis moved before Luna could draw breath. He caught the boy, pulling him close as he twisted, rolling across the cobblestones just as the creature's claws raked through the space they had occupied. The strike met stone instead, leaving a jagged scar of shadow in its wake.

He landed hard, the child still cradled against his chest, his body curved protectively around him.

A man who placed a child before himself.

Moon, she was in trouble.

The creature turned, smoke curling off its limbs as it hissed, eyes burning red. Luna didn't hesitate. Her daggers flashed into her hands, their silver edges catching the faint light as she moved.

The shadow lunged, claws outstretched. Luna ducked low, spinning beneath its reach, her movement fluid as water. Her blade caught along its side, the cut burning bright against the dark. The thing roared, swung again. She leapt back, feet gliding over the cobblestones.

Her motion steadied into a familiar rhythm. The dance of battle. Power stirred beneath her skin, a faint glow blooming at her chest.

When it lunged again, she met it head-on, crossing her blades and driving them into its core. Light burst through the shadow's body, tearing it apart from within. It let out one last distorted scream before collapsing into smoke.

Silence fell, broken only by her ragged breath.

Luna lowered her blades, air misting from her lips. The last wisps of shadow faded into nothing.

Solis was already on his feet, one hand resting on the boy's shoulder. He bent slightly, his other hand brushing the child's hair. His voice came low, gentle. "You're safe now. Go home."

The boy looked up, eyes wide with something between fear and awe, then gave a shaky nod and ran.

Luna watched him disappear into the misted street before turning back to Solis. Moonlight traced his cheek, painting him in pale gold and shadow. He looked up, a faint smile ghosting across his lips.

"Never thought I'd be saved by the princess herself. Maybe I should have worried more when we fought on the battlefield."

She forced her gaze away. "Try not to need saving again, Prince. I'm not in the habit of rescuing Solarans."

His smile deepened. "I'll try to remember that."

But even as he said it, she saw the look in his eyes—soft, unguarded, impossibly kind—and knew she would never be able to forget it. Guilt coiled in her chest for being so cruel to him.

Just like before, he didn't hold her gaze for long, as if the very act of looking at her too long might ruin him. He never realized he was already ruining her.

Solis turned his head toward the ground.

Luna followed his gaze. Where the creature had stood, the earth was scorched black. An eclipse mark had burned into the cobblestones, the center still faintly smoking. Solis crouched, brushing his fingers across the mark, his lashes low as he studied the charred surface.

Luna knelt beside him. "Every village in Selvaran that's been attacked bears the same mark," she said quietly.

His voice came low. "So does Solara. The same symbol. If it isn't Selvaran, then who is it? Who would want to destroy both realms?"

The silence between them deepened, heavy with questions neither could answer. For a breath, their world narrowed to the scorch mark and the sound of their mingled breaths.

Then Solis's voice broke through. "I'm going to be honest with you."

Her heart skipped. Was he finally going to confess what lingered unspoken between them?

The way he turned his head toward her made her forget to breathe. Moonlight caught the edges of his hair, gold turning silver, and she despised how much she longed to reach out, to feel the warmth of him against her palm, to trace the line of his jaw.

He drew in a low breath. "I surrendered to Selvaran because I wanted this war to end. That part is true. But I also came here to find answers. My father reignited the war, believing your people were behind the attacks on our villages. I wanted to find the truth for myself, to see Selvaran with my own eyes."

Her gaze dropped to the blackened mark between them. So that was why he risked himself—not for glory, but out of a duty that weighed on him like chains.

Yet he still refused to acknowledge what shimmered between them. Looking at him too long made her chest ache in ways she dared not understand.

"Honestly," she said, masking what she felt, "I'm not angry about what you did. Giving yourself up to an enemy kingdom to end a war no one comprehends—that's brave."

To test the pull between them, she added, "And I already know you're not here just to get close to me. Even if you can't seem to stop flirting."

Solis tilted his head, that maddening grin curving his lips. "Flirt with you? I don't recall being that desperate."

There it was. The man was in denial.

"Don't pretend you weren't," she retorted. "You practically melted under my charms. You should've seen your face in the garden."

He laughed, the sound low and rich. "Do not flatter yourself. My standards are far higher than a little princess from the moon."

She arched a brow. "Good. I'd hate to be within reach of that outrageous ego of yours."

He leaned closer, voice dropping low, his breath brushing warm along her cheek. "It's not like you could reach it anyway, short one."

Luna's jaw dropped. "I'm not even that short."

"Does it hurt to look up all the time?" he asked, grin widening. "Princess, I can't stay on my knees forever so you can meet my eyes."

Her pulse flared. "Being on your knees suits you, Prince. It'll keep your ego in check."

He raised a brow, amusement glinting in his eyes. "If you want me on my knees, you only have to say so. I'd gladly stay there for you."

Her heart stuttered. Moon help her. He was impossible. She rose quickly, hoping he wouldn't see the heat rising in her cheeks. And the man said he wasn't flirting. This was absolutely flirting.

"Let's go before another one of those creatures shows up," she said, clearing her throat. "Next time, I might let it eat you."

He chuckled, the sound stirring something deep within her. Her flush deepened.

"So vicious."

She said nothing, hoping he couldn't hear how fast her heart was racing.

He rose and fell into step beside her. After a quiet moment, he spoke again. "Princess, what do you say we work together?"

Her brow furrowed. "Working together? Doing what exactly?"

If he dared ask her to betray her realm, she would let the Vorraken eat him. Such a shame for such a striking face, but so be it.

"Oh, I don't know," he said, that infuriating smirk returning. "Solving this mystery, perhaps? You want to protect your people. I want to protect mine. We might actually make progress if we don't try to kill each other in the process."

That wasn't a bad idea.

"Are you admitting you need protection, Prince?" she asked, the corner of her mouth lifting despite herself. Working together might finally bring their realms peace.

"Look who has the high ego now," he murmured. He extended his hand. "Partners, then?"

She hesitated for only a breath before taking it. His grip was firm, steady, unbearably warm—and he didn't let go.

Neither of them did.

Their eyes met, and the air thickened between them, quiet and fragile and electric. For a heartbeat, the world stilled.

Then Solis swallowed, breaking the spell that had gathered around them. His throat worked as if even breathing pained him. He withdrew his hand and turned his gaze aside. "We should go," he said, his voice tight, almost restrained.

Who was he trying to fool? She had felt it too. Whatever burned between them was real.

"Why are you running, Solis?" she asked softly. She had to know. She had to know why he couldn't face it. Engaged or not, he felt something for her—and she knew what she felt.

He stilled. For a heartbeat, he didn't move at all. Then he turned away from her, the moonlight carving the hard line of his jaw.

"Princess," he said quietly, each word sharp as glass, "whatever you think this is… we can't."

The words cut deep. She bit back the ache rising in her throat.

"What this is?" she said, forcing a scoff. "Don't flatter yourself, Prince. I never wanted you."

Because lies were safer than truth. Because they both knew this could never be. He was the sun. She was the moon. Two forces destined to chase each other yet never collide. Her hands trembled. Foolish of her to think he would ever choose her.

Solis exhaled slowly, his gaze dropping. Then he stepped past her, his voice low. "Exactly. Forget it."

Yeah. Forget it. That's what she told herself.

If only she could.

TWENTY-NINE

SOLIS

The first light of Moonrise spilled through the high windows of the throne room, pale and soft as silver mist, cold against the warmth of his breath. Solis stood before the dais beside Khael, King Orion, Queen Astrid, and Luna. Her skin caught the light, smooth as porcelain. He forced his gaze elsewhere, his fingers flexing at his sides as he waited.

A sealed letter rested in Orion's hands, the crimson wax of Solara already broken.

Orion read it aloud. The sound carried through the hall like slow water over stone. It was a Selvaran custom Solis still didn't understand. In Solara, King Leo never shared his words so freely. Every decree was guarded like a secret. But here, truth was spoken into open air. Nothing hidden.

Even more striking was the queen's presence. Astrid stood beside her husband, her voice threading through his as if it belonged there. In Solara, queens were never permitted inside the council chamber. Even Calista had been barred, favor or not. Politics belonged to men. Solis had been taught that all his life. Yet watching Astrid's quiet authority, the grace with which the court followed her voice, he knew his realm had been wrong.

Perhaps one day, when he became king, he could change Solara too. Maybe somewhere in that dream, without Calista as his queen. He would sooner forfeit his crown than be bound to her. Maybe then, another face might sit beside him—one he couldn't look at now, not without unraveling. After what had happened last night, because of his own cowardice, because of the way he had turned her away, that dream was only that, an illusion of his own heart. But he still wanted It.

He was still lost in that reverie when Orion's voice broke through the hush.

"King Leo has agreed to the terms."

The words hit harder than Solis expected. His father had chosen peace. Chosen him. For a moment, something twisted in his chest, an ache he thought long dead. He drew in a slow breath and held it until the feeling dulled.

"King Leo has also agreed to the Celestial Summit," Orion continued, "but on one condition. The prince must be released first and allowed to return home before the event."

Khael objected at once. "Once King Leo has his son, he could revoke his promise. We cannot release him until the ceremony concludes."

Orion inclined his head. "Then Solis shall remain here until the day of the ceremony."

The decision should have felt like a sentence, yet instead, Solis felt something akin to relief. He didn't have to face Calista. Didn't have to see his father. Didn't have to return to the gilded cage that had never felt like home.

For now, he could remain here, in this realm of moonlight and frost. He could pretend this was where he belonged. Pretend he could be with her.

His traitorous gaze drifted toward her before he forced it away. She said nothing, but he caught the faintest curve of her lips, quickly hidden. Perhaps she didn't mind his stay either. Whatever existed between them was a silent, perilous game he couldn't stop playing. Though every rational thought reminded him he was engaged, desire for the princess fractured reason like glass. His heart beat against its cage like a trapped bird.

"Prince Solis."

Slowly, his gaze lifted to King Orion.

"You must forgive the delay. I take no pleasure in keeping you from your home, but the safety of my people must come before all else. For now, it is best you remain here."

His heart faltered. One beat, then another, rapid and uneven beneath his ribs, though his expression remained composed. "You owe me no apology, Your Majesty. I understand your reasoning."

If only Orion knew the truth. Compared to Solara, this was paradise.

And then there was her.

Don't look at her, you fool.

When the court was dismissed, Solis wandered the marble halls with no destination in mind. The echoes of his footsteps followed him like ghosts. For the first time in his life, there were no expectations, no orders, no duty. Just silence. And it felt incredible.

He told himself he might return to his chambers, read a book, maybe just think. He had never felt so free. But then a sound stopped him mid-step.

A sharp twang. Then another. And faintly—

"Jerk."

He froze. That voice. The corner of his mouth lifted before he could stop it. He knew that voice.

"Jerk," it came again, sharper this time, followed by the soft whistle of an arrow slicing through air.

Curiosity stirred in his chest. Without meaning to, he followed the sound down the corridor until he reached the open doorway of a training hall.

And there she was.

His little Starlight.

Bow in hand. Eyes fierce. Hair falling loose over her shoulders.

Another arrow flew. The string sang as it buried itself dead center in the target.

That's my girl.

"Jerk," she muttered again, reaching for another arrow.

Solis leaned against the doorway, the smile on his face refusing to fade as his heart fluttered—each beat sharp and aching, almost painful in how beautiful it felt—watching her take her anger out on a piece of wood.

Each shot was precise, her movements fluid as water, but that faint scowl on her face… that was his undoing. She didn't even know what she did to him just by existing.

He tilted his head, admiring the lethal grace in her form. A violent little thing.

"Moon help the man who truly deserves that word." A quiet laugh slipped from him as he stepped into the room. "I wonder," he said, voice low with amusement, eyes glinting, "what that poor target did to earn such a name."

She jolted, startled. Her eyes widened, then narrowed to slits.

She said nothing. His gaze flicked from the target back to her.

"Well? Cat got your tongue, Princess?"

Without warning, her bow snapped toward him and loosed an arrow. It sliced through the air—so close he felt the wind brush his cheek—before striking the wall behind him with a heavy thud.

Solis froze. The air still trembled where it had passed. She had actually shot at him. The princess of Selvaran had aimed straight for his face.

And gods, he didn't mind. It was maddening. He should have been furious, but she left him without a shred of composure. The sharp focus in her eyes, the slight pout of her lips, the fury rolling off her like heat. She looked like she wanted to kill him, and somehow that only made him want her more.

She was devastating. Dangerous. Real. No crown. No mask. Just fire wrapped in moonlight.

A deep ache unfurled inside him. He wanted her to look at him like that again, because that look unraveled him piece by piece. He craved it more than he should.

He tilted his head, a mocking smile tugging at his mouth—one he knew would rattle her even more.

"Missed."

She said nothing.

Her glare deepened. A flush rose to her cheeks. He loved how easily he could draw that color from her, how easily it was becoming his new favorite shade. Well, second favorite, because those violet eyes that burned with the promise of murder had already claimed first place.

She was so beautiful. Infuriating, impossibly beautiful.

Her anger only made her more breathtaking.

And he knew, without question, he was in trouble.

She nocked another arrow, deliberately ignoring him. The tip aimed squarely between his eyes.

He smiled, crossed his arms.

"Shoot as many times as you want, Princess. I'd take a thousand arrows to see that expression again. Nothing like fury to spark a fire."

"You're insufferable," she shouted, as if she hadn't just fired an arrow at his head.

Solis gave her his sweetest smile.

"It's all part of my charm, darling."

She snorted. "Charm. As if you have any." She tilted her head, the movement almost feline. "What are you doing here anyway? Nothing better to do, Prince?"

He shrugged, eyes tracing the bow in her hands. "I thought I might challenge the almighty Princess to a little competition."

The laugh that slipped from her lips made his chest tighten. Sun above, he would do anything to hear that sound again.

"Did you forget what happened the last time we shot arrows?" she said. "I seem to recall a certain little prince who couldn't even hit his target."

He smirked, meeting her gaze. "I was eleven. And in my defense, I'd never held a bow before. I'm not the same prince you met back then, Princess."

Her mouth curved, those infuriatingly perfect dimples appearing on her cheeks. Gods, have mercy on him.

"Do you want to bet on it?" she asked.

"Fine," he said, his grin matching hers. "Let's bet."

Luna arched a brow, voice light with challenge. "On what?"

"Loser does whatever the winner asks."

Her eyes narrowed, a glint lighting her starlit gaze. "That's a dangerous wager, Prince."

He stepped closer, voice lowering just enough to stir the air between them. "Afraid you'll lose?"

Her mouth opened, then closed. She lifted her bow again, confident, sure of herself. "Since you clearly have no idea what you're up against, I'll go first."

"Oh, how generous of you," he said, crossing his arms, waiting.

She rolled her eyes, drew her arrow, and fired. The arrow struck the center clean—perfect aim.

She stretched out her hand, offering him the bow. The smirk she wore was a victory flag.

A quiet laugh rumbled in his chest as Solis took the bow, testing the string. She was right about one thing—when he was a boy, he'd never shot a bow. That changed when his father forced him into the regiment at fifteen, made him shoot arrows until his fingers bled and the sun sank beyond the horizon. A prince must excel at everything. Failure meant pain. Pain meant punishment. There was no space in the king's heart for a son who fell short.

He nudged the memory away, notched the arrow with muscle memory, sighted the target, and released. It struck dead center, splitting Luna's arrow by a hair.

Her lips parted, eyes widening. "You've gotten better."

Three years of torn skin and spilled blood. He'd had no choice but to get better.

He said nothing, only watched astonishment spread across her features. Then she shrugged, the motion light, careless. Solis wondered what it felt like to live that free.

"Almost impressive."

That made him laugh. His little starlight would never admit defeat. "Almost?" he teased, handing her the bow. "Let's see if you can do better."

She said nothing, simply took her stance again. Her violet eyes fixed on him. Without looking away, she loosed the arrow. It split his clean in half. Fierce. Deadly. Devastating.

A grin broke across his face, amusement striking his chest. "So competitive."

He took the bow from her but didn't lift it right away. Instead, he stepped closer, closing the distance between them, catching the faint scent of lavender on her. It was calm. Familiar. Like home. His breath brushed her cheek as he leaned in, his voice a whisper.

"But I can do better."

Heat rose along her cheeks as he drew back, giving her his most infuriating smile. He lifted the bow, never taking his eyes off her. The string snapped; the arrow whistled through the air and struck the target with a sharp crack. Her soft gasp told him he'd hit true.

He tilted his head, lowering the bow. "Did you like that, Princess?"

Those violet eyes melted into his, as if she could see straight through him. She stepped forward in silence, wrapping her fingers around his hand. Her touch seared through his skin like sunlight on snow.

"If you're trying to seduce me, Prince, you'll have to do better than that."

With one smooth motion, she slipped the bow from his grasp. The loss of her warmth left him hollow, aching for more. She drew two arrows from her quiver, raised the bow, and fired. Both struck dead center.

He lifted a brow, quiet pride stirring within him.

She turned, offering the bow back to him. "Your turn."

He took it, grabbed two arrows, masking his fondness behind a grin. "Easy."

He drew the string back. As he steadied his aim, movement flickered at the edge of his vision. She reached into his space; her breath grazed his neck. Warm. Dangerously close.

"I almost missed that. I was distracted," she whispered, voice low and teasing.

"By what?" His pulse stumbled hard.

"By you."

He forgot to breathe.

The arrows flew wild, missing the target entirely.

She didn't move away. Her lips curved near his ear. "Got you, Prince."

He exhaled, heat crawling up his neck.

A soft laugh slipped from her as she turned away.

He dropped the bow, caught her arm, and drew her back against him. Her eyes widened as their bodies collided, her breathing uneven against his. His gaze fell to her lips—so close it set his entire body alight. The ghost of her breath brushed his skin, sending a shiver down his spine. An urge to taste her rose like fire through his veins. For one suspended moment, he nearly gave in.

But reason clawed its way back. He forced his composure, gripping it like the hilt of a blade, letting the tension between them die.

"You cheated," he said, masking the chaos inside him, hoping she didn't realize how easily she could unravel him.

She shrugged, a teasing spark in her eyes. "You never said I couldn't."

His shoulders shook with quiet laughter. "Remind me never to play anything with you again."

"Come on, don't be like that," she said, her tone light, though her gaze lingered on him too long, each second pounding against his ribs. Her eyes lowered.

"So," she murmured, "I suppose I should claim my prize."

His throat tightened. "What do you want, Princess?"

The air thickened, charged with something dangerous and beautiful. Her nearness undid him. Then her arms slipped around his neck, and the world vanished until there was nothing but her warmth and the sound of their uneven breathing.

Was he even breathing? He couldn't look away. Her lips brushed his—and he almost forgot his name.

THIRTY

LUNA

That voice.

"Princess."

Luna shoved Solis back so fast her palms stung. Her hands dropped to her sides as she turned away, heat rising along her neck. Solis stepped back too, his bronze skin deepening to a burnished crimson. Her heart hammered, and the sudden loss of his nearness felt colder than frost.

Khael stood in the doorway, arms crossed, expression carved from iron. Luna had no idea how much he had seen. She had only been testing Solis, trying to see how far she could push him—but it had gone further than she meant. The idiot claimed he felt nothing for her, yet clearly he did.

"What are you two doing?" Khael's voice cut through the air, low and sharp.

"Nothing," Luna said quickly. "I was showing the prince how well Selvaran can shoot a bow."

Khael's gaze dropped to the bow lying on the ground—nowhere near either of them. A miserable lie, and they all knew it. Luna bit back a groan.

He took a step closer. His gaze swept over Solis, cold as a blizzard, stripping him down to something less than human. Murder simmered behind that stare.

But the obstinate prince didn't back away. Defiance flared in him like a flame catching wind. He lifted his chin, meeting Khael's stare head-on. Luna wanted to sink into the floor. Why couldn't the two of them behave like civilized men? They'd been at odds since the day Solis arrived.

"Don't you have something better to do, Prince?" Khael asked, voice sharp as cut crystal.

Solis offered a half-smile, humor flickering in his eyes. "What can a hostage prince do in his enemy's land? It's not like I can wander wherever I please, is there?"

At this rate, she would need an entire shield wall to keep them apart.

Khael let out a mirthless laugh. "Such a sharp tongue. I look forward to the day I make you lose it."

Solis's mouth parted, ready with a retort, but Luna stepped between them, glare slicing through the tension. "We were just about to leave." She turned to Solis. "Didn't you say you wanted to go to the library?"

He arched a brow, catching her meaning at once.

The library. The eclipse mark.

"My little starlight—not only dangerously beautiful, but clever as well."

Her heart stumbled. Why did he have to say that now, of all times? Khael looked ready to hang him from the castle gates.

"Still want to go?" Solis added smoothly, pretending the idea had been his all along.

She nodded, seized his hand, and pulled him from the training hall at a pace that made it look like they were fleeing for their lives. Khael didn't follow, but Luna could still feel his glare scorching between her shoulder blades. She needed to find a way for those two to coexist—otherwise one of them would end up buried beneath the courtyard.

Once they reached the corridor, Luna slowed and released Solis's hand. Her eyes flashed toward him. "Do you have a death wish? Why would you provoke him like that?"

Solis shrugged, the corner of his mouth curving. "What fun would it be if I didn't?"

Luna groaned.

She turned to leave, but his voice halted her. "I thought we were going to the library?"

Another groan slipped out.

"There it is again," he said lightly. "That sound—it's becoming one of my favorites."

Gods. And this fool claimed he felt nothing for her. He couldn't stop flirting if his life depended on it.

She faced him again, eyes cold enough to freeze the river outside. "I only said that so Khael would leave us alone—and so you two don't murder each other."

"Well, Princess," Solis said, amusement threading through his tone, "I thought it might be the perfect opportunity to research the eclipse. Since we're partners now. And as for Khael—I doubt he could stand against me."

Luna inhaled sharply through her nose, her cheeks puffing slightly as she exhaled.

That tiny gesture drew a grin from Solis, making her glance anywhere but at him. She refused to face those bright blue eyes or that insufferably handsome smile.

"Gods, you're irresistible when you're annoyed," the flirter pressed on, voice dripping with amusement. "I'm starting to lose count of how many things I like about you."

Her pulse stuttered. Heat crept up her throat. Was this his way of getting back at her for earlier? Because it was working. She forced herself to meet his gaze.

"Can't you stop? I thought we had nothing going on, and here you are—nonstop flirting!"

"Who's flirting?" He tilted his head slightly, maddeningly charming. "I'm just testing your patience."

Forget Khael murdering him. She was going to do it herself.

"Fine," she said, spinning so fast her cloak flared behind her like a streak of midnight. She stormed off, boots striking the marble.

Solis followed, grinning the entire way.

THIRTY-ONE

SOLIS

The library of Selvaran was unlike anything Solis had ever seen. A glass dome arched high above, revealing the night sky in all its glory. Stars shimmered beyond the curved panes, moonlight spilling in a pale wash across the marble floor. There were no windows here, only the soft glow of candles and lanterns that shimmered like captured starlight, their light blending with the moon's pale gleam. The aisles stretched upward into shadow, tier upon tier of shelves heavy with books. The air smelled of parchment and ink, old and sacred, as though time itself had settled here to rest.

At the center stood a long, curved desk carved of dark wood polished to silver by age. Behind it, a woman with jet-black hair tied into a severe bun bent low over an open book.

Her glasses had slipped halfway down her nose, the candle beside her trembling as if afraid to disturb her focus.

Solis slowed his steps as they entered, his voice dropping to a hush, instinctively reverent. "Your realm truly knows how to honor knowledge."

Luna looked back at him, a small, proud smile tugging at her lips. "What did you expect? Selvaran is a kingdom of scholars. Solara prefers to honor steel and flame."

That part, he thought, was painfully true.

She moved between the shelves, her fingers brushing the spines of books older than either of their realms. "The ink in each book is made from the moon's sap," she said. "They say the oldest texts whisper when the moon is full."

His eyes lit with wonder. Books had always been his refuge. While his father worshiped conquest and power, Solis had found solace in pages and words. The Solaran Royal Library was vast, but this—this was alive. "Do they truly whisper?" he asked.

Luna shrugged, a hint of mischief in her tone. "I'm rarely here long enough to find out."

The smile that curved her lips made him laugh before he could stop himself. The sound echoed faintly between the shelves, drawing a few curious glances. He straightened quickly, clearing his throat. "Well, Princess, perhaps tonight you will."

She rolled her eyes but said nothing, leading him toward the center desk. Her steps made no sound against the marble, her movement fluid as her own shadow. Solis followed, half admiring, half curious how someone could move like that.

"Excuse me," Luna whispered to the woman at the desk. "Where can I find information about an eclipse?"

Without looking up, the woman replied, her tone brisk and dry, "Aisle twenty. Top shelves."

"Thank you," Luna said softly before turning to Solis.

He offered a faint smile. "After you, Princess."

They walked in silence between the towering shelves. Luna led him to a narrow aisle lined with books. Dust drifted in the light, soft as snowfall.

"Well, Prince," she said, turning to face him. "Let's start looking."

Solis ran his fingers along the spines, tracing the faded Selvaran script carved into each one. He could read the words easily. His father had made certain of that. Leo Aurelius would accept no son who couldn't master the language of his enemies. Failure was not tolerated.

His hand stopped on a single book bound in deep blue leather, the gold lettering faded almost to nothing. The moment he touched it, the faint scent of parchment shifted to something sharper. The sound of a belt hitting flesh. Blood in the air.

He blinked, and the library was gone.

He was sixteen again, standing in his father's chamber. His mother sat at the edge of the bed, her hands clasped in her lap, her eyes full of quiet fear. King Leo lounged nearby, reading a parchment, his expression as cold as the blade he favored.

"Stand in the center, boy," his father had said. Solis obeyed.

He remembered the sound of his mother's voice, soft and trembling. "Leo, he has just returned from the camps. Let him rest for one night."

"Duty does not stop because of travel," King Leo said. "He must remember that if he ever wishes to be king."

He set the parchment aside and rose. Solis's blood turned cold as he saw the man unbuckle his belt. The scrape of leather filled the air.

His mother tried again. "Leo, please. If he has marks again—people will talk."

The king turned to her, his voice sharp as steel. "Say another word, and you will face the same punishment."

Solis's breath caught. He wished she would stop. She did. She sat there, holding back tears as she watched, like she always had, because there was nothing she could do to stop him.

King Leo circled him. "You will recite the Book of Governance, word for word. Miss even one, and you will bleed for it."

He had tried. Gods, he had tried. But the words blurred together after the first . One mistake, a lash. Two mistakes, another. He lost count as the sun fell beyond the windows. Still, the belt struck, again and again, until his back burned raw and his breath came in ragged gasps.

It had been a game to his father. One he was never meant to win. Not even the finest scholars could recite a tome word for word, and King Leo knew that.

When it was over, the air reeked of sweat and blood. His father finally closed the book. "That will do for today. Tomorrow, we will start again."

Solis blinked hard until the memory receded. Until he was no longer in Solara but in Selvaran again, surrounded by books and silence. He could still feel the sting on his back, the ache of each lash like it had never healed. His breathing came shallow and uneven.

"Solis."

The sound of her voice pulled him back. He looked up. Luna was standing in front of him. At some point, his knees had hit the floor. Her hands cupped his face, her touch soft, grounding.

"Solis, where did you go?" she asked.

His name. Not Prince. His name. It felt like air after drowning.

He caught her wrists before she could pull away. "I'm fine," he said quietly. "Just tripped."

Her brows furrowed, but her lips curved slightly. "On thin air? You're awfully clumsy, Prince."

Prince. She was back to the word Prince again. Disappointment slipped through him before he could stop it. He wanted to hear his name on her mouth. He wanted it again. And again.

"Call me Solis," he said.

For a moment she said nothing. The air between them seemed to still. Her hands were still on his skin, her thumb brushing over his cheek as if to soothe him. Her violet eyes searched his face.

"Solis," she repeated at last. The sound of it stole his breath. His name had never sounded so soft in another's voice, like a prayer whispered into the dark. For the first time in years, he felt whole.

He rose and pulled her into him. His arms wrapped around her, and she did not pull away. Neither of them did.

They stayed there, caught between shadow and moonlight. Her arms slipped around him, her head resting against his chest.

"Are you all right?" she asked softly.

"Yeah," he murmured. "Never better."

For a moment, he allowed himself the selfishness of it. Just her, just warmth, just silence. Was it wrong to want this?

Her hands traced slow circles along his back. "Good."

The silence grew heavy with words neither of them could say, but he knew she felt it too. It lingered in her touch, in the way she leaned into him, in the quiet that seemed to hold its breath around them. He wondered what would have happened if Khael didn't interrupt them. Would they have ended this game of endless chasing?

Then the sound of a whip reminded him of the duty he bore. He flinched. His father would have disapproved of this. *Love was weak.* Solis repeated it as he forced himself to let her go. He wanted her but want was not a luxury he was allowed to have. Not now. Not ever. They had a mission to complete—a truth heavier than the feelings they both pretended not to carry.

"Should we go back to looking?" he asked, glancing down at her.

She looked up, those violet eyes calm as the center of a storm, light against all his darkness.

"Yeah," she breathed.

They separated slowly, though part of him ached to draw her close again.

Luna cleared her throat and climbed the ladder to the second tier of shelves. The faint gleam of her daggers flashed beneath her cloak. Dangerous little thing, he thought. Even here, surrounded by books, she was lethal. His little starlight made it so hard not to desire her.

For a while, they worked in silence, the soft rustle of pages and the faint scent of parchment filling the air. The deeper they went, the older the books became—spines cracked, lettering faded by time. The sight stirred something warm in Solis. He wondered how long these words had waited to be read.

He traced his fingers along the rows, searching for anything that might hold an answer.

"Anything?" Luna called softly.

"Nothing yet," he said. "Most of these are celestial studies—constellations, lunar phases."

"Keep looking. It has to be here somewhere."

Then his hand stilled. The book was bound in black and silver, a faint crescent intertwined with a sun engraved across the cover.

"I think I might have found something," he said.

Luna came beside him. He opened the book; it felt heavier than it appeared. They leaned together over the pages. The eclipse mark appeared in one of the s, linked to a fallen star and a fragment of shadow said to summon creatures born of darkness.

Solis looked up, meeting her eyes. "A fallen star. Do you know anything about it?"

She shook her head. "No, but I saw a book earlier that mentioned one."

She disappeared between the shelves and returned carrying a volume half-charred, the title barely legible: *The Legend of the Fallen Star.*

Intrigued, Luna sank to the floor, spreading the book open across her knees. Solis joined her. Their elbows brushed, a quiet spark catching beneath his skin. He leaned closer, drawn to her warmth, and she did not move away.

Together they read:

The corruption of the shadow shard of the fallen star could open a portal to the shadow realm, summoning creatures born of darkness—the Vorraken. Known for their swiftness and hunger, the Vorraken were soul-stealing wraiths born from the Realm of Void, an existence between life and death. Once summoned, they remained in the world of the living, devouring souls. The more they consumed, the stronger they grew.

Legends spoke of a darker truth: mortals could become Vorraken when marked by shadow. The Cursed lost themselves slowly—first their memories, then their minds—until nothing remained but an empty shell. The transformation could take years. When the soul was wholly devoured, the body transformed. Wherever these abominations appeared, they left behind a scorched eclipse mark. It was said that, if skilled enough, a shadow wielder could create their own Vorraken from a living being, seizing both mind and will. Only those with the Blackest heart could wield such corruption.

Luna's breath caught. "So that's what happened in the village. Those creatures—the Vorraken. Someone's summoning them, or causing them to appear by using the shadow shard."

Solis nodded. "Whatever the cause, these Vorraken can devour souls. And if the legends are correct, the corruption spreads through the mark itself. The mark might be some kind of passage."

Their eyes met. Then she gave him her most adorable smile, dimples flashing like light through clouds. *Duty*, he reminded himself. *Duty.*

"Am I not the best investigator ever?" Luna said. "I found our answers."

Solis's shoulders shook. His little starlight was radiant with awe. He repeated the word duty several more times in his mind, but it failed him. She had him completely. "Fine. You are. I would never doubt your brilliance again, my clever little starlight."

"I'm not little," she pouted. "Admit you doubted me."

"Fine. I admit it. I underestimated you. The Princess of Selvaran is far more brilliant than I gave her credit for. Her intelligence rivals no one." He dipped his head in mock reverence. "I bow to such greatness."

Her laughter broke through the quiescence of the library, earning them a few disapproving glares. She didn't seem to care.

"Solis, don't do that again."

"Do what?" he asked, smiling.

"Whatever you just did."

Her body was close enough that her warmth brushed against him. His fingers twitched. He wanted to touch her, to hold her in his arms, but he stopped himself. Duty. Still, a little teasing wouldn't hurt. He couldn't help but find this entertaining. When was the last time he'd felt any kind of joy? When was the last time he had truly lived?

"Well, perhaps we can finish reading before your adoring audience throws us out, great investigator."

She nudged his ribs with a light punch. "Stop calling me that."

"What? I thought that was what you wanted, great investigator."

"Call me that again and I'll make you regret it," she said, pushing against him.

He wanted her to make him regret it. It would be well worth it.

The nearness of her face made his heart stumble. He looked away before his sheer willpower betrayed him.

He lifted the book again, turning its brittle pages in search of an answer. She leaned against him, breaking what little resistance he had, while reading the next passage aloud.

When the star fell, it shattered into eight shards scattered across both realms. Each carried a unique element—ice, fire, shadow, wind, earth, illusion, nature, and time.

Solis's gaze lifted. "Do you think there's a record of where they were last found?"

"I'm sure there is," she said, eyes bright.

They searched until he found another book tucked between the shelves.

"Great investigator," he called out. "I think the title belongs to me now."

She rolled her eyes but joined him on the floor again, the book open between them. Their knees brushed as they leaned close, the candlelight gliding over her hair in a fleeting ember tones.

In Solara, four shards were recorded—fire, time, wind, and earth. Their exact locations remain unknown. In Selvaran, the remaining four—illusion, shadow, nature, and ice—were last sighted. Each shard holds a will of its own, choosing its wielder and binding through generations. The magic can be inherited, passed down through blood, or seek a new host when its bearer dies. The seven shards are linked to one another, but the shard of shadow stands apart—its power corrupted, its magic severed from the rest, dividing light and darkness.

He flipped through more pages.

Centuries ago, when the realms were one. An eclipse, born of the shadow shard, brought darkness to the world. The seven celestial warriors who bore the elements of light fought beside the moon priestess—marked by a crescent moon upon her chest—and the sun heir. They found the shadow but failed, causing the realm to split in two. The moon priestess vanished. The sun heir lived on. A prophecy rose soon after: seven warriors would rise again, forge a shield for the light, and only then would the darkness be destroyed, restoring balance to the world. To forge the light—

The page ended abruptly. Torn.

He turned to the next, but half of it was missing.

To restore balance, all eight shards must meet again. Light must meet dark. Only then can the darkness be conquered.

The shadow shard… like Lucien's and Calista's shadow magic. Was there a connection? Solis felt the answer pulling at him like a thread. The shards' power could be inherited. Inherited. Where had Lucien come from again? Solis racked his mind, searching, but found nothing. No one knew where Lucien came from.

Solis ran a finger along the edge of the page, reading aloud, hoping the words would spark something. "Their power can be passed on… like a legacy."

Was his magic tied to the fallen star? The sun heir—was that his ancestor? And the moon priestess… Solis's eyes widened. His gaze dropped to Luna's chest.

"You're the moon priestess."

Luna's hand rose to her collarbone, fingers brushing her crescent mark. Her voice came soft and quiet. "I was told."

The crescent shimmered faintly, pulsing with silver light. Had it ever glowed this vividly before? It felt alive, as if it were calling to him.

"So whoever wields the shadow shard is behind the attacks."

"And if that's true," Luna said, her violet eyes meeting his, "then that person created the Vorraken… or caused them to appear."

Solis chewed the inside of his cheek. He shouldn't hide this from her, but telling her might only complicate things. Would she hate him if she learned Solara might be behind it all? And why would Lucien want his own realm destroyed? Why did he ignite another war? Did he possess the shadow shard himself? Solis had never seen Lucien use his magic—but he had seen Calista's.

There was a connection. He could feel it. Keeping it from her was no longer worth the cost.

"I think I know who has it."

Her jaw dropped. "You do?"

Solis stared down at the book. "I'm not completely sure, but I have a feeling. There's a duke in Solara who can wield shadow magic. I'm sure you can guess who. I'm engaged to his daughter."

The word engaged tasted bitter on his tongue. He hated saying it aloud—especially to her. Another reminder of why whatever existed between them could never be. Luna deserved far better.

He saw the change in her before she spoke. Her shoulders stiffened, and she turned away. The distance between them widened. "So she's your fiancée."

"I'm not with her because I want to be, Luna."

"But you still are."

And he hated himself for it. "Well, we're not here to talk about my engagement. We're here to stop whatever's destroying our realms."

She turned back, facing him. "Then from now on, it's strictly business."

"Strictly business."

"So what now?"

"We need to figure out how to stop the attacks. The prophecy said we need the warriors and the light. You're already here, which leaves the warriors."

"The book says the shards respond to each other. If we find one, we can use it to trace the rest."

"Exactly. Then I suppose our next step is obvious." He leaned back, hating that it had come to this—mission and duty. "Finding the first shard."

She nodded. "Before the wrong person does."

"Where do we start? The realms are vast."

"That's true," she said. "But if the shards are connected, finding one might lead us to the others."

"Then we'll figure it out together," he said quietly. "Right, partner?"

Because partner was the only thing she could be to him. And he needed her to be something.

Luna's lips curved. "Yeah. Partner."

Relief washed through him. Partner. At least he could be that.

Solis held her gaze a moment longer. The word lingered between them. Something shifted inside him, undeniable and dangerous. He wanted her—and he could not have her.

THIRTY-TWO

LUNA

After the library discovery and their official declaration of partnership, sealed with the decree that nothing between them would go further than that, Luna now stood outside the palace gates with Solis and Nova, waiting for Khael.

Another attack had struck a village near the border. They needed her to respond. Solis had decided to accompany them, claiming the palace bored him and that he might uncover more clues about the shadow shard if he could see the Vorraken. Against her better judgment, Luna agreed to let him join.

Now, judging by the look in her men's eyes, she wasn't sure it had been a good idea. Their hatred for Solara ran deep—just as it did in Khael. The journey would take days, and Solis and Khael already had enough conflict to last a lifetime. Luna doubted she could endure days of them exchanging verbal daggers, so she had brought Nova along for the sake of her sanity.

That, as it turned out, was an epic mistake. Nova had a talent for mischief, and at the moment, she was wielding it mercilessly.

"So, princey," Nova said, rocking on her heels, her eyes bright with mischief. "How are you liking Selvaran so far? I heard you and the princess have been spending plenty of time together."

Luna averted her gaze. She refused to be part of this conversation.

"Selvaran is wonderful," Solis replied smoothly. "Just as wonderful as its princess. Dark and gloomy at times, yet full of wonder at others."

"Gloomy?" Luna muttered. "I am not gloomy." She was doing exactly what he'd asked of her—focusing on their mission.

She turned, hands on her hips. "Well, prince, if I'm so gloomy, you don't have to come. I'd hate to ruin your royal day by being such a royal pain in the ass."

"Princess, if you insist on being a royal pain, I'd be delighted to assist you. It would be my honor to keep you on your toes."

"I'm about to shove those toes up your—"

She stopped. Khael was descending the stairway, his black leather uniform gleaming under the moonlight, the white in his beard stark against the darkness. His silver eyes carved straight through Solis.

"I hope no accidents happen to you, prince," he said, voice level.

It sounded like he wished for one. Luna cleared her throat. "We should get going. The villagers need us."

Khael brushed past Solis, deliberately slamming his shoulder into him. Solis staggered a step, then smirked. He actually smirked.

She pinched the bridge of her nose. Oh, moon above. This was going to be a very long trip.

Mostly, the journey passed in silence. The village lay north of the castle, near the frozen mountain peaks. It wasn't far; if it had been, Khael never would have allowed Solis to come. He still didn't trust the prince, and technically, Solis was still a hostage, even if he never acted like one.

They reached the village before Moonfall. The air grew sharper as the night deepened, and Luna was grateful for the fur cloak draped over her shoulders. From the corner of her eye, she saw Solis dismount with effortless grace, his hair falling across his brow as he took in every detail.

It never failed to amaze her how much he admired their villages. Even now, he examined the place as though it were the most extraordinary thing he had ever seen.

They set up camp near the forest's edge, stationed guards at every perimeter, and settled in for the night. The Vorraken had been sighted nearby. Precautions were taken.

Luna and Nova sat by the fire. Nova spoke, but Luna barely heard her. Her traitorous eyes drifted toward a certain prince sitting alone at the edge of camp, a book open in his hands.

The soldiers around him glared with open disdain, but Solis never looked up. One passed close by and spat on the ground beside him.

Filth.

Another muttered as he walked past.

Monster.

Disgrace.

Shame.

The insults circled endlessly, yet Solis kept reading, unmoved by their contempt. The men were forbidden to harm him—Luna had made certain of that. She had gone to her father, demanded the prince's protection, and extracted a promise that Khael would keep him safe.

Khael's response had been simple. My men will not harm him, but I cannot guarantee his safety against the Vorraken.

And he had kept his word.

The next day, they spotted the Vorraken—hundreds of them. An entire village overrun.

From the hilltop, they watched in grim silence. Nova stumbled back while Luna swallowed hard. This was beyond anything they had seen before. When had they multiplied so quickly? Usually, they found only ruins and a few stragglers left behind. But this—this was devastation.

Her focus shifted to Solis, who stood beside her, calm in the face of ruin. Heat radiated from him, fury blazing bright beneath his composed exterior. It startled her. These weren't even his people, and still he cared. He cared despite their hatred, even after the insults hurled at him again and again.

She steadied her breathing. Now was not the time to admire him. They were partners, nothing more.

Nova stayed behind in camp while Luna, Khael, Solis, and the others advanced toward the village.

Fire erupted from Solis the moment they arrived. The Vorraken ignited in waves of flame as he charged forward without hesitation. Fearless. She had forgotten just how devastating he could be on a battlefield. A claw strike. A sidestep. Fire. Burn. Every movement efficient, controlled, lethal. The air reeked of smoke and shadow.

She moved beside him, releasing her own light. Her daggers flared with power, though something felt different this time. Before, her magic had been a soft hum, calm like the wind. Now it pulsed outward, sharper and fiercer than before as if her light recognized his.

His fire surrounded her, licking at her skin but never touching. Gentle, almost tender. Her light flared in response, drawn to his. Two lights moved as one. They dodged, struck, fire and moonlight entwining in a rhythm of destruction and grace.

Around them, her men fell. A soldier stumbled, and before the Vorraken could strike, Solis was there, flame blazing in his palm, reducing the creature to ash. He protected the same men who had despised him, showing mercy where none had been shown to him.

A strange feeling rose within her, like color after rain. A fragile hope. A longing for him. She could not help but fall for the man who could burn the world to ashes yet heal it all the same.

Another man fell, and Solis was already there, shielding him. Every time. He threw himself between blade and soldier without hesitation.

Then a portal tore open in front of a distant Vorraken and reformed behind Solis. Luna opened her mouth to shout for him to move, but it was too late. A long claw dragged across his back. Solis staggered forward. His fire burst outward. The Vorraken collapsed, but blood darkened the wound. The creature had left its mark.

Another portal. Another Vorraken. Five. Ten. Twenty. Solis fought them all. Fire against shadow.

Rage tightened inside Luna. She recognized exactly whose magic that was. Khael. She scanned the chaos until she found him standing far off, watching as the Vorraken struck Solis again and again. He had promised.

Her focus snapped back to Solis.

He took another slash along his arm yet fought on just as fiercely, never slowing. If this continued, he would be covered in wounds. Without a second thought, she sprinted to his side.

She intercepted a strike aiming for his ribs, her back pressing against his. If Khael wanted Solis dead, then he could lose her too. She refused to let Solis fall.

The Infuriating prince had the nerve to grin. "Bored, princess?"

A deflection. Fire. Ash.

"No. Just trying to keep you alive," she said. A dagger caught a claw. Light shattered the shadow. "I would hate to bury you so soon. Not after we agreed to complete this mission."

Solis burned a Vorraken lunging at her right, then dragged his fingers briefly along her arm as he pulled back. The heat didn't scorch. It welcomed her. Was this what it felt like to be touched by an Aurelius?

"Ha. I am sure my downfall would be pleasing for your commander. Mission or not." Blood streamed from the gash in his arm, yet he kept fighting as if pain were only an inconvenience. Had he simply lived with it for so long? She remembered the scars across his back. Luna swallowed. Solis was tragic. A man hiding behind sarcasm and fire but broken beneath it.

"You know why he's like that," she said quietly. "You're more alike than you think." If Khael understood how similar he and Solis truly were, maybe he would not try so hard to kill him.

"Well, if he wants to end me, he'll need to try harder than this."

As if she would ever let that happen.

They fought until the last Vorraken fell. Only then did Luna storm toward Khael, fury thundering through her.

"Khael, you promised you would keep him safe. You promised."

The commander turned away, surveying the destruction. "I promised I would not kill him. I never said the Vorraken wouldn't."

"Well, opening portals to trap him is helping them kill him."

Khael's expression hardened. "If he cannot handle a few Vorraken, then he does not deserve to live. Selvaran has spent years fighting these creatures, along with those filthy Solaran soldiers. Excuse me if your little prince is too soft for war. At least now the Solaran get a taste of what Selvaran has endured."

Anger surged through her. Khael wanted to punish Solis for something he had no control over. Solis had been a pawn since childhood. A boy brutalized into a weapon he never wanted to be. And for what? To be dehumanized by men like Khael while he was still bleeding inside?

"Khael," she snarled. Her voice shook with fury she could barely contain. She would not allow him or anyone else to harm Solis again. Solis deserved peace. He deserved happiness. She would not let anyone take that from him. "You are forbidden to harm him. As your princess, you will obey me. If I see or hear of another incident, I will have you punished."

She hated using her authority against Khael, but some lines were not meant to be crossed. And Khael had crossed it.

They set up camp again that night. Nova and Luna helped Solis wrap his wounds. Without the barrier of his cloth, his old scars surfaced beneath the firelight. They crossed his body like fractures in a shattered vase. The new wounds twisted over the old, creating a map of pain and survival. Even though Luna had seen them before, the sight still carved an ache through her chest. Nova gasped.

"Prince, your skin is like a ripe apple. Bruised, but still sweet, I'm sure."

Solis huffed a low laugh. "Nova, please don't actually try to taste me."

Nova batted her lashes. "No promises. Especially when my princess here refuses to admit she wants you just as much."

"Nova," Luna warned.

Nova only shrugged. "Speaking the truth."

Then her eyes widened. Luna followed her gaze to a thin cord peeking from Solis's folded clothes. Before Nova could reach for it, Solis moved with such a startling speed that Luna barely caught the motion. His hand closed over Nova's, pulling it away.

"Nova, I never took you for someone who would steal my clothes."

Nova curled her fingers around his and tugged his hand against her chest. "Oh, but Prince, how else am I supposed to keep your scent with me?"

The idiot grinned, all teeth. "Charmer, are you?"

Look who was calling who. As if he hadn't spent every chance in Selvaran flirting with Luna.

While he was distracted, Luna slipped the thin cord from his clothes. Her breath stalled when she saw what hung from it.

Her pendant.

Her moon pendant.

The one her mother had given her.

Solis froze the moment he realized what she held. His shoulders locked. His voice faltered. The composure he clung to splintered. "It… it is not what you think."

The words stuck in her throat.

Not what she thought? The fool had carried the token of their broken engagement for eight years. Eight years. Her fingers trembled around the pendant as the truth settled in her chest.

His throat worked, the tension in his eyes telling her he had kept it for a reason she had always known.

Solis tore his hand from Nova's grasp, snatched the necklace from Luna's hold, and stepped back, putting space between them as if distance alone could stop him from unraveling. His shoulders sagged. Nova's brows lifted in confusion, but Luna barely noticed. Her heart was pounding too hard, echoing in her ears.

She rose, closing the distance between them until only a few feet remained.

"Why… why did you keep it?"

Solis said nothing. His head lowered. He refused to look at her.

His fingers curled inward around the pendant, tightening until his knuckles blanched, as if he were trying to keep himself from breaking.

Nova must have sensed the shift because she slipped away quietly, leaving them alone. Luna fought the urge to reach for him. Her fingers twitched uselessly at her side.

"Solis. Why did you keep it?"

His head bowed. His shoulders trembled. When he finally spoke, his voice was thin, almost breaking.

"Because I needed something to hold on to. Because the world took everything else from me, and this… this was the only piece of light I had left. It reminded me of the stars. It reminded me of you. Of the boy I used to be before they broke me."

His body shook. "Keeping it made me feel like I could still be free. Free like the stars above. Free like I once was. Even if it was a lie… I needed something to believe in."

Her heart stopped. It felt as if the world stilled around them. He had held on to her even when she had let him go.

She stepped forward. Then another. The space between them closed. She wrapped her arms around him from behind, resting her cheek against his back.

"You are free, Solis," she whispered. "Freer than you've ever been allowed to believe."

"Then why do I feel so broken, so caged?"

"Because the world misunderstood you. Because you deserve better than all of them. Because you are more than this world ever offered you."

She felt his breath tremble. His ribs shuddered beneath her hold. She had never been more grateful that the soldiers and Khael were nowhere nearby. Solis needed space. He needed to break where no one could weaponize it.

She held him as his composure shattered, letting him grieve for everything he had lost.

The prince of steel could break after all.

THIRTY-THREE

LUNA

After Solis calmed, they sat in silence by the river, moonlight brushing over them and the rush of water filling the spaces they could not name. His head stayed bowed, thumb moving absently over the pendant she had once given him. Luna nudged the water with the tip of her boot. A firefly drifted past, its glow pulsing through the cool air. Across the riverbank, a frog flickered pink, then green, before disappearing into the reeds. Solis lifted his head, eyes narrowing as he scrutinized it before finally speaking.

"How does it do that?"

"The creatures in Selvaran are magical," Luna said, following the glow until it vanished.

"All of them?"

"Well, they feed off the magical plants here. That's what gives them their glow."

His focus dropped back to the river. "Selvaran never ceases to amaze me."

She said nothing.

Luna chewed her lip as the urge pressed against her chest. She wanted to ask him about whatever this was between them. She knew it was real. It had been real for a long time, even if they kept pretending it wasn't, even if they kept pushing each other away. She was done running from it.

Her gaze dropped to the pendant in his palm.

The way he held it… as if it were the most precious thing he owned.

Was it because she was precious to him, or because the pendant was the only piece of comfort he had left in a world that kept taking from him?

She had to know.

She swallowed. "Solis."

"Hmm?" His eyes stayed fixed on the current pushing against the rocks.

"Is there something wrong with me?"

His head snapped toward her. "Why would you ask that?"

"Because… I… this… thing between us… it feels like—"

"There's nothing wrong with you." His voice came out barely a whisper. "If anything, everything's wrong with me. I'm the one they broke. I'm the one they carved into something I never wanted to be. You deserve someone whole… not someone who's still trying to remember how to be human."

She reached out, took his hand, and set it gently on her lap. "You're not damaged. You never asked for what they did to you. You're more than the monster they forced you to become."

He exhaled slowly but didn't answer. She brushed her thumb over his knuckles, grounding him.

"Don't sell yourself short, Solis. The world doesn't understand what it owes you. You showed mercy to men who mocked you, saved lives you had every reason to abandon. That isn't broken. That's someone who knows how cruel the world can be and still chooses to meet it with kindness."

He drew in a slow breath, his gaze fixed on their entwined hands. "When I saw a falling star, I thought I had no wishes left. There was nothing inside me brave enough to hope." His fingers tightened around hers. "But now… now I wish for a different life. One where you weren't the moon's princess and I wasn't the sun's prince. One where we weren't bound by crowns or realms, just… two souls who found each other."

Her breath vanished. She leaned closer, fingertips brushing his cheekbone. "Then why can't we choose that life now? Don't you want me the way I want you?"

His gaze tore from hers, dragged back to the river as if looking at her hurt. "You have no idea how much I want you. Wanting you isn't the problem. It's what I could do to you if I let myself have you… I burn everything I touch. I can't burn you too."

She cupped his jaw and guided his face back to hers. "Solis… I'm not something fragile you can scorch. If you want me, take me. I'm choosing you. You could burn the world down and I'd still choose you. There's no crown, no duty, no title that can take me from you."

The river's light caught in his eyes, turning them a shade of blue too beautiful for the sorrow living inside them.

"Princess… you don't understand. I'm not pulling away because I don't want you. I'm pulling away because you're the only thing I can't taint. You're more than a desire. You're the only piece of my life that still feels sacred. I can't have you. Not until I become someone worthy of you."

"I'm already yours, Solis." If only he knew she already belonged to him.

A tear slipped down his cheek. She barely caught the words as they left him.

"I don't deserve you."

THIRTY-FOUR

LUNA

Their return to the castle was met with urgent news. King Leo had sent a reply. Nova was dismissed while Luna, Khael, and Solis entered the council chamber to deliver their report to King Orion.

They arrived just in time. Nobles circled the king like restless birds. Luna stayed near the wall, Solis beside her. His face held that quiet stillness she had come to recognize, unreadable to everyone but her. King Orion lifted a hand, and the chamber fell silent.

After the river, Solis had become impossible to ignore. His presence lingered like a song that clung to the air long after the last note faded. She was a fool, perhaps, to want someone already bound by another… but the heart never bends to reason. Reason had never meant anything to her. Not where he was concerned.

Her father sat at the head of the table, the silver crown on his brow catching the light like frost on steel. His voice carried through the room with the steady weight of distant thunder.

"King Leo has sent his terms. The prince is to be returned to him at the Celestial Keep for the Celestial Summit. He guarantees Selvaran's safety only if his son remains under our protection until that day. The ceremony will take place in three days."

Three days.

The words sank through her like stones to the bottom of a riverbed. Three days until Solis returned to the world that carved him into something he never wanted to be. Three days until he left her.

Luna's breath paused in her throat. She turned toward him, searching for a flicker of reaction, and found it. In his eyes, a quiet ache shimmered, mirroring her own. It felt like staring into a reflection rippling on water, close enough to touch yet never meeting. Her fingers tightened with the urge to reach for him, to anchor him before he slipped away again.

But she kept them still.

Not here.

Not under her father's gaze.

Not with Khael watching every breath between them.

Maybe Solis had been right.

Maybe in another life, they could have what they wanted.

No crown.

No realm.

No duty standing between them.

Only them.

But reality was far too cruel to let them have that.

"Khael," King Orion said, "have the army ready to march. We cannot afford carelessness. My wife and daughter's safety come before all else. The Keep's magic forbids soldiers within its walls, but I want them stationed outside. If anything happens, they will act on my command."

His attention shifted to Solis. "Rest assured, you will be safe here. I trust you have been treated well."

"I have, Your Majesty." Solis's tone was calm, a mask of steel holding back a storm he refused to show. Luna wished she could tear that mask away and remind him he did not need it here. He was safe in Selvaran.

"Excellent." A faint crease formed at the corner of her father's eyes. "Selvaran will stand beside Solara for the first time in decades. Let us hope our people remember peace better than they remember hatred."

Someone should tell Khael that.

Khael stepped forward. "Your Majesty, you need not fear for their safety. I will stake my life upon it. If you permit it, I will send the soldiers ahead through the portal and open another when the time comes. Should danger arise, I will bring you home."

"That would be wise," King Orion said with a nod. He rose from his chair. "Now, I should check on my queen. She has already changed her gown five times this morning."

A soft ripple of laughter passed through the nobles as Orion stepped away from the table. He paused in front of Luna. His tone softened.

"My daughter, the tailors will deliver your gowns soon. Nova will help you choose. Try not to argue with her this time."

Then his gaze found Solis. "As for you, Prince Solis, your father has sent attire from Solara. He insists the prince of light should not wear the colors of the moon. A shame, truly. I thought the outfit suited you very well. But we must agree. Your people will want to see that their prince still belongs to them."

Solis inclined his head. "Of course, Your Majesty."

Luna clenched her teeth. He does not belong to them. They forfeited that the moment those scars were carved into his skin. Solis was more Selvaran than Solaran. He belonged here. With her.

Her father left the chamber. The nobles followed soon after, and then Khael — but not before giving Solis one last cold stare.

After the journey, her men had softened toward Solis. He had saved their lives and they were grateful. Some had even begun speaking to him as though he were human.

But Khael.

Khael never changed.

He still wanted Solis gone, and Luna could not fathom how to get the stubborn old man to show Solis even a trace of kindness.

Luna stood unmoving after everyone left. Solis remained beside her, the weight of the truth settling heavily in her chest.

Three days. Only three days before he returned to Solara, and she would be left chasing the memory of him. He was leaving her.

She felt Solis take her hand. Without a word, he led her outside, his grip firm around hers. He didn't speak.

Her gaze fell to the hand holding her own, then lifted to the boy who owned it. His eyes were blue as a dawn she had never seen, bright and unguarded when he was with her. Perhaps that was why she could not look away. That color belonged to stories and oceans she had only read about, to dreams that had never belonged to her world. Yet it lived in him.

"Solis," she whispered. Even his name sounded like a goodbye.

He smiled faintly. It never reached his eyes. "Don't give me that look."

"What look?"

"The one that tells me I would be a fool to forget the princess of Selvaran."

She huffed, though her lips curved despite the ache tightening her chest. "Well, it is true. I am impossible to forget."

He laughed quietly. "Painfully impossible."

Silence settled between them, thick with what they refused to say. Luna bit her lip, the question burning on her tongue. "Solis… do you wish to go home?"

He turned away. His voice fractured. "I do not know what home means anymore. In Solara, I am a son my father is ashamed of. But here… your father has shown me more kindness than mine ever has."

The memory of his scars flashed through her mind. The person meant to protect him had wounded him beyond measure. Her gaze dropped to his hand, warm around hers. Too warm for someone who lived a life so cold.

"You belong here more, Solis," she murmured. She added, trying to lift the heavy air between them, "Besides, black suits you better than gold."

That made him smile. "It does, doesn't it?"

She made him smile. She wondered how often he hid it back in Solara. Whether he even got to smile like this there.

Then came the question that cracked something inside her.

"Do you wish for me to stay?"

The words hung between them like a lantern trembling in the wind. She lifted her head, but no answer came. If she said yes, would he stay? If she dared to admit she wanted him to? He was promised to another, yet some part of her wanted to be selfish. Was it so wrong to love?

The air stilled as she searched for her voice.

Moonblossom petals drifted in through the open window, scattering across the floor like soft rain. One brushed her hair. Solis reached to pluck it free.

"I was hoping you would say yes," he murmured. "Because I would have stayed."

Why did he have to say that? When every part of her yearned for him. Her breath caught as she swallowed the tears rising in her throat.

He looked away before she could speak. "Three days," he said quietly. "It will pass quickly."

"Yes," she answered, her voice raw. "It will pass quickly."

And then he would be gone.

Neither moved as the unspoken words lingered. Then he stepped closer and pulled her into his arms. His head rested against her shoulder, his warmth filling her. She never wanted him to let go.

His voice slipped into the quiet between them, weighted with something she could not name. "Even if the stars forget their light, I will not forget you. You're the song that stays when everything else falls silent."

Her heart stuttered. She forgot how to breathe. The world blurred until all that remained was the sound of his heartbeat against her.

When he finally pulled back, he did not release her. His hand found hers again, guiding her down the corridor. His warmth was a quiet promise against the cold of the night.

They walked beneath the colonnade in silence. Servants passed, staring, but he did not care, and neither did she.

A forbidden love.

His steps matched hers, the rhythm weaving into the fragile calm between them as he held her hand like it was the string keeping them together. Her pulse quickened. She knew she should stop this, draw the line that should be drawn, but every sensible thought dissolved the moment he looked at her.

"You do not have to walk me back," she whispered when they reached her chambers.

"I know," he said, stopping beside her. "But I want to."

Something in the simplicity of it made her heart tremble. He spoke without armor, without pretense, honest in a world that had forgotten honesty.

He smiled, that quiet, devastating smile that made the palace fade around them. Then he lifted her hand and pressed his lips to her knuckles, closing his eyes.

"I know we shouldn't," he said softly. "But if I can borrow time, even for three days, I want to spend every heartbeat beside you. When it ends, let it end beautifully."

THIRTY-FIVE

LUNA

A blink. Another. Moonlight spilled across her lashes as her thoughts drifted in the quiet space between dream and waking. His voice lingered in her mind, soft as breath against silk.

She had dreamed of him beneath the moon. He had been warm, warm enough to turn a lifetime of waiting into a single heartbeat.

She was in trouble. The prince had rooted himself in her thoughts. Why did he have to be so charming, so impossible to ignore, so painfully irresistible?

She shifted on the pillow and lifted her hand, brushing her fingers over the place where his had held hers. Had that really happened? Had he truly walked her through the palace like that? People would talk. Her father would know. Khael… she refused to imagine his reaction.

A creak stirred the room, breaking her reverie. The door opened. She did not need to look to know it was Nova.

Luna pushed herself upright, stretched, and yawned. Morning had arrived. No more dreaming of him.

Yet her wandering thoughts kept replaying his words.

Her lips curved despite her best effort. Foolish prince. He spoke of love as if it were poetry, as if every moment were a verse that refused to fade. He had spoken like a man offering his final breath. Dramatic to a fault—but the memory of it haunted her sleep.

Nova passed her with a tray of bread and fruit.

"You look like someone who had a dream she cannot forget," Nova teased. "Who were you dreaming of, princess?"

Luna caught herself smiling. Curse that prince, making her look like a lovesick fool.

She cupped her cheeks to hide the rising heat. "Do I?"

Nova climbed onto the bed and crossed her legs. "Tell me, princess. What did you and the prince do in that dream of yours?"

Luna gave her a small shove. "I was not dreaming about anyone. Especially not who you think."

Nova giggled, rose again, and returned with a folded bundle of silk Luna had not noticed. "Your mother sent these for the ceremony. She said you should choose one before the tailors arrive."

She spread the gowns across the bed.

Luna shifted closer, unfolding each one with care. Silk shimmered beneath her fingertips, shades sliding from pale starlight to deep, quiet blue. All were beautiful, yet none stirred anything in her.

Until she saw it.

A gown of deep violet. The color of her eyes beneath the moon. Dark and luminous, as if the heavens had borrowed the shade.

My little starlight.

Heat crept up her neck. Why could she not stop thinking of him? Her fingers traced the silk.

"This one," she said softly.

Nova tilted her head, hand beneath her chin in dramatic thought before she straightened, her grin blooming mischievously. "Oh, princess, it is perfect. The prince will fall head over heels when he sees you in it."

"Who said I wanted to impress him?"

"Your face did."

Her palms met her cheeks. Heat rushed beneath them, like a fever returning for its due. She was smitten, and she hated how obvious it was.

"Do you know where the prince is?" she asked.

Nova arched a brow, amusement slipping across her features. "What prince are we speaking of?"

Luna gave her a pointed look. "There is only one."

Nova didn't answer at once. She sat on the bed, kicked her legs, and stretched out the moment as though savoring every heartbeat of Luna's suffering. "He was spotted in the courtyard at Moonrise. I believe he was training. Running laps like he is chasing something he cannot catch." She winked.

Luna wanted to strangle her.

She walked to the window and peeked out. Beyond the marble arches, she saw him, a solitary figure moving through the courtyard's silver light. The moon gathered in his hair, turning gold to argent fire. He moved with the rhythm of a forgotten melody, every step a verse, every breath a quiet prayer. It looked like a dance.

A warmth stirred inside her. She wanted to know what it would feel like to be in his arms, moving with him through the wind.

His name trembled on the tip of her tongue, but she swallowed it back. Instead, she stood there like a fool, simply watching him.

Nova's laughter shattered her reverie. "Careful, princess. Fall any deeper and you might tumble right out that window or straight into a certain prince's arms." She sang the last words like a lullaby.

Luna tore herself from the window, smoothing her expression into something resembling composure. "I have more dignity than that."

She absolutely didn't.

Nova leaned back on the bed with a wicked grin. "Dignity is overrated. There is nothing wrong with admiring the man you love."

"I am not admiring anyone. We just… have a connection, and we are trying to understand where we stand."

A breeze slipped through the window, carrying the scent of moonblossoms. Luna closed her eyes and breathed it in, remembering the warmth of his hand brushing her hair. Her heart refused to forget him. She doubted it ever could.

She ignored Nova's latest jab and drifted back to the window, drawn helplessly to the man in the courtyard. Something inside her broke open like a song she had never learned yet somehow knew.

Her heart knew it.

"Oh my moon," Nova said, dragging her back to reality. "Just go see him already. If you do not go down there, I will shout his name out that window."

"I am not that desperate," Luna said, though her voice wobbled.

"Of course not," Nova replied. "You were clearly admiring the moon. Not that gorgeous piece of man beneath it."

Luna's jaw dropped. Words deserted her.

Before she could recover, Nova stood, smoothed her gown, and sauntered to the window. "Fine then," she said sweetly. "If you will not go to him, I'll call him to you."

"Nova, don't you dare—"

Nova leaned out. "Sol—"

Luna slapped both hands over her friend's mouth. "Shut—"

Too late.

Solis had already turned. His gaze lifted toward their window.

Luna's heart leapt into her throat. She yanked Nova down so fast they both hit the floor, her pulse hammering in her ears.

"Do you think he saw us?" she whispered.

"Oh, he definitely saw us," Nova said, entirely too calm for someone who had just sentenced Luna to death.

Luna covered her face with both hands. "I am going to murder you, Nova."

"You should thank me instead. Go to him. You only have two days left. Make them count."

She was right. Two days, and Solis would be gone. Two days before distance swallowed whatever fragile truth lay between them. He would be in one realm, she in another, meeting only when duty forced their paths to cross, pretending their hearts had not tangled.

Luna's legs carried her out the door before she even formed the decision. The air met her cold and sharp, brushing her skin with the sweetness of night. A shiver ran down her spine as she stepped into the corridor, the marble cool beneath her feet.

Moonrise echoed faintly through the palace halls as servants stirred awake, but she ignored them all. She moved toward the courtyard, her heart a steady drum beneath her ribs. She needed to see him.

And then he was there.

The sight of him stole her breath. For a moment, the world fell silent. Moonlight traced his features, turning his eyes a deep, startling blue, like dawn reflecting across frozen lakes.

When he turned fully, surprise flickered across his expression.

"Princess." Disbelief threaded through his voice. He swallowed. "Why are you in your nightgown?"

Luna blinked. Then she glanced down.

Oh moon.

The thin silk clung to her skin like spilled moonlight, revealing far more than it should.

Heat climbed her throat. She folded her arms across her chest, as if her hands alone could shield her.

Solis reacted instantly. His head snapped upward, gaze shooting to the sky as if refusing to risk even a glance. His jaw tightened. His ears flushed red. Silence thickened. Embarrassment swept through her, but beneath it something else stirred.

"Have… have you never been with a woman before?" she asked, curiosity threading through her nerves.

His reply stunned her. "I haven't. I do not believe in lust for lust's sake. When I give myself to someone, I want it to be with the person I love. Someone I want to share my life with."

She stared. Speechless.

If an ideal man existed, it would be Solis Aurelius. Who had that kind of restraint? Who carried that kind of heart?

Her blush deepened as he crossed the courtyard. He gathered his cloak and returned to her, stopping close enough that she felt his warmth brush her skin. He draped the cloak over her shoulders, fastening it carefully without letting his gaze stray even once. Only when the fabric settled did a quiet breath leave him, as though he had finally allowed himself to exhale. His restraint both startled and disarmed her.

Then he reached out, the barest touch tilting her chin upward. His lashes lowered, his voice sinking to a whisper.

"You deserve more than a flicker of lust, Princess. You should be treasured, not devoured. A man ought to fall to his knees before he ever earns the right to see you like this."

Her breath vanished. "Would you fall to your knees for me?"

"I will do whatever you want me to."

For a heartbeat, she nearly melted into him. His touch felt like a vow without words, soft as moonlight skimming still water, reaching for her with a reverence that undid her.

"Solis," she breathed, his name slipping from her lips before she could catch it.

His gaze lowered to her mouth as he spoke. "I am sorry. I did not mean to frighten you. I simply did not want you walking around like that."

Because he cared. Because she meant more to him than a passing glance or a fleeting desire. His eyes held restraint, not hunger. Solis possessed control born of strength, not indifference, and it made her respect him. It made her love him, painfully and recklessly, more than she should.

"Solis."

He smiled faintly. "Keep saying my name like that, and I might lose my mind."

A soft laugh escaped her. "Is the great peacock lowering his ego for little me?"

"There is no ego when it comes to you." His fingers brushed a strand of her hair. "We should go inside. It is too cold for you to be out here like this."

"Perhaps," she said, teasing. "It depends on whether you will come inside with me."

"I will." No hesitation. None.

They walked side by side beneath the moon. Even in silence, the pull between them hummed like a thread drawn taut between two hearts.

A prick. Then pain. The sharp sting caught her off guard. She flinched, a soft whine escaping her.

Solis stopped at once. "Are you all right?"

"I think I stepped on a rock," she muttered.

He dropped to one knee in front of her without a breath of hesitation. "Which foot?"

"The right," she whispered.

He took her foot gently, examining it with deliberate care. "There is a cut," he murmured. "Walking barefoot was not your brightest idea."

"Tell me about it."

Then he did something that unraveled her entirely.

Solis turned his back to her. "Get on."

Her breath hitched. The prince of Solara, kneeling, offering to carry her.

For a heartbeat, she could only stare. Then she leaned into him, her arms slipping around his shoulders. When she settled against him, a soft breath escaped from him, his ear flushing crimson. His hands steadied her by the thighs as he lifted her with effortless strength. She had never been carried by a man before, let alone a prince.

And of course it had to be him.

The world shifted when he rose with her, as if they were the only beings left in the universe. Her breath caught at the sudden closeness. His back was warm beneath her, solid and strong, and she could feel the muscles in his shoulders flex beneath her palms. Every step sent a gentle sway through her body. It felt like she was floating in a dream she never wanted to wake from.

The sting in her foot faded, replaced completely by him. His strength. His warmth. The impossibly tender way he carried her.

Her cheek brushed the side of his neck. Heat pooled low in her stomach. She had seen warriors carry injured comrades before, but nothing had ever felt so intimate. The angle of her arm shifted as she held onto him, and her palm settled over the left side of his chest. She felt the steady thrum of his heartbeat beneath her hand, its rhythm falling into step with her own.

She became painfully aware of everything about him.

The soft rise of his breath.

The faint tremor of restraint that passed through him each time her body shifted against his.

"What were you doing up so early?" she whispered, her lips close enough to ghost the curve of his ear. She had to fight the urge not to tilt her head and press her mouth to the warm line of his neck. She wondered what he would taste like.

Solis inhaled sharply before answering. "Could not sleep," he said. His voice was calm, but she could feel the tension beneath it.

She said nothing. Her head rested on his shoulder, letting the steady rise and fall of his breath cradle her. His scent wrapped around her like firelight drifting through pine, something warm and unmistakably him.

They entered the palace quietly. A few maids covered their mouths as they whispered behind their hands, their eyes widening at the sight, yet Solis showed no concern for their murmured astonishment.

At her chamber door, he paused. The corridor stretched in stillness, washed in argent moonlight that softened every edge of stone and shadow.

"I do not think I can walk inside," she murmured, still held securely in his arms.

"Princess, if you wanted me in your room, you could have simply said so," Solis replied, his tone threaded with mischief.

She tapped the top of his head with feigned irritation. "Please. If I wanted you in my room, you would be tied and gagged so I could finally have some silence."

His grin sharpened. "Is that how you prefer your men, Princess? Bound and wordless?"

Her cheeks heated. "Put me down, Solis."

A quiet laugh escaped him. "I am teasing." Keeping one arm firmly around her, he opened the door with his free hand and carried her inside with effortless grace.

He brought her to the bed and lowered her gently onto its edge. Then, kneeling, he lifted her right foot into his hands to study the injury. "A bit of ointment will help. You may not want to walk today."

"Hmm."

"Where do you keep your ointment and bandages?"

She pointed to a nearby drawer. "Always there. Nova is very clumsy."

"Are you certain it is not you who is clumsy?" he asked, a faint smile touching his lips as he crossed the room. He retrieved the ointment and bandages before returning to her side.

He knelt once more, his expression softening as he took her foot in his hands. Cool salve brushed her skin as he worked. He wrapped the bandage into a neat, seamless line.

Silence settled between them, warm and unspoken. She found herself watching him despite her better judgment. The slope of his shoulders. The concentration etched along his features. The quiet, almost reverent care in every movement. It unsettled her, stirring something she was no longer able to deny.

When he finished, he looked up at her. "Rest. I'll bring you breakfast."

Her brows rose. "You will bring me breakfast?"

"Of course."

Had Solis forgotten he was a prince?

Yet true to his word, he returned shortly after with a tray of warm bread, fruit, and fragrant tea. He set it beside her with unthinking grace. When she asked for a book, he retrieved it. When she wanted more tea, he poured it. Anything she requested, he fulfilled without hesitation, as though service were not beneath a prince but a privilege.

And all the while, Luna found her gaze drawn to him. The way the morning light threaded through his hair like spun gold. To the ease of his smile. To the quiet patience in every gesture.

She had never encountered a man like Solis. Not in this palace. Not in this life.

THIRTY-SIX

LUNA

The next day passed like petals drifting down a river, slow, beautiful, and impossible to hold.

Solis proved to be the strangest man she had ever known. Since the moment she injured her foot, he had remained faithfully by her side. He brought her breakfast again, endured Nova's merciless jokes with surprising ease, and read to her whenever she grew tired. He never once sat on her bed, though a foolish part of her wished he would. His restraint only made her want him more.

She learned he loved to read, but after he was forced into the regiment, he had lost the time for such pleasures. A quiet ache stirred within her, pity for the boy who had been shaped by blood and glory instead of the worlds hidden between pages.

When she could finally stand, they spent their afternoons in the garden beneath the old white willow whose branches shimmered beneath the moonlight. Sometimes they spoke. Other times silence carried them. Being with him was enough.

That evening they decided to draw. Luna sat cross-legged across from him, parchment balanced on her lap, her tongue caught between her teeth in fierce concentration. "Look, Solis," she announced at last, lifting the parchment with pride. "I drew you."

It was a circle with two uneven dots for eyes and a wide grin beneath straw-like hair.

He let out a soft laugh. "Drawing is certainly not one of your many talents, Princess."

"Then let us see you do better," she said, pretending to pout.

Solis leaned back against the tree, the bark rough beneath his shoulders, lantern light flickering over his face. With quiet focus he began to draw. She tried not to stare, but her gaze betrayed her. The delicate furrow in his brow. The faint tilt of his head as he searched for the perfect angle.

Curiosity tugged at her. Slowly she leaned closer, peering over his arm as the pencil moved in steady strokes. Her knees brushed his, the touch sending a quiet jolt through her. She saw him swallow hard, though his focus stayed on the parchment, his hand suddenly still. When he paused, she caught a glimpse of the sketch.

Her breath hitched.

He had drawn her — her eyes, her hair, the faint curve of her smile — captured with such attentive care that words deserted her. He was gifted. And she found herself wondering what other talents he kept hidden behind that calm restraint.

Her gaze lingered on the drawing until she felt his attention shift. When she looked up, he was already watching her.

"You are staring," she murmured.

"Am not."

"Yes, you are," she teased, batting her lashes. "See something you like, Prince?"

He chuckled, shaking his head. "Not if you keep doing that."

A strand of her hair slipped forward. He reached up and tucked it behind her ear, his fingers lingering a heartbeat longer than necessary. Her heart stumbled.

Everything around her whispered how little time they had left.

"It is getting late," she said, steadying her voice. "We should go have dinner."

"Yes," he replied, though his eyes did not leave her. "We should." Longing lived quietly in them.

That night they ate with her parents, laughter and conversation filling the hall. Solis barely touched his food. Even as King Orion addressed him and Khael's brow tightened with thinly veiled disapproval, Solis's gaze kept drifting back to her, as though the world had narrowed itself to the sound of her laughter.

The next day passed the same. They spent every waking hour together. Each time their hands brushed, the ache of parting grew sharper, until even silence between them became painful.

Luna wished time would stop, if only long enough to keep him in Selvaran a little while longer.

But time, like the river, never obeyed.

And when the morning of the Ceremony arrived, her wish fractured beneath the weight of truth.

Solis was going home.

THIRTY-SEVEN

SOLIS

The Moonrise of the Celestial Summit felt worse than a thousand blades piercing through him.

Solis rested against the marble pillar, eyes lifted to the silver sky where the moon climbed with quiet grace. Its light poured gently over the world, calm as breath, patient as time. In that glow he felt something he had never known before, a peace that wrapped around him like a whisper. It felt like home. It felt like her.

Everything reminded him of her. He loved her the way the moon loves the sea, quiet but illimitable. He loved her smile that could calm storms, her laughter that lingered like spring rain, the soft sigh she gave when the world grew still. She had become the pulse beneath his skin, the thought between each breath, the one thing he could not let go.

Could he still call Solara home? All he had ever known there was pain. Love had been a language long forgotten, a word without meaning, until her. Until Luna. She had shown him warmth beneath the cold, light within the silence. Now that he had touched it, he could no longer remember how to live without it.

High above him, the stars burned against the endless sky. Some shone fierce and steady; others trembled on the edge of fading. One fell across the heavens, swift and unbound, leaving behind a silver trail that disappeared too soon. He closed his eyes and made a wish, the kind whispered only to the heavens when the heart has nowhere else to place its longing.

A wish for her. For the girl with eyes like twilight violets, holding both the light of the moon and the pull of the sea. In their depths he had found the calm of night and the ache of forever.

At half-light, when the moon stood midway to falling, Khael would open the portal to the outer ridge of the Celestial Keep. When the ceremony ended, Solis would return to Solara, and she would remain here beneath her moon. Living her life. A life without him. Would she remember him when the stars changed their places? Or would he fade like a dream she once had beneath the silver sky?

And he would be bound to another, a woman he could not even bear to touch.

He looked toward the rising light and thought, not for the first time, that the heavens were cruel.

To let him find love only to take it away.

Standing in his chamber, Solis adjusted the cuffs of his shirt. The white fabric flowed over his skin, silky and smooth, yet cool as glass. It was the color of Solara, not the black he had grown accustomed to in Selvaran. Not the color of the realm where he had found peace.

A long cloak rested on his shoulders, white embroidered with gold. The royal crest of Solara, a lion crowned by a blazing sun, was pinned at his chest, gleaming faintly in the half-light.

He lingered for a moment, his gaze tracing the obsidian walls. This place, once foreign, now carried the warmth of home. The thought tightened quietly inside him.

When he stepped into the corridor, the sound of his boots echoed softly across the marble floor. Servants passed by, bowing politely, though their eyes lingered longer than courtesy allowed.

It was always the same. His golden hair and blue eyes marked him as someone out of place, a flash of sunlight in a kingdom of night.

He offered them a small smile.

That was all it took.

Two of them turned pink at once. One leaned against the wall with the back of her hand pressed to her forehead, sighing as if overcome, while another clutched her friend's arm and whispered something that made them both giggle uncontrollably.

Solis bit back a laugh. Even the servants of Selvaran were as dramatic and strange as their princess.

He would miss it all. Their laughter, their shyness, their harmless theatrics. Even this, he thought, was a kind of love.

He turned the corner and entered the throne room.

And forgot to breathe.

Luna stood beside her father, draped in a gown of midnight violet that glimmered with the faint shimmer of stars. The fabric moved like liquid dusk, tracing her form with effortless grace, as if the night itself had been woven to adorn her.

He took a step, then another, the distance between them shrinking yet feeling endless. For a moment, he wished her parents gone, wished Khael would simply fade from sight. All he wanted was to draw her close and forget the world that waited beyond this hall.

Her violet eyes found him and held him still. Each breath grew heavier, each heartbeat slower, until even the air between them felt like a wound he could not heal.

She was the moon given form, and he was the fool who would chase her light even if it led him to ruin.

When her gaze met his, there was no need for words. In that single look, he saw everything he could never say.

"Prince, stand beside me," Khael said. "It is time."

Solis obeyed, though his gaze never left Luna. She bit her lip, as if she wished to speak but did not. His own voice caught in his throat, the words of every confession he would never say.

Khael raised his hands. Light gathered around his fingers, swirling like silver smoke. The air trembled. The scent of cold iron and burning stars filled the hall.

The portal opened, a circle of light rippling in the air, bright as the heart of a moon.

The guards stepped through first, then the queen. Luna turned to follow but paused at the threshold. Her eyes found him again, violet glimmering like wet petals under starlight.

Her lips moved soundlessly. Wait for me.

He would wait a lifetime for her. No—more than a lifetime. He would wait through every age, every rebirth, every turning of the stars. He would wait until time itself forgot its name if that was what it took to find her again.

She stepped into the light and vanished.

King Orion followed. The portal shimmered, and only Solis and Khael remained.

"Well, Prince," Khael said, amusement twisting his tone like a knife. "A pity we never met on a battlefield. I would have relished watching you crawl for mercy while the light bled from your eyes."

Solis arched a brow. "How romantic. I did not know I haunted your dreams, Khael. If you must fantasize, be subtle. You sound obsessed. I am flattered, truly, but you are not my type."

Khael closed until there was no air between them. The smell of iron and cold filled the space. His smile was a blade. "One day I will strip the flesh from you piece by piece," he murmured, almost tender. "I will keep you breathing just long enough to beg me to finish."

Solis returned a smile that did not reach his eyes. "I can hardly wait."

He turned and walked toward the light. The portal's glow painted his face gold and white before it swallowed him whole.

Cold met him first, sharp enough to steal breath. Then came light, soft and endless.

When his vision cleared, he stood beneath an open sky. The moon hung low between day and night, painting the world in silver and gold. Soldiers ringed the clearing, their armor catching the half-light like scattered stars.

Before him stretched the Celestial Balance, the sacred land between realms, the only place where the Sun and Moon shared the same sky, suspended in an eternal twilight.

The horizon glowed in rose and amber hues. Twin towers reached for the heavens, one crowned in gold, the other in silver. Between them, a vast window of stained glass shimmered with color, a sun entwined with a crescent moon.

It was neither day nor night. The sky lingered between both, as though reluctant to choose.

King Orion took his queen's hand and moved toward the waiting carriage. Luna remained beside him.

"So this is it," she whispered. "The Celestial Keep. It is beautiful, isn't it?"

He looked out at the horizon where the towers shimmered like a reverie suspended between two worlds. Even the air felt balanced, each breath woven from opposing light. Then he looked at her. "I can name something far more beautiful," he said softly. "And she is standing before me."

She turned, startled. Moonlight kissed her skin. A faint blush rose beneath its glow, though her smile trembled with sorrow. "I did not know the prince of Solara could be such a poet," she murmured. "I thought you had never been in a relationship before… except for the one you are in now."

The quiet ache in her voice struck deep. He wanted to tear his treacherous heart from his chest for being the cause of it.

He raised his hand and touched her cheek, the gesture light, careful. "There is only one woman I have ever fallen to my knees for," he said. "And it is not the one I was promised to."

A tear slipped down her face, glimmering like a pearl caught in moonlight. He brushed it away with his thumb, gentle enough to break him.

For an instant, he wished he could offer her every heartbeat he had, just to ease the hurt in her eyes.

He wanted to tell her she had become the pulse of his silence, the warmth in his cold, the peace he had searched for his entire life. But the truth felt too heavy for words.

So he remained silent.

And she understood.

Without speaking, she turned and walked toward the carriage where her parents waited, her gown trailing behind her like a fading whisper on the wind. Solis followed, each step heavier than the one before, his heart tightening with the quiet grief of something precious slipping out of reach.

Above them, the sky of the Celestial Balance shimmered in eternal twilight, held between sun and moon, forever close yet destined never to touch.

They rode in silence. Luna never spoke, and that quiet pressed against him like heat over desert sand, relentless and aching for rain.

When the carriage stopped at the entrance, King Orion, Queen Astrid, Luna, and Solis stepped out. Khael followed. The Selvaran army remained behind; the ceremony was meant only for royals and nobles, a symbol of unity rather than strength. Soldiers would have been a reminder of war, and no one wished to summon that shadow.

Solis assumed it would be the same for Solara. His father would come without soldiers, pretending, at least for today, that peace mattered as much to him.

Servants dressed in silver greeted them at the gates. Their faces were veiled. These were the Keepers of Balance, attendants of the Celestial Keep, as enigmatic as the realm they served.

They led the group through vast marble halls toward the heart of the Keep. Voices echoed ahead, announcing their arrival.

What met Solis's eyes stole his breath.

The great hall opened directly into the twilight sky, with no ceiling above, only the boundless shimmer of the Celestial Balance. Floating lanterns drifted like stars set loose, casting both the glow of firelight and the cool sheen of starlight across floors etched with the emblems of both realms. Golden ivy and silver nightbloom climbed the outer walls, their vines intertwined in perfect harmony, symbols of what this day was meant to promise.

Nobles from both kingdoms filled the space. The air held elegance and unease in equal measure. Solis felt it, the strained peace of two worlds learning to breathe the same air.

Nervousness stirred through him. It had been years since he attended any gathering, even in Solara. His father's relentless demands left no room for banquets or joy. The only company he had known were his parents, Commander Korven, Argus, and… Calista.

Calista.

He scanned the crowd. Most faces were strangers from Selvaran, though he recognized several Solaran nobles. Then he found her near the edge of the hall, her back turned. She wore a pale blue gown; her blond hair coiled into a loose bun. She had not noticed him yet.

Relief washed over him like wind across sun-scorched sand, a fleeting breeze in a world built of fire.

Then his father's voice sliced through the moment.

Solis looked up.

King Leo approached, his presence filling the hall with bright authority. He was dressed in white and gold, the golden

girdle around his waist inscribed with celestial runes.
Solis flinched at the sight of it. That same belt had struck his
back more times than he could bear to remember.

Beside him walked Queen Aurora, her gown of ivory set
with sunstone crystals that caught the light as if flame slept
beneath the silk.

"King Orion," King Leo said smoothly. "It is an honor to
meet again under peaceful skies."

How ironic. His father had been the one to rekindle the last
war, spilling Selvaran blood across the border, yet here he stood
speaking of honor and peace.

King Orion's expression remained composed. If he felt even
a fraction of the resentment he deserved to feel, he hid it well.
He extended his hand.

"It is," Orion replied. "My moon, this must be the esteemed
Queen Aurora."

The kings clasped hands.

King Leo inclined his head. Queen Aurora bowed with
practiced grace, and Queen Astrid mirrored her. Etiquette
demanded Solis and Luna bow as well, but from the corner of
his eye he saw Luna stifle an eye roll.
He nearly smiled at the familiar defiance.

He felt his father's attention shift to him.

"I see you have kept your word," King Leo said to Orion.
"My son has been returned unharmed and well."

Solis swallowed. The heat in his father's gaze carried
promises of punishment—for daring to secure peace, for

allowing himself to be captured. He could already hear the accusations waiting for him back home.

Weak. Unworthy. A disgrace to the Aurelius bloodline.

They pushed against his skull like the phantom sting of a lash, memory cutting clean through him. His jaw tightened. The old ache crawled beneath his ribs, steady as breath, unwelcome as ever.

A gentle hand brushed his arm, pulling him back.

"I am dying for a dance," Luna said lightly. "May I be excused?"

Queen Astrid nodded. Luna seized Solis's arm and led him away before anyone could object.

At the center of the hall, Solis tilted his head, a small smile forming.

"I never thought you wanted to dance with me so badly, Princess."

Her eyes nearly rolled out of her head. "Please. I only said that to rescue you from your father. He was staring at you like a Vorraken staring at its next meal."

A quiet laugh escaped him. "He does have that talent."

He lifted her hand and set it against his shoulder. She startled but didn't pull away. His other hand took hers, fingers brushing lightly before settling into place.

"I thought you wanted to dance," he murmured. "So dance with me, Princess."

A faint blush rose to her cheeks. "Alright."

He guided her easily, steps sure and patient. Within moments he felt a tap at his boot, then another. He stifled a laugh.

"How ironic. You fight like a storm, yet dance like one too. My feet may not survive the night."

She pouted. "I never claimed to be good at dancing."

"Then allow me to teach you."

The music swelled around them, violins threading with soft flutes. Their movements gradually found rhythm. Her gown swept the floor like twilight unfurling across dusk. He spun her, and the silk flared in a circle of violet light before he caught her again, his palm settling at her back in a warmth he could not hide.

Her breath hitched. His held still.

For a heartbeat, the hall vanished. There was only her, her violet eyes, her warmth beneath his hand.

When the music ended, his chest tightened. He wanted to hold on to her, to stay inside that small pocket of stillness where the world had fallen away.

"What is it?" Luna asked quietly.

He forced a smile. "Nothing. Just wondering how many more times you plan to step on my toes before the night ends."

She laughed, light as chimes. "I told you I am not good at dancing with others."

"No kidding."

"The music is over," she teased. "You are free to dance with whoever you like now, Prince."

"And miss another opportunity to have my feet destroyed? Never."

"You are quite the flirt."

"Only on special occasions."

"Like this?"

Like when I am with the most beautiful woman in the room."

Her blush deepened. He caught her hand again, unwilling to let it slip away.

Call it greed, but for once he wanted to choose for himself. And he would choose her. A thousand times over.

The next song rose in a slow swell, and he drew her toward him. Her gown swirled like liquid moonlight when she spun, then drifted back against his chest.

He forgot everything else. The Keep. The ceremony. The watching nobles. There was only her heartbeat against his own.

When the song faded, a nobleman in Selvaran blue stepped forward and bowed. "Princess Luna, may I have the next dance?"

Something in Solis twisted. Harmless request or not, the thought of another man's hand resting where his had been made his pulse stumble.

He smiled, though his tone sharpened just enough to warn.

"The princess has already promised me the next dance."

The nobleman hesitated, then bowed again before retreating. Few dared to challenge the prince of Solara.

Luna turned to him, her brows lifting. "You know you cannot keep me glued to you all night, Prince."

"If you wished to dance with him, you could have said so," Solis replied, his voice calm though his pulse was anything but.

Her lips curved. "I thought stepping on only one person's toes tonight would be enough."

He chuckled. "So you wish to injure only me, Princess?"

"Maybe it will make you humble. Your confidence is unmatched."

"Not my fault my charm is irresistible."

She clicked her tongue. "Please. You cannot resist me either. You refuse to let me go."

"Thinking highly of yourself, Princess." His smile betrayed him.

He drew her close again, closer than he meant to. The next melody began, slower this time, its rhythm languid. They swayed in silence, her head resting against his chest, her breath warm against the fabric of his tunic.

Around them, the nobles blurred into a haze of light and shadow, drifting like distant stars. Yet the only one he saw was the girl in his arms, shining like the heart of the heavens.

When she finally grew tired, he guided her toward the tables for a drink, his thumb brushing her knuckles, his hand lingering in hers a moment longer than he intended.

"Your Highness."

No.

Not that voice.

Solis turned, the air tightening in his chest as Calista approached. His hand was still holding Luna's. Calista's gaze fell to their joined fingers at once, the way a fox studies a rabbit before deciding where to sink its teeth.

"Someone looks like he is enjoying himself," she said coolly. Her green eyes swept over him, slow and calculating, before she hooked her arm through his, curling possessively around his sleeve.

"Are you going to introduce me to your little friend, Solis?"

Luna's expression told him everything. Her hand slipped from his, and the loss struck like heat across raw skin.

He shoved Calista's arm away and reached for Luna, but she shifted back, denying him. His pulse stuttered.

Luna said nothing.

He swallowed the ache in his chest. "Princess, this is Calista. My fiancée." The word tasted like ash.

Calista leaned in, attempting to rest her head on his shoulder. He stepped aside, refusing her touch. He was no longer the boy she could intimidate. Yet nothing he did could erase the hurt in Luna's eyes. He had put that hurt there.

Calista gave a dangerous casual smile, her voice dripping with false sweetness. "So this is Princess Luna. A pleasure to finally meet the woman who has taken up so much of my soon-to-be husband's time." Her smile sharpened. "But I will take him back now."

Luna lifted her chin, violet eyes flashing. "If you do not want him to wander off, keep him on a leash."

The words hit him clean across the ribs.

His brow creased, trying to understand why she was pulling away from him. His hand twitched at his side. He stepped forward again, reaching for her fingers, but she turned and left him standing there.

His eyes followed her, drawn as irrevocably as the sun to the horizon. His mouth parted, yet no words reached the air.

"That is an excellent idea," Calista murmured beside him. "I will keep that in mind for the future."

He said nothing. The way she looked at him made his stomach twist. Disgust rippled through him like bile.

A tug at his arm pulled him off balance. Heat brushed his ear.

"If you ever let another girl touch you like that again, I will make you pay dearly. Do you understand me?"

His eyes leveled hers. A cold calm settled over him. "I do not belong to you. Speak to her like that again and you will regret it."

Her lips curved, amusement brightening her gaze. "A few weeks in Selvaran and suddenly you have a backbone. It will be delightful when I break it."

"Then break me. There is nothing left that is not already broken."

He walked away from her.

"You seem to have forgotten who you belong to," she called after him. "That is fine. I will remind you soon enough."

He no longer cared. Whatever pain she promised was nothing compared to the hollow ache swelling through his chest, a silence that felt like loss long before goodbye.

THIRTY-EIGHT

LUNA

Luna walked until the music and laughter behind her dissolved into silence. Her pulse thundered in her ears, louder than anything around her. At the far end of the corridor, she pressed a trembling hand to the cold wall, trying to steady her breath.

Her chest ached when it shouldn't have. She told herself she didn't care. She shouldn't care. Yet the image would not leave her mind. Calista's arm looped around Solis's, possessive. The way she leaned into him as if she had a right to every part of him made Luna's eyes sting.

Fiancée.

The word cut through her with the precision of a blade drawn in silence. She had known, of course, but hearing it from his lips and seeing it with her own eyes was something else entirely.

She sank onto a marble bench beneath a glowing lantern. Its silver light washed over her shaking hands. "You are such a fool," she whispered.

She wanted to be angry at him. For standing there. For saying nothing. For letting that woman touch him as if he belonged to her. But the anger refused to come.

Because when she saw him… truly saw him… she had seen everything.

The stillness in his shoulders.

The pain behind his eyes.

The way his body went rigid the moment Calista touched him.

It lived in the silence between his breaths. Solis did not love that woman. Luna knew it. This was duty, not devotion. Yet knowing the truth did nothing to ease the ache. He was still going to marry her.

She lifted her gaze to the twilight sky where hues of gold and violet bled together. Her voice came out thin, almost lost to the wind. "You cannot protect me by breaking my heart, Solis."

Because she knew exactly what they were. Something forbidden. Something fragile. A love the heavens would never grant them.

Tears slid down her cheeks, warm and soundless, like rain vanishing into the sea.

"Luna."

She thought she imagined it, but when she turned, he stood there, framed in lantern light. Calista was nowhere in sight.

"Why don't you stay with your fiancée, Prince?" she said. Her tone tried for sharpness, but the tremor beneath it betrayed her.

He didn't answer. He simply crossed the space and lowered himself beside her, his shoulder brushing hers in the quietest plea.

"I used to think duty was everything," he said quietly. "That my choices didn't matter. Being born with a crown meant my life was never mine to live."

"I know." Her fingers tightened in her lap. "You are speaking to a princess."

"Let me finish." His tone steadied, though something raw cut through it. "I thought my dreams were meaningless. That every wish would be buried beneath obedience. I wasn't a person. I was property of the crown. When they arranged my marriage to you, someone I had never met, I was angry. But I accepted it. When they canceled it… something strange hurt inside me, and I didn't know why."

Luna's breath caught.

He offered a faint, self-mocking smile. "I accepted that too. Then my father pushed Calista on me and I hated her, but I accepted that as well. Obedience was easier than defiance. I have been a coward all my life. I never chose anything for myself, not once… until I met you."

His exhale trembled. "And I don't regret it."

He took her hand and lifted it to his lips, pressing a kiss against her skin. The touch was reverent, almost trembling. Luna didn't pull away.

"You reminded me how to breathe." His voice lowered as he gently toyed with her fingers. "Before you, I was existing, but only the way a flame burns when no one tends it. Dim and waiting to die. Every breath I took belonged to someone else. I was a hollow thing wearing a crown."

His gaze lifted to hers, and something in his voice cracked open. "But you lit something in me I thought was gone. You made the world feel endless again. You made me want to live. You are my reason, Luna."

Her throat tightened. "What are we going to do?" she whispered. "You are engaged. I cannot pretend you aren't."

"I will ask my father to end it."

Her head snapped up. "How?"

"By giving him something he cannot refuse."

She searched his face. The resolve there frightened her. "Do you even know what you're doing?"

He brushed his thumb across her knuckles, slow and steady. "No. But isn't that how life works? You never know where the path leads. Only who you want walking beside you."

Something soft inside her splintered. She rested her head on his shoulder, her hair brushing his collar. "Solis, being an heir is miserable, isn't it?"

He laughed quietly, a warm, fragile sound. "It is," he said. "At least most of the time."

Her voice fell to a whisper. "Because of the crown, we cannot be together."

His breath warmed her hair. "And because of the crown," he murmured, "we found each other."

His thumb traced slow circles on her skin, the rhythm patient and certain.

"Solis," she whispered. "If you could be anything, what would you be?"

He thought for a long moment. "Anything but a royal," he said softly. "But truthfully… I don't know. The crown is all I was ever allowed to be."

"That is sad," she whispered.

"It is," he replied quietly. "Isn't it?"

Then his voice dropped, laden with quiet certainty. "But I will fight for us. I will make this real. Losing you would be like losing the part of me that finally learned to live."

Her heart trembled. She turned her face toward him, close enough to feel the warmth of his breath. She leaned in. He met her in every motion. His hand cupped her cheek. Their foreheads touched. Their lips brushed—

"Your Highnesses."

He froze. The tension locked through him like steel run cold.

She jerked back so quickly she couldn't reclaim the breath she'd lost.

Her gaze flicked to Solis's face. He blinked slowly; desire and disappointment carved plainly across his features.

Was it because they had been interrupted?

He said nothing. His throat worked.

A servant stood annoyingly few paces away, bowing low. He could not have picked a worse time to interrupt them.

"Your presence is requested."

Well aware.

She met Solis's eyes. "I suppose we should go."

"Seems like it."

He rose first and offered his hand. When they reached the doors of the great hall, he paused. He lifted her fingers and pressed a quiet kiss to her knuckles.

"Can you wait for me?" he whispered.

"I can."

She would wait a lifetime if she had to.

He leaned in and brushed a soft kiss to her forehead, the warmth settling into her skin like sunlight remembered after a long winter.

Then he let go of her hand and walked into the hall.

THIRTY-NINE

LUNA

The sound of voices swelled as Luna and Solis stepped back into the great hall. Nobles had gathered before the twin thrones at the head of the chamber, sun and moon carved into gleaming stone, eternal symbols of the two realms standing side by side beneath the dome.

The Celestial Keep had summoned them. Its magic always seemed to know when it was needed. It could shift to the moment, sense deceit before words found breath, and shield those within its walls whenever danger crept near.

Luna wondered what it would be like to live in such a place, a castle that could feel every unspoken thought, every hidden need, every quiet wish left unsaid.

At the center, before the twin thrones, stood King Orion and King Leo. Her mother had stepped aside to grant Orion room to speak, while Queen Aurora, Solis's mother, stood poised and luminous beside King Leo. Luna moved to her mother's side as Solis joined his family. A daughter of the moon and a son of the sun, heirs of two worlds that had crossed paths for centuries without ever finding peace.

The chamber quieted when King Orion lifted his hand.

"Today," he began, his voice deep and resonant, "we stand upon the threshold of two realms long divided by blood. Yet on this night, we gather not as foes but as kin beneath the same heavens, in the name of peace."

His words flowed through the hall like a slow wave. "Let the stars bear witness to this vow. From this day forth, Selvaran and Solara shall not stand as rivals, but as mirrors of the Celestial Keep upon which we gather, the sun and the moon bound in unity."

Applause followed, gentle at first, then swelling through the vast chamber. Yet beneath the sound, Luna sensed what lingered unseen. Many faces did not smile. Their claps were sharp; their eyes shadowed with disbelief. Peace would not come so easily.

King Leo stepped forward. His voice was commanding, fierce in a manner that left no room for doubt. It carried none of Solis's quiet warmth, the kind that glowed like a candle in stillness. King Leo's fire was the kind that could devour a city and still hunger for more.

"King Orion speaks wisely," he said, his tone steeped in polished civility. "War has brought nothing but grief to both our lands. It took almost losing my heir to understand its cost."

His golden eyes flicked toward Solis.

"Peace is not forged by hope alone. It is built through strength, tempered by restraint, and sealed by sacrifice. We make this vow not for our reign but for the generations that will follow. Tonight, the sun and the moon shall stand as one."

Tonight.

Not forever. Not always. Only tonight.

The word settled uneasily in Luna's chest. Why not from this day forward? Why something so fragile?

Her gaze found Solis. His expression mirrored his father's, composed and still, yet she saw the tightness in his shoulders, the quiet storm beneath his calm. He understood the meaning as well.

This was far from over.

When King Leo finished, King Orion stepped beside him. Their hands met, a gesture of unity between sun and moon. The hall erupted once more in applause, louder yet hollow, as if the nobles clapped only to honor crowns, not promises.

"Now, my guests," King Leo began.

"Before we dismiss everyone."

The voice sliced through the noise.

Luna's head snapped toward it. Solis had stepped forward, walking toward the center of the hall.

"I would like to request an audience with both kings," he said. He stood tall, unyielding. The idiot. What was he doing? Had he finally snapped?

Her pulse quickened. Her father's brow lifted in quiet curiosity. King Leo looked ready to incinerate the floor.

The chamber fell still as Solis dropped to one knee, head bowed.

"We can no longer turn from what is unfolding between our realms," he said, his voice steady as flame. "Shadow beasts walk our lands, creatures born of neither sun nor moon but from another realm. No one knows who commands them. Yet they spread. Villages have burned. Families have vanished. Our people are crying out. Both realms bleed from the same wound."

He lifted his head. "So I ask permission, from both kings, to investigate these attacks. To uncover the truth behind them. To bring our people home or to deliver justice for those who never will."

He said nothing of the shadow wielder. Nothing of the magic corrupting the land. Not a single treasonous name left his lips. Why? What was he protecting? What he had spoken already skirted treason. He had accused both kings of failing their people. If King Leo had not planned to kill him before, he surely did now.

A vein pulsed along the king's throat.

Yet Luna felt pride rise inside her. She and Khael had fought those creatures for a year, losing men in silence. And now Solis, reckless and audacious, was forcing Solara to act.

If she had not loved him before, she did now. Entirely and without reason. Her sun.

Solis continued.

"And if I succeed in uncovering the cause of these attacks, I ask for a reward."

A reward. Of course he did. What was he plotting now?

A ripple of disbelief swept the hall.

"Outrageous," a Selvaran noble shouted. "A prince demanding reward for his duty."

"Duty?" another retorted. "I do not see you on the front line."

"An insolent Selvaran dares insult our prince."

The room erupted. Solaran and Selvaran nobles snapped at one another like wild dogs.

"Silence," King Orion commanded, raising his hand.

The hall quieted, tension thrumming through the air.

"Solis, rise," her father said, his tone gentle. "You need not plead. I grant you permission to enter Selvaran and investigate these attacks. And if you succeed in saving my people, which is no small feat, you shall have my gratitude. You may ask for whatever your heart desires."

Luna glanced at King Leo. He had not spoken. Fire burned behind his golden eyes. The muscle in his jaw tightened.

His gaze fell cold on Solis. His voice struck like tempered steel.

"My son. If you solve this case, I will grant you anything you desire."

A lie offered for show. Luna could see it clearly. He would never forgive this. She prayed he would not dare touch Solis.

A faint smile touched Solis's lips as he met King Orion's eyes.

"Then, Your Majesty, if I succeed, I ask for your daughter's hand in marriage."

Chaos detonated.

Luna's mouth fell open. He had declared his heart before every ruler, every noble, and—saints help her—before Calista. Fury would hunt them both.

Gasps became shouts. Order shattered like glass. The Celestial Keep trembled, its ancient magic stirring as though even the walls sensed the storm he had unleashed.

Through it all, Luna could only stare at him, her heart burning and breaking at once.

King Orion cleared his throat, and silence fell.

"Enough." His voice cut through the remnants of chaos. His gaze settled on Solis. "I have treated you with respect. But to ask for my daughter's hand while you remain promised to another is an insult, not only to her but to Selvaran."

Luna swallowed hard. She had never seen her father angry.

Solis turned toward King Leo.

"That is why I ask my father to dissolve my engagement, so I may choose my own bride."

The air vanished from Luna's lungs. Her world tilted. Was this his idea of daring King Leo to refuse? In front of every noble?

King Leo's fury radiated like heat from molten stone. The fire in his eyes sharpened.

"Do you dare mock this court?" he said. "Do you dare turn a vow of peace into spectacle?"

Solis did not look away. "No, Father. I would make it real. End my engagement to Calista and allow me to restore the bond that should have been."

He rose, shoulders squared.

"Peace cannot exist without commitment. Words are empty when no action follows. Selvaran deserves justice for what Solara has done. Solara deserves justice for the shadows that now strike without reason. We can no longer stand divided while our people suffer."

If he had not signed his own death sentence before, that speech sealed it.

He paused. The chamber held stillness like a held breath.

"If peace is what we seek, let it begin with me. I offer myself to Selvaran's princess. Let my vow be the first act of unity between our realms."

Offer himself… to her.

It took everything Luna had not to run to him.

Silence pressed through the hall, absolute and immovable.

Her heart thundered against her ribs. He had defied his king, his blood, his crown — before two realms.

And he had done it for her.

FORTY

SOLIS

Most would call him a fool for this. To risk everything for her.

But love had no borders, no lines he would not cross.

He saw the fury in his father's eyes, the promise of the storm waiting for him once he returned to Solara, yet fear did not touch him. Love had made him brave. Love had made him reckless. Love had made him a fool, and he would remain one gladly, for her.

His father's voice cut through the silence, low and lethal. It demanded obedience, commanded him to bow again. His arms trembled, but he did not move. He did not bow. A sun does not bend.

"You would throw away the alliances I built? Have you any idea what you've done? The promises that hold this realm together, for a girl you barely know?"

He did.

Duke Veyra was one of the most powerful men in Solara, second only to the crown. His influence ran deep, his loyalty among the nobles unmatched. Dissolving his daughter's engagement was not merely personal. It was political defiance. A humiliation that could fracture Solara's foundation and destabilize his father's rule. It would ignite conflict across the realm.

Yet this was the perfect opportunity to determine whether Lucien was connected to the shadow attacks. Let's see how far he could push the duke to reveal his true nature.

Solis stood firm. "I understand, Father. I mean no disrespect to Duke Veyra."

He did.

He scanned the chamber. The duke was nowhere to be seen, though by rank he should have stood beside the throne. Where was he? Calista was present, her fury unmistakable. He did not care.

"But alliances built on fear will crumble," Solis continued, his voice steady. "Are we afraid of Duke Veyra, Father? Or are we Aurelius, heirs of Solara's fire?"

Gasps rippled through the nobles. He had spoken the unspeakable. To imply the Aurelius line feared another house was near treason, a blade against Solara's pride. He struck precisely where it hurt.

Silence stretched before King Leo replied.

"You speak of choice, yet you have shamed your crown, your house, and your blood. For what? Another realm? Duke Veyra is a loyal servant of Solara, and you reject his daughter? Tonight, we may end a war with Selvaran, but you have begun another within our own walls. You call this peace?"

Yes. It was peace. Peace for the realm if Veyra was behind the Vorraken. Peace for himself. He could finally choose whom he belonged to.

Love was not weak. Love made him strong.

Solis did not waver. "Calista will marry someone who deserves her love."

He doubted anyone deserved Calista. He pitied the man forced to try.

King Leo's fury ignited. "Love is for fools, boy," he snapped. "And fools die young."

A threat.

Solis opened his mouth to respond, but another voice carved through the hall. Cold. Too calm for the man behind it.

"If this discussion concerns my daughter, then perhaps I should be present for it."

There he was.

The temperature in the hall dropped to a chill, as though even the Keep recognized what Lucien was.

Solis turned and found Duke Veyra standing there. He had not seen him enter, had not felt his presence. Veyra inclined his head in a faint bow before stepping forward, smooth as shadow.

"I apologize for my lateness," he said, his voice cool. "Some matters required my attention." His focus shifted to the moon king. "King Orion, it is an honor to meet the ruler of Selvaran. I have long heard of your wisdom."

King Orion regarded him carefully. "Then it seems my people have failed me, for I know little of you, Duke Veyra. Though I can see why you would be involved. We find ourselves in quite the dilemma. Two daughters, one prince."

"It appears so," Veyra replied. He turned to King Leo. "My liege, if I may offer a suggestion."

"You may," King Leo said, his jaw tightening as his gaze burned into Solis.

"I suggest we grant the prince his request."

What?

Solis's brow creased as he tried to understand what Lucien was planning.

Murmurs swept the chamber, stunned. Even King Leo blinked, struggling to grasp what he had heard.

"Elucidate, Duke Veyra," King Leo demanded.

Veyra clasped his hands behind his back. "The future is not built in a single night. The prince is right. This conflict between our realms must end. The truth of these attacks should be," he paused, "found." The word carried a quiet humor, as if the idea itself amused him.

Lucien stepped closer to Solis, lowering his head slightly, predatory in posture. "So let him earn his reward." He straightened. "But…"

There it was. The word that doomed the moment.

"But fairness must go both ways. If the prince insists upon his freedom, then my daughter should be granted hers as well."

Calista had her freedom. Solis simply wanted his.

Veyra turned to the hall, his voice calm, carrying through the vast chamber. "The prince shall have his wish. But to make it fair, my daughter will join the search. If she uncovers the truth before he does, he will marry her. The nobles here will stand witness. If he succeeds first, then he may wed the princess of Selvaran."

He turned to King Orion. "It seems fair, does it not, Your Majesty? Should not the one who wins your daughter's hand prove himself worthy? Let the prince and my daughter both pursue the truth. When it is found, the outcome will decide whom he marries."

King Orion nodded. "Fair enough, Duke Veyra. If both seek the truth, then let it decide the outcome. I will honor this agreement."

Murmurs rippled through the hall, but before they faded, another voice rose.

"Then I would like to speak for myself."

Every head turned toward Luna.

"You speak of fairness, Duke Veyra," she said, her tone challenging. "Yet I hear no voice from the one whose hand is being discussed. Do I not have a say in my own future?"

That's his girl. Pride rose through him like heat.

A faint smile touched Veyra's lips. "Of course, Your Highness. The princess of Selvaran has every right to be part of this."

"Then allow me to join them," Luna said. "Let me take part in the search as well. If I find the truth before they do, I will claim my own reward."

Veyra tilted his head. "And what reward would the princess of Selvaran desire?"

Luna met his gaze without hesitation. "If I win, I will choose whom I marry. No king, no noble, and no realm will decide it for me."

The hall fell silent.

King Orion's expression softened, quiet pride in his eyes. "Then it is decided," he said. "Three will embark on this journey. Let truth choose its victor, and let fate decide what peace will cost."

Fate would decide their future.

But Solis had already made his choice.

He would not lose.

FORTY-ONE

SOLIS

The Celestial Summit ended soon after, but Solis's thoughts had not left her. The princess with black hair and violet eyes lingered in his mind like a shadow he could not shake.

As King Orion, Queen Astrid, and Luna made their way toward the carriage, Solis moved before he could think. His legs carried him with a speed he didn't know he possessed. He reached the steps just as the guards bowed and the door began to close.

"Luna."

His breath came uneven, but he didn't care. Eyes turned, whispers stirred, yet none of it mattered. The world narrowed to her.

When she appeared in the doorway, his lungs eased, as though he had been holding his breath since the moment she walked away.

He stepped forward, and she met him halfway.

"Leaving so soon?" he asked.

A faint smile touched her lips. "Miss me already?"

"Don't think too highly of yourself, princess."

"I would never," she said softly. "Why are you here, prince?"

He opened his mouth, but the words tangled somewhere between his chest and throat. He did not know why she always managed to steal his voice.

"Just to test my father's patience," he said at last. "Can you see how livid he is behind me?"

Luna leaned slightly to the side, peeking past him, then looked back. "If fury had a name, it would be him."

A grin spread across his face. "Guess I am in trouble."

Her smile was worth any punishment his father could give. Dimples curved her cheeks. "Guess you are. Be careful, prince."

"I do not think careful is in my vocabulary."

"Then make it," she said, turning toward the carriage. As her foot touched the step, she glanced back. "See you soon, prince?"

"As soon as I can."

He saw the faint tremor of her shoulders, a soundless laugh escaping her without turning back.

This was goodbye. He wasn't sure when he would see her again.

Just as she began to disappear inside, his heart called to her. "My starlight."

She froze and turned. Her gaze tested every shred of resistance he no longer held. "Yes?"

He took a step toward her, then another, each stride heavier than the last. She slipped away from the carriage, violet eyes meeting his. The starlight of his universe. The stars he had always dreamed of. His reminder that it was okay to dream. That wanting wasn't wrong. That he was allowed to love.

She met him halfway until she stood before him. Her gaze gleamed with unspoken questions, but nothing he could say would reach what he felt for her.

He moved before reason could stop him. He pulled her close, tilted her head back, and kissed her.

She melted instantly, her hand sliding to his cheek as she kissed him back.

A cough broke the moment.

Solis blinked. He had forgotten her parents were inside the carriage. Luna had stripped him of all logic.

His heart raced so fast it hurt to breathe.

She smiled against his lips. "You could not leave without a little grandeur, could you?"

He returned her grin. "No. It's not the peacock way."

Her shoulders shook, dimples flashing. "No, it isn't."

They parted soon after, and he watched the door close with her behind it as the carriage rolled away. Only then did he turn toward his own carriage, where his father waited with a look sharp enough to flay him alive.

The carriage door shut behind him with a heavy thud. Solis sat across from his father. King Leo said nothing. His hands rested clasped over one knee, his silence pressing heavier than stone.

Solis leaned back, his gaze fixed on the passing landscape. The sound of wheels on cobblestone was the only thing that filled the carriage. The twilight skies of the Celestial Balance faded behind them, replaced by the blazing blue of Solara.

Sunlight brushed his skin like a lover's touch. After days beneath cold skies, its warmth stirred through him, quiet and familiar, as if the sun itself remembered his name.

He lifted a hand toward the window. Light spilled across his palm, and he felt energy hum beneath his skin. The sun was the lifeforce of the Aurelius bloodline. Its flame called to him. In Selvaran, that call had been muted, buried under shadow. Now, with Solara's radiance upon him, his fire stirred. It wanted to rise.

The sun called his magic to life.

A spark flickered on his fingertips, small flames dancing like fish beneath water. He was watching them when his father finally released his rage.

"I should have left you in Selvaran to face the consequences of your folly," King Leo said, his voice low but searing. "Never in the history of the Aurelius line has a son brought such shame to his blood. To claim you as mine is a stain upon the crown."

Solis did not answer. The flames vanished from his hand like the warmth slipping inside his chest. This was nothing new. He had been a shame to his bloodline for the last eight years.

Leaning back, he stared at his reflection in the glass, the ghost of a son his father refused to claim. All his life he had chased that shadow, believing obedience would make him worthy. But the chase ended here.

He turned slightly as a small motion caught his eye. His mother sat beside his father, her fingers twisting together in her lap. Her eyes remained lowered, flickering nervously.

He reached out and took her hands, rubbing his thumb along her knuckles. Her skin felt cold against his warmth. When she finally looked at him, he saw the tears she tried to hide. She feared what awaited him. The old scars along his back burned faintly, a reminder of what punishment in Solara meant.

Compunction stirred within him for making her worry.

He drew a slow breath. His voice came steady as he tried to ease his father's illimitable fury. "What is done is done, Father. We must accept it."

King Leo gave a low laugh, though no trace of humor touched it. "Accept that?" he said. "You would have me accept the humiliation you dealt me before King Orion and the nobles of both realms? You stood in the Celestial Keep and defied your own father, your own crown, before our enemies. Tell me, boy. Was that your idea of honor?"

The words struck like a blade, but Solis did not flinch.

"Do you think love can hold a kingdom together?" the king pressed. "Do you think hearts win wars?"

His father's words burned through the air, but Solis held his gaze.

"No," he said, calm and quiet. "Love alone does not hold a kingdom. But neither does fear, and neither does pride."

"The shadows are spreading across our lands," he continued, his tone even. "You can pretend it is Selvaran's curse or another realm's burden, but people are dying. Villages are burning. Your silence saves no one."

King Leo's jaw tightened. His golden eyes narrowed.

Solis did not look away. "You may see my words as rebellion. I call them duty. I will not stand idle while our people suffer. If that makes me a traitor to your pride, then so be it."

King Leo leaned forward, the golden crest on his cloak catching the light.

"You forget who you are speaking to," he said, each word slow and precise. "You forget what you are."

The air in the carriage thickened. His father's voice lowered, almost a growl. "You stand before your king and speak of duty as if you invented it. You speak of mercy as if it could replace a crown. Do you think you bear the weight of Solara alone?"

He paused, his gaze sharp enough to wound. "You are my son, born of fire and blood. But the moment you chose to defy me before King Orion and his cursed court, you made yourself a spectacle. You shamed your mother. You shamed me. You turned the Aurelius name into jest."

Solis's voice remained calm, though the air around him tightened. "I remember exactly what I am," he said. "And that is why I cannot be what you want me to be."

He met his father's eyes, unflinching. "You call it defiance. I call it choice. I will not marry Calista to strengthen your throne, and I will not trade a lifetime of chains for your approval. I am not a weapon for your pride."

His gaze flicked briefly to his mother, then returned to the king. "You taught me to stand my ground, to never falter, to burn brighter than any who came before me. I am only doing what you raised me to do."

His words hung in the stillness, but Solis did not stop.

"I am an Aurelius," he said. "The blood of the sun runs through me. I was not born to crawl beneath shadows or bend to fear. I am the sun, and I do not bow to darkness."

For a heartbeat, silence consumed the carriage. The kind that hummed before a storm.

Then King Leo leaned back. A quiet laugh slipped from him, low and dangerous.

"It is about time you spoke like a man," he said, his tone almost amused. "Not a boy hiding behind ideals."

Solis's mouth curved slightly. "Am I not your son? How could I be anything less?"

King Leo smiled, sharp and joyless. "For your sake," he said, "I hope this defiance is worth what it will cost you."

Neither spoke again for the rest of the ride. The carriage rolled through Sunfall, the light of the realm spilling through the windows like liquid gold. Solis sat in silence, watching his mother's trembling hands. He wished he had spared her this. But the weight of what he had done was his to carry, and he would not turn back.

Not now.

Not ever.

FORTY-TWO

SOLIS

The carriage wheels ground to a halt before the golden gates of Solara Citadel. His home. Yet it felt nothing like home. Not anymore.

Guards stood in rigid formation along the marble path, their armor gleaming beneath the blaze of Highflame, where the sun burned at its fiercest.

His father stepped out first. No words came from him, nor did he glance at Solis.

Solis followed in silence. The thick hot air struck him like unspoken judgement. After so long in Selvaran, the heat felt foreign, almost hostile.

The guards parted, forming two perfect lines, hands pressed to their chests in salute. Solis lifted his gaze and found

Argus among them. A faint smile flickered across his friend's face. Solis returned it. It had been too long since he had seen him. Every part of him wanted to cross the line and embrace him, but duty kept them both still. Beside Argus stood Commander Korven, face as inscrutable as ever, though Solis could have sworn he saw a brief glint in the man's eye. Pride, perhaps, that the prince had returned home.

They advanced down the aisle. One by one, the guards bowed their heads in fealty. Solis almost laughed at the absurdity of it. Loyalty to a throne that cared nothing for them. To a realm that sent them to die for a lie his father and Lucien had wrought.

He fixed his gaze ahead, on his mother's back. She walked beside his father, spine straight, elegant as ever. Warmth spread through his chest. He had missed her. Compunction pressed beneath his ribs. He should have written. He had failed her as a son. She must have been so worried, and he had not even thought to ask Argus to tell her he was safe.

At the top of the steps, the nobles awaited them. Lucien was nowhere to be seen, though he had attended the Celestial Summit with them; he should have returned by now. Solis's brow furrowed as he scanned the hall. No sign of Calista either. Where were they?

As he passed the nobles, whispers rippled through the crowd.

Disgrace.

Shame.

Traitor.

Moon lover.

The last one almost made him smile. Moon lover. They hurled it like an insult, but it felt more like a compliment. She was his moon, and he would bow to her anytime.

King Leo moved like a blade drawn from its sheath as the great doors of the throne room opened before him.

Solis followed, knowing his fate was about to be sealed. He could feel the heat emanating from his father's body. The Aurelius flame responded to emotion, and his father's was on the verge of eruption.

Inside, pillars of clear marble veined with gold rose toward the open dome. Light scattered across the floor where the emblem of the lion and sun—the royal crest—gleamed beneath their feet.

The sight sickened Solis. Lions were meant to be brave. His father was a coward, betraying his realm, his people, and his own son. Glory was a jest. A mockery of what the crown should have stood for. Kings were meant to serve their people, not rule them with fear, yet his father ruled like a mad king.

He lifted his head as he stepped to the center of the hall, awaiting the judgment he knew would come. The king ascended his throne. The nobles gathered along the edges, eyes fixed on him like hawks circling prey, each waiting for what would happen next. A prince who had defied a king stood among them, and no one dared to breathe.

The doors slammed shut behind him with a resonant thud. Solis squared his shoulders, refusing to waver. He had dug his own grave, and he would face whatever consequence awaited him. His gaze locked on the man seated upon the golden throne, daring him to pass judgment.

King Leo leaned forward, his fists gripping the carved arms of the throne until his knuckles turned white. The look in his eyes promised pain. Solis met it without fear.

Their eyes leveled, fire meeting fire.

"My lords." King Leo's voice rang deep through the throne room. "The Celestial Summit has ended in success. An alliance forged with Selvaran. All thanks to my son. The prince who has proven to the world—"

A pause followed. The stillness of the chamber deepened as his father's gaze hardened.

"That Solara's authority can be challenged. That a king is nothing but a jest. For all it took was my own son to stand among our enemies and defy everything Solara has stood for."

The room grew cold. Every noble's stare cut into Solis. He had robbed them of glory again. If Solara withdrew its word a second time, his father's word would be rendered meaningless. The people would see them for the tyrants they are. It could ignite a civil war.

Solis almost smiled at that. Good. Perhaps the realm needed an awakening.

His hands remained clasped behind his back as he endured his father's rage.

"My son thinks courage is born out of cowering before his enemies," Leo said. "He thinks that love could bring peace to this realm. Well, love is a dead man's dream. Let it be known that foolish courage and true bravery are not the same. One strengthens a kingdom while the other... burns it to ash."

From the corner of Solis's eye, he saw Argus step forward from where he stood beside his father. The frustration on his face said everything, the refusal to let Solis take the punishment alone. But before Argus could move, Commander Korven seized his son's arm, holding him back. Argus turned, meeting his father's gaze with silent fury, but Korven did not yield. There was nothing they could do for Solis without making it worse. Argus gritted his teeth and stepped back into position. Solis was grateful to him. He couldn't bear to see Argus punished as well.

He turned his focus forward as King Leo descended the steps, marching before the nobles until he stopped in front of one. Lord Crestholm. A lower-ranking noble. No man of real power, but Solis knew why his father had chosen him. It was to disgrace him, to show that even a lesser man could pass judgment on a prince. This was the price for shaming his father.

"Lord Crestholm, tell me what becomes of a noble who has forgotten his place?"

The lord's gaze darted between Solis and the king. His voice shook. "He is to be whipped or..." He paused and swallowed hard, his throat bobbing. "Or... or burned, Your Grace."

The lord stepped back, head bowed as he finished the last word. No other dared to speak.

"Ah." King Leo's tone dripped with mockery. "Yes, of course. A punishment worthy of the crime. Now tell me, what of a prince who forgets his?"

The color drained from Lord Crestholm's face. He stammered; eyes fixed on the floor. "I… I dare not say."

King Leo's gaze swept over the gathered lords one by one. Each lowered his head. None dared speak against the crown prince.

"No one?" The king's voice deepened, echoing through the chamber. "No one dares challenge a prince, yet my own son dares challenge a king."

His father turned toward him. Solis did not flinch. He met his father's fury with silent defiance. The air between them felt like a storm waiting to break.

Solis said nothing.

King Leo turned and ascended the dais. "When a prince forgets his place, it falls to a king to remind him." When he reached the throne, he turned to face the court, his gaze sweeping across the nobles before settling back on Solis.

"Prince Solis," he said, "before two realms you brought shame upon the crown. You defied your king. You disgraced your kingdom, and for that, you will atone. A prince is not above the law. He is not above his king. Since you have forgotten, I will remind you. Fifty lashes."

The words hung in the air, absolute as the cold in his father's eyes. Solis did not plead or break. He held his head high, showing his father the courage a lion should have.

Footsteps approached from behind. Hands gripped his shoulders, forcing him to his knees. His knees struck the marble with a sharp crack. Pain shot up his legs, but Solis refused to cower. He was the sun. The sun does not waver. He lifted his head, proud and unbroken.

The rod scraped across the floor. Then came the first strike. Wood met flesh with a crack that echoed through the throne room.

Solis gritted his teeth, refusing to falter. The second came just as fierce. Pain flared across his spine, but he kept his head high. The hall remained silent as stone. No one dared breathe as the prince of Solara took his punishment.

"Harder," King Leo commanded. "Let them see that a crown without discipline, without obedience, is no crown at all."

Pain cracked through his back as the next blow landed. Then another. Each harder than the last. Sweat beaded along his neck. The fabric clung to his back, soaked in crimson where skin tore. The metallic scent of blood thickened the air. Yet Solis did not fall. His head remained high, his chest heaving, his back burning.

He did not know how many lashes it took before his body finally faltered. His palms struck the ground as he fought against the heat of his agony.

"Leo."

His mother's voice broke through the quiescence. Solis looked up and saw tears running down her cheeks as she pleaded with the king. "Please. Let him go. Please, spare him."

King Leo said nothing. He ignored her as though she were air. Solis bit back his anger. One day, he would make his father pay for every tear his mother shed.

When the next strike came, Solis forced himself upright. He met his father's gaze, cold as stone. He did not care that his back was on fire. Nothing hurt more than seeing his mother weep for him.

When the final blow landed, Solis held his composure, defiant to the last bone in his body.

Water dripped down his back as Argus cleaned the wounds. His father had dismissed him like a dog after humiliating him before the entire court. Solis felt no compunction for what he had done. For the first time, he had chosen for himself—and he had chosen her. The sting of his injuries burned as Argus pressed the cloth to his skin.

"You're an idiot," Argus said. "A pure idiot. Tell me, was she worth fifty lashes or just forty-nine of them?"

Solis let out a low laugh despite the ache tearing through him. "Fifty—and more. I'd take another fifty for her if that's what it took."

Argus snorted. "Listen to you. A few nights in Selvaran, and she's got you singing like a tavern bard."

"Well, if singing is what she wants, I'll give it to her."

Argus shook his head, a grin tugging at his mouth. "Now I have to meet the girl who made my little brother take fifty lashes for her."

Solis stared at the wall as Argus wiped the last of the blood from his back. "She's different. I've never felt this way about anyone before. It's not her beauty that captivated me—though yes, she is beautiful. It's the way she makes the world feel less hollow. When I look at her, it isn't desire. It's recognition. Like remembering something I'd lost and never realized I needed."

Argus's hand stilled. He dipped the towel into the basin, letting out a quiet sigh. "Then I hope she's worth what it'll cost you."

Solis said nothing.

She was.

FORTY-THREE

SOLIS

The bruises on his back still ached, but it had been worth defying his father for her.

Argus and Solis were out running drills with their men when Calista appeared. She lingered at the edge of the hall, silent as the soldiers trained beneath the brutal heat.

Swords clashed. Boots struck the stone. Dust rose like smoke. Solis's blade felt weightless in his hand as he dodged Argus's strike, a deft pivot to the left, a bend of the knee, and a cut toward the thigh in one seamless motion.

Argus countered, his blow knocking Solis backward. He fought with both speed and brute strength.

Solis grinned. "Not going to go easy on me, are you?"

"I didn't realize you wanted to be babied, little brother." Argus adjusted his stance with a low laugh. "Would you like a hug as well?"

He lunged, his sword striking Solis square in the ribs. Solis bit down on the pain and swung low, but Argus parried like water flowing around stone. Solis shifted his footing and landed a clean strike across Argus's bicep.

"A lot of talk for someone who missed his strike."

"I'm sure the bruise on your side will bloom nicely by morning."

They kept at it until Sunfall, both ignoring Calista, who never left her place at the wall. Her green eyes tracked Solis through every movement, burning into him. When they finally stopped, her voice cut through the hall.

"Boys. I need to speak with Solis. Alone."

Argus breathed through his nose, chest rising and falling. "Anything you have to say to him, you can say here."

Calista tilted her head, the corner of her mouth curving. "I think this is something Solis might prefer to hear in private."

Solis steadied his stance. "Whatever you have to say, you can say it in front of Argus." His gaze met hers, unyielding.

"Even if it involves a current mission?"

His body went still, the sword balanced loosely in his hand. Did she know something about the warriors? His mind raced, trying to decipher her game, but no answer came. He exhaled. "Argus, give us a moment."

Argus lowered his sword and stepped back, clearly irritated by Calista's presence.

Solis followed her toward the far counter of the hall, away from the others. When she reached for him, the hunger in her eyes sent a chill through his bones. He jerked back before she could touch him.

"I'm not here for your little games, Calista. Just tell me what you want."

The smile never left her face. She withdrew her hand, letting it fall to her side, and studied her nails.

"A little bird told me a story," she said, her voice lilting like a song. "Something about a fallen star... and a shard of—"

She paused, the grin widening as though she found her own deceit amusing. He found nothing amusing about it.

"Fire."

The word struck him like a blow. She had found one of the warriors. Solis closed the distance between them until their eyes leveled.

"Tell me where the warrior is."

Calista clicked her tongue and shook her head. "No. This will not do. You will have to earn it."

A muscle on his jaw ticked. "I already told you, Calista. I do not have time for your games. Either tell me, or I am leaving."

He turned, but she seized his arm.

Desperation threaded her voice. "Solis, I know our engagement was not something you wanted. But for me, it was real. I have never felt this way about anyone. Do not make me cruel. Do not turn me into someone you will not like."

Too late. If only she knew how deeply he despised her.

He stopped mid-step and looked over his shoulder. "I do not love you, Calista. I never will. Stop playing games with me. I am not your toy."

Her expression hardened, the softness and desperation gone, replaced with pure malice. "But you are." Her tone dripped venom. "And I will make you beg for me. Beg for us. For now, I will give you what you want. It will be worth it in the end."

Solis grabbed her and shoved her against the wall, teeth flashing like fangs. "I will never beg for you. I will never want you. If you think I am your plaything, you are delusional. I am a prince, Calista. A prince does not bow to a noble. Do not test me."

She gripped the fabric of his shirt, fingers trailing down his chest as she leaned close, her breath hot against his skin. "Oh, but you will."

Her laugh was cruel. "The warrior is in Cindarlis. Red hair. Full of fury, like you—but do not worry. I will burn that flame soon enough."

It took everything in him not to lash out. He drew a slow breath and released her, turning away without another word. He had gotten what he needed. She could keep her games.

He left her against the wall and rejoined Argus.

Later that night, he wrote to Luna, asking her to meet him at the border. They had a mission to complete, but that was not the whole truth. He simply wanted to see her. It had been a week, and he already missed her.

As he undressed for bed, a knock came at the door. Frowning, he opened it to find a guard standing in the hall.

"Your father summons you."

Solis's mouth went dry. What could his father want at this hour? He had done nothing to displease him since the throne affair. Taking a steady breath, he left his chamber and made his way to his father's study. The king had spent most of his hours there of late.

He knocked once and waited. A deep voice called him to enter.

His father sat behind his desk, eyes fixed on parchment. Solis stood at attention, hands clasped behind his back. Despite their differences, he still respected the man, but this time he would not let his father break him.

King Leo did not look up. His eyes scrutinized the paper before him, as if Solis's presence were nothing more than air.

"I thought I could beat the weakness out of you. I was wrong." He turned a page as if discussing the weather. "This is the only way. You made me do it."

Confusion flickered through Solis. "What did I make you do?"

"Go to the dungeon, my son. Remember, this is your fault. You made me do it. I will break that weakness from you, even if I have to shatter every ounce of love you have left."

Solis's eyes widened. His heart slammed against his ribs. He turned, shoved the door open, and ran.

Something was wrong. His mind raced.

Who?

Who had they taken to punish him?

Argus? No. Argus had been with him that morning.

His pulse thundered as he reached the southern tower. He pushed past the guards and descended the narrow steps into the shadowed depths of the dungeon below.

What he saw there broke him.

FORTY-FOUR

SOLIS

He couldn't breathe.

It could not be real. It could not.

"Mother?"

His mother was inside a cage, screaming, shadows whipping through her body. His body lurched forward, his hand reaching for her…

I'm sorry, Mother. I couldn't protect you.

But something wrenched him back, dragging him to his knees.

Air deserted him. Shadows seized his body, pinning him to the ground and forcing him to watch. Lucien sat in a chair in the corner with a smirk carved across his face.

"Well. Isn't it the crown prince of Solara. What an honor."

Solis couldn't speak. His will was gone. His body refused to move. He was trapped. Helpless. Worthless.

"You're not going to be able to speak. Not yet. So be a good little pet and watch what happens when you dare to defy me."

He tried to break free, but the shadow rendered him powerless. He reached within, calling for fire, but nothing came. His magic vanished the moment Lucien's shadow took hold. The darkness in his veins bound him like iron.

He tried to scream, but no sound came. His ears burned as his mother's screams echoed through the dungeon. This was his fault. He had caused this.

Punishment for humiliating Lucien.

For defying the crown.

For ending his engagement to Calista.

His mother suffered for his choices.

Some lessons were crafted to cut deeper than death.

He would have torn his own flesh apart rather than watch her suffer. It should have been him in that cage. Tears streaked down his face as her cries bled into his bones, splintering what remained of his soul into a thousand shards. He shut his eyes, unable to watch any longer.

Please. Please make it stop. Please.

But it never stopped.

He had never known shadow could seize a will and freeze a body until Lucien used it on him. Now he understood why they feared Lucien.

Because Lucien was the reaper.

The floor scraped his knees. The stone was cold beneath him. Nothing cut deeper than the ache in his heart.

His body shook as he tried to block out the screams.

It felt like eternity before the shadow finally let him go, like a puppet given back its flesh. He collapsed. His hands flew to his ears, trying to shut out the sound.

Was the screaming his or hers?

He could not tell.

A footstep entered his vision. He lifted his head and met the green eyes of Lucien Veyra.

Lucien studied him like a cat toying with its prey.

"Did you learn your lesson, prince?" Lucien's head tilted, voice soft as poison. "Or do I need to teach you another?"

"Please. Make it stop." His voice shook, breath ragged. "Please. I'll do anything."

His mother whimpered in pain. His fault. All his fault. For choosing his own selfish greed over duty. Love was weak. His father had taught him that. Why couldn't he learn?

His mother paid the price for his foolishness. He let the pain consume him, burying himself in it until numbness was all that remained.

He was a sun in an eclipse.

Lucien knelt in front of him. A cruel grin spread across his face.

"Anything?" His voice pressed like the edge of a knife.

Solis forced the word out. "Anything. Please, let her go."

Lucien gripped his jaw and tilted his face up. "I know you've heard the prophecy: shadow against light, the chosen one who can rid the world of darkness." He snarled. "That moon princess threatens everything I am. I will not allow her or those warriors to live. Bring them to me, and I will return your mother. Fail, and your mother will pay for every mistake. Understood?"

Solis's gaze fell to his mother in the cage, her fragile body trembling. "Yes."

"Good." Lucien straightened and dusted off his hands.

"Now go and be a good little pet and apologize to my daughter. Beg her to take you back. Break her heart again, and I'll shatter every bone in your mother's body."

A gelid cold spread through Solis's chest. "I'll do whatever you want. Just—please—don't hurt her."

"Then go. Prove your devotion before I decide your mother is not worth the trouble."

Solis forced himself upright, trembling, and turned toward the stairs. With every step, the sombre weight of his failure grew heavier. He left his mother in the hands of evil. He had failed her as a son.

He would fail Luna too.

He would have to play a part—earn her trust, break her heart, betray the warriors.

He would have to become what Selvaran feared most, what they accused him of:

A monster.

For his mother, he would become it.

THE SHADOW REALM AWAITS.

ACKNOWLEDGMENT

Writing this book has been a remarkable journey. It was often stressful and exhausting, yet still one of the most meaningful experiences of my life. I want to thank my husband for being my greatest supporter. Honestly, if it were not for him, *Of Moonlight and Fire* would never have been completed. He stood beside me through every moment of this process, giving me the confidence I needed to reach the finish line.

I began writing earlier this year after losing my daughter. Through grief, I poured whatever strength I had left into a fantasy world that had lived in my mind long before it ever touched paper. My husband played a tremendous role in that healing. During moments when we could not laugh, we talked about *Sun and Moon* and where the story might go. Because of those conversations, we were able to find pieces of joy again.

Most of the characters in *Sun and Moon* were imagined by both my husband and me. He chose many of their names and shaped their personalities. Even though my name appears on the cover, this book belongs to us both. The idea of the twin realms and their magical elements came from him. I added the Vorraken, the shadow magic, and the darker path the story eventually took. The original version was written for a much younger audience, but as the direction of Book Three unfolded, I rewrote the entire series into what it is now.

I hope you will not hate me too much by the end of Book Three. I am sorry for the pain it brings, but the story demanded it. Thank you for reading, and for stepping into the world of Sun and Moon with me.

ABOUT THE AUTHOR

J.N. Wynn lives in California with her husband and their two cats. When she isn't writing about celestial realms and star-crossed heirs, she can be found reading fantasy romance, playing story-rich games, or exploring new ideas over a strong cup of coffee. She owns more than two hundred fantasy novels and loves escaping into the world of magic and myth.

Connect with her online:

TikTok: @jnwynn_author

Instagram: @jnwynn_author

J.N. Wynn